# GOLEM SONG

ALSO BY Marc Estrin

*The Education of Arnold Hitler*

*Insect Dreams: The Half Life of Gregor Samsa*

*Rehearsing with Gods: Photographs & Essays on The Bread & Puppet Theater*
(Co-Authored with Ronald T. Simon, Photographer)

unbridled books

# GOLEM SONG

marc estrin

This is a work of fiction. The names, characters, places and incidents are either the product of the author's imagination or are used fictitiously, and any resemblance to actual persons living or dead, business establishments, events, or locales is entirely coincidental.

Unbridled Books
Denver, Colorado



Library of Congress Cataloging-in-Publication Data

Estrin, Marc.
Golem song / Marc Estrin.
p. cm.
ISBN-13: 978-1-932961-23-2
ISBN-10: 1-932961-23-2
1. Golem—Fiction. 2. Paranoia—Fiction. I. Title.
PS3605.S77G65 2006
813'.6—dc22
2006023571

1 3 5 7 9 10 8 6 4 2

*Book Design by SH • CV*

First Printing

*Man thinks; God laughs.*

Jewish proverb

# contents

## april



## may



## june

## *July*



## *August*



## *September*



## *October*

# *November*

*april*

# 1. ST. KRIEGER'S 911

Stately? No. Ahh, but plump? Decidedly. Therefore, Alan Krieger, RN, will allow himself a clandestine, but full five minutes off to relieve his tired, poor, abusèd feet, feet yearning to be free of the great weight thrust upon them.

Down plops the great tush—*Whump!*—onto the overstuffed couch in the staff room.

Out comes the dental floss, mentholated, waxed . . .

Spool—*Wwwwwah!*

Cut—*Tsip!*

But wait—he speaks:

*"O! that this too too solid flesh,"* and begins the procedure, *"wou meld, Faw an eolfe iel ioo a . . ."*

Alan dug into the periodontal recess behind his right incisor and sawed the floss mercilessly back and forth into his gum. Drawing it slowly out, he listened, and felt for any mini-telltale tiks or toks that might proclaim a palpable hit—but there was only the white noise of thread against flesh and enamel. He held the string up for inspection, frowned, and smelled it.

"A little bloody, but still good."

He wound the used floss around his index finger, lifted the little coil off its digital spool, and put it in his pocket. But his probing tongue tarried—unsatisfied.

"It's a phantom limb in there. A goddamn phantom piece of limb. Wait! Can a phantom limb belong to someone else, not me? Satanic Ma with her drumsticks for lunch! *Ess, ess, mein Kind.*"

Alan surveys the local scene for leavings: "Hmmm. Think I'll just have a bite of this abandoned brownie. Who'll ever know? But I'll have to eat from the bitten end so as not to draw attention. . . . Good thing I don't believe in the germ theory of disease. . . . Mmmmmmm . . . machine manna from the Promised Land."

Alan slung his lower extremities, one—*Oof!*—by one, onto the coffee table, scattering a pile of old magazines and sending the brownie's erstwhile partner, a half-cup of cold coffee, gracefully into space and onto the tiled floor, where it landed bottom down and stayed there, coffee quivering.

"Yammering Yahwehs! What are the odds that Alan Krieger could have so calculated the torque as to spill not one drop? A thousand to one? A million to one? Jesus Christ Twinkletoe couldn't have done better, as is clear after any reading of the synoptic gospels."

And leaning forward with difficulty over his impressive abdominal bulk, Alan swiped at the only reading material not pinned down by his feet. After several tries, he succeeded in shifting it within left hand's reach.

"The *Catholic Worker.* Ah, yes, the *Catholic Worker,* 'Price 1¢.' One fucking cent! Can't even buy a piece of DoubleBubble for that anymore. Must be supported by Rome. Wait, what's this in small print? 'Subscription: 25¢ Per Year.'? The gonifs! That's more than twice as much as buying individual copies! What would Dorothy Day say? What would Peter What's-his-name say? Who's the sucker that subscribes to this thing?" He squinted at the address label. "Oh, it's me."

Alan Krieger, RN, took a sip of the slimy miracle coffee and, newspaper in hand, slipped off into Talmudic fugue state.

*. . . fix'd his canon 'gainst self-slaughter.* Would that be the Bloomian canon or the boom-boom cannon, oh Everlasting, you sly hedgehog?

Considerations interrupted!

"Code green in Chapel, code green in Chapel," the intercom intoned.

"Ah, that *bel canto nasalissimo* . . . nothing like unconscious self-parod—Hey, wait a minute! Code green! OK, Krieger, up off your fat ass, though only approximately two-thirds of the allotted respite has been used, or is that 'have been used'? *Oi.* Oof. Code green—in the Chapel? O, rare! Friar Lawrence, I come."

Alan slid from between coffee table and couch, knocking over the miracle paper cup, and made his way into the hall.

"Let me the fuck outa here!" came a loud voice from behind an oaken door fifteen feet ahead. "You think my Father in Heaven can't send down legions of angels to smite you motherfuckas?"

Alan grabbed an IV stand, abandoned in the hallway, and took it on as partner to his modified cantor—in code green you never know when you might need a vertical iron bar on wheels. He cautiously pushed open the Chapel door.

"Krieger! Wait for security," his supervisor called as she strode quickly down the hall. But Alan was never one to be supervised. He stepped gingerly over the threshold, and two terrified elders slipped out behind him to freedom. It was *his* turn.

There in front of him was a huge man, midthirties, black-bearded, muscular arms straining, in a robe that was not the property of St. Vincent's. He held before him the Chapel cross, ripped from the wall, the object of a zombied contemplation. Had he been yelling at the cross? It was possible. He looked up at the newcomer and his pole. John Brown eyes. William Tecumseh Sherman.

"You!" the black man whispered.

Alan thought, Who, me?

"You! The man with the scythe!" He looked down at the short, fat man with pity. "I can heal you, my son."

"You can?"

"If you have faith. Come hither; draw nigh to God."

Security burst through the door behind Alan, followed by Supervisor Goldtooth, two ER docs, one psychiatrist, and behind them, still outside, unable to penetrate the Chapel crush, a gaggle of nurses, medical students, and curious EMTs.

"Stay back," ordered Alan, serious, imperious, and the crowd froze behind him. The man with the cross surveyed the scene in front of him. There was silence in the heavens. The master of this ceremony addressed the room.

"Do you still reject me, children of man?" He shook his magnificent head with compassion. "Children of man . . ."

"And how should we call you?" asked Alan.

"I am he who cometh in the name of the Lord."

Alan's heartbeat quickened, his neck hairs stood on end, and his t-shirt—his Great-Seal-of-the-United-States t-shirt featuring his beloved northern elephant seal, *Mirounga angustirostris,* half a ton of silver-skinned, well-blubbered muscle—effortlessly silver—without Alan's heartbreak of psoriasis—and a nose as Hebraically Cyranosical as his own, twelve feet of submarine torpedo capable of forty miles per hour underwater, and thus legal on interstates and freeways when such are built under the sea—that very t-shirt felt clammy.

*Freeze frame at the beginning,*

for in the beginning is the end. Here we have a little green man—round, but little if seen from a distance. Green eyes and greenish complexion, green hospital scrubs. A little green fat man, attending code green: Alan the Warrior, né Krieger, servant to Science à la Frankenstein, a jumbled blend of creator turned creature, of creature turned monster, of creature turned monster in search of love, Alan Krieger about to do a shtick.

There is much here to be considered.

. . . . . .

Alan assumed the Eyegor position, hunched.

"Master He," Alan cried, his free hand turned up in supplication.

He-Who-Cometh-in-the-Name-of-the-Lord stared, then rose to the stature of John Brown. Higher: Moses on the mount with horns. Then his eyes melted to those of Mohandas Gandhi.

"Child, do you trust in God?"

"I do, Master He, I do."

"Come hither."

"I'm already hither."

The man reached down and laid a huge hand on Alan's neck, closing his eyes and swaying to and fro.

"Father, Father, give me the Word, that I may heal this poor sinner."

More swaying, more pressure on the neck.

"Give me the Word. . . . In the name of Our Lord Jesus I say unto thee, Rise up, child. Rise up and walk!"

A second silence in heaven—just long enough to tense the Chapel to a high-pitched trill. Then Alan began to straighten up along the IV pole. Slowly he rose to his full height—five foot eight and a half. It was an impressive performance—Martha Graham unfolding as a Georgia O'Keeffe lily in a Walt Disney nature film. He stood there, relatively magnificently tall. Master He did not seem to know what to make of it.

"Good work, man! Now make me walk," Alan prompted.

"Walk," the Master said doubtfully. "In the name of Our Lord, rise up and walk."

"I'm already risen, Master." Alan took a hugely limping step and grabbed the pole for balance.

Master He started weeping. Weeping and wailing. "Shit, shit, shit! Oh, muhfuckin shit!"

It is pathetic to see a tall man weep.

"Sit, Master, sit," Alan said. "Please. Want a cup of coffee? A sugar wafer?"

He-Who-Cometh collapsed at the table. Alan backed up to the

door and, in answer to the silent inquiry of would-be spectators and the proffered blowdart of 10 mg Haldol, he deftly placed the DO NOT DISTURB sign on the outside handle and closed the Chapel door. He drifted back toward the weeper while inspecting the room.

"Holy water? What else we got here? Want to hold a candle?"

"I had the crown, and I lost it. I had the Word—and I have forgotten it."

"Hey, no way. Look how tall I am."

He stretched on tippytoe and did a limpy *pas de bourrée.* "See? Big. Soooo big."

He-Who-Cometh peeked out from between his hands. The vision of a disabled, overweight male ballerina on point, cavorting, was too much for him; he covered his eyes again. Alan collapsed into the chair opposite as He-Who spoke into the muffler of his hands.

"He chose me as the guardian of His people, to reign over the redemption of man and the world."

"What a nice idea."

He-Who looked up at the face close to his own.

"The day is drawing near, the hour of splendor . . ."

Alan knocked hard on the table right between He-Who's elbows, jolting him out of his reverie, and whispered in his patient's ear: "The nearer the hour of redemption approaches, the stronger does Satan become."

He-Who nodded. Alan pulled his handkerchief from his back pocket and wiped his patient's nose.

"Here, bubbie, sorry, sorry, don't cry. Just listen up. Will you listen up?"

He-Who raised his eyes to meet Alan's. The nurse took the man's long fingers in his little fat ones and stroked them gently, hypnotically.

"I want to tell you a story. OK?"

"OK."

"A long time ago, when the black death danced in Amsterdam, and Nieuw Amsterdam—poof!—became New York . . ."

"Here. We're in New York . . ."

"Oriented to place . . . there burst upon the scene in Jerusalem a strange, eccentric man with rabbinic training, a manic-depressive kabbalist named Shabbatai Z'vi."

"He took Lithium?"

"No, dear, Lithium didn't exist. I mean, it existed, but . . ."

"I take Lithium. . . ."

"Oriented to diagnosis and meds. Allah be praised. Shabbatai Zv'i claimed he was the Messiah, the real thing now, not the false Jesus messiah of sixteen hundred years before. He had come—as Isaiah had predicted—he had truly come. Jews all over received the word, and in Frankfurt, Prague, Mantua, Constantinople, and even Amsterdam—in fact, *most* in Amsterdam with its twenty-four thousand corpses—there was hysteria and rioting. People ran naked in the snow, they whipped themselves and each other, they sold all their possessions—the long-awaited hour was at hand. Shabbatai Z'vi's plan was to go to Turkey to convert the sultan. You know what happened?"

"No."

"Guess."

"He wasn't the real Messiah."

"How do you know?"

"Because I'm the real Messiah."

"Praise the Lord," Alan observed.

"Praise the Lord." It seemed they agreed.

"HEY, MAN," Alan shouted, "PRAISE THE LORD!"

He grabbed two glass ashtrays—PROPERTY OF ST. VINCENT'S HOSPITAL—and clacked them over his head like a middle-aged Carmen.

"Praise Him in His holy emergency-room Chapel!"

*Clack, clack.*

"Praise Him with cymbals and ashtrays!"

*Clackety-clack, clack.*

He tossed an ash tray to He-Who, who made a successful stab at the ill-thrown object. He-Who's eyes narrowed and lifted at their lateral edges, smiling all by themselves, without help from the rest of his face. Then, as he watched Alan's Gymnopédie, he broke out laughing.

Alan, meanwhile, was too out of breath to join in his mirth. He collapsed in a pew, puffing, puffing, and puffing led to coughing from two-pack-a-day bronchioli.

"*Aakkkk. Haaaarrrg!*" Alan smashed chest with fist and sprang up to look for a drink. The only liquid at hand was lurking in two vases of flowers, or, better, in an open bowl of holy water. Alan grabbed it from the table that served, for those with enough imagination, as altar. He took a great slug of God's miracle, and lo, though still puffing, he stopped coughing and dropped the bowl back onto the table, where it stood, meniscus quivering.

"Drink?" he asked his client.

He-Who shook his head in slow amazement. Alan, with dignity uncompromised, continued to address the black man. "Let all that live glorify the name of God!"

He-Who stared at him. "Man, you something."

"So are you, man, so are you." He put his hands on He-Who's great shoulders. "And now it's time to exorcise your demons. I want you to fast and pray while I go back to the ER and schedule you for a ritual bath. And remember Shabbatai Z'vi."

"Shabbatai Z'vi? Oh, yeah."

"Mr. Messiah there was given the choice of converting to Islam or having his head chopped off. Guess which one he picked? 'He who hath an ear, let him hear.'"

"I got it, man."

"OK, so then rise up, my son, and repeat after me Psalm 131: 'Lord, my heart is not haughty,' C'mon, man, say it, 'nor mine eyes lofty,' up, up, 'neither do I exercise myself in great matters, or in things too high for me.' All right, don't rise up, don't say it. Just sit there smiling."

"Hey, man," He-Who noticed, "you're standing up. I cured you. Like I said."

And for the third time there was silence for a short space in heaven.

"So you did, man, so you did. Here, I'll write you a prescription for whenever you get home."

Alan ripped a page off the inappropriately Jewish calendar hanging with chutzpah on St. Vincent's own wall.

"Listen. If ever I-Am-He-Who-Cometh tries to come, I want you to tear off a corner of this paper, roll it up in a little ball, and swallow it with a full glass of water, got it? Then read what's written here in the middle."

And in the middle, boxed, inscribed in small caps with his Claritin ballpoint pen, he wrote, OH LORD, MAY I REMEMBER ALWAYS THAT MAN AND GOD ARE NOT ONE.

He offered his hand, and the black man took it. Grateful tears filled Alan's eyes.

"If ever I-Am-He-Who-Cometh tries to come, you look him in the eyes and say, 'Go now, and do not come back . . . ever. You must never, never come again!' Blow him a kiss as he leaves, OK?"

"OK."

"Here's my card if you need me."

"OK, Alan Krieger, RN."

"OK . . . ?"

"Thomas J. Brown."

"Any relation to John?"

"Yeah. He's my brother."

"I see. All right, wait here, and I'll send someone in to talk to you more and give you some little white pills. OK?"

"OK."

"You'll like them."

Thomas J. Brown nodded, sitting there with the prescription in his hand.

Alan walked out of the Chapel, pushing the IV pole in front of him and closing the door behind him. He shushed the crew of enthusiastic fans, signaling them down the hall, out of Chapel earshot. When the group had turned the corner, it broke into decorous applause.

Alan bowed slightly and said, "I'll see you guys later. I'm ten minutes over."

Alan's supervisor, Gloria Gant, otherwise known as "Goldtooth"—for her gold tooth—nodded with uncustomary approval. "You saved us a lotta whad'ya call it? Sooris?"

"*Tsouris,* my dear. With a T-S. As in Eliot."

Alan rolled the IV pole back to its former hallway haunt.

"Sorry, guys, I gotta get uptown to my sweetie-in-laws' for seder. That's Jewish for celebrating that y'all got creamed with plagues while *we* got passed over for smearing our doors with blood. The universal precaution."

And Alan Krieger, RN, waddled out the door like an endomorphic Gary Cooper.

# 2. NOTES FROM UNDERGROUND, AND OVER

*"I am a sick man. . . . I am an angry man.*
*I am an unattractive man.*
*I think there is something wrong with my liver."*

—Fyodor Mikhailovich Dostoevsky,
the doctor's son, *Zapiski Iz Podpolia*

Alan Krieger had nothing wrong with his liver, nor was he likely to, since he didn't drink or do injectables. Unattractive? Beauty must be in the eye of the beholder, for Alan had acquired not one but two lady friends—though overweight is not exactly chic.

As Alan has just trod down the steps and through the turnstile, one's attention turns, then, to "underground." *Podpolia,* in Russian, refers not to subways but to the crawl space under the floor of a house, and Dostoevsky has evoked in this little masterpiece an irate, claustrophobic consciousness in strained polemical battle with some imagined enemy, the condition, he thought, of modern man.

Unlike Dostoevsky's antihero, Alan Krieger, RN, was neither narrow-minded nor without character. Nevertheless, there was something *podpolye*-ish in his heart as he stood waiting to be transported.

Ecstatic discharge from the nether regions of the downtown express as it disappeared into darkness. Old Sparky, Alan thought, the festival of lights come round for Passover. The uptown platform—his—was filling up with huddled masses yearning to go home and watch TV.

What a card, old God. Execute all those lil Egyptian firstborns? *For I will go through the land of Egypt in that night, I and not an intermediary*—the Big Ham. He could have had Jews avenge themselves. But no. No Jewish Fists allowed. Why? Afraid of His People punching themselves in the face? Punching *Him* in the Face? He kept everyone in the dark that night, without responsibility or blame for all those little corpses.

What the . . .

Alan gawked at the lipstick kiss on his shoulder, and gazed back at the poster he had been leaning on. A blond male model, shot headfirst, recumbent in his briefs, foreshortened, looking for all the world like a god on a slab, featuring a pudendal mountain under pesticide-free cotton. At the peak of the mount, as if planted by Sir Edmund Hilary's wife herself, a full-mouthed press of lipstick, yum. This was the attestation that had transferred itself (less passionately) to Alan's shoulder. Sex in the age of mechanical reproduction.

"Gaak," he mugged, and did his best to undo the affection with a handkerchief still wet with the tears of Thomas J. Brown. He only made things worse. Yet damn! he was aroused.

What am I gonna tell my little poopchen?

Tell her the truth, Alan.

She'll never believe me. She'll think I'm two-timing her.

She'll believe you, she'll believe you. Who would kiss *you* on the shoulder?

A downtown train pulled in, filled up, and went sparking away toward West Fourth. Alan walked to the edge of the platform to peer into the darkness for his uptown express. The Cyclopean eye was not yet visible.

Look at all that shit down in the tracks. Paper cups and plastic bags and shards of . . . Shards! Sparks and shards! Chin up, Alan, for even here is the Lord.

He turned to the fourteen-year-old Puerto Rican standing to his left.

"*Buenos dias, muchacho.* Do you know about the sparks and shards of God?"

"No man, never heard of em."

The kid put half-a-dozen would-be passengers between himself and Alan.

"Even down on that rat-infested track . . ." Alan began his lecture to no one in particular. . . .

And he jumped back from the brink. The uptown express had snuck up, invading his kabbalah space. The crowd surged toward the narrow doors, gathering him into itself, squeezing him along as one might a molecule of Pepsodent.

"Ah, Truth," Alan sighed. "Rush hour on a New York subway!"

The car doors began to close.

"Oh no, you don't!" Grab that door. Umph! "Lemme in. O! that this too too solid flesh would melt. Yours, sir, not mine."

Conservation of mass yields to oomph of energy.

Wah. All right, now we can leave. Yowsah. Uptown Seventh Avenue Express en route to Debbiebubbie. Guess I don't have to worry about falling with all these pillars of salt in support. Lessee if I can tummy-waggle my way over to the hang-on. Ummm, no. Guess not. What if I suck in my splendiferous gut, go two-dimensional, and slither my profile over away from the door to the seats?

"Take it easy, buddy."

"Chill out, man, chill out. Just trying to promote the general welfare, you know. You probably don't know."

Speaking of welfare, that is one good-looking young shvartza now sitting in front of me. Mmmm mmm, chocolate one, how the unprejudiced Alan Krieger, here above, would like to eat *you!* Uh-oh. He-Is-Risen rises in the pants. I'd better avert my eyes. You'll never find God looking down.

THE NUMBER OF KIDS WHO DIE FROM GUNFIRE EVERY DAY: 10. THE NUMBER YOU CAN CALL TO HELP STOP IT: 1-800-WE-PREVENT.

Down boy, down down down. Look up, Alan, look up up up!

NO SPITTING NO SMOKING.

Better. Spit. I'll think of spit. How embarrassing. 'Death and the Maiden.' That's good too. Maybe I should write her a note and let it fall unobtrusively on her lap. Ah, *negrita mia,* for you I might die. . . .

Now if I just edge in a little closer, just a bit, excuse me, my pulchritude, no hanky-panky, just want to stake my claim for your likely-soon-to-be-emptied seat, yes. Down, boy!

Ah, tis a fair thought to lie between maids' legs, but at the moment, I mainly want to plant my fat ass on that red Naugahyde the better to people-watch, my dear. Oop, this guy's also getting up, and the guy next to him, and that makes three empty places right here in front of me, and we're slowing down, and we're slowing down, ladies and gentlemen, and Killer Krieger sinks right down, threatening contenders with his mass and tectonic determination, and he's got it, fans, he's got the space he had in mind, though, alas, minus the dark but fair previous occupant, which he might also have liked to possess.

How quaint the ways of synchronicity, though. At the moment of Alan's maximum mental drool, Elantha Thompson, a fourth-year student at Columbia Presbyterian, had been engrossed in Conyer and Evart's *Diseases of the Parotid,* an area of particular interest for her intended career as ENT surgeon. Her father was home on 96th Street, dying of his own parotid, metastasized. NO SPITTING. Alan, however, had focused more on her breasts than on her book.

And synchronicity is easily trumped by the stochastic. For who is steering ineluctably toward the seat at his right? Yet another also luscious, if somewhat galapygeous, dark young maiden.

"Galapygeous," thought Alan. There's a two-dollar word. The only known benefit of studying vocab for the State Scholarship. Never used it since. Pop would have killed himself if we hadn't won scholarships. Use "galapygeous" in a sentence. "Yet another also luscious, if somewhat galapygeous, dark young maiden." Wait. That's not a sentence.

Onward, nevertheless, northward. Sic transit gloria mundi. Let me check out the environs and settle in. What more do the placards have to say to me today?

DOES YOUR WARDROBE GET MORE RECOGNITION THAN YOU DO?

No, sir. Alan Krieger, RN, is Mr. Popular of the ER set.

IF YOUR JOB LEAVES SOMETHING TO BE DESIRED, IT'S TIME TO DO SOMETHING ABOUT IT.

As he was about to seriously consider that proposition, the door between cars whooshed open, and in swaggered two youths of color, fully equipped with acoustic accoutrements.

*I'm unna take that muhfuckin ho,*
*I'm unna shove her out the do . . .*

Something to be *desired?* Goddamn straight! Get rid of that fucking rap music and its filthy trumperies! Get rid of those ill-bred louts plus boom box now taking up more than their share of seats. Fashionable duds, $150 sneakers, perhaps stolen at gunpoint from some poor kid in the schoolyard. Violence for morons who can't handle diction. Seducers of the people! But what care I, who has little big tush seated next to me, and a bar to my left so she can't push me off?

TRAIN FOR A NEW CAREER IN 7 MONTHS.

ENT surgeon, no doubt. At St. Vincent's. And, wow, look at that Hasid over there, far as he can get from the peckerheads. Where the hell's he going? Are there still Hasidim in the Bronx?

"Hey, mista, ya got a light?" his neighbor inquired.

"Huh?"

"You got a light? Fire? *Lumbre?*"

"You talking to me?"

"Yes, I'm talkin to you, who the hell else yo u think I be talkin to?"

"But it's no smoking," Alan observed. "See the sign? NO SPITTING NO SMOKING."

"So?"

"So? Whad'ya mean, so? So 'no smoking' means no smoking. Or maybe you wanted a match for something else?"

"No, man, I just wanta smoke. *Fumar,* y'know?

"You mean you're gonna sit here in this crowded car—smoking?"

"You bet yo fat ass I am."

"*My* fat . . . But . . . but it's against the law to smoke here. Look at the sign. NO SPITTING NO SMOKING."

"Who put up that sign?"

"I dunno. The subway people . . ."

"What right they got to tell me what to do?"

"What right? I don't know. It's the rules."

"Sheeesh!"

She turned away to look for other help. But Alan was percolating, unprepared to drop it.

"What about just being considerate of the people around you?"

"Hey, man, you smoke?"

"Well, yes, but . . ."

"Then who you talking about?"

"Well, everybody in the car."

"Is cigarettes legal?"

"Yes, but . . ."

"You sayin I can't do something legal? Who you?"

"It's not who I am, but . . . I mean, I smoke two packs a day, and it's hard for me to even get to Pelham Parkway without . . ."

"You live on Pelham Parkway?"

"No, I live . . ."

"You a Jew, man?"

"None of your business. Yes."

"You so full o shit." She leaned across the way. "Hey, bro, you got a match? Thanks a lot."

"Whad'ya mean?"

"Whad'ya mean, what I mean?"

"About being full of shit."

"Scuse me, mistah, our station comin up. Have a nice Jewish holiday, whatever it is."

The car made a halfhearted attempt to empty out.

Sweet girl. At least she could have blown a little smoke my way. I'm such a goddamn good Jewish boy. She smokes, those guys blast their rap music and take up extra seats. Everybody does his thing . . . but me! Play by the rules, Alan. Well, *I'm* gonna have a smoke too. Freedom now, we shall overcome, I have a dream. OK, surgeon general, tie yourself to the mast, stuff your nose with earwax, here goes. Ahhhh. Shabbatai Z'vi embraced impurity to rescue the divine sparks imprisoned in the Kingdom of Evil, so why shouldn't I?

Pop died of Chesterfields, twenty-two milligrams of tar. Am I such a dope? No sir, ladies and gentlemen, it's Marlboros for me—only sixteen milligrams. So let's see, if he died at fifty-eight, I should live twenty-two sixteenths longer, what is that, let's say twenty over fifteen, four-thirds times say, sixty, four times sixty is 240, divided by three is eighty. Well, hot shit, eighty. Who wants to live longer than that? Isn't science wonderful? *Sapere aude*. Thank you, Imannuel Kant, and fuck you, surgeon general, and by the way, anybody else in this car who doesn't understand freedom and the American way.

"No smoking in the train, mister."

"Hey, baby, I've come a long way."

Alan took the card he was handed.

"Freedom for me. Freedom now. Whad'ya think? Huh? What are you, deaf? I'm talking to you."

He inspected the card he'd been handed.

Oh. He *is* deaf. OK—my chance to memorize the American Sign Language alphabet before he comes back for his spare change. Now, what's the likelihood this guy is really deaf? He didn't say, "Naw smawkii itha traen," like Helen Keller. On the other hand, maybe he's recently deaf. On the third hand, four legs good, two legs bad, he's probably not deaf at all. Let's see what he does with the kids in the corner. Ah, deaf but not dumb. The doctrine of avoidance. What's the change situation like? Yes, something down there. A quarter will do. Damn, they're tokens. Buck and a quarter each. I could get away cheaper if I just gave him a dollar. Too showy. Besides, I don't want to be pulling my wallet out in front of those kids. Hey, Alan, don't be such a cheapskate.

"Here's your card back, Mister. Sorry, I only got up to 'C.' A. B. C. See? I get it right? Say, I only have a subway token, would that be OK?"

Not a smile. Maybe he *is* deaf, or he has a great act.

"Here you go."

"God bless you."

"Well, that *would* be nice. I am, after all, one of the Chosen People. I said, *I am, after all, one of the Chosen People*."

Oooowie, that was one mean Hasid look. Black as his beard. Look how he just gives him money. No muss, no fuss—thigh-warm Hanukkah gelt. Whoops, wrong season. Actually, that guy probably doesn't even have thighs. Probably just limb structures made of challah dough. Or clay. Pop used to tell me how orthodox Jews tied a black ribbon around their waists to separate the upper body from the lower. How did he know that, the old commie? Never was in a shul in his life. The upper half is spiritual and belongs to God—excuse me, Hashem—the lower half is animal and belongs to the devils. So, you demi-evil satyr with your black eyes and black hat over there, what do you do with your wife at night? Huh? Do you take your hat off in bed? What do you do with the black belt, Hasid-*san?* Take it off? Does just your lower half copulate while the real you studies Torah with a flashlight? Oooop. He stands, ladies and gentlemen, a Jackson Avenue *yidl*. He puts a Jewish wag tilt to his fedora, gives me a final gentle glare, what's with him, what did I do? Musta been reading my sick mind.

And right on schedule, the underworld erupts into the overworld. Play of the modes. Out of the tunnel of Pluto, up into the open plenitude of Sol. In darkness let me dwell no more. Jackson Ave., comin up.

StonewallMichaelJesseGlenda, have mercy upon us, and let there be a net reduction of car population!

And the doors open, ladies and gentlemen, and eight, no nine, get out . . . and two get on. . . . And thus the universe continues its inexorable path toward maximal entropy and heat death. . . .

As the car depressurized, a wave of fatigue—staved off by the recent testosterone rush—caught up with its intended, and Alan's eyes began forthwith to glaze.

Split, oh Alan, split into Alan One at rest, and Alan Two, ever watchful for getting off at the right stop. Do not fail, A2, or I shall wind up in the wilds of Gun Hill Road or beyond, and be late besides. Einstein was a piker with his twenty-minute naps. I shall recover in twelve. Alan Two, peel your eyeballs for Bronx Park East and take heed, for Pelham Parkway is next. Be sure to wake me, OK?

Resting several chins on bullock chest, Alan Krieger dozed, dreaming of matzoh, sweet charoset, and bitter herbs.

## 3. THIS IS THE BREAD OF AFFLICTION

His Alan Two warning system intact and functioning, Alan One got off the train at Pelham Parkway and made his way through the unnerving whole-body egg-slicer gate, down the long and sticky stairway, out onto the trestled jungle of White Plains Road. Confronting him immediately at the foot of the steps, there it was—Bunsen burner of the psyche—Daitch's Supermarket.

Oh, cosmic geographers and imps of perversity, Daitch's!—where my less-than-sainted mother offered me up as a filial sacrifice and made me confess to the owner the filching of a five-cent pack of gum. Effective, if brutal, pedagogy from a brute of a mother. Could have been worse. Is worse.

But in the mid-distance, thar she blows. It's Debbieland, home of Debbie Goldenbaum, sometimes known as Goldenbum, siren demoness of the Alhambra.

Moorish music up and fade.

Is this a building or what? Six interconnected six-floor apartment houses ring-a-rosying around a lush courtyard with fountain, topped with genuine tile roofing, no doubt from New Jersey and not Granada. Beautifully landscaped without even a Filipino gardener. Alan, Alan, stop and smell the spring flowers, though unlike Ferdinand the Bull, you still have your taurine orchae and so would rip the shit out of those toreros before they returned the favor. I think.

Ferdinandrogen at the Alhambra, ladies and gentlemen, will now recite a poem titled "Ethnic Cleansing, or Not in My Neighborhood."

*In fourteen hundred ninety-two,*
*Columbus sailed the ocean blue,*
*While back in Spain, oi gottenyu,*
*There wasn't left a single Jew.*

A neat trick, worthy of the Exterminator. I can't believe I grew up with that. Bang bang bang on the door. Who is it? "The Exterminator." The Exterminator! And we'd actually let him in!

OK, 756 Pelham Parkway. He bounds up the three steps into the hallway. He smells in the gnarly old cabinet standing against the textured walls—mmmm, ancient socks of murdered kings—he's past the elevator, at the foot of the stairs, ladies and gentlemen, and contemplates his aerobics for the day. Three flights of seventeen stairs, fifty-one steps, no more, no less, a number that masquerades as prime, but that, under its skirts, divides rather nicely.

And now we need a chant to accompany us up the stairs, something in precisely fifty-one syllables, and of a nature to elevate us weightlessly to the fourth floor. How about the world's greatest piece by the world's greatest composer, none other than Jan Dismus Zelenka's masterpiece and top hit, *The Lamentations of Jeremiah?* An a one an a two an a one two three: *In-ci-pit la-men-ta-ti-o Je-re-mi-ae Pro-phae-te.* Two more steps to go on. Must have been only fifteen syllables. Something a bit longer, perhaps, for the next selection. *Pec-ca-* (just a minute, have to walk around) *-tum pec-ca-vit Je-ru-sha-lem, prop-ter-e-a in-sta-bi-lis fac* (and here we go round again) *-ta est.* Hm. Two steps up, fifteen to go. Let's try *Je-ru-sha-lem, con-ver-ter-e ad Do-mi-num De-um tu-* (damn! One extra. I'll use it to get around to her door) *-um!*

Apartment 4K it is, land of the somewhat free and home of the could-be-braver Debeleh the Yum-Yum Goldenbaum, social worker extraordinaire, mother of sorrows and font of pity. Mezuzah on doorframe, marker of sacred space within, and also don't kill my firstborn. All right. The Norns have woven my fate. Let's see what destiny is mine. Knock knock knock. Silence? Let's announce ourselves a bit louder.

But the door swung open.

"Alan!"

"Debeleh! Wanna boogie, little schmoogie?"

"Alan, mmmmmmwah. We can boogie right over to the table. We've been waiting for you to start."

"Hi, everybody." Alan performed his signaling-through-the-flames wave. "Isaac, Jane, and . . ."

"Alan, this is Beverly and Ed Rothman, friends of Jane's from Providence, and this is Seth and Joshua and Ruthie."

"Hi, kids. Pleased to meet everybody. Providence. How providential. Home of my favorite balladeer, H. P. Lovecraft. Nice you could make it to a seder so far from home. Sorry to keep you waiting, but I had a date with a nutcase."

"Alan works in an emergency room," Debbie explained to the Rothmans.

"The guy thought he was the Messiah. But I secretly knew he couldn't be 'cause he was black, and even *I* know the Messiah is white, blond hair, blue eyes—the gaunt white whale suffering the children."

The elder Rothmans seemed a little startled, but as no one else was taking shelter, they concluded the best course was just to smile politely. The children remained suspicious.

"Good timing, Alan. We're just now ready to start. Sit next to Debbie, there, good, and let the seder begin." Isaac held the Haggadah booklet in his left hand, picked up a matzoh with his right, held it high, as if bidding at an auction, and began to read: "*This is the bread of affliction which our ancestors ate in the land of Egypt; let all those who are hungry enter and eat thereof; and all who are in distress, come and celebrate the Passover.*"

. . . . . .

The seder—annual rehearsing of the Exodus in which Israel, once a nation of slaves, was humbled and awed by the power of its God. Four times the Bible adjures the Jewish father to pass this history down to the children. Alan's role, self-appointed and usurped from others smaller than he, was that of the wicked son who asks, "What mean you by this service?" as if he were a stranger, not a Jew. A good line for a straight man but only the beginning of Alan's capacity for mischief.

"Can I ask a question?"

"Alan . . ."

"Sorry. *May* I ask a question?"

"Certainly," answered Isaac. "What else is this service about? Freedom, free discussion, free action. The Haggadah is always open to discussion."

"OK, then. Here's the question: Do I really *like* matzoh, or do I just use it as a vehicle for butter?"

"Alan, cut it out!"

"*Because we were slaves unto Pharaoh in Egypt,*" Isaac continued, "*and the Eternal, our God, brought us forth thence with a mighty hand and an outstretched arm.*"

"''Scuse me,' said the Elephant's Child."

"Alan?"

"I have another question. Or rather a comment, Isaac. There is absolutely no evidence outside biblical assertion that the Jews were ever *in* Egypt . . ."

"Al-an!" Debbie elbowed him in the ribs.

". . . or that any of this stuff ever happened."

"Isaac, don't bite," warned Jane. "Let's go on. We heard this last year."

"OK, OK, I'll be good I just thought the Rothman kids should know this fact. Jews should not be ahistorical. After all, ten plagues—ruining crops, polluting the waters, massive starvation, killing of every first-born child in one horrific night—don't you think some of that might show up in the extensive Egyptian writings covering the putative time of the Exodus?"

"Alan . . ."

"Yes, Jane?"

"You want Jewish freedom? Then shut up and listen."

The service proceeded with Alan biting his tongue and playing footsie with Deb under the table.

"In front of you," Isaac instructed, "you see a plate with the symbolic foods of the Passover meal. It is time to begin eating, and by eating to bring the lessons of the Exodus from our minds into our very bodies. Please pick up the bitter herb—symbolizing the bitterness of our oppression—"

"None for me, thank you."

"Alan?"

"Firstborn children often don't eat *at all* before dark, since all our Egyptian cohorts died during the night and we were saved only because of the blood on the doorpost. And since here there is no blood—I looked as I was coming in, there's only a teensy-tiny scroll that might not be noticed in the sixty-watt dimness of the hall—and even though I was *second*-born, it seems prudent of me to continue my fasting through the meal, especially since my brother *ainé* is in Vermont, and I'm the one they'd be looking for."

"Debbie, where did you ever get such a meshuggener?"

"In an emergency room, where else?"

"Hey, I'm not meshuga, I'm the wicked child."

"Now," Isaac said, "dip the bitter herbs in the charoset—symbolizing the mortar we were forced to use to build Pharaoh's monuments."

"So if the oppression is so bitter," the wicked child demanded, "and the mortar such a load on our backs and spirits, how come it's so ground-nuts-and-honey sweet?"

"Why don't you tell us, Alan?" Jane said sarcastically.

"Isaac? What do you think?"

"Are you the simple child," he said, "or do you know the answer?"

"Presto, change-o. The simple child transforms into the wise child. *Ecco:* Slavery is bitter, but its orderliness and security can also become sweet to the slaves, going along and getting along. Voilà! Slavery's just gotten a bad name in the liberal press."

"Alan, that's ridiculous. You're stuck in your wicked-child costume. This isn't Halloween."

"Everyone lift your wine glass," Isaac continued. "*Baruch atoh adonoi elohaynu melech ha'olum boray p'ree hagaofen. Blessed art thou, O Lord our God, King of the Universe, who created the fruit of the vine.* Drink."

"*Oi, gottenyu,* Deb, a glass of Manischewitz even Mr. Manischewitz couldn't drink."

"You love it, you hypocrite. Twelve hundred calories a glass."

"Let us now fill Elijah's cup over there at the end of the table. Elijah, the prophet from the village of Tishbi in Gilead . . ."

"Will he come take a sip?"

"Of course. In spirit."

"So, are you going to show the children later that there is less wine in the cup?"

"Alan," said Isaac, unusually forceful, "the whole point of Pesach is to look toward the coming of Elijah, toward the Passover that will redeem all people from all pharaohs and turn the hearts of the generations toward each other. Alan, is this important—crucial—or not?"

"It is important. Crucial."

"OK, then," the elder continued, "Elijah challenged the injustice of the king. His disciples had a vision of him being carried into the skies on a chariot of fire. So we associate him with the end of days, with the coming of the Messiah, when all humanity will celebrate freedom. Let us open the door, then, that the prophet may come in! Josh, will you open the door?"

"Wait, Josh, first I have to go pee. But before I go, I will demonstrate a great magic trick taught to me by an old rabbi in sixteenth-century

Prague. It's called 'pulling the tablecloth out from a fully-set table without breaking the dishes thereon.' I haven't done this in seventeen years, so I'll just begin with the children's table here . . ."

Alan approached the small table butted up against the end of the larger one and pulled it back an inch to free the tablecloth. He positioned the dishes closer to the center and took hold of a side of the cloth.

"Now, remember I haven't done this in seventeen years, but we'll just see what happens."

Little Ruthie started crying. Beverly Rothman leaped up to protect and comfort her.

"There, there, sweet child," Alan consoled, "you'll remember this your whole life."

He pulled the cloth sharply floorward, and the dishes remained in place.

"Neat," said Seth.

"Neat? It's a goddamn miracle, and all you can say is 'neat'? What are you, a TV generation?"

He stalked out of the dining room, tablecloth in hand, slamming the door behind him.

"Leave it open for Elijah," Debbie yelled.

From behind the door: "Just a minute."

The company waited expectantly.

"Alan?"

From behind the door, fierce knocking.

"AS GOD THE LORD OF ISRAEL LIVETH, BEFORE WHOM I STAND, IS THIS THE HOUSE OF GOLDENBAUM—ISAAC, JANE, AND DEBBIE?"

Ruthie started to cry again. The door flung open and into the room jumped a strange fat figure, hooded and cloaked, looking much like Nurse Krieger but more embroidered.

"BE NOT AFRAID, SAITH GOD THE LORD. THOUGH THOUSANDS LANGUISH AND FALL BESIDE THEE."

"Is it Elijah?" Ruthie asked her mother.

"Me? Elijah? Vatayou, kidding? I'm Gimpel Shweig, come vit good news—for me. Harken and perpend. It says here" (he pulls a crumpled bus transfer from out his pocket and reads), "it is an old Jewish tradition that 'if a single male happens to come into the seder room ven the door is opened for Elijah, he is to be given the hand of the daughter of the house in marriage.'"

"But the door wasn't open for Elijah," Debbie observed. "We were waiting for Alan to open it when he came back from the bathroom."

"Besides," Isaac added, "my daughter is not available. She is already betrothed to a demon who lives on the other side of the river Sambation."

"*Oi,* forgive me, I'm sorry, I'm sorry, I must have gotten the directions wrong."

He backed out the door bowing and scraping.

BAM, BAM, BAM, another pounding on the door. In peeked a nose and glasses, checking more carefully this time round, and finally emerging, disheveled in his toga, a stooped old man clinging to his broomstick staff. His glittering eye held Isaac fast.

"Oh, my swineherd, I am your king back from the seas. Can you direct me to the faithful Penelope Goldenbaum-Krieger?" He surveyed the room.

"No one by that name here," said Joshua Rothman, who at thirteen was old enough to jump into the game.

"Is this Ithaca or not?" the Wanderer retorted.

"The Bronx. It's the Bronx," little Seth yelled out. The wise child.

"The Bronx? That's not the wine-dark sea out there?"

"Nope. The Bronx River."

"Fershluggener map. Sorry to bother you."

He slammed the door behind him.

"Alan, get back in here and sit down," yelled Isaac.

After a moment, Alan reentered. "Hey, I had a cup of Manischewitz.

Was it Isak Dinesen who called man an ingenious machine for turning wine into urine?" He moseyed back to his seat at the table and sloppy-kissed his sweetie. "Did Elijah come while I was gone?"

Once the Rothmans had taken grateful, expeditious leave, Alan, Deb, Jane, and Isaac stretched out in the living room, talking, leaving the dishes for Elijah.

"You know," Alan was saying, "the thing that gets to me is how cowardly we all are, sitting at our clean tables with clean napkins and clean children. We wouldn't know what to do with an Egyptian overseer if one had his sandal planted right in our *punims*. My God, what did even Moses do—and this was before God was on his case—pow! right in the kisser. Who here would do that? That's why I like the take-no-shit Israelis. Here, Isaac, throw me that Haggadah."

Isaac reached over to the lampstand.

"Here you go."

"Lessee. Page 38. When you open the door for Elijah, you're supposed to tell him, *Pour out thy wrath upon the heathen who will not acknowledge thee, and upon the kingdoms who invoke not thy name. Pour out thy indignation upon them, and let thy fierce anger overtake them. Pursue them in wrath and destroy them from under the heavens of the Eternal.* 'Them' is all the goyim. How come you didn't read that part?

"Alan, those verses were added in the twelfth century in fury at the pogroms of the Crusades. The Crusades are over. The Holocaust is over. We need peace in this world, not more war."

"Famous last liberal words, Isaac. You sound like my goddamn brother."

"We appreciate your passion for truth," Jane said, "and your impatience with our mindless conformity."

"Actually, we Buddhists go in for mindlessness."

"But I don't appreciate the cruelty implicit in it," she continued, "and finally the stupidity of your position."

"So what's so stupid?"

"What point were you trying to make, Alan?"

"*Oi.* You must be Jewish, Jane, you answer a question with a question. The point is freedom, overcoming oppression. It's *the* question."

"So?"

"So first of all, we have to have our facts straight. Were the Jews in Egypt or not?"

"Why is this important?"

"Were we oppressed by the Egyptians or weren't we? Who was Moses? *Was* there a Moses? Did the Angel of Death kill all the first-born? Did the locusts create a famine? Did the Red Sea part for us and drown our pursuers?"

"Who cares?" Deb put in.

Alan couldn't believe his ears.

"Whad'ya mean, who cares? If none of that happened, who is *us?*"

"Alan, *us* is the people who celebrate that story," says Deb. "You and me, for instance."

"But we don't *believe* it, do we?"

Jews in a room. Sitting with text. Study the book, they say, the books, the books within the books, the books beyond the books, the wordless books beyond the mystery of words. In the Bronx, it was growing dark.

"It doesn't have to be factual to be true," her father said.

"You think there was 'a man in the land of Uz, whose name was Job'?" his daughter wanted to know. "Does it matter? Does it matter that a real Jonah would be mangled and digested in hydrochloric acid before he was puked up on the shores of Ninevah?"

"No."

"So your position is stupid," Jane said. "None of the truths you're insisting on are important. What is important is the story."

"A *gemish* of old folk tales and fairy stories: tyrant persecution of a people whose existence is historically unexplained; a baby in a basket—which couldn't have happened in Egypt since pitch was not used in Egypt before Ptolemaic times; a princess who finds the baby and rears him as her own—a modified virgin-birth motif with inverted humble-to-noble household. Which baby turns out to be the savior of his people, magic-flight motif, passage through water, overturning of underworld power, and so on. The patriarchs enter the underworld of Egypt, and what comes out is the People—us. OK, let's accept the story—but let's *really* accept it. Who is this God who has chosen us as His People? What does it mean to serve him? I'm not talking 613 commandments, keeping a kosher house, and not fucking your neighbor's wife. I'm talking style, attitude, altitude. I'm talking what key is God in?"

"Alan, calm down, we're low on Rolaids."

"I'm talking let's look at how He models behavior. *And the Lord hardened Pharaoh's heart that he hearkened not unto Moses.* So the yiddles had to suffer even longer while the Lord got to make *potchky* with frogs and locusts? I'd rather be governed by a three-year-old."

"Symbolic plagues, sweetie, remember? This didn't even happen, according to you."

"OK, what about nonsymbolic plagues? Like Joshua fit the battle of Jericho. The destruction of every man and woman, every old person and every child, every ox, sheep, and ass—including yours if you had happened to be there. The only things on the 'save' list were silver and gold and goblets for the I-Am-Who-Am treasury. It takes an entire Chapter 12 to list all the lands that got smote. Good thing there was no war crimes tribunal."

"There's no clear archaeological evidence for any of this," Isaac responded. "You said so yourself."

"I'm talking story. *Teaching* story—true or not. And the teaching is clear: God—if we believe in Him—wants our enemies utterly destroyed. Passover night aside—this night being different from all others—He wants *us* to destroy them. How can anyone read this otherwise? If I were a *real* Jew—fart shittr, give me torture and decapitation of the neck and head, wringing of the teeth, extraction of the brain by the heels, partial, or even total suppression of the spinal marrow . . ."

"Alan, down, boy," said Jane. "Think where you're going. Are *you* ready to do what you say?"

Deb tried another tack. "Alan, you know why we're commanded to get rid of the *hametz* before Passover?"

"You cleaned all the leaven out of the house? Really?"

"We weren't maniacal about it. But we got rid of the obvious things—the bread and the cookies. I took them to the soup kitchen."

"OK, why?"

"It's *tradition* to clean leavening or leavened things out of the house," Isaac said.

"But why?"

"I'll tell you my theory," Deb said. "See what you think. Leaven is symbolic of what lifts us up all year, makes us work harder and love more. It's the swelling impulse of our souls."

"So why get rid of it?" Alan asked.

"What if our souls swelled with no reminders of restraint? We'd become obsessive, possessive, aggressive. Our love would turn to jealousy and lust."

"Yum," says Alan.

"So once a year we clean out the leaven and eat the bread of an oppressed people."

There was silence as the party considered the meaning of the party. But someone will always argue.

"Good whyfor, Debeleh, my zaftig Talmudic flower. But actually, I eat matzoh all the time—with sweet butter, in the image of God."

"It's not great for your diet, Père Ubu."

. . . . . .

What is it with Jews? From *pilpul* to *tsimtsum,* from Talmudic disputation to God as a zero-dimensional point, making room for the world. Capital *CH* chutzpah of the mind, soul armored in brain!

Consider the intransitive Yiddish verb *zikh arayntrakhtn,* literally to think oneself into something, to consider a matter in depth but also perhaps to turn oneself into the thing being thought of. For what else could be the meaning of his parents' fortieth wedding anniversary, with a banquet table featuring forty pounds of chopped liver sculpted as a bust of Mel Brooks? You are what you eat: it was surely Alan's father and not bad old Ma who had brainstormed that orgy of terminal Jewish thinking.

The spirit as meat. Circumcision, the essential corporeality of Jewish essence. No abstract spirituality here. Shamus, pass the knife.

*Tell me why,* Alan would often sing for reasons unclear,

*Tell me why*
*There's no meat behind my fly—*
*Drunken rabbi . . .*

Stormy weather indeed.

While escaping Egypt, his ancestors had accomplished an even more grandiose dodge—a retreat from small and myriad myths, from puny idols, from merest representation. *Einziger, ewiger* was their God, ubiquitous, invisible, and unrepresentable. What Hitler sought to annihilate in the "myth of the Jew" was precisely this: a race freed from myths.

Dangerous folks, the mythless ones: the atheist Marx, the antireligious Freud, the lensmaker Baruch Spinoza. Dangerous to themselves and to the goyim. There is a story that F. Scott Fitzgerald would haunt Jewish delicatessens just to hear the word *knish*. No wonder his marriage was shaky.

"If God were living on earth," the Yiddish proverb goes, "people would break His windows." No wonder Alan was hyperkinetic.

“Don’t worry,” they say, those Jews. “God has protected us from Pharaoh and Haman. He will protect us from the Messiah too.” This is serious levity. No wonder the house must be emptied of *hametz* on Passover.

Words and meat, and the consequence of each. The story of Alan Krieger.

## 4. *BEI* URSULA, OR SHIKSA *SCHICKSAL*

And afterward, down into the depths. Or rather, up into the depths, for the subway at Pelham Parkway is a steel structure thirty-five feet off the ground, a sub not sub until shortly after Jackson Avenue. Then, then, things become closed in and chthonic, and match the darkness of Alan's deceit. For, having just taken food with the Jews, he was now off to play with the Germans, or at least one German. And this surreptitiously: the Goldenbaums were under the impression he had to go cover a sick colleague's shift.

Southward, then, to Greenwich Village and its chief inhabitant, Ursula Franke, supermodel shiksa of psychiatry. Alan trudged, shaking, up the filthy subway stairs and thought to accost the phone near the newsstand at the top.

Goddamn! Three phones at Sheridan Square and now the last one is smashed! Fuckin dopeheads. What do they do, carry hammers around with them? And why the fuck doesn't Ma Bell fix them? Gone to the hairdressers? NYNEX outta bucks?

"Hey, who smashes these phones, Mr. Newsstand?"

*He* probably does. Supplemental income. No answer.

Have to go back down to the station. Descent into the Pit. Very deep is the well of the past. Should we not call it bottomless? Actually, Alan, it's only sixteen piss-soaked steps. Where's the phone? Ah. Looks intact, but you never can tell. I should use my rubber gloves and rubber dam, but no, I'll brave the receiver. What ho, a dial tone! And now six-eight-five-A-L-A-N. Yowsah! Of course it could be M—or O. And ring.

And ring. And ring. And ring . . . damn, I should have called from uptown. She's probably . . .

*"Allo?"*

"Urs! My little bear. I thought you were out."

*"Alan! I just got out of the tub. What are you doing calling? I thought you'd be at a seder with your family."*

"Hey *kleine* shiksa, howja know it was Pesach? And what do you know from seders?"

*"You think they call me Doktor for nothing? And from Universität Freiburg,* noch, *the honorable Martin Heidegger, rector emeritus?"*

"They teach you Jewish holidays in Freiburg?"

*"No. It's a standard calculation. You look for the first Sunday after the full moon after March 21 . . ."*

". . . which happens to be Bach's birthday . . ."

*"Then the stone is rolled away from the cave and the groundhog comes out and if he sees his shadow, it's spring.* Richtig? *Oh, no, that's Easter. Aren't they the same thing? Actually, I heard it all day on the radio on BAI."*

"The Brains Against Israel station."

*"Bad Alan."*

"Merely acute. Anyway, now that you're all clean and warm and cozy naked under your silk kimono, wanna hear the news? I just got raped. Raped and rolled."

*"Where are you?"*

"Down at the station."

*"Which station?"*

"Sheridan Square, *dummkopf,* what other station?"

*"I can't hear you."*

"Sheridan Square. Can't you tell the sound of the Seventh Avenue express going by?"

*"Don't yell. Could be any station."*

"I'll be right up."

I should really get a cell phone. What if they get this one? *Non est qui con-sol-e-tur e-am ex om-ni-bus ca-ris e-* (shit, one extra syllable) *-jus*. Why can't they ever get these stairs right? Ah, the bright lights of quaint old Greenwich Village. The smell of spring and dope in the air. The crossing of Seventh Avenue, requiring daring second only to the crossing of the Red Sea.

"Maniac! Fuck you too!"

Sheridan Square—"the heart of the Village"—a triangle. Alan had often pondered this. Four against three, a typical Brahms tactic. But more likely reflecting the corralling mind of General Sheridan, commander of the Army of the Potomack. But of course it might be an effect of the Stonewall Inn on Christopher Street and its famous Stonewall gang, makers of '69. Alan wouldn't put anything past them, especially concerning geometry.

Do modest *tuchas,* Alan. Smile at the nice man, but look demure. And it's left onto West 10th Street, home of Ursula Long-Legs, girl psychiatrist, and her totally offensive fat pug, Ophelia. The perversity of *Homo* so-called *sapiens* to have bred such a pathetic abomination from the noble wolf. $1300 a month for a fourth-floor walkup, and not even an outside bell. I am reduced as usual to yelling like an idiot to have a key thrown down. Ma! Ma! Throw me down a quarter for a Good Humor. And down it comes, sailing down, wrapped in a handkerchief so it shouldn't break the skull of any passerby. So considerate, my mother.

Alan approached the ornate brownstone and mounted its very first step. He craned his neck toward the top floor and felt his double chin expand to glorious oneness, its sulcus unaccustomed to the air.

"Gak. I can't yell with my head at this angle. And I can't afford a chiropractor either."

He stepped back onto the sidewalk and retreated to the curb, reducing the angle of incidence.

"Hey! Yo! Urs! Wooohoooo! Ursula . . . There you are, my little scrumchkin. . . . *Muchas gracias!*"

Lock one . . . and lock two . . . why the fuck they use two locks with the same key I'll never know. Lessee . . . any mail in her box from strange males? Nope. And creak creak creak creak, what do they do with the twelve times thirteen hundred bucks a month? Ought to be able to put in a bell and clean the goddamn hallways.

Now slow down, Alan. You don't want her to think you're all winded just climbing four flights. We don't want to bring up the weight and shape issue now when Bathsheba is just out of the bath. And—I think I'll stand here a minute before knocking, although she probably heard me coming up, quiet as Godzilla. Be still, my heart. Nymph, in thy orisons be all my sins remembered. Whoops. The door opened in front of him to an obbligato of shrill barking.

"Alan."

"Ophelia, quiet. Shhh. Don't you even knock before coming in? Oh no, you're supposed to say that to me. But I haven't come in yet."

"Do come in."

"Nice little Snorty. No. Down. Keep your slobber to yourself."

"So, Alan, what kind of a Jew are you if you don't go to a seder tonight?"

"A bad Jew is better than a good German, I always say."

"I hope not too bad because I made you a Jewish present."

"Chocolate-chip challah, my favorite."

"Guess again."

"Halavah? Potato knish? Pastrami on rye no seeds with coleslaw?"

"Here."

"A cassette box."

"He's brilliant. Next. What's in it?"

"It doesn't sound like much when you shake it."

"Actually, it's not a Jewish present. It's a Catholic present. A Catholic-to-Jewish present. Here. Sit down. I'll play it for you. Actually, I'll play the CD I made it from."

"Ophelia is snorting. I won't be able to concentrate."

"She's not snorting. She's breathing. If you didn't have a snout, you'd snort too. I'll put her in the bedroom."

"For the moment."

Ursula made for the CDs.

"Don't put that on."

"But it's Zelenka, your favorite, the first recording of his Requiem. Straight from Prague. Just released. Not available . . ."

"Doktor! You don't look like a doctor. You look like an enigma from the *New York Times* Fashion section. But Doktor, I just got rapped, raped, and rolled! Don't you care? I almost lost my pecker not to mention twenty bucks."

"I thought you were kidding."

"Do I ever kid? Especially about peckers? Listen. Get out your pad. You up on your rap?"

"What kind of wrap?"

"A kind of racist Ogden Knosherei, consisting of cheap rhymes and illiterate scansion."

"Ah, *Rapmusik*. I know it exists, but I can't say I've listened."

"You elitist, racist *Mutter*. It's the slaves' revenge, the new pedagogy for our younger generation. Here, I will perform a rap in your very living room. So, where you're sitting is one side of the subway car, and this here's the door, and I'm coming down from the Bronx to see my shrink, and in swagger three African American young people, all duded up, serenading the car with their ghetto blaster."

"*Rapmusik*."

"*Jawohl*. Now, *theme*: 'a neoconservative is a liberal who has been mugged.' Ah, but what about a *radical* who has been mugged? What then? Something newer than neo? A hyperconservative? Bernhard Goetz? But let us not postpone the performance. I offer you a simulacrum of the boom in the box that you may judge its finality for yourself. You go boom chick boom chick . . ."

"Boom chick boom chick."

"Keep it up. It's the entire musical setting of the text, which sounds as follows.

"Concerning white women, for instance:

*How you spell girl, girl, with a G?*
*Well, you know I spell girl, girl, with a B!*
*Cause I know what the fuck you fo*
*Ain't no mischance you called a ho.*
*Hey, a brother like me, he need only one thing,*
*And that thing a target for mah .44 ding-a-ling!*
*Ain't my vernacular simply spectacular?*
*I'm a killa, a Godzilla, that's the ganze megillah . . .*"

"OK, Alan, I get the point."

"You don't get the point. That's only the rap. You forgot the rape and roll. We're leaving 42nd Street, and here comes a legless black man scooting slowly down the aisle. He's looking around but fixes his glittering eye on guess who. Jesus, give me an I AM DEAF guy any day. He's on his way toward me.

"'All folks on this here car,' he says 'rich an po, white an black, happy an sad, dreamers or people who sleep through the night, I am no ordinary person.' No shit. 'No,' he says, 'I am not an ordinary beggar come to ask for yo pity and coins. I am special, a gift from the gods of self-esteem. Learn from me that you can lift yoself from whatever holds you down, holds you back.' He's getting closer. 'Stan up and shake yo fist at the darkness. Look aroun you, what you see?'

"I'm outta here next stop. So I begin to gather up my psychic entrails, and he says, 'You, ma friend, you're gettin ready to go . . .'

"And I say, 'Me? Yeah, I get out at 14th Street.'

"'I know what you thinkin,' he say. 'Ma brain know what you thinkin. You thinkin this guy really got some rap. You sad you cain't stay no longer. You thinkin he might have somepin portant to say to you. So how bout a little money fo Unca Sammy here?'

"And I say, 'I'm sorry, I don't have . . .' OK, here comes the rape 'n roll part. The boom boxers see fit to intercede.

"'Give him some money, man,' they say. 'The guy ain't got no legs.'

"The linguist among them translates: '*Dinero, hombre, ahora.*' I will act out the rest, complete with R-rated gestures.

"'Now, just a minute,' I say, 'you can't make . . . Here's my stop . . . I have to . . . Look, the door's opening.'

"'We hold the do' open fo you, man. The train don't leave with the do' open.' This from the third, hitherto silent, mechanical engineering student. 'Pull out dat wallet from yo too-tight pants and lessee what's in it.'

"'I can see into yo pants, *hombre*.' The linguist again. 'I know what's in yo wallet. I know what's hangin tween yo legs too. A lot o de former and ain't too much o de latter.'"

"He reaches down into the front of my pants, gives my ding-a-ling a tug (That was the rape part), then slides his hands around to the rear, and pushes my wallet out from the inside.

"'Hey, you can't do that,' sez I to meself, sez I.

"'Thank you, brother. Ten bucks ain't too much fo de portant lesson from Unca Sammy, is it? Let's make it twenty.'

"'Hey, looky this sporty condom,' says the engineer. 'Um um um, plastic ribs an a strawberry smell! You got some plans fo later, bro?' Do I, Lady Bertram?

"'Gimme that.' I snatch it back heroically.

"'I see you, Jewish bro,' says Uncle Sammy. 'I see you better'n you see yosef. I see you better'n you see me. You a dangerous man.' That's what he said—me a dangerous man!"

"Al-an. *Du*. You so dangerous! But come on, I take you out to dinner anyway."

"I'm not hungry. It's late."

"We'll have our own little seder—over at 17 Barrow. They're still open. I have an urge for snails."

"Snails? You're going to eat snails?"

"*Ja*. They're symbolic of your sense of humor and the slowness of the people who couldn't get their act together to get out of Egypt.

Sauteed in garlic. Symbolic of the bitterness of the killing of the second-borns."

"They were too slow to have first-borns? But what about my rape?"

"Minimal. Par for the course north of Fourteenth Street."

"I won't eat snails. They're not kosher."

"Where does it say that?"

"Deuteronomy 23:4."

"*Scheiße!* You're making it up. You can't kid me."

"All right. But they don't have cloven hoofs."

"They do—very tiny ones. How do you think they move? We're off. It's only a couple of blocks."

Down the stairs and out the door and down the steps and onto the street.

"I'm not eating snails. And I've never seen a grown Ph.D. slide down a banister."

"Alan, you sound like an old Jewish mother."

"I am an old Jewish mother. You haven't met Shlong."

"*Schlang. Das bedeutet* 'snake' *auf Deutsch.*"

"Yeah. Shlong my snake. He thinks I'm his old Jewish mother. Hey, slow down. Let's enjoy the spring air."

Alan's German romantic excuse to avoid puffing.

"Why is that?"

"What?"

"That he thinks you are his mother?"

"I got him when he was a baby, a wee suckling dove, and we just bonded that way. Remember Konrad Lorenz and the ducks?"

"My father was a friend of Konrad Lorenz."

"So you know his ducks?"

"No. They were living in Vienna, and besides, they were geese. Careful crossing. Here, hold my hand."

"Did you know this was the scene of the worst rioting in New York history?"

"When was that?"

"1863. The good people of Sheridan Square tried to lynch a bunch of newly freed slaves. See those lampposts there?"

"Why?"

"Congress had just called for a draft for the Army of the North, and Mom and Pop didn't want to see their sons go off to die for the coons."

"What are coons?"

"Blacks. Shvartzas."

"Ah, *ja*. Hasn't changed all that much, it seems. What happened?"

"Apparently a bunch of crazy abolitionists from Grove Street attacked the attackers, and the police attacked everybody, and the shvartzas escaped in the melee without so much as a by-your-leave."

"You wanted them to stick around for a greeting line? It always astounds me, the racism in America. In Germany . . ."

"You lynch Turks."

"Skinheads lynch Turks. People as a whole are quite tolerant."

"Even when the Turks take their jobs?"

"Jobs Germans don't want to do."

"Nice. Shitwork to the swarthy shitworkers while the Aryan race supervises in its lyrical, romantic, blond, blue-eyed way. Guess there are some things we shouldn't talk about."

"Guess so."

"I have a present for you," he said.

*"Ja?"*

"Two presents."

"What are they?"

"I'll show you in the restaurant," he said. "Where is it?"

"Next block, turn right. 17 Barrow."

"What kind of food is it?"

"Different kinds. *Wunderbar*."

"You've gone there before?"

"A couple of times."

"Recently?"

"Yes."

"With who?"

"Different friends."

"Like who?"

"You don't know them."

"Penis-people or vagina-people?" he needed to know.

There it was, at 17 Barrow—a restaurant called "17 Barrow." Paucity of imagination, he thought. Alan held open the heavy planked door.

"Two for dinner, please," Ursula said.

"Huh? Penis people or . . ."

"Alan, quiet. In private is one thing . . ."

"It's dark in here. What are they trying to hide?"

"It's called atmosphere, dummy."

The hostess led them to a table for two in the corner. Plaid tablecloth. Candle in chianti bottle with wax drippings from central casting.

"Thank you, miss, that will be fine. Alan, hang my coat over there. *Danke.*"

Alan and the waiter made converging beelines to the table as Alan returned and almost intersected.

"Excuse me!"

"No, excuse *me*."

This could have gone on but didn't.

"Well then, hi, my name is Jaime, and I'll be your server this evening. Can I interest you in a drink before dinner?"

"Just a menu, please," Ursula said. "And water will be fine. Thank you."

"I'll be back shortly."

"Thank you."

"I don't eat vegetables," Alan advised.

"You can put them on my plate if you're discreet. I'll eat them if I have room."

"You'd leave some?"

"If I'm stuffed."

"What about the starving children in Europe?"

"They eat better than you do."

Alan was too absorbed in the menu to promote the clean-plate club with his usual fervor.

"Mussels in White Wine, fashioned with bits of onion, garlic, and tomato. Too expensive. Moroccan Chicken Charmoula, a double breast of chicken marinated in a cilantro and cumin-spiced citrus juice, roasted and served on a bed of almond couscous. $18.95. No way. Ever see that cartoon of a woman in a funeral parlor? The funeral director says something like, 'And for only a few dollars more, we can have him laid out on a bed of cilantro.' Never touch the stuff. Tastes like soap. Grilled Pink Sea Bass in Jicama Salsa . . . What's jicama?"

"You'll like it. It's very mild and crunchy."

"Possible. Gorgonzola Polenta with shrimp and tomato. Bombay Chicken Salad in sweet curry dressing tossed with raisins, grapes, and toasted hazelnuts and served with a mouthwatering chutney and slices of kiwi. Ursula, these people are nuts. They'd eat their grandmothers if they could call it something foreign. Oh, wait—here's something that doesn't sound too disgusting. Crêpe de Maison, a choice of buckwheat or whole-wheat crêpe filled with smoked sausage and Munster cheese, topped with sweet apples and maple syrup. Sounds like a cheese dog from the wrong side of the class struggle. Now, if they would only use white-flour buns, a good Zion frank, Velveeta, and some Heinz sweet relish, I could get enthusiastic—at one-quarter the price and without the maple syrup, which reminds me of my brother."

"Would you mind acting the gentleman," Ursula asked, "and ordering my snails when the waiter returns?"

"Hey, you're paying, you order. He has to know who's boss around here."

She placed her menu on the table and looked at her date.

"What are my presents?"

"Do you know what today is?"

"First day of Passover, Thursday, April 4th, last year of the twentieth century."

"Factually accurate, but no, that's *not* what today is."

Jaime returned, pad in hand.

"Are you ready to order? Would you like to hear the evening specials?"

"No!" Alan barked.

"Yes, we'll have the Escargot Bourguinon and a glass of—do you have Pouilly Fumé?"

"We have Pouilly Fuisse."

"That's fine. And the Crêpe de Maison with a Coca-Cola?"

"Diet Pepsi."

"You're so virtuous."

"Diet Pepsi," Jaime noted. "Will that be all?"

"Yes."

"Thank you."

He swished away to the kitchen.

"You did that very well," said Alan, admiring her savoir faire.

"*Danke*. What's my present?"

"It's April 4th. Think."

"Nothing is coming."

"Ursula Franke, you're an embarrassment to your profession. In honor of the thirty-second day before the birthday of Sigmund Freud, I hereby present you with . . ."

"Oh, what a darling little couch. *Echt Wien.* For my one-inch patients."

"And . . ."

"A white beard."

"A genuine artificial Sigmund Freud pastie. It will go beautifully with your hair in the summer. I tried to get you some coke, but they weren't selling it on Pesach. And crack just wouldn't do. Too low class for my little Brünnhilde."

"Alan, you're so thoughtful."

"Put it on."

"Here?"

"We have to see if it fits. What if I have to return it?"

"But everyone will stare at me."

"So? Is this the Village or what? I bet no one stares. They'll just assume you're a male transvestite dressed as a female dressing up as a male German psychiatrist."

"Austrian."

"German, Austrian, they're all Krauts. And they all look alike. Like you. Put it on."

And so she did.

"Darling, it's you!"

She shook her head incredulously. "Oh, why do I have this thing for Jewish men?"

"Cause they assuage your Aryan guilt."

The strains of a Hungarian rhapsody grew threateningly closer.

"I can't believe it . . . gypsy violinists. Get outta here, you guys, I'm trying to talk with my German friend. She'll have you committed—she does that."

"Alan!"

"Look, if I drive them away, at least we don't have to tip them. Besides, it's hard to hear what you're saying, and besides they have shitty technique. Say, you know why a violinist is like a Scud missile?"

"Why?"

"Both are offensive and inaccurate. How can you tell if a violin is out of tune?"

"Tell me."

"The bow is moving. What's the difference between a violinist and a seamstress?"

"Can't guess."

"A seamstress tucks up frills."

"Know any flute-player jokes, Mr. Flute Player?" she asked.

Alan rebuked her: “Of course I don’t know any flute-player jokes. Flute playing is no joke. We descend directly from Dionysus and Pan, very respectable. On the other hand, I know a lot of viola jokes.”

“Why do you reserve brain cells for this stuff?”

“My fuckin brother is a violist, wouldn’t you know. What do violists use for birth control?”

“I can’t imagine.”

“Their personalities. That was made for Walter. If you drop a violist and a watermelon off the top of the Empire State Building, which will hit the ground first?”

“Alan . . .”

“Who cares?”

“Alan, you’re beginning to show some hostility here.”

“Why, thank you, Dr. Franke. Your check is in the mail.”

“You sound like Attila the Hun cranking up for attack.”

Alan stared at her in disbelief at her uncanny perspicacity. “Unbelievable! I used to have a portrait of him (taken by Alfred Steiglitz, I believe) hanging over my bed when I shared a room with my beloved brother.”

“That would be just like you.”

“Savior of the downtrodden, the despisèd and rejected.”

“Attila was downtrodden?”

“Well, despisèd and rejected anyway. He certainly has a bad press these days—sheer racism, if you ask me. But his mother loved him, and his troops adored him. Know how he died?”

“No.”

“Some hanky-pank in a tent with a younger woman. Quite suspicious.”

“I know something about Attila even you may not know,” she said.

“Oh yeah?”

“He murdered his brother.”

“That’s exactly fuckin why I hung his picture over my bed.”

“What *is* this thing about your brother?”

"He was the good brother, the smart one, Mr. Straight-As, class president, shortstop, batted third in the lineup. You know what my parents called me? 'Trade School.'"

"So you were jealous?"

"Me, the fat, ugly slob, jealous? Never. Just cause I couldn't even ride a fucking bicycle? Jealous? No way. 'Don't get mad, get even!' was my motto."

"What did you do?"

"Took my hunting knife and carved up his bed, his mattress, his half of the room. Sliced up his new catcher's mitt."

"Your parents must have loved that."

"And memorized nasty poems to quote at him. Want to know about Walter? I just so happen to have a letter of his, where the fuck is it? No, that's the Passover Haggadah, . . . buried somewhere . . . hey, goddamn, that's my renewal application, they're gonna expire my nursing license, I need to . . . Ah, here it is: letter from my beloved asshole brother. I will perform this document for you in my best Walter-bullshit imitation:"

"Here are your dinners, folks," Jaime said.

"Thank you. Snails here. Thank you. Pepsi goes with the crêpe. Thank you."

"Thank you, Jaime. A nice boy. He is a boy, isn't he?"

"Alan!"

"So listen. Here."

"Not too loud."

"*Lyndonville, Vermont*. That's where he lives, in fuckin beautiful university paradise with his fuckin beautiful wife and fuckin beautiful children.

"*Feb. 8—Martin Buber's birthday!* Always showing off. Usually with ironic references. *Alan.* Note no 'Dear Alan.' *I have in hand your second letter urgently asking for financial contributions to AIPAC and to the State of Israel.*"

"You've been carrying this around in your pocket for two months?"

"I haven't figured out how to respond. Driving up to Vermont and propping an open bottle of urine against his door and ringing the bell and running away won't do it. *I let the first one go*—I'd written him about a month earlier, when Hezboola-boola started lobbing Katyushas across the Mason-Dixon Line—*I let the first one go, hoping to avoid a take-no-prisoners (your style) spat with you . . .* 'Spat.' Typically marginalizing and demeaning, Jekyll to my Hyde . . . *but I can't ignore the vicious accusations you've made in this one about me and Anne, or your ridiculous truth claims about the Middle East situation.*"

"What did you say?"

"Wait. You'll get the picture. *I want to make my position clear once and for all, so that at least this issue will never again come up between us.* Yes, your highness, I'll try to control my insolent mouth in the future. . . ."

"Eat your crêpe before it gets cold."

"*You ask how I, as a Jew, can be so critical of Israeli survival. You accuse me of being a cowardly, self-hating anti-Semite married to a repulsive shiksa in contempt of my and my children's heritage, repudiating the heroic struggles of my people. . . .*"

"Want to taste a snail?"

"Get away with that! *Alan, you may equate struggle exclusively with violence. I see the larger—and far more important*—he only sees the most important things—*and far more important—struggle as being a moral one: the huge effort to carve out, over the millennia, the possibility of kindness among people.*"

"It *is* the more important struggle."

"*The cumulative actions of Israeli Jews in this century, while 'victorious' in the military sense, have been nothing short of disastrous with respect to this larger struggle. My support is for the moral and ethical possibilities of Judaism, and in this I am more true to, and loving of, our tradition than you with your JDL-type swagger and machismo. 'My* support . . .' Talk about swagger. . . . *Israel's outrageous policies of a thousand eyes for an eye is stolen right out of Goering's book . . .* This crêpe is not too bad. . . . *and should be condemned by any friend as well as any enemy.*"

"Swallow your food, I'll understand you better."

"No. Chewing and snorting is thematic. Ophelia does it."

"Chew with your mouth closed."

"How am I supposed to recite? *In praising and supporting Israel's campaigns of terror against the Palestinians, its enormous crimes against humanity committed daily, you are helping provide a green light which colors all American Jews in ghastly, shameful tones. You call for support and funding for Israel's continuing occupation of the territories, for expansion of its network of controlled roads, for its theft of common water supply, for ever more illegal settlements, and for its unconscionable policies of gross collective punishment which make a mockery of every professed American value of democracy, self-determination, and human rights. Even South Africa undid apartheid; you want me to support its continuation.* Thank you for the history lesson, Professor Krieger, but just who started this whole business? And who was almost exterminated?"

"Alan . . ."

"Wait, here's the best part. Here's the part even I can't respond to: *Let me say this to you once and for all: I believe ever more strongly that the price of a Jewish state is Jewishly unacceptable. The existence and practices of the State of Israel are a violation of every conceivable remaining value for which Judaism might stand in history. I find the brutal militarism and horrifying racism of the Israeli state and its supporters profoundly abhorrent, as is the implied message to the world that Israel reserves the right to create another Holocaust in retaliation for its own.*

"What this guy needs is a Katyusha shoved up his ass. He'd change his tune fast. *Alan, do not ask me ever again to support the State of Israel. Yes, I am a Jew. I value my traditions. But the State of Israel, morally bankrupt and mortally endangered by its victories, has triumphed over Judaism, and has deeply polluted the Jewish people, their history and their fate. It may even succeed where Hitler failed—and for me, the extermination of Judaism is too high a price to pay for the security of any state. Do I make myself clear?* Clear enough, my brother . . . *In biblical struggle, Walter.*"

Alan was actually foaming at the mouth. Ursula reached across the table with her napkin and dabbed at his face. He drew back reflexively and fixed things with his sleeve.

"That's a strong letter. I can see how you might find it upsetting."

"What is this? Active listening? Cut the shit. I mean, do you agree with him? Better say no. . . ."

"Jewish brothers fighting. It *is* the Bible story."

"No kidding. And who gets to win—always? Me. The younger brother. Isaac over Ishmael. Jacob creams Esau. Joseph rules. Aron fronts for Moses the Mealymouth."

"But the Jewish essence is *bei* Moses."

"What do you mean?"

An athletic, vivid-eyed black man in an Afghan sweater strode up behind Ursula, stopped, and peeked around to see if she were actually she. Alan eyed him with distrust.

"Urs!"

"Calvin! Nice to see you. Calvin, this is Alan Krieger. Alan, Calvin Alswang."

"Pleased to meet you."

"Are you here alone? Where's Denise?"

"We've been having a little difficulty."

"Calvin! Serious?"

"Trial separation."

"*Schade.*"

"*Genau.* Let's talk about it some other time. I don't want to bore—Alan, is it?—with news of the weird."

"Be sure to give me a call, OK?"

"I will. Tomorrow night good?"

"After eight."

"You're on. You may regret it."

"Never. Psychiatrists have infinite capacity."

"But you're not my psychiatrist," Calvin said.

"So do real friends," she answered.

"OK, real friend, *bis Morgen*."

*"Tschuß."*

*"Tschuß."*

Alan let several beats of silence ring out between them and chewed on his crêpe.

"Who is that?"

"Calvin Alswang."

"I know. I memorized his name. Who's Calvin Alswang?"

"Just an old friend."

"How old? No. How friendly?"

"Very friendly. What do you mean?"

"I mean you've slept with him?"

"Alan, first of all, no, and second of all, it's none of your business."

"How come he knows German?"

"Learned it in the army. Intelligence. He was stationed in Frankfurt."

"When you lived there?"

"That's how I met him."

"Were you his tutor?"

"A little."

"Is he the penis-person you came here with before?"

"Alan, cut it out. I don't like interrogations."

"Let's just go."

"You haven't finished your crêpe."

"I'll stick it in my pocket."

"Jaime will give you a doggy bag."

"I have a snake. Will he give me a snakey bag?"

"You never know until you ask."

Alan knew well that snakes don't eat crêpes. At least not dead ones. So he wrapped it in a Kleenex from his jacket pocket, figuring he'd wash it off later, and sat quietly while Ursula signaled Jaime for the bill and paid it with plastic. Calvin waved as they went out the door. Alan belched out a startling "Baaaaah!"

"E-flat. My lowest note. My fundament, like the River Rhine. Boy it's nice to get out in the so-called fresh air."

"What was wrong with you?"

"I don't know. Maybe the snails got to me."

"You didn't have snails."

"Just the sight of you picking them out of their little homes with your tiny satanic fork."

"I think of it as Neptune's trident."

"Hhmph."

"Sure it wasn't Calvin?"

"Shiksa thinking."

"I'm a shiksa."

"Worse, a shiksa psychiatrist," he said. "Say, do you mind if we swing by B&N on the way home? I want to buy you a shiksa psychiatrist educational Passover present."

"Sure. It's a nice night."

"Angel of Death passing over and all. What did you mean by that *bei* Moses remark?"

"Which?"

"That the Jewish essence was *bei* Moses."

"Oh, *ja*. Well—you know Schoenberg . . ."

"Know him? I went out with him!"

". . . in *Moses and Aron.* This business about no half truths, no representations, no Aron giving the people what they can understand. Only a unique, eternal, ubiquitous, invisible, and inconceivable God will do."

Alan snorted.

"No, really. I'm not joking," she said. "It's behind all anti-Semitism."

"What do you mean?"

"I mean what a cruel invention—such a God, your God, spying on every misdeed, purer and mightier than all those little gods on altars and dashboards. Six hundred commandments, isn't it, to satisfy Him? Who is perfect enough? Do those little old men, shuffling in their black coats, do their wives with shaved heads think they are perfect enough?"

"Jewish mothers—dangerous."

"Jewish mothers? What about Jewish sons, Alan? What about the ultimate Jewish son, that schizophrenic rabbi from Nazareth? Renounce the world, turn the other cheek, render good for evil, give all you have to the poor, love thy neighbor as thyself? You think these are ideas that can play in the world at large? You know what you get? Hypocrisy, guilt, resentment—and pogroms!"

"But we stood *against* Jesus. We tried to hold open the space for a *true* Messiah."

"Like Marx? Like Freud? The perfect society? Conversance with the creative depths of the unconscious? Think you can sell that on American TV? If you sow too much wind, you will reap the whirlwind."

"Anybody ever tell you you're too intellectual?"

Ursula stared at him with an undecipherable expression concealing God knows what.

"Alan . . ."

"I'll think about what you said. I will."

"We talk about this."

"We do. We will and we do."

They walked in silence for several minutes, the tension trailing off behind them like the spoor of snails. Alan stopped and looked up. Ursula followed his eyes to a huge bookstore's brightly lit facade.

"You ready for the Barn of Nobles" he asked, "where the elite meet the effete?"

She nodded. "What are we looking for?"

"A continuing-ed classic for a shiksa whose entire command of Yiddish consists of the word *shiksa*. Let's see . . . religion? Judaica? Humor? Let us be deductive, Dr. Watson. Given that this is a goyish establishment, albeit with a ungoyishly large collection of books, and that it's stock arrangement is probably done by an even more goyish digital computer with a gloriously goyish lack of sense of humor, I would think Religion subsection Judaica. *Bei mir bist du shane,* please let me explain. . . . And here in section 17 we see . . ."

"What is the title? I'll help you look."

"Something like *A Goy's Guide to Yiddish Expressions*. Something like that. Arthur Naiman. Nothing under N. Could it be my Jewish/goyish prediction meter is off? Let's hie us ho to Humor."

"From Religion to Humor?"

"A natural connection, especially for a second-born, wouldn't you say? Aha! Voilà! The little white book with the red-and-black spine. *Every Goy's Guide to Common Jewish Expressions, Also Recommended for Jews Who Don't Know Their Punim from Their Pupik. You* don't know your *punim* from your *pupik*. And right there on the front cover is a picture of you, slim, blond, and beautiful, standing outside the circle of us, the big-nosed ones, you looking lonely and dejected. This book is calling to you. You may not know it yet, but you'll see. $4.95 it's worth."

"You're upset because I played scholar-psychiatrist and you didn't like it?"

"No way, eetsway. I loved your monologue. Anti-Semitism 101 from the horse's mouth. Makes me think I'm worthy of a European intellectual."

"Wait, wait, don't turn on the light yet. I will perform the opening of *The Creation,* and when I get to the word *Licht,* you scream and bellow in C major and then flip on the light. Ready?"

"Idiot!"

Ursula hit the switch in the hallway.

"And God saw the cockroaches!" Alan said. "Look, aren't they cute?"

"Not when you get up in the middle of the night with bare feet."

"An *echt* New York sensation. Hey! what are you doing?"

"I'm trying to perform *Endlösung*. Damn, they're fast. If I had gotten that one, I could have tied it to the hood of my car. . . ."

"If you had a car. . . . Ever go to the Bronx Zoo and look at the tropical roaches in the reptile house? They're this big. You could scoop them out and wear them for hiking boots."

"What a thought."

"These little Blattids were scurrying into cracks when the stegosauruses turned on their kitchen lights. They think insecticide is a kind of vitamin. They'll be here after we're all radioactive corpses. I don't kill roaches; I worship them *in saecula seculorum.*"

"Amen. Not me."

"Not you? Roaches are your totem animals."

"You've got the wrong Ursula."

"Ursula Franke? Born 7/11/43 under the sign of Cancer—*Krebs*?"

"Crabs are not roaches. How did you know my birthday? I never . . ."

"I looked it up in the AMA directory."

"*Schlau!*"

"So I've got the right Ursula, Ursula the Cancerette, votary of house and home."

"Well, they may be ancient and honorable, but they're not exactly cuddly."

"Not cuddly? They *invented* cuddly!"

Ursula kicked off her shoes.

"*Sed te absolvo*—for the moment," he said. "I do not, of course, speak for God."

"And I forgive you—*and* God. Want something to drink?"

"I only do Manischewitz."

"How about a glass of milk?"

"No. I'm finished eating or drinking ever again after watching you suck snails. That was the single most goyish thing I've ever seen."

"I know Jews who eat snails."

"And I know CEOs who eat the body of Christ. It's not who eats what . . . it's, I don't know. You have to have been there. You need to get the feel of it."

"Of what?"

"Jewish/goyish. And ta-daaa. Voilà, your present."

"Instructions for Goys 101?"

"Correct. You're off to a good start. Hang in there. You'll like this. It's some stuff from Lenny Bruce."

"Who's that?"

"*Gottenyu!* Did they build a wall around West Germany too?"

"I can see we're into high ethnochauvinism here. And did *you* ever hear of Wolf Biermann?" she demanded.

"Yes! I can even sing one of his songs. Nya nya nya nya nya."

"I give up. You're a superior being. Who's Lenny Bruce?"

"It doesn't matter for the moment. A Jewish comedian. OK. The key section in your present—since it's a guide for goys—is the exposition and development of the concept of goy."

"I know the basics: goys are non-Jews."

"Right. Them. But if you're going to hang out with Jews, you have to be a little less objective and definitional about it. From our point of view, goys are where the pogroms come from. Goys are the stupid, insensitive, and violent folks out there. But it's subtle. There are all kinds and levels of pogroms. Lime Jell-O, for instance."

"Lime Jell-O is a pogrom?"

"You'll see. You're a quick study. You have a Jewish soul, I can tell. So here, I'll read you from page 49."

It was an intense lesson, being tutored and grilled by a trio from Hell—Lennie Bruce, Arthur Naiman, and Alan Krieger all at once. Ursula hacked her way through a jungle of Talmudic distinctions: the Jews Count Basie, Eugene O'Neill, and Beethoven versus the goys Eddie Cantor, Milton Berle, and Henry Kissinger.

"OK," she offered, "the pattern is becoming clear. Passionate blacks are Jewish soul brothers, and silliness or violence is goyish."

"Blacks, maybe," answered the teacher. "But you're on to something. Now Goyish 102. It gets more refined."

More refined was hardly the descriptor. It takes a refined soul to intuit the grave distinction between cherry Kool-Aid (goyish) and black-cherry soda (Jewish).

And then the intergoyish distinctions: lime soda goyish but lime Jell-O *very* goyish. And on into dangerous goyish, like trailer parks and the U.S. Marine Corps. The student was zinging along now, into the high realms of theory.

"Lime Jell-O. Thin, and a cool color. Lime soda even more," she recited. "And trailer parks—stereotypical scenes of violence—though I have to say they are the closest thing to sixteenth-century East European shtetls I know."

"True. We might need a second edition annotated by Dr. Seraphicus. But you're doing quite well, and you're ready for graduate-level Goyish 201."

Where Ursula encountered the mysterious distinctions between balls (goyish) and tits (Jewish), and the odd (to the unthinking) fact that all Italians are Jewish.

"You getting it?"

"I think I'm getting it."

"Good. Then on to your Ph.G. exam. You identify Jewish or goyish and put them in the right piles. Sort of like the ramp at Auschwitz."

"Alan, stop being cruel. Or I won't play."

"Sorry. Marlon Brando?"

"Jewish as Stanley Kowalski, even though violent, and goyish as Mark Antony, even though articulate."

"Bingo. Student of the Year award. You will therefore understand Naiman's Aggadic commentaries: *Talk is Jewish. Silence is goyish. Thin is goyish. Fat is Jewish. Blue is Jewish. Green is goyish. Atheism is Jewish.* Got it?"

Ursula nodded slowly as angry light began to glow behind the glitter. Alan sang out Naiman's text—with motions: "*Computers are Jewish. Rifles are goyish. California is goyish. France is Jewish. The '30s were Jewish. The '40s and '50s were goyish. The '60s were Jewish; the '70s goyish—*"

"Alan . . ."

"*Teddy Kennedy is Jewish. Nancy Reagan is the most goyisha person who has ever lived. Marie Osmond is second. Tricia Nixon is third. Richard Nixon, however, is too much of an open maniac to be a goy.*"

"Alan, stop."

"What about Clinton? George Stephanopolous?"

"Alan, I mean it. You can't have all the good people for yourself."

"Jesus—Jewish, of course."

"This is all your *verdammte* Chosen People bit come home to roost. It's what gets you in trouble all the time."

"We *are* the Chosen People."

"Alan, what does that mean?"

"Jewish *sechel, yiddishe kopf.* We're passionate and smart."

"So are the Berrigans. So is Susan Sarandon."

"They're Jewish."

"They're not. You're so arrogant and stubborn!"

"And you're antisemitic."

"What? *What?*"

"What did your father do during the war?"

"He practiced psychiatry."

"Where?"

"In Frankfurt and Bonn."

"And who was chancellor?"

"What has that got to do with anything?"

"It has everything to do with anything. All the responsible Germans left. All the good Germans stayed behind."

"That's stupid."

"Where was your father killed?"

"Leave my father out of this, Alan! Get your oedipal rocks off somewhere else!"

"A stoning of fathers, huh? Like they did to mine?"

"Who's 'they'? What do you mean? When?"

"Nineteen sixty-eight."

"What happened?"

"So-called community control. The shvartza school board wanted all the Jews out of the schools those Jews had built so carefully, so brilliantly, over thirty years. Poisoning their children with their Jewishness, you know. They just fired a whole bunch of teachers—bam. No notice. Pack up and move out. My father was in the Teachers' Union, leading a strike."

"And?"

"And he was stoned."

"What do you mean?"

"What do you think I mean, LSD? Someone threw a rock at his head."

"And?"

"And he died of a heart attack in his wheelchair two years later."

"You never told me."

"You never asked me."

"You've got tears in your eyes," she whispered.

"Precious bodily fluids . . ."

"Come here. Let's stop fighting."

"Hey, fighting is the Jewish thing to do."

"Yeah, but I'm not Jewish, remember?"

"Can I ever forget?" he asked.

"Come here, *mein Schatz*."

"You trying to seduce me?"

"No, I *am* seducing you. Turn out the light."

"What about the cockroaches? They'll come back and crawl all over us."

"You've converted me."

"You don't want to stay up and read?"

"Unh-uh."

"I hear the Angel of Death passing over."

"That's a police helicopter. . . . You'll get to interview the Angel of Death later. . . . There's a good Henry Jekyll. . . ."

It may not have been standard Freudian technique, but as an intervention, it was effective.

## 5. KRIEGER DOMESTICUS

Alan took the elevator to the top floor of a tan brick apartment building adorning the east side of the Grand Concourse. Occasionally he cardiovasculared up the stairs, in grudging obedience to Scott, his doctor, that six-foot-six mountain of muscle who shamed him at each checkup, with his jock bike parked in the hallway outside his office and photos from his mountain expeditions displayed ostentatiously on exam-room walls. But no steps today, not this morning. Late to bed, and a sinful bed at that, duplicitously snuggled in and around Ursula's lankiness, emptied of precious bodily fluids and filled with insomniac guilt over little Debeleh.

Elisha Graves Otis, hosannah in excelsis! If Einstein had had Scott for a doctor, he'd never have hit on general relativity. I'll bet that guy's never taken an elevator in his life. I'll bet he rappels down the side of his building to go to work and has his wife throw his bike down to him.

Alan watched the floors slip southward through his spacecraft's porthole. As the fifth floor went by, the state-of-the-art (1950) automatic leveler took over to guide the vehicle to a precisely positioned stop.

A right turn from the elevator and down the hall brought him to 6F—home, or at least his mother's home. Key in latch and key in latch, and—voilà, Valhalla! Except standing in the kitchen, putting on her coat, was not Brunnhilde or even Fricka but—

"Hey, Ma. How ya doin?"

"How should I be doing?"

"You're looking grim as Grendel."

"Don't give me any of your *mishegas*. Where were you last night?"

"I went to Deb's for seder, you old atheist."

"Seder goes on til eight in the morning? I'm going shopping. Anything you want?"

"Um, yeah. A can of Reddi-Wip."

"Alan, you'll make yourself sick with all that fat."

"Fats to the fat, Ma. Classical Hahnemannian homeopathy. Make it a large can."

"I'll be back in a little while."

She left, pulling her shopping cart behind her, an empty, rolling, collapsible cage—like her life, he thought, like her life.

Thirty-six was maybe a little old to be still living with one's mother, but to Alan's mind he was living in *his* room even if in *her* house, in a realm not much dirtier but territorially distinct. "I am a serious, cultured person, unlike my mother," it said.

The walls were floor-to-ceilinged with books—the great works of all periods. No less-than-literature volumes here. The exalted Germans and towering Russians took eye-level pride of place. And there were shrines, little face-out areas of shelving, sometimes decorated with statuettes or postcards—Buddha and Beethoven, Jarry and Rabelais, Einstein and Dostoevsky, George Steiner and Samuel Beckett, Shakespeare, Joyce, and Dylan Thomas, Wittgenstein and Spengler, Heidegger, Schopenhauer and Bloch—and the mysterious cover of Alexander Theroux's *Darconville's Cat.* And music galore. Old vinyls, cassettes, and CDs, arranged by composer, from Adam de la Halle to Zelenka. The complete works of every major composer except Brahms, multiple versions of favorite pieces, all three completions of Mahler's Tenth, closely compared—and his pride and joy, a 1922 edition of *Grove Encyclopedia of Music and Musicians* in six volumes. His "reference section" included a 1911 *Britannica,* read through up to J, and a 1945 twenty-volume edition of the *Oxford English Dictionary,* whose volumes he would often take to bed with him to read, caress, and smell.

His stereo was low-end: "I'm interested in the music, not the sound." His word processor did not compute: A good ol prewar Underwood with a ten-year old ribbon. This last seemed important, as if the ghost of ancient keystrokes might somehow hallow those of the present. "Good enough for Cervantes, good enough for me."

His fifty-five-gallon aquarium contained one large, quite lovely boa constrictor, the envy of the younger set at 840 Grand Concourse, which often knocked on the door to come play with Shlong, who, being a Buddhist boa, accepted all stroking with equanimity.

"I used to have a cat, kids—Myshkin. A thoughtful beast with few demands—no tai can-do lessons, no car insurance, no psychiatrist bills—just Science Diet Maintenance. An Enlightenment beast. And of course, 'Clean my box.' He died, defenestrating after a black squirrel in the canopy of my tree, only two stories down from my window."

The richness of Alan's room was complemented—in a yin-yang sort of way—by a mattress on the floor, covered with grubby sheets and a torn army blanket, a reading chair so overstuffed as to be overflowing in three places, and a squalid folding chair at a small desk whose laminated top was rising up at the corners, as if in prayer concerning the cigarette burns upon it, inflicted, it seemed, by graduates of the School of the Americas, but it was only Alan being careless. Which didn't reduce the half-dozen ashtrays and three or four coffee cups arrayed around the floor filled with butts, some drowned in caffeinated puddles. The wall surfaces, such as were left, and the windows, and naturally the book spines were as nicotine-stained as a wino's quivering thumbs. Reading Alan's copy of *The Magic Mountain* was an olfactory as well as a literary experience.

Alan entered his kingdom and pulled the cord to raise venetian blinds so filthy that even Shylock's servants would have balked at cleaning them. "Hey, man," Alan would say, "they're hard to clean."

He reached into his aquarium-turned-terrarium.

"Shlongy-boy, my little malic symbol. Are you growing any legs yet? Let's see."

Palpation of possible clavicular and pelvic areas.

"That mean Man, making you crawl on your belly! He'll come round. Just keep saying your *bruchas*."

He cranked open the window and looked out over the great, sunny expanse of boulevard, park, and river, already dotted with black and Latino strollers and a few old Russians. In his earlier years, it had been Jews. To the left, the great, gray granite County Courthouse, its bas-relief scales of justice gleaming gold, and beyond that golden gleam, symbolizing and concentrating it, Yankee Stadium, home of the powerhouse plutocrats, the team his commie father had always despised in favor of the Dodgers, the perennial underdogs to be fought for, the impoverished abolitionists of the national sport, liberating Jackie Robinson from the Negro Leagues. But Alan was a steadfast Yankee fan in the face of his father's passion and polemics. Take that, Laius! Before books, before his father's death, his room had been plastered with eight-by-ten glossies—some even signed—of Yankee stars from the '30s on.

"Stay out of my room, Pop, if you don't want to be politically assaulted."

Walter's room, on the other hand, had been festooned with pages from *Natural History* and *Field and Stream.* A country kid from the west Bronx. No wonder he ended up in fuckin beautiful Vermont. It had also been filled with sports equipment—bats and sticks and helmets, gloves and balls and masks and skates—for unlike Alan, who could root like the dickens, Walter could actually play, yet another thorn in the cap of sibling rivalry. But, as is the biblical norm, the younger brother had triumphed in the end: Walter's old space was now a stockroom for Alan's overflow—years and years of old *New York Reviews* and *Emergency Medicine* magazines; paperback classics too numerous for his crowded shelves; "less-than-literature" and "airport" books not worthy of sacred space, stacked in ignominious piles on an ever filthier floor; clothing too dirty to wear but never cleaned; furniture—broken and yet to be fixed; several ancient dried accumulations of Myshkin poop; and the treasure of this rat's nest: an old, dust-covered Macintosh Classic that Walter had once given him in a much-resented attempt "to improve your chances of getting published." May the Luddite gods of the underworld stick number-two knitting needles in his eyes.

Walter's room was also the bucolic setting for the Alan Krieger Roach Motel—"It's So Wonderful, Why Should You Ever Want to Check Out?"—actually a mini-grand hotel, modeled on Grossinger's. Its many windows and doors—cut into the gessoed walls of small-medical-equipment boxes and drawn in stylish Catskill Quatorze—opened upon the advent of great free food, stocked daily from the leavings on his mother's plate, his mother, who, although the ur-teacher of the clean-plate club, was herself a very bad student. Initial plans for an outdoor, roach-Olympic-sized pool filled with Dr. Brown's cream soda had been scrapped after the enterprise proved fatal to the first swimming party. The indoor dining room, however, was a smashing success. Ma's scraps were placed in a plastic pill-counting tray at the center of the complex, a device that enabled the more fun-loving roaches to enter through a hinged cylinder like children in a Burger King playpen. Most, however, just went through doors and windows, straight for the goods. Alan washed out the tray every week or so to minimize the smell. But then, it was in Walter's room that these Blattid goings went on.

Alan walked into the kitchen, opened the fridge, grabbed a half-empty can of Reddi-Wip, and sneaked back into his room, though there was no Ma to spy on him. He closed the door, plopped down in his chair, stuck the nozzle in his mouth, clamped his teeth and lips upon the white crenellated plastic, and tipped his head back and the red-and-white can up toward his right ear. Xhaaaaaaaaaaaaaawwww . . . That sound, like the exhalation of cosmic love, the sweet white ejaculate filling his oral cavity, bulging his cheeks . . . and then the slow, dulcet in-suck, his cheeks contracting unto gauntness as the stream of cream departed his connisewer mouth for the philistine, tasteless esophagus. Could heroin be better?

Eyes closed, he reached over to his left and flipped on the stereo, with its WBAI default—"We Be Against Israel," Alan often noted, but still home to . . . Wha? My God . . . the third movement of the Ninth. Why art thou cast down, o my soul?

As Reddi-Wip sank stomachward, late-Ludwig's gorgeous, inward, mystical contemplation sank upon a weary Alan with its flowering serenity, its slow, human miracles, timeless, beyond decay . . .

*the veil of Maya gently blown aside,*
*til earth and water reveal fire and air,*
*and all turns mist dispersed at morningtide,*
*as disembodied souls dissolve in prayer.*

Alan drifted with the blissful, sinuous variations, adagio and andante, protecting himself subtly from what was to come. And then it came, the most gargantuan fart in music, the terrifying *Schreckenfanfare,* blowing off all sublimity in the Master's attempt to ward off passive death. Alan twitched greatly in his chair, then got up to dispel the sacred and accept the secular, walking around his room like some boss considering whom to fire. The symphony's themes were reviewed and rejected by basses and celli until at last the "Ode to Joy" melody appeared, a tune Alan had always thought as gross as beer-hall bawling. But even he could not resent the increasingly complex set of songful variations growing through the strings and winds, joining forces with the brass to ease the *Schreckenfanfare* back again, this time prepared—and preparing for the entrance of the bass.

*O, Freunde, nicht diese Töne! Sondern, laßt uns angenehmere anstimmen, Und freudenvollere.*

OK, OK, Ludwig. Let's have it. Dump heaven for a sermon on brotherhood—see if I care, schmuck.

The orchestra began the "Ode to Joy" theme, and the chorus cried out its first and overarching word: *Freiheit!*

"What?"

*Freiheit!*

"Fuck *Freiheit*—where's *Freude?* This is the 'Ode to Joy.' Ah, yes—Lennie Bernstein, that over-reaching Hebraical bagpiper. The infamous No-More-Berlin-Wall concert. How dare he change the Master's words? Jewish chutzpah unalloyed!"

Alan began pacing fiercely around the room, his fury only slightly abated by the meliorating fact that it was *Freude* that remained the *schöner Götterfunken* and that all became normal after the initial outburst concerning freedom. Normal except for a performance uniquely inspired by the historic moment.

To turn the double fugue into a triple fugue and at the same time illustrate the *Götterfunken,* Alan wound up his beloved Nunzilla and set her waddling across his desk, shooting sparks from her mouth. As she approached the edge, Alan considered whether to rescue her from a plunge into the abyss but decided to let her experience the fall of Man like everyone else, though as a nun, she had never indulged her fleshly parts, or at least Alan hoped not. Over the edge the doll went, bouncing off the iron rim of the decrepit folding chair unfolded ("No worse than Glenn Gould's," he defended it to visitors) and landing on its back on the floor, undulating sexually as the key performed its ever-slowing gyrations. The sparks fell still. Alan stuck a smoke in her mouth.

The chorus sang, *Seid umschlungen, Millionen!*

He sank into his chair, and meditated on the messianic age.

*may*

## 6. HOW COULD ANYONE NAMED MARTHA NUSSBAUM LOOK LIKE THAT?

Four days later, back at the Alhambra, there was a knocking at 4K, D. Goldenbaum's door.

"Shhh. Don't let them know we're here."

"Al-an . . . !" She pushed him on the shoulder and shook her head. "Who is it?"

"What if it's the gestapo?" he whispered.

"It's me," came a familiar voice from out in the hall.

"Daddy."

Deb went to the door.

"Can't be too careful these days," Alan demurred.

"Forgot my book. Oh, hi, Alan. Didn't know you'd be here. Sorry for interrupting."

"First sign of Alzheimer's, Mr. Uh . . . what's your name?—forgetting books. Oh, no. Second sign. First sign of Alzheimer's is forgetting relatives' names. What's the book?"

Isaac picked up a volume from the foyer table—yellow star on brown—and flashed it at Alan.

"Rosenzweig."

"What is it?" Alan squinted at the title. "*The Star of Redemption?* Vat does zis book shoah?"

"Too much to tell you. I'm late for dinner. Jane'll have a fit."

"No, no. Now I'm interested. Yellow star and all. Gimme a two-minute précis. I'll write you an excuse note for Jane."

"*Oi.* May you have an inquisitive son-in-law. Let's see. It's about the relationship between Judaism and Christianity."

"Jews versus goys? We win. If the Messiah's already come, how come the world is like it is? QED. TKO."

"Is this the simple child again?"

Isaac did his famous disappearing act.

"Where'd you get that father?"

"Flea market in Tel Aviv."

"They let you bring him back through customs?"

"Duty free."

"You have no duty to your father?"

"Only to protect him from rebellious prospective sons-in-law who would eat him alive. But now, for your delectation . . ." Deb pulled a videocassette case from her backpack.

"The Wednesday Night Video Series presents—ta da!—"

"Oh, right. *That's* what we're doing tonight. What is it?"

"Hold your horses. You ready?"

"Do we have popcorn?"

"I'll stick it in the microwave."

Deb walked into the kitchen. Alan yelled after her.

"Can you put some Reddi-Wip on it?"

The popping kernels inflating the sealed bag were cousin to the Xhaaaaaaaaaaaaaawwww blowing up his cheeks, though they sounded different, a form and content twelve-tone variation.

"No," Deb yelled from the kitchen. She ripped open the two bags, poured them into a large mixing bowl, and returned to the couch. "But I'll put brewer's yeast on it if you want."

"I'd rather sprinkle it with mouse dung."

"It's already buttered and salted by Orville Redenbacher. Take it or leave it."

"I'll take it. What you got there?"

Deb turned on the TV and put a cartridge into the VCR.

"What is it?"

"Hang on a sec. You'll see."

She plopped down on the sofa next to him.

"Hollywood almost made a great picture once, but they caught it in time."

The FBI announced its intentions to enter without a warrant, obviously intent on attacking the homes of slow readers. A lion roared. And then—

ADOLPH ZUKOR
PRESENTS

Fredric March
Miriam Hopkins and Rose Hobart
in

*Dr. Jekyll and Mr. Hyde*

A Rouben Mamoulian Production

"When MGM made another *Jekyll and Hyde* with Spencer Tracy, they bought the rights from Paramount and stuck the Mamoulian negative in their vaults. . . ."

Alan didn't hear the rest of Deb's little history of competition and resurfacing. He was startled, even bowled over, by paranoia. Why this? Why me? What is she trying to say? He checked the corners of his mouth to see if he'd been salivating. No, that was with Ursula. Does she know? Does Deb know? The little monster in the man?

He let it go and settled in, part of him remaining on guard, outside, wary. Still . . .

The title sequence music was Bach. Ach, Bach. The G-minor fugue. String transcription, but still . . . Yeah, yeah, get on with it, please. Ah, organ, hands on organ, that's the real sound. Alan capitulated.

A plan to separate human good from human evil! Yes. If you could only do that, and leave the better half free to build a new world. "It's the things one can't do that always tempt me," says Jekyll. He talks about the girl, the blond girl, her leg, her leg dangling in his mind. Beware, Henry Jekyll, beware. "There are no bounds"? Beware.

"You know this girl stuff isn't in Stevenson."

"Really?" exclaimed Deb. "This is the only version I know."

"Yeah, well, that's cause you're a girl."

Alan watched through flame and bubbling liquid. His eye caught the skeleton in the corner of the lab. Truly Mr. Mamoulian was a master. And then the agony of transformation. Jekyll-March, the matinee idol, now a dark, fanged monster with wide-set eyes. What are his first words? "Free! Free at last!"

Hyde looks at himself in the mirror, laughs, stretches, dances, and gets gleefully dressed. Out into the London rain, agile as a cat. He opens his mouth for a drink from heaven. Such happiness, such boundless joy in the created world. Alan shoved in a handful of Orville Redenbacher.

Mamoulian's pregnant plot played out, with Alan attending half to the film and half to his own turbulent thoughts. "You ain't no beauty," the poor girl says.

"That's for sure," Alan answers.

And Hyde: "Under this exterior, you'll find the very flower of a man."

Hyde's dark, wild-toothed face against Ivy's white bosom. "They'll lynch him, just you wait and see. He's lost."

Alan watched, gaping, as the upright, exemplary man of science vainly mixed his beakers. Then the horrifying end, the caped fall from crucifixion. Civilization gathers round and stares amazed at the metamorphosis of monster back to man, calm and beautiful—in death. Free at last!

. . . . . .

"Why did you pick that?" Alan asked, cautiously.

"I thought you'd like it."

"Why?"

"Oh . . . a lot of reasons. Bach. And you're a leg man."

"I'm hungry." Alan snarled like Hyde and bit into Debbie's left tricep. "What's in the fridge?"

"Nothing *you* would eat. Some Pepsi."

"Diet?"

"Is this the Golden Tree Fat Farm? Vad'ya tink?"

"On the other hand, let's go pray at hamburger Mecca. I need to sink my canines into about ten White Castles. Maybe twelve."

"I'm on a diet. So, by the way, are you. But I'll watch you eat if you chew with your mouth closed."

"I promise."

"You're not afraid to walk up there at night?"

"Who would attack Mr. Hyde?" Alan cackled and leaped around, swinging his arms. "I'll take my cane. I'll give 'em such a *potchky* they won't know what hit 'em."

"I don't know why I put up with . . ."

"OK. No more beast!"

"What are the chances of that?"

They walked up to Allerton along White Plains Road.

"Free at last," Alan muttered.

"Yes?"

"Suppose the Jews could drink a magic potion and be free at last—what would happen to the world?"

The downtown express rumbled past, overhead.

"And how come it's called a subway if it's over our heads?" Alan asked angrily. "Maybe our heads are pointed down? People in Australia think our heads are pointed down."

"Supposing the Jews could be free at last . . ." prompted Deb.

No answer. What *was* he thinking? They walked in silence like double-Beethoven, both with hands clasped behind backs. East turn on Allerton—to the promised land.

"If people have to choose between freedom and hamburgers, they will choose hamburgers. Thus sayeth the preacher," said the preacher.

White Castle Hamburgers lay dead ahead. Buy 'em by the sack. They may be small, but so was Immanuel Kant. Alan pushed open the door, bowed to his mistress, who struggled to get under his arm and past his paunch. The celestial burger energy bouncing off white tile and stainless steel was staggering, as usual. Utopia. They plopped themselves down in the nearest booth.

"A dozen for me. How many for my sweet patootie? Oh, you're on a diet."

"I'll take two, just to keep you company and assuage your guilt."

"I have nothing to Hyde," he snarled, set his hands to claws, and made for the counter to order. Deb pulled a book out of her pack and got four minutes of reading in. Grab it while you can.

Alan returned cautiously carrying a tray piled with fourteen burgers, barely clothed in wrappers, as if modeling en masse for Victoria's Secret sandwich. Two paper cups of Diet Pepsi, filled to quivering menisci, demonstrated Alan's skill at surface tension and get-everything-you-can instinct, his doctrine of excess. He placed the kill delicately down on the sticky Formica and took in the cover, spine, and back of the book that was open between them. Actually, he took in only the author photo on the back—an elegantly gorgeous blond with long neck and elfin smile. It took Deb a moment to realize what he was looking at. She turned the book around and checked the image.

"Mmmm. Martha," she said. "She's a looker."

"Who's Martha? More chick-lit?"

She turned the book back around and held it up to him. Martha C. Nussbaum. *The Therapy of Desire: Theory and Practice in Hellenistic Ethics.* Nice trees on the cover. Dead, though.

"*That's* Martha C. Nussbaum? How can anyone named Martha C. Nussbaum look like *that?* Who is she?"

Deb read from the back cover: "Ernst Freund Distinguished Service Professor of Law and Ethics at the University of Chicago."

"By God's rattle, I'd like to be *her ernst Freund!*"

"She'd never go out with you. Too classy."

"Well, then, I'd never go out with *her*. What a goyishe *punim!* Anyway, I've got you, my sloe-eyed fastness. But," Alan inquired, "is she Jewish?"

"How do I know? Nussbaum. Sounds Jewish."

"Well, what's the book about? Desire, huh? So why don't you just do it, as Nancy Reagan advised—or did she advise, Just don't do it?—so what's it about?"

Deb launched into an exposition on how the Hellenistic thinkers saw philosophy as therapeutic intervention for the soul—a discourse Alan would normally relish. But while pretending to listen, nodding his head and smiling, this is what he was thinking: My God, I've been waiting for this woman all my life. It would take decades to do all the gene-splicing needed, but here she is. . . . I've got to have her.

"Um-hum."

". . . extirpation of anger. On the other hand, not to get angry feels like some kind of diminution of one's humanity . . ."

I could write her at the University of Chicago, maybe look her up on the web at work, check *Who's Who in Academia*. . . .

". . . remedies for anger . . ."

She'd make me an honest man—everything in one package, no more two-timing. . . .

". . . might be really important for you to read."

"Me read this?"

"I'll give it to you as soon as I'm finished."

"Well, it might be interesting."

"You can at least read the chapter on Seneca—'Anger in Public Life.'"

"OK. If you say so."

"Your dozen burgers are getting cold, dear. And by the way, if I may ask a question usually asked by you, do you know what today is?"

He looked at his watch. There was no date on it.

"May 11th," she informed him.

"May 11th? Why didn't you say so? Let's have a hearty birthday toast to Richard Feynman!" He very carefully lifted his cup of Diet Pepsi.

"You'll spill it."

"That's true."

"No, May 11th is the day before May 12th. And what's May 12th?"

"I don't know. Someone's birthday? Five days after Brahms's birthday, not that he matters?"

"What is May 12th?"

"I don't know."

"It begins with M."

"Mischief Day? Monster Day?"

"Getting warm."

"Malfeasance Day? Megalomania Day?"

"Muh, muh . . ."

"Mutha's Day? Mother's Day! My poor mommy. I forgot all about her."

"As usual."

"Well, what do you want, I should obsess over my mother?"

"Did you get her a Mother's Day present, as if I didn't know the answer?"

"Well, er, gosh, um, I . . ."

"Don't you think you should have something to give her when you get home?"

"What? What should I get her?"

"How do I know? She's *your* mother."

"Got anything here I could give her?"

"Stop at the drugstore and get her a card. That's all. That'll do it."

"Couldn't I just give her a free lecture about Jewish mothers?"

"Alan . . ."

"She'll think it's funny. It's a standing joke between us."

"Don't say I didn't warn you."

"*Te absolvo,* my sweet child."

## 7. MOTHER'S DAY NIGHT

Drugstores contain many types of drugs, but Hallmark cards are the drug most frequently sold, with annual revenues of $4.3 billion. Alan was basically clean—except for nicotine, a virgin unspotted, almost, and so perhaps a tad hypersensitive.

OK, Walgreens. Let's see, cards over there. Good! Mother's Day still with us. Holy moly Shazam! I can't believe it. I can't fucking believe it. Let's see—one two three four five six seven eight nine ten times one two three four five sections, that's fifty columns times one two three four five six seven eight nine ten eleven twelve thirteen rows. That's fifty times thirteen. Fifty times ten is five hundred plus three times fifty—six hundred and fifty! Six hundred and fucking fifty! Six hundred and fifty different Mother's Day cards! How can you have six hundred and fifty . . . oh, I see: categories. Different categories.

Soooo . . . here's MOTHER like my mother, I guess, though who could be like my mother? . . . then what else? MOTHER-TO-BE. I wonder if they have "Mother-that-was"—there's a million-dollar idea. HUMOROUS MOTHER-TO-BE. How about humorous plain Mother? But she's not all that funny. OTHER MOTHER. Nice rhyme. GODMOTHER and GODMOTHER ADULT. Is that like X-rated? Let's see. Nope, stodgier. NEW MOTHER, ah, poor thing, should be in the condolence section with little packs of Valium attached. Oh, here's a good one: LIKE A MOTHER. A Mother's Day card for my "Like a Mother"? No, that would be too mean. I mean I'm mean, but I'm not *that* mean. *Gottenyu*—FRIEND'S MOTHER! One isn't enough? You have to adopt more? I can't deal with this. FROM MOM TO CHILDREN—for Mother's Day? What a rabid guilt trip!

I know you won't remember to send me a Mother's Day card, so I'm sending one to you, hope you feel terrible, love Mom. CARDS FROM BOTH OF US—for the frugally minded, no doubt. CARDS ACROSS THE MILES. Dear Mom, thinking of you from *Challenger II*. Can you see me waving? SISTER, SISTER'S FIRST. RELIGIOUS SISTER. For Mother's Day? Our Lady of Fornication? Ah, NANA, ooo-la-la. Oop. We're in the unspeakably hip section—CARDS SUITABLE FOR SINGLE PARENT. Love them '90s! And last but not least, ladies and gentlemen, more lethal than a speeding bullet, more powerful than a TV commercial—it's SUPERMOM, who years ago, in the Orient, learned the secret of clouding men's minds. How the hell am I going to choose? This is a Ph.D. thesis project. Limit the search, Alan. Back, back. Back, like the aging Goethe, to the simple realm of basic MOTHER.

OK, so then we've got only one two three four and a half sections of ten times thirteen rows. A little less than half the total, the exact arithmetic is beyond me at this hour of mental and spiritual exhaustion, but say three hundred cards to go through. Only three hundred? Well, we'll do an adjectival inspection for relevance to our very own mother. Courage, Alan. "Gentle"? No. "Tender"? No. "Soothing"? *Oi, oi, oi.* "Guiding"? By contrast, perhaps. "Sharing." A little less would be appreciated. "Understanding." Possibly. Though what she understands is unclear. "Patient." Like an adder. "Kind." Yeah. To quadrupeds. "Undemanding." Gimme a break. Must not be Jewish. "Dependable." Like death and taxes. "Strong." You bet, two hundred proof, pH one point oh. "Warm . . . generous . . . giving . . . thoughtfu"—though what kinds of thoughts they're not saying—"kind"—didn't we have that one before?—"unselfish." Am I on the wrong planet?

This is the fundamental question asked by hostages. And hostages are usually ignored.

"Hey buddy, am I on the wrong . . . I'm talkin to you, don't walk away from me."

See?

"Asshole!"

Jesus, I'm only one row across section one. Two hundred ninety cards to go, I'll never make it. "Always there." Well, God knows *that's* true. "Never too busy." On the other hand, might it not be better to have been a latchkey kid? But they don't hire corporate execs with rolled-down stockings. Oh, look at this. How sweet. She "always finds the sunshine." And if the rains do come, she "keeps only the rainbows." Ipecac ahoy. Here's a mom that "always shows concern for others" and "expects very little in return."

That's it. I've had it. My cup of irony runneth over. We're going to do this by the random method and grit our decaying teeth at the result. Close your eyes, Alan. Now spin twice around, moving in a trajectory to your right as you spin, trying not to make a fool of yourself by poking your finger into someone's *pupik*—there! Got it! My finger directly on a card without falling on my face. Oh, praise to your semicircular canals, Alan, for their faithful service all these years. . . .

Why, it's Snoopy! Yes, Snoopy, why not? It matches her literary level and is thematically appropriate, though she won't get the obvious reference. What does Snoopy have to say to my sainted mother? Ah, a riddle. A conundrum, as it were. "What does a mother stand for?" Snoopy, my comical friend, do you really want to ask that question? Are you prepared for the answer? But . . . I give up. What *does* a mother stand for? Open the card, and the answer is . . ."She's so busy she doesn't have time to sit down." Good try, old droopy-nose, but avoidance will get you nowhere. You have to get up pretty early in the morning to hoodwink me, and it's already 8:14 P.M. But Mother Legree will like such innocence and take it as a compliment. $1.49? For this devious piece of shit? That's three and a half White Castle hamburgers! Well, this, plus a small bag of Hershey's Kisses to support her habit and perhaps absolve me of all but one passive peck ought to do it for under five bucks. *Laudamus te,* oh Deborah, who hath spared us the heartache and nitroglycerine of another forgotten Mother's Day.

. . . . . .

Domestic terrorism follows hard upon the interplanetary kind:

"Hi, Ma, I'm home. Hi, Shlong. Shlong, say hi. The only boa constrictor on the block who's lost his tongue. And you know, he never writes either."

"Where were you? You were off at five, right?"

"Stopped off to see someone. Happy Mother's Day."

"Who?"

"Now, now. Do not pry."

And with a Cyranoish bow, Alan handed her a cream-colored envelope.

"For me? Alan! You never remember Mother's Day. Or you don't believe in it or something. What happened?"

"I was contacted by the netherworld. Open it."

She did. After washing her hands. Which were shaking with joy.

" 'What does a mother stand for?' "

"I don't know. What *does* a mother stand for?"

Opening the card.

" 'She's so busy she doesn't have time to sit down.' Alan, that's cute. Thank you, thank you. Kiss!"

"You point to your cheek, Ma. Is that what they call body language?"

"Don't be so smart. Just give your mother a kiss for Mother's Day. It won't hurt you."

"Great minds think alike!" Alan evoked his well-planned evasion. "But not just one kiss . . . no, one hundred, all over the table. General Hershey's cavalcade of dreck . . ."

"And twenty on the floor. I haven't mopped."

"They're wrapped, they're wrapped. Don't have a cow!"

"A cow I have already! Won't even kiss his own mother on Mother's Day. When you were little, you used to kiss me. Now you're such a big man, Mr. Big Nurse, you don't know how to kiss anymore."

"I never kiss older women. It's bad for my psyche. It's kind of like kissing my mother."

"So who's an older woman? And how old is that shiksa you told me about? Want a kiss? A Hershey kiss, you don't have to be afraid."

"If there's any left over. She's twenty-eight and an M.D.-Ph.D. from Freiburg."

"What do you mean, if there's any left over? You expect me to eat a hundred kisses?"

"It wouldn't be the first time."

"You know, you really should call me if you're going to be late. I made supper. It's cold now."

"Where is it?"

"In the icebox. I put it in the icebox."

"Then of course it's cold."

"It was cold before I put it in the icebox."

"So cold, hot, what's the difference? It gets to body temperature eventually, then turns to shit, if it wasn't already."

"I cooked a dinner for you. Are you saying it's, you should excuse me, shit?"

"Ma, do you know a worse cook than you? Shlong, do you know a worse cook than Gargamelle here?"

"Well, Juliet Child I'm not, but I don't cook shit."

"What did you make me for dinner?"

"Hot dogs and string beans, Del Monte, like you like."

"Then I take a piece of Wonder bread and fold it around a wet hot dog, right?"

"And we have catsup and mustard. And some whipped butter for the string beans . . ."

"Ma, did you ever eat in a good restaurant?"

"Well, we ate Chinese a lot, we used to. Yeah, I've eaten in a good restaurant."

"And you always get the same thing."

"So I like shrimp with lobster sauce. What is that, a crime?"

"Ma, you don't have the most adventurous palate."

"Adventure? You should eat what you like."

“Ever have snails?”

“What?”

“Snails.”

“Like with things on their heads and shells.”

“Yeah, snails.”

“What do you mean have them? Crawling around?”

“No—have them, eat them.”

“Eat them?”

“Yeah, sauteed in garlic sauce.”

“I should eat a snail? What are you, crazy?”

“People eat snails.”

“Shvartzas in Africa, maybe. Not anybody I know.”

“No. Nice people eat snails.”

“Who? You?”

“Yeah, I’ve eaten snails.”

“I don’t believe it.”

“Ma, drop it. I’m sorry I mentioned it. So where’s the hot dogs?”

“I told you, in the icebox.”

“Can I give a piece to Shlong?”

“Why?”

“I wanna see if he eats it.”

“Why?”

“I just wanna see.”

“So if he doesn’t eat it, you’ll blame me. I know you. How do you know he’s hungry?”

“Last time I fed him was last month.”

“So? He doesn’t eat much. You don’t move around, you don’t need to eat. How do you even know he’s alive?”

“Well, let’s just take him out for a run. Doesn’t smell like dead meat.”

“Alan, I hate it when you touch him. He’s slimy.”

“He’s not. He’s dry. Here, feel.”

“Get away.”

"Hangs over my neck like the world's biggest stethoscope. Let me listen to your heart."

"Get away with that. Alan, why are you so mean to me? What did I ever do to you that you need to be so mean to me?"

"Don't get me started."

"What did I do to deserve this kind of treatment on Mother's Day?"

"Yeah, well, that's it—Mother's Day. You know what Mother's Day card Oedipus sent Jocasta? It came from the Mother/Wife section at the Aesculapius Drugstore in downtown Thebes."

"I don't know who Jocasta is, and you know I don't know who Jocasta is. So why do you . . ."

"Shlong, did you hear that? My own mother! Ma, sit down. I want to tell you a story."

"You're going to make up something ridiculous to make fun of me."

"I wouldn't. I'm going to tell you one of the deepest stories of Western culture—including the west side of Kiev, your motherland."

"Alan, sometimes you frighten me. Really."

"The feeling is more than mutual. OK, ready? Once upon a time there was a little boy named Oedipus. He was called Oedipus because Oedipus means funky-foot. Nowadays, we would call him 'impaired'—no, that was ten years ago—nowadays 'differently abled.' Does this sound familiar yet?"

"No. He was a cripple?"

"You could say that."

"Such a shame."

"But he wasn't born a cripple."

"So what happened? He got his foot stuck in something?"

"Close. Here's the deal. His pop, Laius, was king of Thebes, and his mom, Jocasta, was the queen."

"Jocasta was Oedipus's mother."

"Right. For the moment. Anyway, Laius was reading the astrology column of the palace newspaper, and he noticed a scary thing."

"What?"

"There was a prophecy that said, 'If the king of Thebes happens to be reading this, I hope you know that your wife will give birth to a son . . .' "

"How nice . . ."

"Not so fast. 'A son who will kill you . . .' "

"No! What son would kill his own father? I wouldn't believe it."

" '. . . and marry your wife, his mother, after you are good and dead. Laius, this means you.' "

"Marry? With going to bed and everything?"

"Everything. Except safe sex."

"Well, I'm sure he didn't believe everything he read in the newspaper."

"Who knows? But with a forecast like that, it's better not to take any chances."

"So?"

"See, I knew you'd be interested. So he looks at Jocasta's pregnant belly and thinks bad-father thoughts."

"Like?"

"Like when his son is born, he takes the little tyke and abandons him up on a mountain. And to make sure the little bugger doesn't crawl back down home when he learns to crawl, he spikes his foot to a tree stump."

"That's terrible! What did his mother say?"

"What she said was so horrible, it was never recorded, that's how horrible it was."

"I can imagine. I would never have let your father do that."

"That's the difference between being married to a king and being married to a *schlimazel*. Ma, even *you* couldn't boss a king around. Probably. Anyway, Baby Boy Oedipus—that's what it said on his bracelet—was rescued by a shepherd. . . ."

"It's a good thing."

"Maybe. Was rescued by a shepherd, and brought to the king of Corinth . . ."

"Another different king?"

"You get an A . . . who, being a good liberal, raised him as his own son. Nice palace, nice people, lots of Corinthian capitals. Then, one Saturday night when he was a differently- abled teenager, Oedipus and his buddies were tooling around in the limo, and they decided to take in an oracle. So up to old Delphi, and guess what?"

"What?"

"The Delphic Oracle told Oedipus the same story his pop, Laius, had been told: that he was going to murder his father and make you know what with his mother."

"*Gottenyu!* What did he do?"

"Well, he was a good boy. He wasn't Jewish, but he was a good boy."

"He told his parents everything."

"Quite the contrary. That very night he went home, packed his things, and after the king and queen—who he wasn't attracted to anyway—went to sleep, he climbed out of his bedroom window and hitched to Thebes."

"Why Thebes?"

"To get away from his like-a-father and like-a-mother. He didn't want to kill him and *shtup* her. They'd been nice to him."

"But Thebes was where his real father and mother were."

"You're cookin with gas, Ma. But *he* didn't know that. He just thought he could get a cheap apartment, maybe find a job, establish residency, take the SATs, maybe get into Thebes U and become an engineer."

"Or a doctor."

"Or a doctor. Actually, probably a doctor."

"Sure. A psychiatrist."

"You like this story—I can tell! So he gets dropped by a traveling salesman at the Phocis exit, walks away from the freeway to a place where three roads meet—this is a good place to start hitching—when all of a sudden he hears, 'Out of the way, you dirty hippie!' and he gets hit by a whip. Some mucky-muck and his bodyguard goons tooling along want the road to themselves. Well, Prince Oedipus is not used to being treated this way, not since his stepsister pushed him and his tricycle off the sidewalk, so he whips out his sword, takes a swipe at the chariot, and accidentally snags the right common carotid of Old Boopkis, who goes, 'Gaaaa!' and starts pumping out the red stuff. His companions aren't too happy about this, so they screech to a halt and jump our hero."

"There were a lot of them?"

"Five against one, Mother mine. But fortunately, he's already hot, he's a great fan of Toshiro Mifune, and guess what? He kills them all, whap whap whap whap and whap. Leaves a mess, but what the hell. Better to be on the right side of the class struggle. It's a public highway. But here comes another chariot. Time to skedaddle, let me tell you. Feets do yo stuff. And by that evening, he's jogging unevenly along Delphi Street, just about at the gates of Thebes, when he hears a crowd moaning. Oh, no, oh, no, *oi, oi, oi!*"

"What was the matter?"

"The Sphinx had just eaten the valedictorian of Thebes High School. Chomped him right at the neck, spit out his head, and scarfed him down. You know what the Sphinx is?"

"Of course. Like next to the pyramids."

"Another Sphinx. Her sister-in-law. This Thebes is in Greece, not Egypt."

"I'll have to look on a map."

"But you know about the Sphinx?"

"Like a lion with a broken nose."

"A lion from the waist down. King of the beasts of the land. This one had wings too. Eagle's wings. King of the beasts of the air. And up front?"

"A whale's face."

"Ma, you're a little Einstein. King of the beasts of the water. You're smart, but you're wrong. Up front this beast had tits like you've never seen."

"Alan!"

"Seriously, Mamie van Doren specials. And a Vanna White goyishe *punim,* with very sharp teeth. She would rub her boobies up against all the young men in town and whisper a sweet nothing in their ears. And you know what the sweet nothing was? A riddle. And when they didn't guess it—she ate em."

"Never!"

"Never say never. She had gone through the captain of the football team, the head of the debating society, the president of the Thebes Junior Chamber of Commerce, you name it. Anyone with leadership potential."

"They couldn't guess the riddle?"

"Ma, can you ever guess a riddle?"

"No."

"So? You're not supposed to be able to guess riddles. That's why they're riddles."

"What was the riddle? I'll try and guess it."

"If you don't get it, I'll have to kill you."

"A man doesn't kill his own parents."

"Who says?"

"I do. What's the riddle?"

"OK, you asked for it. Ready?"

"Ready."

"What is it that goes on four legs in the morning, two legs in the afternoon, and three legs in the evening?"

"A newspaper."

"A newspaper?"

"It's the only riddle answer I know. I thought I'd try it. No harm trying."

"Ma, that's the answer to another riddle."

"I know, I know. I just thought I'd try it."

"Your Einstein brownie points are disappearing fast."

"So? So I'm not Einstein. So kill me."

"How did I ever survive this long? Ma, listen, Ma, Oedipus gets the answer."

"What's the answer?"

"You think I'm gonna tell *you?*"

"Alan, what's the answer?"

"What will you give me?"

"A big mommy kiss."

"Right on my *tuchas?* Just like when I was little? Or on my ear, sucking out my tympanic membrane? No way. So when Oedipus got the right answer . . ."

"You're not going to tell me what it is?"

"No. When Oedipus got the right answer, the Sphinx was so embarrassed, she up and died of mortification. That's the story. It's hard to believe, but that's the story."

"It was something about her? About the Sphinx?"

"No."

"What was it?"

"I said I wasn't going to tell you."

"Just a hint."

"I can't. It's not a politically correct answer. We don't say things like that anymore."

"Alan, you're so mean. How did you get so mean?"

"I came by it honestly. You want the rest of the story?"

"There's more?"

"Remember the prophecy?"

"Oh, he's going to kill his father and marry his mother?"

"Who knows? But young Oedipus was carried into town on the crowd's shoulders, a big hero, and it was a good thing because jogging isn't easy with a bum foot. But at the entrance to the palace, cheering crowd number one meets weeping crowd number two. Pretty chaotic."

"What happened?"

"Laius, the king, was dead."

"And I'll bet that since Oedipus was such a hero, they made him king instead."

"You're good, Ma, you're good. You should become a writer. There was the little matter of Jocasta, the queen. I mean it wasn't that great a relationship, but still, a little mourning time was necessary if only for appearances. On the other hand, Laius was old, and Oedipus was quite a hunk, if you didn't look at his foot."

"How old was Jocasta?"

"Thirty-five, maybe."

"Still in the prime of life. How old was Oedipus?"

"Eighteen, nineteen . . ."

"A little young for her, wouldn't you say?"

"Ma, not only is he a little young . . ."

"Oi, *gottenyu,* I just remembered. Jocasta, she's his mother. Isn't that right? Didn't you say Jocasta was his mother?"

"Good! You get ten negative Alzheimer's points for that one."

"And he's going to be king."

"And after a long day of sitting on the throne together, he will turn to her and say, 'Shall we go upstairs, dear?'"

"She should say, 'No!'"

"But why would she? She doesn't know he's her son. She just thinks he's some quiz kid hunk from out of town who was able to outguess the Sphinx. Besides, her husband is dead, and she has the hots for him."

"Maybe he's not her son. Her son was supposed to kill his father."

"So who do you think the old guy on the road was? Why do you think there was a mourning crowd just after Oedipus arrived in town?"

"It was his father."

"Sad but true."

"This is a terrible story. Why are you telling me this terrible story?"

"This is a Mother's Day story. Did you forget this is Mother's Day? I'm ashamed of you."

"It's not Mother's Day. Mother's Day is over. It's ten o'clock," she said. "Time to go to bed."

"You're supposed to say, 'Shall we go upstairs, dear?'"

"What do you mean? There is no upstairs."

"You know, it's interesting. In all the psychoanalytic writing about the Oedipus complex—you know what the Oedipus complex is?"

"I've heard of it."

"What is it?"

"Stop testing me."

"It's when a boy wants to kill his father and marry his mother."

"That's stupid."

"In all the writing about the Oedipus complex, there is never a mention of a Jocasta complex."

"What's that?"

"A mother who wants to marry her son."

"That's even stupider. Besides, she didn't know. We know, but she didn't."

"Maybe. But maybe not. Her last words to Oedipus might make you think otherwise."

"What?"

"'Doomed man!' she calls him. 'May you never learn the truth of who you are!' Now, why would she say that if she didn't know? But still, she wanted the old in-and-out every night."

"What are you talking?"

"You don't think mothers sexually molest their boy children?"

"No."

"What about you?"

"Never."

"Lots."

"I never."

"Ma, ever hear of denial?"

"No. I mean yes, I heard of it, but I'm not denying anything. I mean you're crazy—I never did that."

"It's my earliest memory, burned into my neurons via the groin. You changing my diapers—so how old was I? One and a half? Two?"

"So you were supposed to change your own diapers?"

"No, I loved it. It's too hard to change your own diapers. And when you were finished wiping away the poopoo, you would swab me down with baby oil, and then you would kiss my little pecker, and it would stand up tall, and you would give it a little suck and say, 'How cute.'"

"Alan, that's sick."

"May have been sick, but it felt great, I'll tell you. And after that, when you would take me in bed with you after Pa was asleep, and open your nightgown, and snuggle me in, and pet me and . . ."

"What's wrong with snuggling your baby?"

"Ma, I'm five years old, six years old."

"You were still my baby."

"And your looking in on my baths, even when I was starting to get pubic hair. That's pubic, not public."

"I didn't look. I just came in to get things."

"Ha ha. You even used to make comments about it. 'Just like your father.' I remember that one."

"I don't want to hear this."

"Always lurking outside the bathroom door."

"Alan, you're sick. Not me, you."

"I could hear you breathing. And then you'd step back up the hall, and yell, 'Alan, are you ever coming out of there?'"

"I'm going to bed."

"Without me? And then will you come into my bedroom with your nightgown open to kiss me good-night?"

"You lock your door."

"As well I might. Would you rather I didn't?"

"You want me out of here? You want me out of your life?"

"It's your apartment, Ma."

"Put it all on me. You're like a little Hitler."

"Interesting you should say that. You know how Herr Schickelgruber got to be his inimitable self?"

"I know, I know. His mother."

"Another ten points. And her name?"

"I don't know."

"Klara. And her parenting style? No answer? Suffocating. Pampering, overprotective, overadmiring, seductive."

"I can go live with your brother and Anne."

"You think you can stand that shicksa saccharine twenty-four hours a day, every day? You think you can deal with Walter's pompous pronouncements about everything? You really want their fucking beautiful children around all the time with their ballet lessons and their Little League?"

"Eric and Sophie are my grandchildren. I love them."

"Uh-oh. Maybe I should be asking Eric and Sophie if they want *you*."

"Of course they want me. I'm their grandma. They call me. They write me."

"With Anne noodging them."

"How do *you* know? They like to kiss me. Unlike some people I know."

"How do *you* know? They're such goody-four-shoes, they'd kiss Henry Kissinger if their parents told them to."

"Alan, maybe this apartment is too small for both of us. Sometimes you go days, weeks, without talking to me, just looking through me as if I'm not here. Or you yell at me, you say mean things to me. This is not a mother's *nachas.* I'm going to call Walter and see what he thinks about my coming."

"Do what you want. First time you meet a swarm of blackflies, you'll be back to civilization fast. I won't rent out your bedroom."

"Good-night, Alan."

"Good-night. I'm gonna hit the sack too. I got a hard day tomorrow. Hey, Ma. Happy Mother's Day."

"Thank you. I liked the card. Thank you for thinking of me."

"Yeah, you're welcome."

"I'm still going to call Walter."

"It's your life."

# *june*

# 8. NOT A VERY GOOD PATIENT

In the early hours of June 6, 1999, on the occasion of Thomas Mann's $124^{th}$ birthday, Alan Krieger was assaulted in the St. Vincent's parking lot by an unidentified assailant. He subsequently named the shaved and sutured lump on his head "the Magic Molehill." Ever Hans Castorp (his self-assessment), he reported on time for his ten-day checkup, as ordered.

6/6/99 *HPI:* 39 y.o. white male RN found unconscious in ED parking lot by security. Hit to occiput c blunt obj. Brought to ED unresponsive to painful stimuli. No other obvious injuries. Regained consciousness in ED. Tetanus up-to-date.

*MED HX:* hypertension, chol. Meds: Lipitor, Lotensin, ASA. Allergy—. Soc: +cigs, -EtOH, -other drugs, lives with mother.

*PE:* Vitals: T = 37, BP 180/92, P 96, Resp 20. Gen: Unconscious male in full c-spine. Unresponsive to sternal rub or nipple twist. Later, alert & oriented X3, but c retrograde amnesia to event. HEENT: Hematoma occiput c 3cm superficial lac to area. Otherwise atraumatic. PERRLA, ext-ocu mvts N, TMs clear, oropharynx N. Neck: c-spine non-tender p x-ray, full ROM. Chest: stble, lungs clear. CV: reg rate, rhythm s murmur, rub, galop. Abd: +bowel sounds, soft, non-tender, o masses. Extremities: atraumatic, full ROM. Back: NT. Neuro: initially unresponsive. Glascow 3. Later A&O X3, Motor, sens, cnii-xii, reflexes intact. C-spine -. Refused CAT scan after A&O. I feel pt is competent to refuse.

*ASSESSMENT:*

1. Probable concussion
2. 3cm lac, head

*PLAN:* Will observe in ED. Wound cleaned. Local c 4cc Marcaine. Stapled. Wound check/staple removal/neuro check,10d.

M. Trabulsy, MD.

"OK, Alan Krieger, 6/16/99, ten-day check and general once-over." Scott heroed in through the door, and spoke before looking up from Alan's chart. Sitting at his desk, he turned and stared at the fat man swinging his bare legs at the edge of the exam table. "Randy get the staples out OK?" Scott got up and checked the wound.

"You like this jonny? You think it's me?"

"So how are you?"

"Why the fuck do I have to wear a jonny for you to talk to me about my head wound? Medical hegemony? The Great Chain of Being?"

"Calm down, Alan. Your pressure's already high. Randy got 180 over 105."

"White-coat hypertension. I get randy over Randy, the siren *smutchie*. Cleavage under lab coats turns me on."

"Well, I'll take it again."

"You? Because you're wearing a Brechtian workshirt—blue, not white? And when you press my flabby limb between your muscular arm and muscular side, think you that homoerotica does not rear its depravèd head? It'll still be high."

"So we have an epistemological problem here."

"Damn straight."

"It's not your blood pressure at all."

"That's likely. A measurement artifact. Your fault."

Scott sighed. "All right. Someone will take it later."

"An unattractive male dweeb might do."

"I'll have Randy eyeball the staff and select. So how's your head? Any symptoms?"

"What's wrong with my head?"

"Cut the shit, Alan. You know the drill. You're here for post-trauma assessment. Let's not play games. You were out for half an hour, you refused a CAT scan. . . ."

"Cats remind me of Myshkin. And I wasn't 'out.' I was resting."

"Resting my ass. You didn't respond to a sternal rub or a nipple twist."

"They twisted my nipple? They twisted my nipple—WITH THEIR BARE HANDS? What if I did that to you? Or to Randy?"

"How's the pain?"

"Where?"

"Under that lump on your noggin."

"Oh, that. Nothing a little Buddhistic nonattachment won't cure. That and some Tylenol 3, ii QID."

"Controllable with Tylenol 3, ii QID," Scott wrote.

"Any memory coming back?"

"Memory of what? Just kidding. No. Not really. It was dark. He was dressed in black, I think."

"That's more than you remembered before."

"There's been one disconnected phrase going through my head though: 'bleached-out, bleached-out.' Weird."

"A TV ad?"

"I don't watch TV."

"New street slang for 'whitey'?"

"Could be."

"You think he was black?"

"Don't remember."

"OK. Maybe it'll come. No nausea, vomiting, excessive head pain, sensory disturbances, vertigo, problems concentrating, memory problems outside of the event, weakness in arms or legs?"

"My biggest problem is that my HMO card was in my wallet, and I'll never get out of here alive."

"Your biggest problem, actually, is your pressure and lipids. And your weight. And your smoking."

"Well, why shouldn't I smoke and suffer obesity, hypertension, and hyperlipidemia in this world? In fact, why don't *you* suffer them? What's wrong with *you?* Here in America, we live off the fat of the land, George, and fat makes lipids and lipids make fat. It's genetic."

"Alan, Jesus . . ."

"As Kafka said, 'The Messiah will come only when he is no longer needed.' On the other hand, somebody better jump in sooner and do some serious kvetching. Did you ever hear that old Salvation Army song, 'There Are Flies on You, There Are Flies on Me, But There Are No Flies on Jesus'?"

"No."

"Want me to sing it?"

"Alan . . ."

"Scott, how am I going to get out of here without following the blue line to debtor's prison? They took my goddamn card. All my cards. Man is wolf to man, Wolfgang. Will you, with your snakes on a stick, run interference in this world of mergers and acquisitions?

"I'll go out with you to the desk and make sure . . ."

"Some wag once summed up American history as the conversion of Eden into money. I don't think that's fair, do you? There's a lot more going on here in this midden heap of blasphemy and cant. Like Velcro, for instance, which may augur the end of civilization. Or at least of *technos*. And the other dross: small-scale morality, libido for the ugly, the Big Fib. But the worst is the disappearance of mermaids from the East River. Did you know that Gerard de Nerval once took a lobster on a leash on a walk through the Tuileries? 'It does not bark,' he said, 'and it knows the secrets of the deep.'"

"Alan, I want to see you again in two weeks. We'll have a dweeb get your pressure. But call me if any symptoms develop. And cut out the fats! OK?"

"Yowsah."

"Get dressed. I'll meet you in front."

Scott walked briskly out the door.

"Whatever you say, Dr. Behrens."

## PAPER TRAIL 1

*VITAL SIGNS (in his own handwriting, on the back of a torn-up Count Chocula box)*

HEIGHT: 5'9"

WEIGHT: 290 lbs.

POUNDS THEREFORE PER INCH: 4.2

***OK, so I'm fat. The more there is to love.***

BODY MASS INDEX: 34

DX: Morbid obesity

***Morbid? Me? Get out. I'm the most life-affirming person I know!***

THIN-SKINNED OR THICK?

DX2: The Heartbreak of Psoriasis.

***Silvery scales? It's not so bad. Bryan and me against the gold standard. I'm trying amaroli—you know—shivambu, taking the piss. Urine as food, medicine, restorative, transforming agent, and immune-system booster. Helps me find the Shiva within. Haven't told Deb or my mother.***

WHAT'S YOUR SIGN, MAN?

*Virgo, man. Virgo is known as the sign of service. For many Virgos, the need to make things better is satisfied by pursuing careers in health-related fields or in other areas such as teaching, labor relations, environmental protection, social work, or religious counseling. Though most of them do have altruistic motives in helping others, it must also be said that Virgos have a tendency to act the martyr when their service or counseling is ignored, and it is not unheard of for them to use guilt as a weapon when they want to elicit the attention and cooperation of others. Like Ma, with whom I share the stars. Appropriate.*

*The Virgin is the astrological symbol of Virgo and, like the true virgin, most Virgos are shy. Like me. Like a virgin waiting to give herself to the perfect lover, Virgos are also idealistic. Like me. Unfortunately, when they allow idealism to get out of hand, nothing is accomplished. The virgin becomes a bitter spinster and talents die on the vine.*

*Mercury, planet of the intellect, rules Virgo, giving Virgos an analytical approach to life. That communication is important to Virgos is aptly demonstrated by the fact that so many of them are very talkative. They love books, magazines, and writing. With a critical eye for organization and detail and their constant search for perfection, Virgos have an irresistible urge to improve everything and everyone, whether they need it or not. Virgos are not above using their inability to achieve perfection as an excuse for their own idleness and unproductiveness. Out of character with their true nature, these Virgos are sloppy, disorganized, and irresponsible. See? Not my fault.*

FAVORITE SIGN IN CIRLOT'S DICTIONARY OF SYMBOLS:

FAVORITE SIGN, PERIOD: Yellow star

*Reinhard Heydrich recommended that the Jews be forced to wear badges following the* Kristallnacht *pogrom in November 1938. The German government first introduced mandatory badges in Poland in November 1939. On July 26, 1941, the Judenrat of Bialystok announced that "the authorities have warned that severe punishment—up to and including death by shooting—is in store for Jews who do not wear the yellow badge on back and front."*

OCCULT MEANING OF FAVORITE SIGN:

The seal of Solomon—two triangles representing fire and water, superimposed and intersecting to form a six-pointed star. Evolutive and involutive consciousness.

Six is the number of creation, symbolizing divine power, majesty, wisdom, love, mercy and justice.

FAVORITE SIGN FROM GOD:

The opening of the ozone hole that the divine effulgence may pour in.

## 9. LISTEN TO THAT LONG SNAKE MOAN

June 25 had been a hard day at the Not-OK Corral. At 2:37 AM., the stars being precisely right, two high-morbidity patients consummated a love-affair by jumping hand in hand from the balcony of the seventh-floor oncology wing at St. Vincent's. It wasn't far to the ER, though they had to be scraped up and assisted. Not a pleasant task, messy and creepy at once. These things happen.

Alan got home late—his mother had already left for her regular Tuesday visit to Old Ma, a woman twenty years more crotchety than she, and entirely in Yiddish yet.

"Falling" was today's secret word made flesh, though no mustachioed duck had manifested. Alan felt the need to consult his *Annotated Poe* concerning that most insidious fatal virus, the Imp of the Perverse, the sometimes overpowering instinct that forces us to act when we know we really should *not*—jumping off some cliff in secret ecstasy, free at last.

Alan got up from his reading chair, and walked to the window, looking straight down six floors, and then along the hypotenuse to sun-filled Joyce Kilmer Park across the Concourse. Had Myshkin really fallen, chasing a black squirrel? Perhaps he too had been prompted by some feline imp, licking its whiskers, and purring, "Why not?"

Maybe someday, Alan thought, but not today.

The Imps scattered and hid among the books, the psychic air freshened, erythrocytes reddened, and Alan, revivified, twitched.

"Let us celebrate, then, our resurrection from the would-be dead, for what is a day without a celebration, and resurrection is as good an occasion as any."

He checked his wall calendar, Chevrolet, 1943. June was the setting for a fresh-faced, blue-eyed family of four (the other quarter child likely hidden in the trunk, away from prying eyes) driving their dark-green Chevy past a levee, though why anyone would go to Mississippi in June was beyond him, especially when the Jews were being ovened only hours away as the raven flies. Still, it was probably better than Death Valley, speaking of death.

Several years earlier, during one of his extended autopsies of Fourth Avenue's book row, he had come across a stack of old calendars molding away at the back of a used-book store. Being a parsimonious fellow, he'd calculated that he could use the calendars over when the universe saw fit to come round again, based on its inscrutable, irregular notions of retro. Thus, 1999 was 1943, day-of-the-week-wise, a year that happened to be represented in his collection. What would we do without Nietzsche?

June 25. Any composers to celebrate with? None that I know of. Philosophers? Novelists? Wait . . . the 25th . . . it rings a bell. Ding-dong merrily on high! Unsilent night! This is the half-birthday of my co-religionist—Jesus—the old gonif who made off with the tradition. But then, *Someone* had to be out there playing baritone in Salvation Army bands. The hidden *lamed-vovnik* disguised as an out-of-work carpenter without whom there would be no bass for the quartet. Hippity-happity half-BD, J. C.

Let's see, what shall we do for the half-birthday cake? Wing-Dings. Drake the Old Spic Killer's Genuine Wing-Dings. We got lots of those. They're sort of a half-birthday-cake affair, though the placement of the hyphen is somewhat ambiguous.

He checked the window again.

Hmmm, looks like three or four kids in the park. Need kids for a half-birthday-cum-resurrection party. I'll recite "The Owl and the

Pussycat" to amuse them. No, better: I'll bring Shlong. He's always good for a laugh. Lessee, we'll need six Drake's Wing-Dings, one for each of them and two or three for me, and a new, large can of Reddi-Wip. . . .

He packed a Krishna ("the Gods Must be Hungry") lunchbox, eighth incarnation of the deity Vishnu, Krishna, that is, not the lunchbox, as blue as a chow's tongue. He also brought one of Ma's Yahrzeit candles, usually reserved for remembering his father's deathday, but he was sure the old commie wouldn't mind.

Displacing the Mac Classic from its cardboard carton, he placed the box in the bottom of Ma's shopping cart, the rainbow apple looking appropriately festive, and the gestalt—a grainy computer image caught in a collapsible cage on wheels—feeling philosophically right.

"Shlongy-boy, we're going out in the midday sun to play with mad dogs and their immigrant humans, and also have a party, some for you. Snake-out! C'mere big guy, ooof, you're getting heavy, soon be asking for the keys to the car. If I had a car . . ."

Alan transferred the snake from terrarium to caged Apple Computer box with the same tender efficiency as he might have offered a comatose anorexic, then changed his mind and lifted Shlong high in the air, uncoiled him, and hung him over his shoulders, supporting his head with his non-Krishna hand.

"My featherless no-ped, little boa that constricts not! Shall we go entertain the *Kinder?*"

Traffic halted as Alan crossed the concourse, though it may have been more the red light than the shoulder-slung Shlong. It takes a lot to turn a New York driver's head. The kids, however, were not as blasé—they came running up as soon as they spotted Snakeman.

"Step right up, little lady and gentlemen, for the First Annual Sissy Hankshaw Memorial Thumb-Sucking Event in Honor of the Half Birthday of Jesus Who Was Called the Christ!"

They didn't see what it had to do with the snake, but they stepped right up anyway. Alan curled Shlong up and placed him back in his box, a true classic if ever there was one.

"Shlong there, a genuine *Boa constrictor domesticus,* will be back in a moment after this announcement: Little bumpkins, how many of you like Wing-Dings?"

Four hands went up and wiggled on the ends of their stalks.

"Me, me, me, me."

"And how many of you like Reddi-Wip?"

The response was even greater.

"ME, ME, ME, ME!"

"And how many of you like sucking your thumb?"

Confusion reigned. One little Puerto Rican boy half raised a hand, then dropped it in view of his isolation.

"Well, let me change the question. How many of you would suck your thumb if it were filled full of Reddi-Wip?"

The old enthusiasm returned. By now two mothers and one father were investigating the situation. Alan decided to play to their fears.

"*Mesdames et Monsieur les parents,* be not afraid. Today is the half-birthday of our Lord and Savior, Jesus who is called the Christ. The 25th of June, I kid you not. You celebrate the infant Christ, why not celebrate the six-month-old? Six months. Cute. Sitting up without support, grabbing for Daddy's spoon, ga-ga, goo-goo."

The adults looked puzzled but not hostile. On to the security section of the talk.

"Grownups all, I have here three unopened packs of Drake's Wing-Dings. Check them yourself—they have not been tampered with."

He passed them around. The more mature actually checked them out. A small crowd was beginning to grow.

"And here, ladies and gentlemen, a new, unopened, large can of Reddi-Wip. You, sir, will you break the seal?"

The father of the Puerto Rican boy bent the plastic tab until it broke.

"It's unfortunate that these days, one has to be so suspicious about gift horses trampling one's children, but it's always wise to be cautious, wise to be cautious. Which of you are the parents of these children?"

Two white moms and thePuerto Rican dad signaled. A fourth child, slim, black, was still unclaimed. Alan signaled him to step forward.

"What's your name, little Tadzio?"

"Hermes Laveau."

Alan's interior eyebrows went up.

"And is your mother or father here, Hermes Laveau?"

"She's over there."

Alan turned in the direction of Hermes's point, and his exterior eyebrows went up even further. Sitting on a bench twenty feet off, interested but easy, was the most beautiful woman—or at least the sexiest—he had ever seen. She was black with lithe limbs and features, a dancer's body—if too voluptuous for Balanchine—in tank-top and Caribbean wraparound, legs crossed, a flip-flop flapping rhythmically against her sole. How beautiful are the feet of them, he thought.

She signaled to Alan that she had been watching and that he might proceed. He addressed the white mom, proximal, who had ended up holding the cake.

"Ma'am, will you do the honors and open the Wing-Ding packs?"

She ripped three cellophanes and handed them over to Alan.

"No, no, *you* give them out to the children. Only one each—I'll take the leftovers."

Four children stood with Wing-Dings in hand. A little white girl began to eat.

"Wait, wait!" commanded Alan. "The best is yet to come. I want you to stick your thumb inside the Wing-Ding."

"My thumb is dirty," said the anxious little girl.

"Right. Everyone to the water fountain."

Hands all washed, the children resumed their positions.

"Thumbs inside Wing-Dings," the staff sergeant ordered.

Squoosh went the thumbs.

"Hold them up for inspection. Very good, very good. Now . . . Reddi-Wip, please."

Mr. Puerto Rican handed over the can. Alan inserted the nozzle into each exposed Wing-Ding end, the same as he would a Foley catheter. With munificent Xhaaaaaaaaaaaaaaawwwws, the can injected its contents into each cake, which expanded to three times its normal volume. Excess Reddi-Wip chased the retreating tip. Alan turned to the surrounding parents.

"They put neoprene in the dough. It makes the eater flexible."

He turned back to the kids.

"Anybody against thumb-sucking now?"

A rhetorical question needing no answer. Nevertheless, "Unh-unh, unh-unh, unh-unh, unh-unh."

"But first we must also placate the source. As the gods need their sacrifice, so do I too enjoy my Sissy Hankshaw Wing-Ding Thumbs."

He held out his two plaintively naked digits; the kids got the point and did him up bilaterally.

"OK. Everybody ready?"

Heads nodded.

"Set?"

Mouths approached tumescent thumbs.

"But first, let's sing 'Happy Half Birthday' to the birthday boy."

Alan led the falsely cadenced chorus . . .

*"Happy birthday, to you,*
*Happy birthday to you . . ."*

. . . and cut them off abruptly.

"That's half the song."

It was unclear that the children remembered who the half-birthday boy was. Nevertheless, "Go!"

Slurp, suck, and gobble. Though no race had been declared, a race was on, and guess who won, even with a double handicap.

"Well, my mouth is bigger."

The kids were happy enough. So was Alan, since during the slurping and gobbling it was Hermes's mother who had been his secret mental Wing-Ding. Though all others might be ignorant of that fact, she seemed to know it, for during the event she had ambled over to the crowd to watch more closely.

"What about the snake?" she asked.

"Ohmigod! I almost forgot! Kids, we almost forgot Shlong! Each one of you can pat him. Don't worry, he doesn't bite, I promise."

The three parents looked wary but signaled their tentative permission. Hermes's mom reached into the Macintosh box and withdrew Shlong for easier petting. As the children stroked, she wound Shlong around her neck and arms and subtly moved with him, setting up a slow resonance that alarmed Alan. He had never before seen such an expression on Shlong's face. When all the children had finished their ministrations, she gently placed the snake in his box.

Alan could barely speak. He did manage:

"Why don't you all . . . take Shlong for a walk . . . in his shopping cart . . . just around the park . . . no crossing the street. . . ."

The kids disappeared with their charge.

Alan sat down at one end of a bench. Though she sat down four feet away at the other, he felt almost suffocated by her nearness.

"Alan Krieger," he offered.

"Calypso Laveau."

They shook hands across the divide. He stared. "You're from Haiti."

"*Naturellement.*"

"You're good with snakes."

"Did you hear him moan?"

"Shlong? Moan?"

"You didn't hear him moan?"

"No."

"You weren't listening."

"Snakes don't moan."

He felt stupid saying that. Obviously they must.

"Do you dance with him?"

"No!"

"What do you do?"

"I pat him. Feed him. Clean his terrarium . . ."

"Why don't you dance with him?"

"I . . . People don't dance with snakes." He felt stupid again.

"Snakes are coolness, peace and power," she said. "Do you dance at all?"

"I . . . no."

"You play music?"

"Why, yes." Alan became animated again. "I play flute. . . ."

"Ah. And what kind of music do you play?"

"Oh . . . Bach . . . Debussy . . ."

"And you don't dance? When you play? When you listen?"

"No. I . . . You're not supposed to dance, you're just supposed to listen."

"Sit still and listen."

"Right."

"And what happens when you listen—to Bach, to Debussy?"

"I don't know . . . my soul goes out to fill their space."

"And what does your body do meanwhile—while your soul's out?"

"Well, it isn't exactly out. It's in. It gets . . . expanded inside."

"Spiritual Reddi-Wip inside bodily Wing-Ding?"

She smiled; he laughed.

"Yeah, something like that."

"Sounds to me like you're suffering from terminal mind-body split. You like rock n' roll?"

"What?"

"You listen to rock n roll?"

"Are you kidding? Mindless cacophany!"

"Metaphysics of the body. No mind-body split there."

It took Alan a few seconds to take this in.

"The screams—Whitman's barbaric yawp finally yawping."

"You don't *yawp* to God. Bach doesn't yawp to God," Alan contended.

"*Tant pis.* Those kids are possessed by the gods!"

"The gods? I thought you were . . . I mean what's that cross hovering over . . . around your neck?"

"It's a cross—a crossing."

"What do you mean? A cross is a Christian symbol."

"Christian for Christians. Not for us."

"Who's us?"

"Us. People who know symbols for what they really are—what this one was before Christians came along. There's no other, *spirit* world—angels and devils and all that—above or below, or even alongside. For us, the worlds intersect. Like a cross."

Alan tried to focus above her cleavage . . .

"Nothing to do with the Christian cross," she said, "some poor Jew in helpless agony. See here?" She held out the cross, as if for show and tell. "The worlds meet and everything important happens right there where they meet. Right there." She pointed. "Life is at the crossroads. We dance there like the kids dancing. They dance like us."

"You're talking evil, voodoo."

She shrugged. "White kids are dancing and learning what blacks already understand."

"Blacks!" Alan gestured as if to say, What have blacks to do with me?

"You'd love to *be* us. Everything white Christians like you want and miss in your own bodies, everything you think is original sin. So thank God for black bodies, eh?" She looked Alan up and down to the point of his discomfort. And then she laughed.

"I'm Jewish," Alan said.

"Worse, maybe."

If Alan had felt shimmeringly tumescent before, he now felt completely deflated. Fat stomach weighed limp on fat, limp thighs. His mind had slumped down onto his basilar process, and his tongue lay dumb in his mouth.

"Sorry," she said and shrugged. "You said you didn't dance. I do."

Alan remained silent.

"The least *you* can do is love those dancing children, with their bodies full of a spirit you don't understand. They're your healing, you know. It's lunchtime. I gotta go gather up my kid. Nice to meet you, Arnold."

She walked off, all body, mind, and spirit of her, a seamless Trinity, a burning bush scattering fiery tablets, untouchable.

"Alan," he said.

The kids came back around—sans Hermes—with Shlong safely in his box, still quivering, for all Alan knew, from his brief encounter with another kind. Man and snake sat there as the park emptied out. The Yahrzeit candle lay forgotten in Krishna's keeping. Alan looked up at his sixth-floor window across the street. The building reminded him of the Texas Book Depository.

## PAPER TRAIL 2

*First Epistle of Ma to the Floridians*

June 20th, 1999

Dear Faigeleh,

A big hello from Lyndonville, Vermont. No, this is not a resort hotel—I *live* here.

I never thought I'd leave New York the way you just went to Florida. But the situation with Alan had become so *farfoylt* I couldn't stay no longer in the same house (*my* house!) with him. When he moved back to save money, I said Alright, it's only for a while. And I wouldn't mind forever even, except he was so moody. Sometimes we would go a month without his saying a word—even when I talked to him, just ignore me. Other times he would yell at me, or lecture me—always so disapproving and judging me. *Me ken meshuge veren*, you know? Walter was worried about Alan even getting violent, and I should come up and live with them in Vermont, but how could I leave New York and everything I know? Finally, last month (our usual Mother's Day!) I realized how much he hates me, and I decided to just go like Walter invited. If I have one son that loves me and the other son that hates me, why should I stay with that one? He thinks I did something dirty to him when he was a baby that he will never forgive. What did I do, change his diapers, wipe his tush, give him an enema? Do Fred and Leonard hate you for that? It may sound silly, but what did I do to deserve this? If you have any opinions, I would like to hear. So here I am in the country, and not in a bungalow colony for the summer, waiting for Jacob to come up from the city like in the old days, but who knows? Maybe forever.

Walter and Anne are very nice to me. They have a big private house on a dirt road and I have my own room in the back with my own bathroom and I can use their kitchen. The children are wonderful, smart, intelligent, beautiful. It should be a *sach nachas*, no? But I hate it. I'm afraid to go out by myself. There are no sidewalks, no people. There are even animals in the woods. It's completely dark at night, no lights, no stores. Walter and Anne took me to a senior center hoping I'd meet a friend. Maybe they thought a boyfriend or something. But who wants to be around old people? Not me! They're so narrow, so stupid, all they do is gossip about who's wearing this or that, or who said this or that, and I heard one old lady whispering, "She's Jewish from New York." All I need is anti-Semitism, *cholileh*, on top of everything else.

Maybe I can visit you for the winter if I get an invitation. Ten feet of snow I don't need either. Give my best to Bernie. *A gezunt ahf dein kop.*

Your loving sister,
Florence

PS My new address is on the envelope, but here it is again.
Mrs. Florence Krieger
c/o Prof. Walter Krieger
RR 2, Box 421
Lyndonville, VT 05851
My telephone is (802) 427-6774 but don't call after 9 or before 7. You probably know that, but just in case.

# 10. ST. ADOLF'S 911

"How was your day at the office, Père Ubu?" Deborah asked.

"Where's your father?"

"Over at Jane's. Why?"

"I don't want him to hear how my day at the office was. Got anything to eat?

"Check the fridge."

"Mmmmm. Hebrew National. Can I throw a couple of these dogs into a pot? Want any?"

"I'll have one."

"Make that four, just in case. Bun?"

"No, plain."

"Diet Pepsi?"

"Sure. So what's cooking?"

"Four hot dogs."

"No, idiot, at work."

"I know, idiota. I'm being called on the carpet by Staff Sergeant Goldtooth, the black-bosomed *balaboosta* thrush."

"Your favorite."

"Yes. Prima diva of affirmative action."

"So not only does she get the job you wanted but she gets to supervise you?"

"So what else? No good deed goes unpunished."

"What was your good deed?"

"It was absolutely transcendent." Alan poured the drinks. "This guy, Eddie—black guy, one of our least favorite GOMERs—gets wheeled in about 3:30 by two nurses, two paramedics, and two cops, all trying to hold him down on the gurney. Tina comes running with the leather restraints."

"What's GOMER?"

"Get Outa My Emergency Room."

"Oh."

"Let me go, you mothafuckas. I'll fuck you all up the ass."

"Eddie, cool it. You're scaring the children."

"Fuck you fuck you fuck you fuck you."

"OK, babe, patent Armani leather to the wrists and ankles. Hey, cut it out. George, hold that leg. Mm mm mm, don't you look good! And such shiny buckles!"

"I'm gonna sue all you mothafuckas. I want all your names. I want everyone's fuckin shit-ass name. I know my fuckin rights. Don't look so snide, you fat white asshole. I'm gonna get you specially. I know where you live, Mr. Fuckin Ass Alan Krieger, you white piece of shit."

"And what is this gentleman's story this fine afternoon, Officer Friendly? Been out at the polo match?"

"Eddie was explaining his theory of melanin to some truckers who seemed doubtful about the doctrine of black supremacy. He got a knife in the back."

"Oh, for more liberal gun laws . . ."

"We considered throwing him off the Willis Street Bridge, but we thought you might be wondering about him, how he was doing. . . . Down low, left side. Vitals are stable. May not be much going on."

"So what are you guys doing here? New York's finest."

"Fuckin shit-ass white racist pigs!"

"It wasn't too cool to beat up on Corporal Mendez while on parole."

"I thought you guys were going to rehabilitate him."

"Well, we're on the case. Somewhat."

"Good, I like to see my tax dollars at work."

Alan approached the patient.

"Eddie, we're going to have to put in an IV and take some X-rays. You got stabbed, and we have to make sure it didn't cut through anything serious."

"Get outa my face, faggot. You ain't doin shit to me. You touch me with your white paws and I'll sue your fuckin white ass off."

"Why didn't you just let him calm down in the rig?" Alan asked. "He would have nodded out soon."

"Yeah, yeah. If he dumped, his lawyers would have showed up next morning licking their greasy chops."

"Eddie, for your own safety, we need to get these tests done. You want to be able to go back to your preaching, don't you?"

"You just try to make me, you bleached-out ball of shit."

"Bleached out?"

"Clorox ain't got nothin on you, you pasty fuckface. Ptoo. Now, don't you wipe that out o you eye too soon. Let it sink in an nourish you, man, heal you, you not be so fucked up."

"Alan, start an IV. If he doesn't want to hold still, we can help him with ten milligrams of Pavulon."

"Ten-four, Dr. Goodman. Soon as I get this *goombah* out of my eye."

"If he's basically OK, I'll sew him up and OTDMF. Set me up."

"Right on."

"OTDMF?" Deb queried.

"Out the door, motherfucker."

"You guys!"

"Dr. Goodman is five foot two, eyes of blue, and she is, baby, stacked like you."

"Hey, Eddie . . . Tighten him down. Hey, Eddie. You comfy?"

"Fuck you, you faggot prick. Fuck you fuck you!"

"Eddie, tell me more about bleached-out. You got that line in? Let me know when. What's with bleached-out?"

"If you had more melanin, you fuckin bleached-out cocksucker, you wouldn't have to ask."

"All right, so I'm asking. You gonna tell me?"

"Melanin is what you don't got. Melanin is the superior absorber of God energy in the universe. If you had some melanin, asshole, you could dance like me—instead of being a fat, ugly, lumbering, melanin-envying bag of fart. You need the color black to be in touch with God."

"Like you?"

"Yessuh, asshole, like me. You don't understand shit about the universe because you are dee-ficient, man. Big time. You suck mah black cock, maybe you get a little connection. You full of terror because you got no color. You don't know what it's all about."

"You mean if I get a good tan, I can get all the women you can?"

"Women want spiritual reality, and melanin is a spirituality superconductor, and you ain't even got a train, man. Melanin got phonons and solitons radiatin the pineal gland, man. You don't even *got* a pineal gland, you pathetic fat prick cocksuckin mothafucka."

"Gimme ten milligrams of Pavulon. Thank you. Hey, Eddie, I got a present for you."

"I'll sue your fat ass right off your legs, you do anything to me."

"Into the port nice and slow. Bye, Eddie. I'll see you in your dreams. I'll take him into the prep room till CT is ready. C'mon, big guy. Let's see what your melanin makes of this."

Alan served up the dogs, three and one, naked on their plates. Deb often enjoyed his combat stories, which made her feel grateful for having only *her* kind of clients.

"Pavulon is an amazing drug," Alan said. "It's kind of like curare—paralyzes the muscles without altering consciousness. You're just sort of trapped inside your body. You can feel, you can hear, you can see—

but you can't move, you can't breathe. Eddie and his melanin wasn't going to kick any technicians. You got any buns for these dogs?"

"Why didn't the doctor just put him out? In the cupboard to your left."

"It's usually used along with general anesthesia. Must not be very pleasant without it. I don't know why Goodman used it alone. I know why I would have. I'd like to torture the fucker. In fact," he said quietly, "I did—a little."

"What do you mean?"

"Don't get upset. I was only teasing him." Alan snatched up the dogs with the rolls. "I didn't really hurt him." He squeezed on the mustard—whooey! "See, on Pavulon he can't breathe, so I had to intubate him and put him on a ventilator, and while I was watching him deal with that fully conscious and completely helpless, I realized it was just me and him and his fucking melanin—alone in a room behind a door."

"Alan, he's obviously just horribly defensive for some reason. He probably needs to be."

"Not at my expense he doesn't."

"Eddie, can you hear me? Can you see me? The Prince of Itches? I know you can. Can you move? Even your little finger? I know you can't. Here, I'll unstrap you. Wouldn't you like to grab me, you poor *schlimazel?* Know what a *schlimazel* is, Mr. Melanin? No? Deprived as a child of the wonders of Yiddish? Poor baby. Listen carefully. A *schlimazel* is the guy the *schlimiel* spills the soup on. That's you. Not very lucky. Except tonight it's not going to be soup but one of the great wonders of modern science. Eddie, you've been a very bad boy tonight, quite unpleasant. You were rude and vulgar and noisy and you scared a poor little child with a cut on his eyebrow. Bad Eddie, bad, bad, bad. You're just going to have to be punished. I don't see any way around it—

see these scissors? Who will ask, Eddie? I mean, you don't have a lot of friends here at ol St. Vince. But hey, they'll love you in prison now. I can make it look just like a woman—they'll be lining up for your butt, Ed. Hey, speaking of buts, there's always a silver lining—you'll have less carnal distraction, you'll be more able to concentrate on lining up the melanin molecules with the big magnetic resonance in the sky. Maybe you could write a book, make lots of money. Now, this will only take a minute."

"Alan, I can't believe this. Eddie may be a creep, but," she shook her head " 'do no harm' and all that, you know?"

"Nurses don't take the Hippocratic oath, only docs. Besides, I owed it to my colleagues who don't have as much imagination."

"I don't want to hear any more."

"It's OK. Nothing really happened."

"What do you mean? It's already happened."

"Want another frank?"

"You ready, Eddie? Now, try to keep very still so I don't damage any more tissue than I have to. Say, Eddie, you do have an impressive set of goodies here. I think this scissors is too small. Hold still, I'm gonna go arrange for them to take you into the OR and use the big cutters."

"That's it. I wasn't so bad, was I? Considering?"

"And he's hearing you and seeing you do all this?"

"You bet. Pavulon. So I leave the room, and then the orderlies come and wheel him down to the CAT scan, and then Goodman sews him up. *C'est tout*."

"His scan was normal?"

"No bad deed goes unrewarded. Boy, these hot dogs are really great! Don't you want some mustard on yours? It's getting cold. Don't gimme that look." He took a big bite out of his second dog. "Deb, sweetie, there is such a thing as justice in the universe."

What could she say?

"Finish chewing," she said. He didn't.

"It's a corollary of the Law of Conservation of Mass Energy. You're not eating your hot dog. This guy needed my little playlet there to offset his karma. You can call up Professor Walter and ask him. Without it he would be unbalanced, and he'd have to pay for it in a future life—with interest, maybe compound interest. I was his secret friend, helping him. Don't you believe in justice?"

"Balancing his karma, were you?"

"Right. But did he appreciate it? No. He's in overnight to stabilize, his Parvulon wears off, and this morning he's up in hospital administration in his jonny telling the story to anyone who will listen—including Big Ted Callahan, chief of operations, who happens to be on one of his rare days away from the golf course. Nobody quite believes him, given him and respectable me, but on the other hand, I'm due to be duly quizzed by Ms. Aurodent tomorrow."

"Are you going to fess up?"

"Well, I thought I'd get a second opinion. Yours."

"What's the first opinion?"

"My opinion: Why should I confess? Management doesn't understand deeper karmic justice. Goldtooth is great on *in*justice, especially concerning melanin people, but there's not a *Yiddisher kopf* in the whole chain of command." He crammed the rest of his hot dog into his mouth. "Fwo why fould uh wion . . ." He swallowed. ". . . a lion submit himself to the law of the ox?"

"Which is the ox?"

"Ha ha. I can see what the second opinion is going to be. If you're not going to eat that, can I have it?"

"I don't know which is worse, your ethics or your eating habits."

"My eating habits? Who is the only living human being who has ever beaten me in a White Castle eating contest?"

Deborah pushed her plate over to his side of the table.

"This may surprise you, but *I* don't think you should confess either."

"Deborah Goldenbaum, you *do* surprise me! I came to be verbally abused. Why not?"

"First of all, you'd lose your job, and probably your license. That would make you disgruntled *and* unemployed, out on the streets and doubly dangerous. I'm serious. This job keeps you in line—somewhat."

"I know you're serious, and you're right. You and I have a stupendous future as partners in crime. So you think I should deny everything to Goldtooth?"

"Is she on your case?"

"Of course she's on my case. Wouldn't *you* be?"

"Just don't get belligerent with her."

"Me? Mr. Mellow get belligerent?"

"I can just see you giving her the whole story just to teach her about the need to put shvartzas in their place."

"Yeah, well, I can see that too."

"Don't."

"Maybe."

"Don't."

"If I promise, will you do the dirty deed with me tonight?"

"Alan."

"What?"

"Sometimes you scare me. Doing things like that. Words games are one thing, but when you . . ."

"It's OK. I didn't really do it. I just made it up. I was testing you."

"Really?"

"Don't you know I'm one of the great actors?"

"I don't believe you."

"Have it your way," he said, shaking his head. And then he finished off Deb's half a dog.

# PAPER TRAIL 3

*Memo to his colleagues in the emergency department, 1997*

EYES-ONLY MEMO

FROM: ALAN KRIEGER, RN, Rotund Necromancer

TO: ER STAFF

RE: PSY-OPS FOR THE ER

DATE: 1 APRIL 1997

*The Problem*

Frequent flyers with chartomegaly. Crocks with complaints like "Every time the subway goes by, my eyes start to water." Dumps with negative wallet biopsies. GOKs[1], LOLNADs[2], SPOTAs[3], GOMERs[4], or worse, OTDMFs[5], those playing with less than a full deck, Terraspheres[6] with or without Q-Signs[7]. You get the picture: the moon-like terrain of rocks—patients here for three hots and a cot, not admissions-worthy, but whose families won't take them back home. What the hell do we do (consistent

[1] God Only Knows

[2] Little Old Lady with No Acute Distress

[3] As in "I spota be in court now, but I'm not feelin too good. Can you gimme a note?"

[4] Get Out of My Emergency Room

[5] Out the Door, Motherfucker

[6] i.e., Dirtballs

[7] You know the kind—mouth slacked open with tongue hanging out.

with our Hippocratic oaths) to get them admitted and off our gurneys?

*The Secondary Problem*

The goddamn admitting docs upstairs who don't want their beds cluttered up by patients without treatable problems, testy bastards who advise us to "be a wall."

*The Achilles' Heel*

Y'all will recall that Achilles' mom dipped him in the River Styx to make him invulnerable. The things mothers will do! Close, but no cigar. She forgot to dip the heel by which she held him. Admitting physicians too have their Achilles' heels—and there is where we must aim our Appolonian barbs. A number of examples will make the necessary strategies clear:

*1. Play dumb.*

WRONG

YOU: Hey, Frank, I've got a fifty-five-year-old white guy down here, hypotensive, cyanotic, confused, and a bit septic. I've got him intubated, on saline, I've drawn cultures and have got a Cipro drip going. He's on his way to the ICU, and . . .

ADMITTING PHYSICIAN: Wait a minute, sonny! What makes you think he has to be admitted?

RIGHT

YOU: Hello, Dr. Feldman, this is Soozie down in the ER. We have a patient who is cyanotic and confused. He doesn't seem normal to me. I was just wondering if maybe you

thought this could be neurological? I mean, maybe he should be admitted or something.
ADMITTING PHYSICIAN: Hold on, I'll be right down.

*2. Utilize elementary child psychology.*

WRONG

YOU: I've got a sixty-seven-year-old female in cardiogenic shock who needs CIC.
ADMITTING PHYSICIAN: She's probably just anxious. We see this a lot. Send her home and have her call my office in the morning.

RIGHT:

YOU (regarding, say, that patient whose eyes water when the subway goes by): Hello, Dr. Feldman, this is Rafael down in the ER. I've got a patient with some weird complaints. He's probably OK to go home. . . . Yeah, I think I'll just send him home.
ADMITTING PHYSICIAN: You may be missing something. Get him admitted, and I'll have a resident look at him.

*3. Choose your words carefully.*

a. Never use the word "chronic." "Unstable" is far better.
b. Use exotic initial diagnoses difficult to disprove and usually requiring extensive lab workups: herpatolenticular degeneration; early Werner's Syndrome, periodic paroxysmal epistaxis without hypokalemia.
c. Avoid weasel words.

WRONG

YOU: Hi, Dr. Feldman. Dr. Trabulsy in the ER. I've got an elderly GOMER complaining of weakness. Says he wants to be admitted.
ADMITTING PHYSICIAN (angry): So what do you want me to do about it? Be a wall! (click)

RIGHT
YOU: Hi, Dr. Feldman. Dr. Trabulsy in the ER. I've got an interesting elderly gentleman with transient delirium, generalized muscular weakness, and evidence of some kind of organophosphate overdose, possibly muscarinic.
ADMITTING PHYSICIAN (intrigued): Hmmm. I'll admit him and be right down. What's his name?

Thus does medical management become more efficient through the careful application of discourse and situational ethics.

AK, RN, RN

## 11. GOLDTOOTH BITES

What room is not an emergency room, what department not an ED? The Latin word *emergere* means "coming to the surface of an enveloping liquid," and where is liquidity that does not envelop? Where, in this undulant life, do things not surface, only to submerge again? Medicine, often solipsistic, has appropriated the word "emergent" to itself—as meaning "sudden" or "unforeseen." But is not "suddenness" only apparent and "unforeseen" the bounty of shortsightedness? In short, what goes round comes round.

"Alan."

"Hey, Julio! How was the night?"

"Man, you don't want to know."

"What happened?"

"You'll find out soon enough, man. When you start picking up the pieces."

"So gimme a hint."

"Just some more gang bullshit, man. Ought to let all these kids kill each other off."

"What'd we do for work?"

"These cars just zoom on up to the door, drop em in the driveway, and drive off."

"Yup, positive taillight sign. No blame, as the *I Ching* says."

"Who says?" Julio asked.

"An old Chinese buddy. OK, Julio, no bloody details. Get some rest, *hombre*."

"Give em hell, *amigo*—and have a nice day."

Ah, today's youth, whose every day is Mother's Day. It was likely one too many epithets about copulation with Mom, and whango-bazango, it's a war.

"Hey, Charlie, hey, Rosie. Why, Mary L. Brown, what are you doin here lyin on a gurney in the hall again? No room at the inn?"

"I dunno, Mr. Man, they just stuck me heah in the muhfuckin hallway for the last half hour."

"Uh-uh-uh, no imprecations about mothers."

"Don gimme any yo smart-ass intellecshul buhshit, creep. Tryin to impress me so I'll sleep wif yuh?"

"Just cause you're strapped down on a gurney, you think I wanna sleep with you?"

"Listen, I know all you Jew boys. You jus in a constant state of excitement."

"Shhh. Everyone'll hear you. Can't give away the big secret of the Chosen People."

"Chosen People, my black ass. What you chosen for?"

"Chosen to run the international banking conspiracy to keep you niggers in line."

"Don't you be callin me nigger, man, I'll have yo ass. Besides, I bet you ain't got twenny dollars in the bank."

"Too true, too true. But even so, I won't sleep with you. I got a thing about sleeping in public with toothless old black women."

"You jus unbutton that fly an I'll show you what a toothless ol black woman can do."

"Mary, the Jews have been persecuted enough, don't you think?"

"Who's persecutin you?"

"Well, you know, like Auschwitz and all that."

"Whazzat? Auswich."

"Hey, where were you during the second World War?"

"Scrubbin floors fo white folks, man. Where were you? You wasn't even a twonkle in you daddy's eye. Talk about persecution! What you know?"

"Nice talkin to you, Mary. Gotta get to work. I hear the children of the poorer, darker classes had a hard day's night."

"Man, we always got a hard day's night. An a hard night's day. Wait a minute. Whazzat Auswich stuff you talkin bout?"

"Death camp, Mary. Death camp."

"Well, shit, man, yo death camp ain't nothin compared to our death camp. How long was Auswich? Fo, five, six years? How many you got dead?"

"Six million. Ever hear that number?"

"Fuck six million, man. We got three hundred, fo hundred million killed on them slave ships. An millions more when they got off. Took like cattle. Killed like cattle."

"Mary, I gotta go."

"Yeah, yeah, yeah, white man always gotta go when black folks start tellin history."

"I didn't do anything, Mary. I wasn't even a twonkle in my daddy's eye."

"An not for three, four years, man, for three, four *hundred*! Ain't no crime in history compare to that. Six million? Kid stuff, man, baby stuff! You owe us big time, man, you owe us big time, an we ain't gonna forget it."

"Yeah, well, the check's in the mail."

"Don't you run off like that Mr. Alan Krieger, RN, with some wise-ass remark bout the biggest crime in history."

"Mary, pipe down and I'll sleep with you—next month."

"You sleep wif me? I ain't gonna sleep wif you. You couldn *make* me sleep wif you. I'm tryin to tell you sompin you need to unnerstan."

"Hey, hey, there are sick children in the next room. Calm down."

"Black folks has lost knowledge of ourself, and we living an animal life. An this proves it was the greatest crime. Not only was we killed and murdered, not only was our women raped in front of their own chillen, not only did massa stick daggers in pregnant women's bellies, slice her womb open—to instill fear, y'unnerstan? Fear."

"OK, Mary, take it easy."

"Easy? I'm talkin the crimes nobody wants to talk bout. But the biggest crime—they told us we was animals, subhumans, gave us despisin names like Prince Orangutang, and Lady Chimpanzee. But mah name's Mary Leocadia Brown, see, Brown, like mah skin, and don't you think I ain't someone to be reckoned wif."

"Mary, everybody in the ER knows you're someone to be . . ."

"But this heah name was given me in the greatest crime ever committed on the face of the earth. You stolen our dentity, y'unnerstan me? Do you? Cat got yo tongue?"

"Mary, I gotta get to . . ."

"The Honorable Louis Farrakhan teaches that *we* are the chosen of God, not you. You Jews masquerading aroun in our garment! Who you think you're kiddin?"

"Not you, Mary, not you. See you later."

"Seven verses in Deuteronomy I do believe, seven verses, thas all you got to prove you the Chosen." Her voice echoed down the hall as Alan Krieger receded.

"Hey, Marge, Sue. Ben, you look like you've had it."

"Better believe it."

"So what's cooking today?"

"We had a dozen kids last night. Some kind of gang thing."

"How jolly. What was on the program?"

"I don't know. I don't really talk to them before they go into rooms. But they were all bloody. There were a whole bunch in the corridor between three and five. Both sides, both gangs. We had to strap them down, they wouldn't stop cursing one another, it was terrible."

"Only Mary Brown out there now."

"Craig and Nancy and Esteban had a stitch-em-up factory going. I think you've got the last of them. So you'll probably be able to get some kind of a story."

"OK, good. Chart? Thanks. Room 17. Evan Prichard, age fifteen. I'm on my way. Let you know if I hear anything interesting."

"Have fun."

"Always. Fun, fun, fun. Which, spelled backward, is 'nuf.'"

"Yo, Evan, my man. What's cookin?"

"I can't talk too good."

"Your mouth looks a little bloody, Evan. Open up. Let's see."

"Hard to open mah mouf."

"Gimme a little peek. Ooooh, nice. Wanna wash out? Here, come on over to the sink. Here's some water. Swish and spit—so I can see a little better. OK, Evan, good boy. Back on the table. Know what? I don't think I want to put any stitches in that. The tongue is the second-fastest healer in the body. Know what's the first?"

"No."

"The eyeball. Slash your eyeball, it's better next day."

"No kiddin."

"Depends on the slash, but it's fast."

"Hey, I won't go for the eyeballs anymore if I'd know'd that."

"Yeah. Stay away from them eyeballs. What happened?"

"Well, this spic was talkin to my sister and I don't like no spics talkin to my sister."

"How old's your sister? Hey, lemme see you open your mouth. Jaw that way. OK, now jaw this way. Good. Still got a good jawbone. Famous weapon, Evan, the jawbone. So this kid's talking to your sister."

"Yeah, so I axed him where y'all from. And when he tell me, I realize he's one of the guys that stomped Eddie and Boolo last week. But all I said was 'Righteous, righteous.'"

"That's all? So how'dja get your tongue busted up?"

"Hold on, man. So I go off, man, and I fetch up Fred an Boolo and Ace, and we go back over there and catch that muhfucka. And when we be beatin on him, Boolo says . . ."

"I know Boolo," Alan remarked. "He was in here last week. I stitched him up."

"You did, man?"

"Yeah, I helped."

"You good, man. A righteous sewin job."

"Thanks."

"So Boolo goes, 'I gotta idea, cuz,' and I go, 'Whuzzat?' and he goes, 'Let's drag him with a rope.' Hey, man, it's hard to talk wif a fat tongue. I gotta tell you all this?"

"I'm interested, Evan. I'm interested in your exploits. And you talk so funny. I'm writing a book about the most interesting characters I come across in the ER."

"Really? I'm gonna be in a book?"

"Sure."

"Don use my name."

"Why not? Don't you want to be famous?"

"No, man, I could get in big trouble. They still don't know who started this whole thing."

"You mean all these guys that were in here last night? You started all that, beating up on this guy talking to your sister?"

"You bet yo ass."

"I'm impressed. So how come you just got a little cut on the tongue?"

"I told you, man, they didn't know it was me."

"OK, no real names. So you said, 'Let's drag him.'"

"I didn't say it. Boolo said it."

"Oh, OK."

"So we put him in Boolo's Mustang and we make it over to the river and put a rope on the bumper, he's got a rope in the back, and we ties this guy on to it and drag him in the street. He sure got the beauty treatment, tore his face half off. Got all dirt and like gravel and shit stuck in his head. Boolo say he looks like a hamburger treat for Tashay's puppies."

"You liked that?"

"Yeah, man. What was he doin talkin to mah sister? And what the fuck about beatin up Boolo las week? At first, you know, when we grabbed him, he tried to act tough, but when we through with him, man, he cryin like a baby. After we untie him we make him kneel down and say shit like, I'll suck your dicks, shit like that. Man, we almost kill him. Then we just drop him near the river til somebody find him or he crawl home. Whatever."

"Jesus, Evan, that's a horrible story."

"Yeah, we bad, we killers. We freedom fighters."

"Well, I sure wouldn't want to meet you guys in a dark alley."

"You better believe it, man."

"So who sliced up your tongue?"

"Everything OK, Alan?"

"Yeah, Dr. Porter. No prob. Little tongue lac. Doesn't need sewing."

"Want me to take a look?"

"He's fine."

"OK."

"Took em about an hour to get the word, and his boys come lookin for us. So we know what's comin, and we ready for em."

"So who sliced up your tongue?"

"Ain't no one slice it up, man. I bit it."

"How's that?"

"I tripped."

"Runnin away?"

"What you sayin? You better watch yo mouf, man."

"Scuse me, said the elephant's child."

"Don you ever call me no coward, heah?"

"Yes, suh, captain, suh!"

"Can I get some pain pills? I ain't gonna be able to sleep."

"What would you like?"

"Percodan? How bout ten, fifteen Percodan?"

"Advil'll do fine. Take down the swelling faster."

"C'mon man, gimme some Percs."

"Not this time, Evan. Gotta do better than a little tongue laceration for Percodan."

"Hey, man, what time you get off, cause I wanna kill ya."

"Gimme a break, Evan. Save it for when I do somethin really terrible to you."

"OK, man, I'm openin your account. . . ."

"Hang in there. You'll feel better tomorrow. Or the next day. Four Advil, four times a day. Here, I got some samples for you. See ya. Power to the people!"

"See ya."

It is not only cardiologists that deal in thickened hearts. *Jerushalem, convertere ad Dominum!*

Whoops, 9:01. Late for my date. Sorry, Mistress Goldtooth, I was late in the line of duty, takin care of a homeboy. Notice how few yeshiva *buchers* we've had in here compared? None, I believe. Why is that, now? All right, Alan. Straighten the tie. Pat back the hair. We'll give the polite version of the knock.

"Come in."

"Hi, Bertha. And Eddie! What are you doing here?"

"Comin to fry your ass, my friend."

"How nice."

"I asked Mr. Fenton to sit in with us for a while. And Dr. Callahan will be here any minute."

"The Great Chain of Being, huh?"

"We just want to straighten out what happened Friday."

"What happened Friday?"

"Hey, looky Innocent Pius the Fourth, you hypocrite!"

"Calm down, Mr. Fenton. You get to tell your story. Ah, Dr. Callahan, good, thanks for coming."

"Hi, Bertha, hello, Mr. Fenton. How're you feeling?"

"Good, good. I smell blood, and I'm feeling good."

"Mr. Fenton came to see me Saturday afternoon, Alan. And I thought we should all sit down and try to work out what happened. Sit down, Alan, it's OK. But Mr. Fenton's got some serious charges."

"I'll bet. Too little melanin among the staff, Eddie?"

"Could be, my man, could be. Why else would y'all undertake yo fuckin gratuitous, sadistic torture when y'all get caught with yo pants down and yo pathetic circumsized . . ."

"Hey, Eddie, you ain't gonna win no converts like that. The guy's insane, Dr. Callahan. It's obvious. You gonna believe . . ."

"Mr. Fenton. Nurse Krieger. Please. Let's just hear your story, Mr. Fenton."

"I got in a little fight, and these cops bring me in, I'm perfectly OK, but Big Shot Alan heah, he strap me down on a table . . ."

"After you were kicking the nurses . . ."

"And without my consent, without my informed consent, illegally, this fucker inject me with some Nazi drug, paralyze all my muscles but not my mind . . ."

"Pavulon."

"Ah."

"Ten milligrams, specifically ordered by Dr. Goodman. It's in his chart."

"Go on, Mr. Fenton."

"So he wheel me in a room where he can get me alone an nobody can hear, he call me fuckin nigger prick and some kinda Jewish cuss-words."

"What were they, Eddie? With your phenomenal recall you ought to be able to dredge em right up."

"Alan, let him talk."

"Man, I can't remember yo foreign Jew language, whad'ya want from me?"

"Point proven, I hope."

"Go on, Mr. Fenton."

"He say I been a bad, bad boy, and he just goin to have to punish me."

"You *were* a bad boy, Eddie, but we don't punish here. We stitch you up and send you *out* to be punished."

"Then he take this huge motherfuckin scissors and he cut off my clothes. Cut em off! Ruined! Hundred-fifty-dollar pair of pants! Hundred-dollar sports shirt! This fucker don know the value of money. What right he got? An then he snip the scissors next to my ear and he say 'Say good byc to your big black cock, Eddie, no more hard-ons for you.'"

"I did not!"

"Shh. Let him finish."

"An he say he goin to make me look like I got a cunt so everybody wanta fuck me in prison. An he take my balls in his faggot hands, and he fondle em and tells me I got big beautiful balls, and then he say they's too big for the scissors he got, so he has to go out an arrange to take me to the operatin room where they got the big cutters."

"You don't believe all this, do you?"

"Go on, Mr. Fenton, what happened next?"

"Well, shit, then they come an wheel me into some kinda room with big fuckin machines."

"MRI to see if there was any . . ."

"An everythin anybody do to me I think is preparation for the big cutters. Man, I'm scared shitless . . ."

"Scared of MRI?"

"Man, what I know what you medical fucker sadists got planned for me? You could pull anything and call it medical appropriate. Circle the muthafuckin wagons, boys, it's peer review. Didn't think I knew bout that, did ya? What a shit-ass joke."

"Did anything else happen, Mr. Fenton?"

"No, sir. They jus took some pictures, decided it was nothin—jus like I said in the first place—and some babe sews up my cut. I wanted to leave as soon as that fuckin drug wore off an I could walk, but they make me stay overnight. Chalk up another thousand bucks in Medicaid fraud! I come up to see you, Dr. Callahan, soon as I was DC'd."

"That's exactly the story he told me on Saturday," Goldtooth observed.

"Mr. Fenton, would you be willing to make a statement to a stenographer, and would you swear to it? Sign it and swear to it?"

"You bet you fuckin ass! I'm gonna get this fucker. He never gonna torture a black man again. Be out on the street, you Jew asshole, like the rest of us, see how you do."

"OK, Mr. Fenton, come upstairs with me." Dr. Callahan stood up.

"Hey, what about my side of the story?"

"I'll be back down as soon as I get Mr. Fenton set up with a secretary. Just hold it for five minutes, Alan, and you'll get a chance to respond."

"With him around?"

"No. He's done for today. Just you and Bertha and me."

"I ain't done, man. I want reparations! I'm gonna sue the shit outa this goddamn hospital. You gonna pay millions. Hundreds of millions. Ain't a jury in the world that wouldn't convict big time. You don't get to do whatever you want to a black man and walk off, you bleached-out piece-o-shit prick. It's over, man. Slavery's over. Time for reparations. An we startin with you, Mr. Alan Krieger, RN."

"Have a good time, Eddie. Get it all down. And be sure to sign it, so we can get you for perjury. Eight to ten, boy. Incredible!"

"What's incredible, Krieger?"

"What's incredible? That whole bullshit story!"

"I find it quite believable, knowing you."

"Look, Bertha . . ."

"I believe the name is Big Mama Goldtooth, the black-bosomed *balaboosta*."

"*Balaboosta? Balaboosta?* A *Landsmann!* You know something, you don't *look* Jewish. . . ."

"I've got big ears, Krieger. And I've got big eyes. I know everything you do. And I hear everything you say. It's called being a supervisor."

"Seriously, you know what a *balaboosta* is?"

"I don't know what it is, but I'm sure it isn't complimentary."

"No, no. It's a term of respect. It means a woman really in charge. Someone you could eat off her floor."

"Well, I don't need you eating off my floor, Krieger. I need to get to the bottom of what went on with Fenton, what's been going on with you, especially with you and black folks, and what kind of reparations we need to be doing."

"Reparations? For what? Three, four hundred million killed? Wanna take it out on me?"

The Emergency Department medical supervisor returned and walked toward the table.

"Oh, hi, Dr. Callahan. Bertha here was just confusing the issue."

"You talking about slavery?"

"I didn't bring it up," Bertha said. "He did."

"When you're dealing with African-Americans these days—correct me if I'm wrong, Bertha—you've got to take that history into account."

"I'm sorry, Dr. Callahan. . . ."

"Call me Ted, please. OK. I blocked you and Alan out of the book for the rest of the morning so we could take some time and discuss what's really going on. We've got Mr. Fenton's story, but given his . . . given Mr. Fenton, how do we know Alan isn't just another white . . ."

"Jewish . . ."

". . . target on his hit list? That's a pretty hard story to believe, wouldn't you say?"

"Not for Bertha."

"From what I've seen and heard of Krieger, Dr. Callahan, I can believe it. I don't know if it's true, but I can believe it. I've watched Krieger carefully over the last several months. This man's a dyed-in-the-wool racist. You ought to hear him talk. . . ."

"Time out." Callahan made the referee's "T." "Alan, give us your . . ."

"Gimme a break! Racist! The first word that comes out of every black mouth. Except for the 'm' word, of course. *I* am not the problem, Bertha. You know, you cry wolf once too often . . ."

"Alan, I'd like to hear . . ."

"Look, I don't have any stake in blacks being the way they are. I have nothing to gain from oppressing poor A-As. What matters to me is I don't want to have to worry that Eddie or his buddies will be waiting for me after work. That's not racism; it's plain common sense."

"Alan, it's stereotypical thinking, that's what it is. I'm surprised."

"I'm not a racist; I'm a realist. Look at Eddie. He's real, and he's violent, and he hates Jews. Think I'd trust him late at night, especially with a gang of friends? No way. I can't even trust him in here. Is that stereotyping? Is that racist? Look at how he's trying to get me fired. That's a life-threatening move these days. Does he care? No. A story like that—I'd be blackballed for the rest of my life. And you know, the funny thing is that that's the kind of treatment—what he made up—that might straighten him out. It's unethical, a slippery slope to be sure, but man, aversive therapy is classical. It's what he needs, I'll tell you. Ever see *A Clockwork Orange?*"

"Yes."

"But instead, we joke with him, we stitch him up and send him out, and I'll give you ten to one he's back here with the same crap within two weeks, and eventually that knife won't miss all major organs, and then he gets to visit the morgue. What good are we doing him? Sheer liberal hypocrisy, man. He needs treatment. Real treatment."

"He needs work is what he needs," said Bertha.

"Who would hire him? He needs more than affirmative action. Only a madman would take him on."

"What do you mean—affirmative action—like me?"

"Forget it."

"No, Krieger. I will not forget it. I want you to tell me in front of Dr. Callahan what you mean."

"Well, strap me down for the sodium pentathol. Ted, write her an order."

"Alan, Bertha, cut it out. We're not here to settle personality issues, we're here to find out what happened with Fenton, so we can do whatever we have to do. Alan, what's your side of the story? What happened?"

"Nothing."

"Obviously something happened."

"He came in with the ambulance crew and two cops after getting stabbed and then taking down a cop who was trying to break things up. I think he was haranguing someone about the color of their skin."

"And?"

"We had to restrain him after he kicked Margaret Goodwin and really hurt her."

"OK, so he's now restrained . . ."

"And shouting obscenities, and threatening everyone, especially me, and thrashing around enough to hurt himself more on the straps."

"Right. Is this what you saw, Bertha?"

"I didn't see any of it. I was in with a patient."

"And then?"

"Dr. Goodman was worried we wouldn't be able to get good pictures, and I think she was also put off by what Eddie was doing to the whole ER, so she ordered ten milligrams of Pavulon, which we put in his IV."

"He quieted down."

"A perfect gentlemen. Amazing. So then I wheeled him into a room to prep him for the imaging, and yes, I did cut off his clothes—they were all torn and bloody anyway—because it was a lot easier than trying to peel them off."

"And?"

"And when I was finished, I wheeled him out to Radiology."

"You wheeled him out?"

"I didn't wheel him to Radiology, I wheeled him out of the room, and John, I think, wheeled him over."

"And that's it? You didn't say any more? What did you say to him while you were cutting his clothes?"

"What I always say to a conscious patient—'I'm sorry I have to cut these off, but it will keep you from getting hurt any further.' Most people accept it. Look, let me cut to the quick, here, Dr. Callahan. I don't want to waste any more of your valuable time. Or mine. Or Bertha's. It's going to come down to who do you believe, Eddie or me? He's set up his story so no one else witnessed this alleged malpractice. OK, we go to court. And? In this corner, we have Eddie Fenton, frequent flyer with major chartomegaly, one of the biggest GOMERs we have—I can get thirty employees to attest to this—threatening to women, offensive to men, a guy with huge chips on both little shoulders, a multiple druggie with a long police record and big-time racist logorrhea. A complete dirtball. Character witnesses? Forget it. And on the other hand, we have Alan Krieger, health professional, scholar, musician, Buddhist Jew filled with compassion for the suffering of all sentient beings. Easily documented. Who do you think a jury would believe?"

"That depends on the color of the jury, Krieger."

"Ooooo. A little racism there?"

"A big lot of racism there," Bertha corrected. "One-third of young black men rounded up."

"And why do you think, Bertha? Is that an accident?"

"No, that's no accident, my friend, that's your way of solving economic problems, all fronted with bullshit, excuse me, about reducing crime. Racist hypocrites like you who support desegregation but won't bus their kids . . ."

"Hey, Bertha, some of my best friends . . ."

"Alan, Bertha, please!"

". . . who are all for equal housing . . ."

"Man, we live in a totally mixed apartment, my poor ol mom and I. And Shlong, my . . ."

"You'd split for the suburbs if you could."

"Like hell. They'd lynch me quick. Big pogrom."

"You say you want equal opportunity . . ."

"Please!"

The medical supervisor was having trouble supervising this one.

"Absolutely."

". . . but when someone like me gets promoted over someone like you, you scream reverse discrimination!"

"Could be the case, couldn't it?"

"Hey!" A big, big "T" from Dr. Callahan. "Alan, I was on the committee that promoted Bertha. Believe me, she was the best of the candidates—including yourself—for many reasons."

"Look, Krieger, excuse me, Dr. Callahan, but Mr. Krieger here is a total crock of . . ."

"OK, cut it out, both of you."

"Dr. Callahan, sorry. But if we want to get to the truth here, we've got to really look at the racism. I admit Eddie's a tough customer, but at least you know where he's coming from. This man here is a snake in the grass."

"Now, don't go maligning snakes. I have a very sweet . . ."

"This man is racist in every way, intentional and unintentional. He's subtle, he's blatant, he's a bigot hiding behind being a Jew. I hear him talk. 'Some of my best friends are black!' *None* of his friends are black. Spanish, PR, Orientals, yes. Never black. How is this guy going to relate to our patients? How's he going to really understand what they're about, what they need? What keeps him from playing out his sadistic fantasies when he gets a chance, especially on someone like

Eddie? I'll tell you one thing—in a which-one-do-you-believe? situation, I believe the person who walks what he talks. And that is *not* Mr. Krieger here."

"Do I get a chance to talk my talk?"

"Go on, Alan."

"I just want to say that there's a war on out there. For a guy like Eddie, it's take no prisoners. And Eddie's the tip of the iceberg. Five minutes before I came in here, I'm treating a kid who tied another kid to the back bumper of a car and dragged him around in the dirt for half an hour. Why? Because this kid was talking to his sister, and he's a 'freedom fighter.' Oh, I forgot, after they finished dragging him, they tossed him into the river. Just another fun night in the big city. Dr. Callahan, maybe you're not on the front lines enough to know what's really going on."

"All right, Alan. I'd like to talk with Bertha, if you'll excuse us."

"I'm not finished."

"You've made your point."

"I just want to say one more thing."

"What?"

"I'm sorry I got so upset. My livelihood—my career—is on the line and I feel like I'm being made to stand in for all the huge black-white problems out there. So I got upset. But I just want to say one thing. Eddie Fenton is a sociopath. At least toward whites and white society. He's going to get killed because we're not really helping him, and he's going to take anyone he can with him. Anyone white. It would be much too ironic if this transparent lie he's laying out were to deprive St. Vincent's of one of the few people who can really understand and articulate what's going on. So please think about what you're doing."

"Would you be prepared to submit a sworn deposition if it came to that?"

"Of course."

"Eight to ten, Krieger," Bertha warned.

"I'll get back to you," said Dr. Callahan.

"When?"

"By the end of the week."

"OK."

Alan stood in the doorway.

"Please close the door behind you, Alan."

"Oh, sure. I was just surprised to see Eddie out here."

"Jes wanted to see how you was doin, man, jes wanted to check on the color o yo pasty white face. Not lookin so good, Nurse Krieger, not lookin so good. Sompin on you mind?"

"Give your statement, Eddie?"

"Sure nuff, boss."

"I can't wait to read it."

"Read it an weep, mah man, read it an weep."

## PAPER TRAIL 4
## APPLICATION TO THE NYU SCHOOL OF NURSING, 1984

SELECT ONE OF THE FOLLOWING TOPICS AND WRITE A CLEAR, SUCCINCT, AND INFORMATIVE ESSAY. REMEMBER: WE ARE SEEKING QUALITY, NOT QUANTITY.

1. Tell us about an experience or event that has had a significant impact on your life.
2. Discuss the most pressing problem that you feel our society faces today and its relevance to you.

I trust the Admissions Committee will not take it amiss if I briefly address both questions, since, for me, they are interwoven and lie at the heart of my interest in the NYU Baccalaureate Nursing Program.

It is finally 1984, the long-dreaded year. Most pundits maintain, with an I-told-you-so air, that Orwell's predictions did not come to pass and proceed to praise the triumph of liberal democracy. I beg to differ. Not only are we well-launched into a totalitarian state but the insidious subtlety and friendly fascism of our condition make it far more dangerous than the one Orwell imagined half a century ago.

This is not the place to catalog the myriad assaults on our well-being, privacy, and health, individual and collective. I will focus on only one aspect of our morbidity/mortality: the simultaneous emptying and mechanization of human contact.

For all its flakiness, the generation of the '60s and early '70s was conscious of the need to "make love, not war," to bond with individuals, to embrace the enemy, to "walk a mile in someone else's moccasins." They were involved in radical reprioritization: being above doing, spirituality above materialism, connectedness above separation, right brain above left.

But now we are immersed in what punditry has tagged the "me generation." Watch out for number one, and live the good, if empty, life. Our role models are fed us by the ubiquitous media, which, for all its pseudovariety, has only one goal: to transform us into profit-yielding consumers. Should we feel something is awry, we can be adjusted with a new generation of low-side-effect psychoactive drugs.

The consequences are already apparent: this is an

age of universal divorce. The family fragments; nations, races, even subcultures are at each other's throats; we ravage our earth as if we were aliens bent on planetary destruction. Orwell's *1984* is child's play in comparison.

As an undergraduate, I was privileged to be an English and music major, constantly experiencing the crucial negativity of artistic creation. "I love the great nay-sayers, because they are the great yea-sayers. They are arrows of longing for the other shore." Thus Nietzsche. Art stands outside the status quo. Art can say "No!" when No is necessary. Those marinated in masterpieces can see through the brainwashing guidance of their own mainstream culture.

Two events/experiences in my undergraduate education changed my life and set me on a path toward nursing. The first was my discovery of the music of Jan Dismus Zelenka, a Czech composer of the 17th and early 18th century. As no other composer before or since, he made me aware of human existence as a wash of unmitigated pain. Where is there balm for such a condition? The second was my reading of Tolstoy's amazing novella "The Death of Ivan Ilyich." In this tale, a landowner is able to take in the enormity of his oncoming death because of the loving attention of one of his devoted servants. *Here* was balm for such a condition. Every nursing student, every potential healer, should listen to this music, should read this book. They are worth many courses in physics, math, and chemistry.

Nevertheless, I am anxious to go back to school as a "nontraditional" student, to fill in scientific gaps and learn the new material that will enable me to become a nurse. "To nurse" comes from the root "to nourish," and specifically evokes the babe at the breast. Such tenderness is exactly what we need now, in 1984, as individuals, as nations, and as a species.

Alan Krieger
February 1984

PLEASE RESPOND TO THE FOLLOWING THREE QUESTIONS.

1. How did your interest in the NYU School of Nursing develop?

I have been a lifetime resident of the city. When I was a child, my father would take me with him down to the bookstores on Fourth Ave. and would point out the various sites of his old alma mater, NYU. The deep companionship of these moments, my subsequent involvement in the many activities of the Village, and my current commitment to nursing as a career make my choice of NYU inevitable.

2. Please tell us how accurately your academic record to date indicates your ability to succeed at NYU.

My record will show that what I enjoy, what I want to learn, I am quite good at. It will also show the converse. I am convinced that my now mature determination to enter the field of nursing will inspire my studies even in those fields I have previously disdained. I have an almost photographic memory, have learned vast amounts of literature by heart, and anticipate no problems in memorizing the consequences of acetylene meeting water or the brachiation of the cranial nerves.

3. Please describe your postcollege or career plans as they relate to your prospective major.

I intend to work as a clinical nurse, hopefully with those most in need. My requirements for money or fame are minimal. Me for the trenches.

*This guy will either be terrific or a disaster.*
*Worth a try? TG*

*july*

## 12. INDEPENDENCE DAY: RALLIES IN BLACK, WHITE, AND BLUE

Thar she blows, first lady of the land. And not once did she stoop to work for the Rose Law Firm.

Alan was taking in the view from Battery Park, the southern tip of Manhattan.

*Give me your tired, your poor,*
*Your huddled masses yearning to breathe free,*
*The wretched refuse of your teeming shore.*
*Send these, the homeless, tempest-tost to me,*
*I lift my lamp beside the golden door!*

Oh, Emma Lazarus, check it out. Got enough wretched refuse yet, old girl? Enough spare change for the homeless tempest-tost? Hope your piggy bank is full.

Fuck, it's hot! I'd take off my shirt if I weren't so portly. I wonder if they know that I know that they know that I know that wearing a shirt with vertical stripes is supposed to make me look taller and thinner?

Thirty-six years in this city, and I've never been out to the Statue of Liberty. If I was in from Des Moines for thirty-six hours, I'd have been there. Well, shit, what am I supposed to do, go out there and climb the stairs? I can barely make it up to my sweetics' apartments. On the other hand, if I did go and climb the stairs, say every day for three or four hours, I'd probably be able to arrive at one bed or another without the embarrassing huffing and puffing. I suppose smoking less than two packs a day would help, too.

Look at those flags. Limp as a nonagenarian cock. Is this symbolic of our national condition? If I broke down and spent the five bucks or whatever to get out there, I could see the broken chains of tyranny at Emma's feet. Wait a minute, she's not named Emma. Emma Lazarus is named Emma. What the fuck is *she* named? Something dumb like Liberty or Columbia? Liberty, that must be it. It's the Statue of Liberty. Like the statue of David. Don't these people have last names? I mean, I wouldn't have been confused if it were called the Statue of Liberty Aronowitz. Libby, it's *you*. A little stern in the face for me—but nicely bookish, that I can say. Enough of staring out to sea, Alan. It's me for the huddled masses, yearning. Let's check out the holiday crowd, especially the younger female members thereof.

Oh, by Jesus, better steer clear of this little mob. Look at them all in their shiny blue suits and red bow ties. Looks like a gathering of the Mortimer Snerd of Color Club. Maybe a little tougher. Maybe a lot tougher. Herr Krieger, let's be outa here.

"Hey, Alan!"

"Enrico, *hombre!* What the fuck are you doing here? This isn't *your* country's birthday. And what are you doin in the middle of . . ."

"What's up, man? Hey, we miss you. The place isn't the same without . . ."

"Shhhh! They'll hear you. Our asses'll be fried."

"No, man, check this out," Enrico said. "I'm takin notes."

"Maybe they'll think you're a reporter. But what's *my* excuse?"

"Chill out, man. You're an interested bystander. This place is swarming with cops."

"Oh, then I'm safe as a babe in me mother's arms. Whoops, I forgot who my mother was."

"*Está increíble.* Shut up and listen."

" *. . . is none other than the black man. The black man is the first and last, the maker and the owner of the universe. Allah is proving to us that the* *white race is not, and never will be, the Chosen People of God. They are the Chosen People of their father Yacub, the devil.*"

"I take it this is Jacob of Abraham, Isaac, and Jacob fame?"

"Who the fuck knows?"

"*Since Yacub bred whites to be specially greedy and vicious, these monsters were bound to try to rule over other peoples. Allah permitted this for six thousand years. But then he arranged for the people of Shabazz to come as slaves to North America, where they could see for themselves the wiles of the white man so as to spearhead his destruction. We have to recognize our true pedigree. We have to reclaim our racial heritage. Whites are the mortal enemy. We must fight to drown the vicious beast in the fiery lake prepared for him.*"

"Does that include you?"

"No, man, *latino no es blanco.*"

"*You are the Black Man, the original man. You are the Black Man, you are African, the quintessence of universal blackness. You will crush the corners of the earth and this world will surely tremble until you, the Black Man, the first and original man, can erect a new society, humane to its core, out of which will emerge, at long last, the first truly human being that the world has ever known.*"

"That humane core makes me feel all wet and gushy inside."

"*Bueno*. It should."

"*You are the royal family on this planet. You gazed into the stars and wrote astrology. You had a conversation—and that became philosophy. You are the ones who created mathematics. You are the alpha and omega of creation itself.*"

"What is this, self-esteem graduate school? Oh, Watson and Crick, where are you now?"

"*I can't hear you, friend. You come up here and speak to the brothers an sisters in the microphone.*"

"I hope he's not talking to me."

"You think he'd call on you?"

"Yeah, why not? I'm a good speaker. Clever. Witty . . ."

*"You know how Jews are always saying they're the Chosen People?"* the new speaker began.

"Whoops. Here comes our fifteen minutes of fame. . . ."

*"But just cause they say it, it don't mean it's true. You look in the Bible, do you find that Jews are the Chosen People?"*

*"No! No!"*

*"Black people are the real Chosen People. We are the Chosen People. Jews are fakes, trying to steal our place. And I got one thing to say to any you Jews might be listenin around the fringes . . ."*

"The jig is up, *hombre,*" Ernesto remarked.

"The jig is up at the mike, you mean. . . ."

*"Bruchator adenoids, muhfuckas!"*

*"Whoowee! Yes, sir! Tell it like it is, bro!"*

The emcee took the mike again.

*"The brother's language may be strong, but his thought is correct. Jews are not really Semitic peoples at all but impostors descended from the vicious tribes of Jakub. The Egyptians had good reason to persecute them because they worshipped their God instead of working."*

"Hard to get a Shabbes goy on Saturdays!"

"What's a Shabbes goy?"

"I'll tell you later."

*"Brother? Yell it out so we can all hear."*

*"But everyone thinks the Jews are victims. When we are the victims!"*

*"Just so, brother. Jewish victimization is part of a great hoax that explains how Jews have come to influence Western civilization out of all proportion to their small numbers. Jews are not victims: they are victimizers. They were the main people responsible for the genocide of the Native Americans. They were one of the main slaveholders of our people before—and after—the Civil War."*

*"Yeah!"*

*"The nuclear age began with the help of Jewish scientists—Oppenheimer and Einstein—but only when Jews in Germany were threatened. And they*

*tested it on a population of color outside Europe—where no Caucasians or Jews could be hurt."*

*"And what about muhfucking Jewish landlords?"* a voice in the crowd inquired.

*"Jew York City."*

*"Jewish doctors inject our babies with AIDS!"*

"This is getting heavy, man." Enrico looked worried.

"It wasn't heavy before?"

"They're gonna storm the hospital."

"They already do."

*"Who caught and killed Nat Turner?"*

*"Jews!"*

*"Who controls the Federal Reserve?"*

*"Jews!"*

*"You're not afraid to say it, are you?"*

*"Jews, Jews!"*

*"Who controls the media and Hollywood?"*

*"Jews!"*

*"Who is squeezing our entertainers, our athletes?"*

*"Jews!"*

*"Am I lying?"*

*"No!"*

*"What you have to say, brother? Come on up here. . . ."*

*"I want to say that I am not anti-Semitic. I am not calling for the extermination, or even the expulsion, of the Jewish people. No. But we got to speak the truth. We got to look truth in the eye. We got to recognize and remove the bloodsuckers from our neighborhoods and from our lives. If we are ever to be liberated, we need to recognize the hands that are holding us down. We need to sever those hands from holding us—so we can be a free people!"*

*"Amen, brother. Tell the truth."*

You getting all this down?"

"There are words I don't know. Bloodsucker."

"Like *sanguijuela*."

"Ah, *sí*."

"I had a patient come in covered with em. Looked it up."

*"What is a bloodsucker? When they land on your skin, they suck the life from you to sustain their own. Now, who were the primary merchants in the black community?"*

*"The Jews."*

*"That's right. Black people are never going to be free until there is a new relationship with the Jewish community along the lines of fairness and reciprocity. Is that anti-Semitism?"*

*"Kill the Jew bastards."*

*"No, no. Then we wind up strapped on that gurney with a needle in the arm. We have got to address the problem of the relationship between blacks and Jews."*

*"Go ahead and kill us, we already dead!"*

*"Push that gutter religion back into the gutter where it belong!"*

*"More lampshades! More lampshades!"*

"This is not encouraging," Alan noted.

*"Minister Farrakhan has tried to reason with the Jews. But they disrespected him. And they lied to him. So now they have to face us."*

*"And we'll eat their be-hinds alive!"*

*"The only way to get respect is to use violence. I'm talkin bout bloodshed and guerrilla warfare."*

*"Two wrongs don't make it right."*

*"But it damn sure make it even, man."*

"Hey, Enrico, buddy. This is getting a bit much for me. I feel like the one missing piece of the lynch-mob puzzle. I'm like see you later, OK?"

"Stick with me, buddy. I protect you."

"Hey, man, you can pass. You got the almost-melanin. But white, pasty, Jewish intellectual-shaped me—I'm a tasty morsel. Look, gimme a call when you get a chance. I want to know what's been happening at St. Vincent's Dysfunctional."

"What's your phone?"

"Here's my card. I'll write my home number on it. Gimme your pen, hotshot."

"Hey, *you're* not deaf."

"Deaf to the cries of suffering humanity."

"The card says I AM DEAF."

"I'm learning sign language. Bought it off a subway bum. Cost me a whole token."

"So how will you learn if I take your card?"

"Got it memorized."

"Really? OK, man, I call you."

"Great. Terrific to see you."

"You too. We miss your big mouth."

"*Hasta luego, hombre.*"

"*Luego.*"

Jesus H. Christ fuckin shit, lemme out, I need some air! That was unbelievable. *Oi.* Goddamn Pepsi! I shoulda known better. Man, I really have to piss! We are forced into purloined-letter mode, the invisibility of the obvious. Let's just kick away all this garbage and salute this flagpole right here. Helicopter shot will focus on the flag, no doubt, limp as it is—like my little shlong.

*Oh, say, can we pee*
*In the midst of this blight . . .*

But officer, there's not a Porta-Potty in sight, and I have benign prostatic hypertrophy, which, of course, is not as serious as malign prostatic hypertrophy; nevertheless, this is certainly a medical emergency, not to mention having drunk a liter of Diet Pepsi. . . .

*We're so proud to be male*
*For to make such a streaming.*

Ahhhhhhh. What could be better this side of paradise? Ummm-mmm. Careful, Alan, don't wet your chinos. Shake and bake. That sun feels good on it. But goddamn, those NOI-sies, or whatever they are . . . they are somethin! I can see em coming, shiny suits and submachine guns. Scarier than Brown Shirts. At least the Brown Shirts didn't wear red bow ties! Wonder what asshole Walter would say if he'd been at *that* seminar. Of course, they don't have such seminars up in the beautiful Vermont woods. Ah, a *Landsmann!* Hebrew National Franks. Looks Jamaican to me.

Alan Krieger, freshly emptied, sauntered up to the hot-dog man.

"I'll have one big one, my good fellow. Mustard and sauerkraut, to celebrate my feeling sour and worrying about neo-Krauts. And one Diet Pepsi, juice of the gods. *Muchas grassy ass.*"

What language do they speak?

He munched his cylindrical prey and waved knowingly to a young man in blue.

"Top o the marnin to ya, Officer Friendly."

Hm. Not very friendly. Guess it's not in his job description to say hello. And I'm white. Pasty, even.

*America, America,*
*God sprayed his mace on thee . . .*

Listen, Krieger, your main objective is not yet begun. Get on the stick. What are you here for, patriotism? No. Your main agenda item is to pluck an American Beauty rose, preferably without thorns. Peel those eyeballs, man. Let's just sit down under this shady tree, chew on our frank, suck on our Pepsi, and check out the ladies.

Black.

Black.

Too old.

Brown.

Ug-ly.

Taken, it would seem.

He drained his can and squinted to the west.

Now, what's that coming down the path in those short, short shorts? Mm, mm, mm. Only in America. But I do have to finish my Hebrew National Frankfurter and wipe the mustard off my face before I make an approach. No sense courting failure when it's hard enough already. These dogs are goddamn good—even if they're putting money in the pockets of illegal aliens. And now, a last slug of this glorious dark fluid with the secret formula, mead of the mighty! Big belch—*urugg!*—and ready to go. Now, where am I going? Nowhere. I'm sitting here, ready to spring. But no, I'd split my pants. I'll just sit and wait for fate. That's how it is on this bitch of an earth.

But look, Alan Krieger, at *that* one! Suntanned bombshell in miniskirt and tank top. If they made tanks like that, we wouldn't have lost thc war.

*Oh, beautiful, for spacious thighs*

This is too good to pass up. Prepare to meet thy destiny, AK-47. But I need to prepare better. Down, down, o pissing tool. Detumescence. Think of auto accidents and pit bulls. There, that's better. More like a civilized Jewish man. OK. Ready again. Better prepared. Well fed. Highly motivated—but . . . too late. Can't approach from behind—they frighten or ignore.

*Attend, attend,* Alan. For here, in postmodernity, now comes a pomo pair. OJ and Nicole. Get with it. Nice figure, yes, yes, a little slim but slinky. Actually, both of them, nice figures. Must be a health-club romance. They probably rub their black-and-white abs together. Wait a minute. Who is . . . what the . . . is that Ursula? It's Ursula and that fucking what's-his-name Calvin! I knew it! I fucking knew it! I can smell those things even before they happen. A hundred yards and heading my way. I can hide maybe on the other side of this tree. Just sit facing away from the path. That goddamn bitch. Cheating on me all these months. With a fuckin shvartza yet. I can't do it. I can't just hide. And if I move now, they'll see me. So up and atom. Be still, my heart.

"Hi, Ursula."

"Alan, hello. You remember Calvin? You met him . . ."

". . . while you were stuffing snails in your . . ."

"Hi, Alan. Ursula's been telling me all about . . ."

"I thought communications between doctor and patient were confidential."

"Alan, you are not my patient."

"Oh. I thought maybe I was paranoid-schizophrenic thinking you two might be making the beast with two backs."

"Al-an . . ."

Calvin thought it was time to take charge.

"Whoa, guys. Calm down."

"So when's the honeymoon?"

"As a matter of fact, Ursula and I *are* going on a little trip. Three weeks in Prague."

"Jesus, Mary, and Joseph K.! What's in Prague?"

"Calvin's doing genealogical research."

"Whose genealogy?"

"Mine, Alan. My family comes from Prague."

"They allowed shvartzas in Prague?"

"My grandfather was Jewish. A rabbi, in fact."

"So where's your hooked nose?"

"My mother looked like Lena Horne."

"Your nose got absorbed."

"Apparently."

"So you're Jewish."

"Yes."

"You don't look Jewish."

"*Mit vos far an oig men kukt oif ainem, as ponem hot er.*"

"You speak Yiddish?"

"*A bissel.*"

"I don't. My mother and father kept it for their secret language. I have to get by on my German."

"All right, Yiddish lesson for German speaker. Let's take it slow: Mit vos far an oig . . ."

"With what kind of an eye?"

"Good. *Men kukt oif ainem . . .*"

"Someone looks at something."

"Someone looks at someone. *As ponem . . .*"

"Something about a face."

". . . *hot er.*"

"He has."

"Right. And all together?"

"With whatever eye you look at someone, that is the face he has?"

"You got it."

"That's a good saying."

"You still think he doesn't look Jewish?"

"Maybe a little more. Your whole family is Jewish?"

"Southern Baptist."

"So? How did you get Jewish?"

"I converted."

"Being black isn't enough? You have to be Jewish too? What, you haven't suffered enough?"

"Is being lynched better than being gassed?"

"Not all blacks were lynched," Alan pointed out.

"Not all Jews were gassed. But that's not the point, and I don't want to get into numbers. For some reason," Calvin continued, "I find myself in deep and permanent mourning for six million murdered Jews."

"The wail of your *zayda*'s DNA."

"Maybe. Probably."

"That's why he's going to Prague," Ursula said.

"And you?" Alan asked her.

"I'm starting to relate to the Jewish experience. . . ."

"*Oi!* Three months with me, and a special introductory book for goys, and only now you're starting?"

"I want to be in Jewish Prague, consciously, as a German."

"There's no Jewish Prague left. And there are millions of Germans—all with guidebooks in hand."

"Unconscious."

"Calvin, I have an interesting assignment for you," Alan said.

"In Prague?"

"No. Here and now."

"Shoot."

"About two hundred yards south of here, there's a little rally—it may still be going on."

"We walked by it. Looked like Nation of Islam."

"Nation of Islam plus miscellaneous unwashed condisciples. I want to go back there with you guys. I want you to listen to what's going on, and then I want to have an Independence Day seminar on blacks and Jews under the shade of some coolibah tree."

"We can save time. I know the story."

"You may know the NOI story—it's in print. But you may not have experienced the enlightening wipe-bummatory discourse of the rabble."

"I hear it every day. It's part of my job."

"What do you do?"

"BATF. I'm the codirector of Project LEAD."

"Lead abatement? You walk the slums?"

"Law Enforcement Arms Database. We track the weapons. I'm a programmer and investigator."

"He basically designed the system," Ursula said. "Did you know only a tiny number of dealers are responsible for half the guns used in crimes?"

"No. OK, so you've heard it all. So then I have a couple of questions for a Jewish black man."

"Shall we sit down?"

"You won't grass-stain those white pants?"

"So I'll get them cleaned."

"It costs, it costs. . . ."

There were times when Alan sounded like his mother. The three of them pulled up a grassy knoll.

"What's the seminar?"

"A couple of questions. First, are blacks taking over the world?"

"Why do you think blacks—we—are taking over the world?"

"I don't have to go over the current cultural worship—music, sports, fashion, language. Right? Right."

"And?"

"Life has made blacks hard, inside and out. But American Jews, and white people in general, are dying a slow death by the softness of mindless conformity. This is a clear and perfect setup for natural selection, *nicht wahr?*"

"But they're—we're—not the fittest, Alan. At *every* socioeconomic level, blacks are uncompetitive. . . ."

"Maybe. But black kids see themselves—and act—like they're the elite. Look at those four strutting over there. You think they want success?—they're out to replace success with a morality of the bottom, perverted, promiscuous, violent. Why should they try to compete? They know a losing proposition when they see it. Better to affirm the barbarian. And everything is set for white kids to follow these pied pipers into delinquency and self-destruction."

"That's a great line, Alan," Ursula said. "I'm sure the *Post* would love a series of scare articles."

"Alan," Calvin said, "it seems to me white society is coming round—slowly, I admit—but coming round to . . ."

"Whites don't *want* to cure black crime, Calvin. Thousands of people would lose jobs if police forces were reduced or prisons closed. Manufacturers who sell weapons, or uniforms and equipment, to law enforcement agencies—like the BATF—would close. And worse, lower crime rates would allow blacks to flourish—and limit white revenge. Yes?"

It was not an angel passing over but the baffled silence of mismatched worldviews. Ursula was first to feel antsy: "There was a second topic in this seminar?"

"Second topic?" asked Alan, jolted from his toxic trance. He stood up and began to pace. "Second and last. But not least. I ask you as a Jew, Calvin, and I ask you as a German, Urs—what is the role of the Jew in this emerging extravaganza?"

"Why should Jews have any special role?"

"Because we are the Chosen People."

"What does that mean?"

"That's what I'm asking you. What are we chosen for?"

"Alan," said Ursula, "I hate to interrupt just when we are broaching your favorite subject. But I have to pee."

"So pee."

"There's no toilet."

"Pee in the bushes over there."

"We can talk and walk," Calvin said, "and we'll come to a toilet, I'm sure. Worse comes to worst, we can head over to the ferry dock. OK with you, Urs? Can you hold a few minutes?"

"See, Alan? That's the difference between a real *mensch*—and you."

"Asking you to curb your natural functions and be uncomfortable? That's a *mensch?*"

"Let's head that way. You were saying?"

"I wasn't saying anything. I was asking you two if you thought Jews had a special role to play in the current situation—whatever it is."

"If you're worried about the fate of the Jews," Ursula said, "it's probably best to soft-pedal the notion of Chosenness. It seems to piss people off."

"Speaking of pee."

"It should be possible," Calvin said, "to be Jewish without basing it on chosenness, and the implied inferiority of others."

"And how do you do that? God chose us Jews as his people. It says so in the Bible. Deuteronomy 7-something."

"Maybe it's a mark of responsibility."

"That's good, Calvin. More responsibility. For what?"

"For living in the world in a certain way."

"What about you, Ursula? If you were Jewish . . ."

"It's hard for me to imagine becoming Jewish, Alan. And what does that really mean? Practicing six hundred something commandments? If that's the case, any nonorthodox Jew isn't Jewish."

"Like me?" Alan stopped pacing. "I spy."

"You spy?" Urs asked.

"I spy with my little eye."

"What are you talking about?"

"I spy with my little eye something blue."

"Something blue?"

He gestured to the west.

"Oh, Alan, thank you! A Porta-Potty!"

"Who's the *mensch* now?"

"You are. Be right back."

In her absence, Calvin sat and Alan resumed pacing.

"Look, Calvin. When the Jews began slugging it out with the Christians in the first century, there was a guy named Celsus, a pagan philosopher, who watched the whole thing ringside, busting his gut with laughter. He compared the Js and Cs to worms meeting in the corner of a manure pile and saying to one another, 'God has made us rulers over everything.'"

Calvin inspected the ground, plucked a blade of grass, and stuck it in his mouth. Ursula came briskly back, all bouncy. It is remarkable what an empty bladder can do for the soul.

"Hi, I'm back. What happened?"

"Worms in a shit pile," reported Calvin, and stood up, unstained by green.

"Oh."

"Want to walk?" he asked.

"Sure."

"Alan?"

"I'm already walking."

The three continued along the path. Step on a crack, break your mother's . . .

"I was thinking in the Porta-Potty that chosenness is just defensive self-infatuation."

"Always thinking," Alan accused. "OK, suppose we substituted some special mission instead of Chosenness?"

"Like a vocation? A calling? *Beruf?*" Ursula asked.

"All right. Good," Alan said. "So what's the Jewish calling here?"

"You tell us," said Calvin. "You're the senior Jew."

"To stop the whole slide into the abyss," Alan announced.

"That's a tall order."

"You'd rather go on that particular ride?"

"How do you intend to abort it?"

"I don't know. But abortion it is—for the false messianic age!"

White follows black as dawn does the night. But dawn does not always bring enlightenment. Oh, for luminous shades of gray. To the north of the snaking path, Al and Cal spied another group of humans gathered in sodality. Ursula had already noticed. And this was what those humans said: "*Last week, before this rally, when I went to get the permit, I talked to a black police chief, and he said, 'Now, David, I don't want to hear the word* nigger.' *Well, Lieutenant Cobey, hear this: Nigger, nigger, nigger, nigger, nigger!*"

"*Nig-ger! Nig-ger! Nig-ger! Nig-ger!*" echoed the flock.

"More democracy in America," Alan observed. "Care to play de Tocqueville with me?"

"You won't believe this, Alan, but we're still not packed. We have to get up at four to get to Kennedy by six."

"We'll be back first of August."

"Have a great trip," Alan said. "I hope you find your *zayda* and your *zayda's zayda*."

"Thanks."

"Alan?" Ursula pleaded. "Try to stay out of trouble?"

"Would it matter?"

"Of course."

Calvin's not so bad, Alan thought. I see what she likes in him.

As he watched them head off for the subway, a familiar name struck his ear.

"*Aristotle, the great Greek philosopher, said that "just as some are by nature free, so others are by nature slaves.*"

A seminar in Aristotle. Free! Isn't America wonderful? Let us approach.

"*White Power! White Power!*"

But maybe not too close.

A bald young man in black leather sprang up to the flag-adorned platform and took the mike.

"*But in* my *mind, the real problem, the more basic problem is the Jew.*"

Perhaps a few feet farther back might be appropriate. Well, there's Officer Friendly. I'll just keep him in sight. Doesn't look as if he's going anywhere. He must be interested in basics too.

"*All the real leaders of the NAACP were Jews. The so-called black civil rights leaders were financed, advised, or led by Jews.*"

"*Martin Lucifer Coon!*"

"*Now a lot of people say, 'Let's go out and get a nigger.' But I say leave the niggers alone. Without Jewish control and Jewish leadership, niggers wouldn't go* nowhere. *And not because they're stupid or illiterate, because they're not. But without Jewish money power, the black movement wouldn't go anywhere.*"

A woman's voice from the crowd: "*The bulk of Jews are very neurotic, psychotic people.*"

Alan clapped internally.

*"I'm not saying all Jews. I know a lot of Jews, I've worked for Jews who treated me great. But I've studied the idea why Jews are so attracted to the Hitler thing. I think Jews have this love-hate relationship with Nazis, and now they are using the same stuff in Israel that's a copycat of the SS, and I just think there's some kind of neurosis that is catching."*

*"Jews are not Caucasians as far as I'm concerned."*

*"More lampshades!"*

Lampshades again? Fuck! Unplug the electricity! Maybe I should buy stock in a Lampshades R Us—we could advertise in *Ebony* and *Reader's Digest.*

Another skinhead, bigger, fatter, joined his colleague on the platform.

*"It's always been Jews that's the problem. Always. In one of the missing books of the Bible, Satan says, 'My own people, the Jew.' That's what he calls them, 'My own people.' The Jew is scared cause he knows our movement is growing."*

*"Hail victory! White Power! Hail victory! White Power! Hail victory! White Power!"*

*"I mean we got our guns, and we know how to protect ourselves on the street if we have to. But the Jews are behind communism, and . . .*

*"Well shit,—they crucified* Christ, *so whad'ya expect? They crucified Christ. In my opinion, Jews did it. And in my opinion, Jews engineered and invented abortion when it was first invented. I'm sure there's a lot more Jews that's murderers than there are whites!"*

I wonder if they can tell I'm Jewish. I mean, do I really look Jewish? My nose is big, but not *so* big. I'm fat—but so are most Merkins. Not this group, though. Oh, there's one fat guy. But I've got glasses. They'll know it's from too much reading—Jewish. If I don't open my mouth, I could look like a furniture salesman, I think. Recliners and overstuffed chairs, that's innocent enough. Officer Friendly, protect and serve.

*"Jews control nine out of ten abortion clinics. They want white women to have abortions, but they encourage blacks to have lots of kids."*

*"They hate us, they hate our Father, they hate our culture, they hate our music, they hate our children. They are the Antichrist, and their hatred won't stop until Christ returns."*

*"Amen!"*

All false messiahs will be destroyed, my friends, no exceptions.

The emcee took back the mike. *"Friends, we are here to deliver the American people from evil. But look around. Where's the TV cameras? Where are they? It just goes to prove my point. What, a hundred of us here on America's own birthday to celebrate America, and where is the Jewish media?"*

*"Covering the coons!"*

By God, they're right, noted Alan. There *was* coverage there! Two channels, in fact.

*"Right! You go home and watch your TVs tonight, and figure it out for yourselves. The American people are brainwashed. This nation needs to be cleansed, revived, a white man's revival!"*

*"Hail victory! White Power! Hail victory! White Power! Hail victory! White Power!"*

*"I want you to join me in singing 'My Country Tis of Thee.'"*

*My country tis of thee,*
*Sweet land of liberty,*
*Of thee I sing . . .*

They sing pretty well for a lynch mob, thought Alan.

*"The Jews, they own this country because they're smart. They have billionaires, trillionaires, and millionaires. They pay the president, they own the country."*

So how come nobody I ever vote for gets elected? Nobody. Not once, ever. Of course maybe if I voted for other people than write-ins . . . But then how would Clarabelle and Captain Kangaroo ever get on the ballot?

*"Now listen here, can I say something about the United States? If the*

*United States would be smart like they're supposed to be following our traditional fathers, but you know what? They can't wait to get a hold of it with their piggy-ass, scummy-ass communism."*

What wings of song! What rhetorical flight! Momentum. Trajectory. Throw weight. A tad whacko, but . . .

*"We gotta kill em all . . ."*

*"Careful. There are informers here in this very audience."*

Uh-oh . . . Officer Friendly, still there? Good boy.

*"Hail victory! White Power! Hail victory! White Power! Hail victory! White Power!"*

*"When I see what the Jews are doing to our people, what they are doing to our women—turning them into men, sending them to work, turning their heads . . . The blacks we can send back to Africa. But the Jews? Put tote bags on their heads!"*

Tote bags? This is getting too surreal for me. All right, Mr. Krieger, I think we've had enough for the day. Besides, I think I see some tote bags over by those bushes. Off we go. Officer Friendly still with us? Whenever I feel afraid, I hold myself erect—shame! How did they ever get away with that adjective?—and whistle a happy tune, so no one will suspect . . .

*"Hail victory! White Power! Hail victory! White Power! Hail victory! White Power!*

All hail the black, white, and blue. What was blue? The swarms of police. The liquid distance to the Statue of Liberty, though it verged on greeny-gray. The abdomen of certain flies, and the color of some birds that ate them. The orgone in the air. The jeans on young and old, and the Rimbaud "o"s of their words. The beards of would-be ladykillers. The tassels on prayer shawls in the park. Baby boys' blankets and the tongues of two chows. The gabardine garments of the Nation of Islam, and the Hitler eyes of many who opposed them. The Diet Pepsi cans tossed in among the irises. The color of Krishna in the copies of the

*Gita* carried by different skinheads. The sound of the Prelude to Act One of *Lohengrin,* even out of one tiny radio. The skin of smoking emphysemics and the hair of women who took care of them. The lips of those who had sucked on blueberry popsicles. The memory, on this American holiday, of JFK's assassination limo. The tattoos on the white skins of young girls and old men. And most blue of all, Alan's mood against the relentlessly luminous sky.

Goethe felt that blue gave birth to anxiousness, tenderness, and yearning. So did Alan. "The deeper blue becomes," Kandinsky wrote, "the more urgently it summons man toward the infinite, the more it arouses in him a longing for purity and, ultimately, for . . . infinite penetration into absolute essence—where there is, and can be, no end." For Alan, there would be.

But for the moment . . .

## 13. PHILOSOPHY IN A NEW KEY

*Oh what a beautiful mornin,*
*Oh what a beautiful day,*
*I've got a beautiful feeling*
*Martha will be easy prey!*

The New School. Well, it used to be new. What—1920 or so? Lot of high-class types, though. Dewey, Levi-Strauss, Harry Belafonte . . . Don't they have some Orozco murals somewhere, and a Thomas Hart Benton? Shit, all I see is splendiferous women. But . . .

*None so fair*
*None so fair*
*None so fair*
*And she's my treasure!*

None so fair as Martha. Here's my dance card, let me smell the envelope for the hundredth time. And for the hundredth time, it smells like offices. Well, what do you expect, she can't be asking her secretary to send out perfumed mail. What if she's allergic? Rest the old butt, Krieger, you rogue.

"*Dear Mr. Krieger.*"

*Dear.* She calls me *Dear.* And she hasn't even met me!

"*Thank you for the fascinating letter and the excellent poem.*"

See, you're fascinating. That is a not-too-common word, and carefully chosen. This woman is a writer and philosopher, after all, precise in her language.

*"I do agree there is a place for righteous anger, even in the economy of love."*

Love. Love! She speaketh to me of love.

*"Your idea that there is an anger-equivalent to* agape *in the* eros/agape *duality seems most pregnant, and I hope you will be able to develop it at length."*

Now, *she* said that, not I. Pregnant. If that isn't a come-on, I don't know what is.

*Oh what a happy forewarning,*
*I'm grateful I am not gay.*
*Martha, on you I am fawwww-ning . . .*

*"Yes, I'll be in New York in July for the New School symposium. I would be happy to have lunch with you on the 21st, and we can discuss all this in more detail. Can we meet in the New School lobby at 12:30? We'll decide what to do from there. Please contact my secretary to confirm. I look forward to meeting with you.*

*"Yours sincerely,*

*"Martha Nussbaum"*

And I to meeting with you, O Helen of Academe. I knew it, I knew it! I just knew she'd see me. Invest thirty-four cents and come up with a million-dollar baby. It's better than Publishers' Clearing House. At least I don't get sent a whole bunch of dreck made in China by slaves. 12:26. Will she come early, *en punto,* a little late, or lots late? You're having your first exam right now, my suave and svelte. At least I think you're suave and svelte. Now that I think about it, I've only seen pictures of your pulchritudinous *punim.* What if she's three hundred pounds with a ravishing, thin *punim?* How will I get out of this? I'm gonna have to spend an hour theorizing with her over lunch and then I'm gonna have to pick up the bill. She's a full professor, and I have to pay the bill? Fuck, I'm unemployed and subject to the disease yclept lack of money! I got twenty-five bucks till the end of the month. 12:28. If you're early, you're anxious; if you're on time, you're obsessive; if you're late, you're resistant and irresponsible. No win, Martha. But I'd rather have her anxious. On the other hand, what if she's anxious but doesn't want to show it, so she intentionally comes late? But not very late. A little late.

Oh my God, that's her. Across a crowded room. I can't believe it. Everything I want in one trim package. Oh, man, long evenings with *that* on my lap, reading Catullus. *Amor vincit insomnia.* She's looking around. I told her I'd recognize her. Oh, God, I hope she's not disappointed when she sees me. I didn't eat all week, and I only lost two pounds. What does she want? Perfection?

"Professor Nussbaum?"

"Mr. Krieger?"

"Yes. Nice to meet you."

"Nice to meet you too. Please call me Martha. I've had enough Professor Nussbaum for today."

"Why? What happened?"

"A seminar on my patriotism article. Or non-patriotism."

"I'm ashamed to say I haven't read it."

"It's just a short piece. But it certainly pulled down a lot of fire."

"What did you say?"

"I was arguing that our primary loyalty should be to humanity as a whole, and not to some parochial national identity."

"So what's wrong with that?"

"Oh, there were all kinds of objections—from silliness like, How can you be loyal to the world at large when there is no world state to be loyal to? to more substantial objections about the way people reach out conceptually from the local to the universal."

"So you can't be loyal to your sweetie and to humanity at the same time? Or is this one of those ethics-class questions about who do you save from a fire if you can only save one?"

"No. Of course you're right. I'm right. And maybe they're objecting just to object."

"What do you expect? They're academics."

"And they're all so polite! So many nice things to say about Professor Nussbaum's 'noble ideal of cosmopolitanism' and her 'moving, provocative, stimulating essay.'"

"And then they rip into you as if you were fresh from drowning and eating your children."

"Well, not quite that. But I see you've had some taste of academia. What do you do?"

"Let's eat, speaking of Susan Smith, and I'll tell you. Where would you like to go? Want to eat in the cafeteria? By the way, you can call me Alan."

"All right—Alan. But no, I don't usually eat *lunch* lunch. I'll just sit with you and eat my Power Bar."

She show-and-telled it from her purse.

"That's a lunch? What have you got against lunch? If it was good enough for William Burroughs . . . Well, at least that thing is empowering and portable. I'll tell you what—since it's so nice out, want to walk to Union Square and one of us at least can have a real lunch al fresco?"

"That's the best idea I've heard all morning."

"Sounds like there wasn't much competition."

"No. Actually, there were some good things. You know Richard Falk?"

"Yes. Let's walk and talk Falk."

"Sure you wouldn't like one little würstchen from that nice man?"

"I don't eat hot dogs."

"This isn't just a hot dog. Please. This is a Hebrew National Frankfurter. You know, like the Frankfurt School, the Institut für Sozialforschung, arch-rivals of the New School. . . ."

"Hebrew National Franks are my one sin in thought."

"Oh, Jakob Frank, do you hear this?"

"But I haven't eaten red meat in ten years . . ."

"It's not really red. That's just food coloring."

". . . and I've been a complete vegetarian for the last year—since I've been thinking and writing about animal rights . . ."

"Hot dogs are vegetables."

". . . so no, thank you."

"A woman of principle."

She nodded and shrugged at once.

"Well, would you mind if I had one? Or two?"

"One of my chief principles is respect for others."

"Well then, two Zion National Beef Frankfurters, my good man."

Martha fingered the Power Bar in her purse, her one-stick cross to ward off vampires.

"Do you ever eat real food?"

"Dinner without fail, and I really tear into it. By then I'm absolutely starving and eat everything in sight."

"Provided it's vegetable or mineral. Keeps you trim."

"That, and running thirty miles a week."

"*Oi!* Is that a job for a good Jewish girl?"

Alan gestured, and they sat down on the grass. He offered Martha his clean white handkerchief to sit on.

"How do you know I'm Jewish?"

"With a name like Nussbaum?"

"I could be German. It could be my husband's name."

"Actually, I know quite a bit about you. It's unfair, of course, but you're a public figure, and this stuff is out there."

"What do you know about me?"

"Well, let's see. You were born in 1947, which makes you more than fifty. Sorry. But I don't know what day."

"May 6th."

"Holy McGracken! I can't believe it. That's Freud's birthday!"

"Yes. I know."

"Mine's Tolstoy's. September 10th."

"How nice."

"Umph, I'm a Dostoevsky man myself."

"George Steiner says that the world is divided between them."

" '*It would be possible to determine two types among men's souls, the one inclined toward the spirit of Tolstoy, the other toward that of Dostoevsky.*' "

"Did you just pull that out of the air?"

"I have a pretty good memory. Besides, Steiner's book changed my life. I bought it at a library sale for ten cents when I was fifteen. I wanted to know all about Russian literature without having to read it."

"Why?"

"So I could impress girls."

"I mean why not read it?"

"The books were too fat."

"What's wrong with fat?"

"Well, when you're fifteen, you like skinny."

"I liked fat. In fact, I'd never read a book if it was less than five hundred pages," Martha said.

"Why?"

"I wanted to impress the boys."

"You must have been impressive."

"I was. No one would come near me."

"Would you like a bit of mustard on that Power Bar? Seriously, try it. Mustard's a seed, like in *Midsummer Night's Dream*."

Alan took a swipe of his, and held his finger out to Martha. A yellow driplet flicked unnoticed onto her crisp white blouse.

"No, thank you. French's mustard is not on my diet."

"Orthorexic! I suspected it."

"So you bought Steiner's book for ten cents, and . . ."

"And after the first chapter I decided I'd better read the stuff he was talking about, or I'd be wasting my ten cents."

"Ummm."

"I didn't want to waste my ten cents."

"Of course not."

"So I spent the next five years reading nothing but classical Russian literature, and then I went back and finished Steiner. Spare change? Certainly, my man. Here you go."

"I never give spare change."

"You don't have Jewish guilt?"

"I'm not Jewish."

"I thought you said you were Jewish."

"I converted. So I get the good part without the bad."

"Contorted, hand-wringing Jewish DNA. The double helix doubled over in knots."

"I grew up without poor people."

"That I knew. In a castle in Philadelphia that once belonged to the Earl of Surrey."

"Brought over brick by brick . . ."

". . . by your father."

"You do know about me."

"*My* father sat around in his underwear with the roaches in the kitchen reading Kierkegaard and Nietzsche."

"We didn't *live* in the Earl of Surrey house; we rented an apartment over the nine-car garage. But I did have the run of the estate."

"Like Tolstoy—one of the world's greatest frauds."

"Why is that?"

"Because he idolized the peasants; mittin in pigshit, and he idolized them."

"I've traveled a lot lately looking at international development projects, talking to poor women in rural India, and my impression is quite the opposite. It's not 'the peasants' but the University of Chicago economists who are both pigs and full of shit and who are unabashedly sucking the blood from the Third World to line their masters' pockets, and incidentally their own. The farmers and villagers know very well what's happening. They have quite a sophisticated analysis, and even some good strategic plans. So I'm a Tolstoyan and proud of it."

"And you have mustard on your blouse to prove it."

"Damn!"

"A little *aqua fontana* on the hanky, oops, you're sitting on the hanky . . ."

"I can do it, thanks."

Martha finger-flicked the mustard blob away.

"Almost passable."

"Well, I'll just pretend it's a summer decoration til I get back to my hotel."

"Makes me hungry, though. Cookie?"

Martha shook her head. Alan lumbered to the stand, a bit stiff in the knees, and returned with two large cookies, both for him.

"I never turn down a chocolate-chip cookie. It's one of my principal principles. Keeps me at optimal weight. All right. Let's get to the good part. So you went to Harvard, snooty, snooty, in 1969 at the height of the youth rebellion . . ."

"And I met Alan—Alan Nussbaum. . . . He was the only other classics major in my whole class."

"What did the Earl of Surrey think of him?"

"You mean Dad? He hated him. Not only was he an impoverished classics student, he was Jewish. They don't like Jews—or blacks—in Georgia."

"Classic triangulation. So you married him. What delicious revenge!"

"He was so much like my father. I was born on Freud's birthday. Of course I married him. And I converted to Judaism."

"My daughter! O my ducats! O my daughter! Fled with a Jew! But you split up. Whyzat?"

"Alan, this is getting creepy. I don't know how we got on all this, but really, it's none of your business. I don't even know you. . . ."

"How come you didn't change your name back to Craven? You don't exactly look Nussbaumy."

"Craven is my father's name. And I feel really Jewish now."

"What's that—'really Jewish'?"

"I don't know . . . preferential option for the poor . . ."

"Are you kidding? That's Catholics! And *they* don't even do it! Let's talk about Jewish."

"Yes, I thought that was on our agenda. You . . ."

"Good. Let me recap, and you kibitz, OK? So. Love. It's generally accepted that there are two vastly different kinds of love."

"Yes."

Alan took a bite of cookie and then spoke around it. "*Eros* and *agape* . . ."

"Right."

"Now, it's also generally accepted that the other side of passionate love is passionate hate, passionate anger."

"'Heav'n has no rage, like love to hatred turn'd,'" Martha said.

"So if passionate love can transform into passionate anger, what can disinterested love transform into?"

"Disinterested anger? No such thing."

"Ha! Let me refer you to the writings of one Martha C. Nussbaum. Why else did I write to you? Professor Nussbaum draws our attention to the assertion of 'rational emotion,' as propounded by the Greeks, especially Aristotle. According to the old man—and according to Martha—emotions are not simply blind surges of affect. No-siree. Emotions are actually considered responses, deeply connected to beliefs about how things are and what is important."

"So *your* anger at whatever, even if it's connected to a rational belief structure, is disinterested?" she asked.

"Yes."

"Then what are you angry about?"

"OK. Last month, just before I was canned . . ."

"You were canned? From what?"

"My job in the ER at St. Vince's."

"Why is that?"

"It's a long story. In a word, for truth-telling. I don't want to get into it now. I want your opinion about disinterested anger."

"All right. Go on."

"Just before I was canned, I'm taking care of this black kid with a busted lip and a cut on his tongue, and he tells me the story of his fun evening on the town, the final event of which was beating someone to a pulp with the help of two or three friends, dragging him from the bumper of a car, and tossing him into the river to sink or swim. I hope this isn't too shocking for a daughter of the Earl of Surrey, even if she is now Jewish."

"I'm from Philadelphia."

"The City of Disinterested Love. So I'm checking out this guy's mouth to see if he needs sewing up . . ."

"You're a doctor?"

"I'm an RN."

"They let RNs sew?"

"In the ER, if you have a needle and thread, you're on. Say, you know the difference between a seamstress and a violist?—no—shut up, Alan. I sew him up, and inside, I'm shaking with rage. Palpable rage. Now, Ms. Aristotle, what am I angry at? Did he hurt me? Did he hurt anybody I care about? Do I give a fig about him or his lethal-injection destiny? No. I'm completely disinterested. This is the animal world. It has less to do with me than with my pet boa constrictor. I'm furious—but I'm disinterested."

"You're not disinterested. For one thing, you're worried the same thing might happen to you. Alan Krieger in the wrong neighborhood, at the wrong time . . . it doesn't take a huge imaginative leap."

"No. It has nothing to do with me. What made me angry was aesthetic revulsion at the bestial state of *Homo* so-called *sapiens.* What a fall was here! From Shakespeare to—them!"

"Who is them?"

"In this case, shvartzas. You know what I'm talking about?"

"And what about you?" she asked.

"What about me?"

"Are you capable of the same thing?"

"Are you kidding? Those kids offend my beliefs in the way things oughta be. Rational emotion. Disinterested anger. QED."

She sat a moment to consider.

"First of all," she offered, "it's a Freudian cliché that we repress parts of our personality that horrify us and project them outward onto those horrible others."

"Freudian cliché—a complete tautology."

"Second, you can't escape your sense of the personhood of the Other. It's built in, like a sense of time or temperature."

"These aren't persons, they're animals. Animals stalking the world of humans. Night raids. Day raids."

"Alan. Did you learn 'Twinkle, Twinkle, Little Star' as a kid?"

"Actually, I prefer the sexy Mozart lyrics. *Ah, je vous dirai, maman . . .*"

"You have a nice voice."

"Wanna hear my falsetto Queen of the Night?"

"Absolutely not. What's that nursery rhyme about?" she asked him. "What do you think?"

To Alan it was obvious. "'How I wonder what you are'—that's what it's about—the connection between humans, even children, especially children, and the universe. Everything in the universe is what it's about. Wanna hear *my* version?

*Scintillate, scintillate, globule vivific*
*Fain would I fathom thy nature specific*
*Distantly poised in the ether capacious,*
*Closely resembling a gem, carbonacious.*"

"Did you make that up?"

"No. It was in my high school *English Review Book* as an example of high speech. And that was *before* LSD."

"OK. So why do humans make that inquisitive connection? We make it all the time, with everything we look at, and listen to, and smell, and touch. How can you say you're separate from 'them', Alan? Where do you think your sense of values, of fall, of justice comes from?"

"From love," said Alan.

She nodded.

"And then we have to take this instinctive sympathy and turn it into action, not books," she said.

"Retributive justice?"

"I'd prefer corrective. Restorative."

"You do what you can." he said wryly.

"So you want me to help you plan a program of disinterested punishment?"

They looked at each other intently.

"I want you to help me clarify the nature of my anger and figure an appropriate response. I also want you to marry me. Whoops, I didn't say that."

"I'm married."

"You're separated."

"I'm seeing someone."

"Who?"

"That's none of your business either." She looked at her watch and stood up. "I have to go, Alan."

"Wait. Wait. I swear I won't bring it up again. And you'll have to admit I've been a perfect gentleman, even treating you to a Perrier in place of a Hebrew National Frank with mustard and sauerkraut, and offering you a chocolate-chip cookie even if I ate it myself."

"A gentleman and a scholar," she said. But she didn't sit back down. "And potentially dangerous."

"Let me just ask two questions." He touched her arm and then let it go. "OK, one—what is the role of a Jew in bringing justice into this here world? And two—would such action require teleological suspension of the ethical, and if so (this could be three), do you *believe* in teleological suspension of the ethical?"

"This is worse than a Grimms' fairy tale. I don't even get to marry the prince if I get the right answer."

"You never can tell."

"Well, let's start with teleological suspension of the ethical, since that's easiest."

"Easy for Henry Kissinger."

"You've read *Crime and Punishment?*"

"Have I read *Crime and Punishment?* I *am* Crime and Punishment!"

"Do you use an ax?"

"No, but what if I did?"

"What do you mean?"

"What, for instance, if I would take an ax to those kids while they were tying that boy to the car?"

"You'd be a murderer."

"Even if I was transcending the ethical for higher ends?"

"Kierkegaard would want you to be entering the religious sphere in doing so. And of course, jury selection probably won't get you a lot of Kierkegaards."

"How do I know if I'm transcending the ethical for the religious sphere?"

"You don't. That's the challenge. And do you know *The Bacchae?*"

"I went out with three of them."

"There's a chorus line toward the end: 'It is not possible to separate the beautiful from the horrible.' "

"A high-kicking chorus line if I ever heard one."

"Look, I think that story you told me is completely repulsive . . ."

"And you ain't heard a half of it. A quarter."

". . . but there's wisdom in the warnings. Who are you to think you know what's right, what the balance should be?"

"So what do *you* feel in your heart chakra? What do you feel in your womb?"

"I told you—disgust."

"But?"

"But I'm not about to take an ax to anybody over it." She turned to leave, but then turned back again. He could see that she was angry now, but her mind was already at the next point of argumentation. "The messenger in *The Bacchae* . . ."

Alan jumped up in enthusiasm.

"I *love* that speech, especially the part about his mother, foaming at the mouth, sticking her foot in his armpit and ripping his arms off."

"So you know the speech. You remember the last lines?"

"Lemme hear em."

He sat down again, arms about his knees, an adoring audience.

"*To know your human limits, to revere the gods, is the noblest and the wisest course that mortal men can follow.*"

"That was terrific. You're a great actress."

"Yes, well. Do you know *your* human limits?"

"No, really. Three lines and I was transfixed."

She scrutinized him as he sat.

"Alan, you seem like a man of great passion—but mixed with a real lack of sensitivity about your own excesses and maybe even cruelty. That's a dangerous combination."

"John Brown. He's a big hero today. Crazy eyes."

"All of this is dangerous, Alan."

"I'm searching for justice. 'If I am not for myself, who is for me? And if I am only for myself, what am I?'"

"You're a religious man."

"I'm a registered nurse."

"Alan, I have to get going."

"What about the role of the Jew?"

"I've got a plane at three-fifteen."

"Want me to drive you to the airport?"

"No."

"Good. I don't have a car."

He wasn't sure, but he thought she might have rolled her eyes.

"Can I see you again?"

"No."

"You have a twenty-something daughter . . ."

"Not for you."

"May I buy you a Power Bar before you go?"

"Goodbye, Alan. Thank you for lunch."

Alan plopped down on the grass with an "Oeuf!" and lay, belly up, eyes closed against the sun. In the play of scintillae and scotoma, white on reddish black, he saw a glittering ax shatter an old woman's skull. That's ridiculous, he thought. Jews don't kill. Not the ones I know. I and Thou. But he followed the neural projection until the last floater floated off to dreamland and the chocolate on his hands, now folded on his chest, fingerpainted and fingerprinted his new white shirt.

## PAPER TRAIL 5
## URSULA'S PRAGER TAGEBUCH

*WEDNESDAY, 7/7/99*

*Gott! To step out of the "modern" ugliness of the Inter-Continental Hotel away from Parizska's glitzy boutiques—and into another century, another universe! From bourgeois splendor,* Wohnmachinen, *to the mystical city of the dead. Not such contrast elsewhere in the world, I bet. We spent today wandering around Josefov, which was once the old Jewish ghetto. So little left, and that, thanks to Hitler's mania for display! The turn-of-the-century slum clearance, the guidebook says, was called "sanitization." Public health? Seems more like a prelude to the final solution!*

*Standing outside the Old-New Synagogue (Staronova, Altneu, a pregnant what do you call it oxymoron!) I thought of Alan for the first time on the trip, his old newness, new oldness, reaching back through centuries of thoughts and images, coming up with outrageous combinations—just like this strangest of structures, a synagogue planned and built by Franciscans—since Jews couldn't be architects. The building reminded me of Alan. Dark, fat, with spikes coming out of his head, and up there in the attic, supposedly, the "corpse" of the golem. I'm surprised Alan never brought up the golem—his kind of fellow, and the rabbi that made him. Inside the building we saw a glass cabinet, shaped like Moses' tablets filled with tiny personal lightbulbs, which light up on the anniversary of the person's death. Paid for by relatives. One for Kafka. The clock that goes backwards—also Alan. There is a legend that the community elders dug into a hill and found this synagogue completely built.*

*The most of the day we spent in the Old Jewish Cemetery, called Beth Chaim—the House of Life. Something about Jewish thought. Once we went inside the gate, it was as though the rule of the outside world stopped—even though we could see it just over the wall. I felt at the mercy of other invisible, hidden, possibly malevolent powers. Calvin less so, less malevolent. Perhaps that's understandable. The ground is most uneven between the gravestones. The guide says there are twelve layers buried here one on top of another, an accumulated ghetto of the dead of many generations. That made Calvin feel an "intense vitality" from the crowd of lopsided stones, but for me it had the scariness of the dropoff at the continental shelf. What is* under *there? Nothing human, that's certain! And the way the ground sinks in places—as if the dead are sucking on the world, ready to swallow us. For me the whole place reeks of evil eye and plague breath. Even unto silliness: spiderwebs hang from tomb to tomb like American Halloween decorations. Calvin thought the Hebrew inscriptions cast some kind of holy spell, and I did seem to be alone among the crowd of reverent visitors in feeling asphyxiated,* ausgekreeped.

*Many of them placed pebbles on the graves, and even paper messages in among the pebbles. The most messages were on the grave of Rabbi Loew—the golem man again.*

*About three o'clock the sky threw up a deathish blackness—my feelings made external? There came (no thunder) a rainstorm that was more than sheets. It was volumes of rain, as if someone were emptying a huge tub over Prague. My Casio (waterproof!) displayed only crippled, amputated numerals. Distortion of time again. I hope it will dry out. The old elder trees were groaning as if they were sound tubes from the dead below. The ground was gulping up the flood streaming down the tombstones with a sinister gurgling, as if getting ready to give birth to its dead. There was absolutely no shelter in the cemetery—as if to say there is also no shelter from death. We ran into a little building right outside the gate to dry off. There was an exhibition of children's drawings from Theriesenstadt—naive, harrowing. More for me than for Calvin, who seems to see every gleam from Jewish souls as positive testimony, even if deluded.*

*Tonight we went to the Rudolfinum to hear Penderecki conduct the Berg Violin Concerto and Mahler Fourth. But first, the Prague Symphony! The true Prague Mozart! Oh, the opening! For the first time, I thought of it not as an introduction to the first movement but as an entire vision itself, an ominous universe lying behind whatever worlds there were to come. That first huge chord, nor major nor minor but somehow rather dark than light. The few isolated moments of sweetness, but so flickering, always sandwiched between fierceness or ominousness or most often ambiguity. Again, I thought of Alan—leitmotif of the day! So chromatic and colorful Alan, yet all his half-steps snaking around toward sinister. I don't* like *sinister. When the tympani entered with its doomful beat, I thought: the Commendatore—knocking for the first time in this very town!—the Commendatore coming—for Alan! He puts out such a dare to the world—Come and get me! Why? So many false cadences in so few measures. Calvin seems so simple and good by comparison. I could barely concentrate on the rest of the work for the looming of this huge black cloud, worse than over the cemetery today. But it's good to be in, out of the rain, the struggle, the anguish!*

*I went to the restroom in the lobby. Everything exaggerated marble and gold—Hollywoodish even for the business elite—as if the bones of so many—and not just Jews—were not under the sidewalks. The toilet had a carousel-like mechanism running around the seat, bringing fresh sitting-on paper automatically out from the wall. The engineering was ingenious, but the thought that your noble predecessor's bottom might contaminate . . .* Großer Gott! *More "sanitization"! Alan would love it. I try to take a picture of it tomorrow.*

*So—a day of much chiaroscuro—in search of Calvin's Judaism.*

*august*

# 14. AUGUST 6: THE BOMB DROPS. BYE, URSULA

*As Proust observed, "everything great in the world comes from neurotics. They alone have founded our religions and composed our masterpieces." If this be true, do we really want to cure them? Especially after sleeping with them? And if we do, how shall we go about the task? Let the credulous and the vulgar continue to believe that all mental woes can be cured by a daily application of old Greek myths to their private parts.*

—Vladimir Nabokov, creator of Humbert Humbert

"Hi, Alan."

"Whoa, I thought you were with a patient."

"I was. He just left."

"How'd he leave? Down the fire-escape?"

"No, *dummkopf,* out the door."

"I didn't see him."

"You're not supposed to. He leaves through another door. Specially designed by high-pay architects."

"This is like the Roach Motel."

"No roaches here."

"No, no, it's an ad. A TV ad. The Roach Motel: they check in, but they don't check out. This is a room people enter but never leave."

"They do leave. Through that door—to my office. So you can have the waiting room to yourself."

"You mean so we can't see one another."

"Patient confidentiality."

"Confidentiality gone mad. You sit in other offices with people who are sick, waiting to see the doctor. God, people sit in the ER with their guts hanging out or their lips falling off."

"There's still a stigma around mental health. Typically American."

"Doctor, do you think I'm sick? My mind makes me out of control."

"Come in and we'll talk about it. You haven't seen my office."

The psychiatrist's office. If psychology explores the *logos* of the psyche, psychiatry pretends to its *iatrikos,* or healing. But where is the medical equipment, where are the research tools to probe, the scanners and electron microscopy to sniff out viruses infesting the mind? A chair, a couch, a desk. Could be some upscale den in Beverly Hills. Downshifted and worse, could be your mother's kitchen without the pots and pans, icebox and roaches.

"Hey, nice. Quite snazzy. I like the quilt. Where'd you get it?"

"Bartered with a patient."

"Big potted plant. *Dieffenbachia*. Swells the throat and shuts the airway."

"Really?"

"You didn't know? I thought it was part of your practice—assisted suicide? Don't they do that over there?"

"That's Holland."

"They learned it from concentration-camp doctors during the war."

"Alan, what do you want?"

"Seriously, didn't they teach you anything in shrink school? We see five cases of *Dieffenbachia* poisoning a week."

"You don't work at the ER anymore, Alan."

"True. But the mind swirls, just being in a psychiatrist's office. Mind if I lie here on this piece of apparently genuine Freudiana? Say, what's with this couch? I thought you were modern and eclectic."

"What sharp eyes you have, Grandma. It's Vienna, 1927."

"Year of the publication of *The Future of an Illusion.*"

"Is there anything you don't know?"

"Yeah. I don't know if we're getting back together now that you've had your overseas fling in Spooky City."

"What?"

"First, I have a little present for you. Hand me my pack. Thanks."

"An empty canning jar. Just what I need."

"An empty *apparent* canning jar. But actually my newest invention, a gift for you and Ophelia, balm for your eternal souls, assuming Ophelia has a soul."

"Is this like the emperor's new clothes?"

"Ursula, open the damn thing up."

"What do you mean open it up? It's open."

"Take off the top rim."

"Very nice. An inverted cone with a small hole at the vertex. Is this supposed to be symbolic, as usual?"

"No. It's thoroughly practical. More than practical—essential."

"I give up."

"You give up too easily. *That* could be a theme. Actually, it's a Not-Very-Bad-Karma Flea Receptacle. Number one off the assembly line."

"And why do I need a Not-Very-Bad-Karma Flea Receptacle?"

"Hitler's willing executioner! I've seen you combing those noble fleas out of that repulsive canine. Dropping them into soapy water—beings that can jump a hundred seventy-five times their own height and walk tightropes in flea circuses around the world. Can you walk a tightrope?"

"So instead of dropping them in soapy water . . ."

"You drop them onto the inverted cone, through the hole, into the bottle. It's a good one-way valve. Like your waiting room: they enter but rarely exit."

"So now I've got a bottle full of fleas."

"And your soul is saved from eternal damnation for not destroying the sanctity of life and the breathing of cute sentient beings."

"And what do I do with the fleas?"

"Empty the bottle where you will. In your pathetic backyard. Or in the pocket of your least-favorite patient."

"But they'll just jump back on Ophelia or another pet."

"You think killing a hundred fleas is going to change the ecology of fleadom? Give them the gift of life and save your eternal soul. Ophelia will itch no matter what. It's her awful destiny. That and snorting. Don't you think it's worth it? Pascal's wager for dummies. Tell me about Prague."

"Prague. Great chocolate-smothered waffles with whipped cream."

"That's all you got from Prague?"

"No, but I thought you'd appreciate it. I actually thought of you while trying to wipe the chocolate off my face."

"That's sweet. You thought of me even though chocolate Calvin of the Firm Bod was at your side?"

"Alan, it's over."

"You've given him up. I knew it. Travel often does that."

"No. It's over with *us*. It was over a while ago. You know that."

"Trial separation—like Kafka—where I don't know the nature of my crime."

"No crime. You didn't do anything. It's you plus me. It just doesn't work."

"But it works with a black converted Jewish gumshoe trying to 'find himself.'"

"Alan, even you, even you can see how stupid that is. You talked with him long enough . . ."

"Why won't you forgive me?"

"It's not a question of forgiveness."

"*Everything* is a question of forgiveness. You know about the Jewish New Year?"

"Some time in the fall."

"Next month, in fact. You know how it works?"

"Not really."

"Well, it's not like on Times Square, screaming and yelling and blowing horns. And then again, it is—the whole noisemaker bit comes from old ceremonies to exorcise evil spirits."

"I don't think of Jews as noisy."

"No, but they *are* interested in exorcising evil spirits. It's just that the evil spirits are inside them. On New Year's Day . . ."

"Rosh Hashanah . . ."

"Very good—for a goyess."

"I've been reading your horrible little book."

"Rosh Hashanah is a day to remember the whole painful history of the Jews in their crazy dance with the Eternal, a kind of forward memory that calls forth the continuity of the generations heading for—what?"

"The Kingdom of God on Earth—just like for Christians. And Muslims."

"OK—but Rosh Hashanah asks you if your life is helping or hindering the Kingdom from coming. It's the big evaluation in the sky—are we measuring up?"

"A tough question. What's Yom Kippur then?"

"Yom, the day, Kippur, of atonement. On that day, naked humans are booked to go mano a mano with God. Ten days before, on Rosh Hashanah, you were put down in pencil in either the Book of Life, or the Book of Death. You have ten days to change the judgment, the final judgment—in ink—on Yom Kippur. Yom Kippur—books closed."

"That's why Jews fast on Yom Kippur."

"That plus a full day of prayer—five separate services, with little break between them. When the body has given up its natural acts, and time has suspended its ups and down—that's when the spirit can be reborn."

"Alan, *scheisse,* you're so goddam convoluted."

"You mean what has this got to do with forgiveness?"

"You try to get *God* to forgive you. . . ."

"Goyish thinking. Too obvious. Jews are trickier. The most fascinating thing about the New Year events is not Rosh Hashanah and Yom Kippur but those ten days in between. The Days of Awe."

"*Ehrfurcht?*"

"Love you Krauts with your revelatory etymologies. The Days of Honorable Fear, just so, *Liebchen*. And the main strategy for processing our fear is? I'll give you a hint: it isn't going to see your shrink."

"I don't know."

"The main strategy is asking and giving forgiveness. Forgiveness. The tradition of the *shtetls* was that in the ten days between Rosh Hashanah and Yom Kippur, people would ask forgiveness of everyone they had wronged that year. All the big and little nasties were brought out into the open, confessed, and made good, if possible. The entire community was cleansed. Purified."

"Probably many people were afraid to beg pardon."

"Or give it. Still . . . interesting, no? Turning toward God by turning toward neighbors? How about that? Earning a place in the Book of Life via—of all things—forgiveness?"

Alan lit up as he waited for a reaction. Ursula passed him an ashtray and opened the window in spite of the air conditioning.

"What has this got to do with us?"

"I want you to beg forgiveness of me," he said.

It wasn't funny enough for her to laugh at. "Alan, get off that couch, and come sit over here. If you were my patient, I wouldn't talk with you like this."

"You probably wouldn't talk at all. Except for 'active listening.'" He refused to move. He was too comfortable.

"Let's just imagine we're colleagues discussing a case."

"Shit, I forgot my pince-nez."

"There is this patient . . ."

"Let's call him Alan."

"All right, let's call him Alan."

"No, let's call him Werther. You know, unrequited love, suicide . . ."

"Are you feeling suicidal?"

"No, Doctor, and I have no plan."

"All right, then, let's call him Werther."

"No. How about Walther? Walther von Stoltzing."

"Alan."

"Walther von Stoltzing wins the prize chicken with the prize song, and it's also the name of my unspeakable brother, but without the von Stoltzing—though he does suffer from the sin of pride."

"You know what? I want to call him Alan. In fact, I want to talk about you."

"Me? Why would you want to do that?"

"To tell you—as a friend—what it's like to be subjected to such narcissism."

"Oop. A psychoanalytic category. I should have known. Proceed, Herr Doktor."

"You think you can listen?"

"You mean can I hear you in the New Age sense? Or do you mean for me to temporarily narcotize my attention-deficit hyperactivity disorder? Actually, I'm well acquainted with Narcissus and *sequelae*."

"I should imagine."

"He's one of my favorite characters, along with Prince Myshkin and Attila the Hun. Would you like me to tell you the story?"

"I know the story. Is this avoidance behavior?"

"Is there something I need to avoid? The story has many interesting details."

"OK, Alan, go ahead."

"As you no doubt know, after Narcissus fell there, plop, at the side of the pond, he turned into the narcissus flower. Now, narcissus bulbs contain alkaloids that may, if eaten, produce severe digestive upset, vomiting and diarrhea, accompanied by trembling and convulsions, and occasionally, if you really pig out, death. In short, narcissus has become the 'death flower,' and it opened the doors to his realm of the underworld. Persephone had just picked a narcissus when the earth opened up and Hades came out to abduct her."

"So?"

"So it would behoove us to investigate the death themes in this well-known . . ."

"And completely misunderstood."

". . . and completely misunderstood myth. Would you care to tell it?"

"No, Alan. You have the floor, as usual."

"Well, let's see, Narcissus was, as we all know, the first centerfold hunk in *Playgirl* magazine. It has been rumored through the ages that he didn't like women—which is true—but he didn't like men either. Or boys. However, because of his great beauty many women fell in love with him. Did he care, this son-of-a-river-god? Huh?"

"No."

"Correct. He repulsed all advances. Now then, Doktor, question number one: What kind of death is involved here? You may make notes on your psychiatrist's pad."

Alan jumped up off the couch and began to pace, his hands folded behind his back in his best Viennese fashion.

"Now, to continue—among the lovelorn maidens was the mountain nymph Echo—certainly the poor pitiful pearl of the early twentieth century B.C.E. Ain't no one who would want to get hung up with her, much less Narcissus, who didn't want to get hung up with anybody."

"This part I don't know about."

"Good. Listen up. It may relate to you. You see, Zeus, that old philanderer, had persuaded Echo to distract Hera from noticing his little absences by gabbing away at her incessantly. Blahdeblahdeblah. And this was big-time stuff—like changing into swans to fuck with birdwatchers. So—when Hera discovered the plot, she was royally pissed. And what did she do? Go after the real culprit? No. She took it out on lower-level management—she stripped poor Echo of her power of speech so she could only repeat the final syllable of every word she heard."

"That *is* interesting."

"Echo became the founder and patron saint of active listening. I hope you've been sending royalties on schedule. Therefore, question number two: What is the nature of the death here?"

"I don't do active listening. I let the patient talk, and I react as needed."

"So anyway, guess who joins the fall-in-love-with-Narcissus club? Don't answer—I know you're right. And since she could only repeat what other people said, and since Narcissus never said anything, Echo was unable to tell him of her love. Is this perhaps symbolic of you and me?"

"You're saying you don't talk?"

"Point taken. OK, here comes the big scene: one day, as Narcissus is walking in the woods, he becomes separated from his companions. He shouts out, 'Is anyone here?' And Echo joyfully answers, 'Here, here.' Unable to see her hidden back among the sumac, Narcissus yells, 'Come!' and back comes the answer, 'Come, come.' I hesitate to describe the cruelty of the following scene. All I can say is that she was so humiliated that she hid in a cave and wasted away until nothing was left of her but her voice. So now, question three . . ."

"The same as questions one and two . . ."

"Of course! Well, as you can imagine, this scene didn't go down too well with the sisterhood. To punish Narcissus, the avenging goddess Nemesis made him fall hopelessly in love with his own face reflected in a pool of water. He gazed in fascination, unable to stop longing for his image, and he too gradually pined away. They don't pine like that anymore. At the place where his body fell, there grew a beautiful flower, honoring the name and memory of Narcissus. Question number four is slightly different: Why did I tell you this story?"

"To display your pyrotechnical defense mechanisms."

"What you mean is that I have not applied 'know thyself' to the narration."

"To put it mildly."

"But do not be impatient, my dear. First comes exposition, then development."

"The development section starts now?"

"If you're still interested."

"I'm taking notes."

"This is where you come in. Siggy tells us that while narcissistic self-involvement is natural in infants—primary narcissism—if the poor kiddies do not outgrow it, much *tsouris* ensues. Am I correct?"

"Sure. Secondary narcissism can lead to the most extreme forms of insanity—people who think that only what pertains to them is real. Everything else is either unreal, uninteresting, or just an object for intellectual investigation. Sound familiar?"

"Alas, dear doctor, self-love is so often unrequited."

"The solution to the problem lies in fulfilling self-love, not renouncing it."

"I have to love myself more?"

"That'd be a start."

"'He that falls in love with himself will have no rivals.' One of Franklin's better gags."

"Narcissists can be dangerous—to themselves and others."

"Sounds like a formula for involuntary commitment, Doctor."

"Alan, I'm not your doctor—but I think you're bordering on pathological narcissism and just barely holding in your aggression."

"'Self-love, my liege, is not so vile a sin as self-neglecting.' *Henry V.*"

"Quote, quote, quote. What a misuse of memory!"

"If it is, you sure ain't helping."

"Want to know something, Alan? Narcissists tend to have shallow emotional relationships, to be promiscuous, and not want to get deeply involved with one person. I wouldn't call our relationship shallow, but it wasn't exactly super-intense either. Most of the time, I didn't have any idea where you were or what you were up to. For all I know, you could have been seeing five other women at the same time. It's like you were avoiding any close entanglement . . ."

". . . which might release feelings of rage."

"That's another trait of narcissists. They always have the answer, can always explain themselves. What's the expression now—'Been there, done that'? They use their intellects for self-evasion, not self-discovery."

"Been there, done that."

"And they think they're omnipotent. That's where they become really dangerous—when they're thwarted, watch out. Narcissists often live in black-and-white worlds of good guys and bad guys. . . ."

"Like Walter."

"There you go. Bad guy. I've never heard you say one positive word about him. To me he seems like a principled and feeling man who has made other life choices than you have."

"Well, as they say, what do you know?"

"I know you hate too much."

"All right, Doctor, your hour's up. Shall we make another appointment?"

"Sit down!" she yelled. She was riled, maybe frightened. "What you need is warning, and so I'm warning you—as a friend. . . ."

"Warning me about what?"

"That it's time for you to make a real descent into the underworld, the unconscious."

"*I have no unconscious!* I don't have an unconscious."

Ursula stared at him. They each breathed through their nostrils. They were each afraid.

"You're dangerous, Alan. And I can imagine you putting yourself in terrible danger just to prove you really exist and are in control. Look at you in your black shirt, black pants, black shoes, black socks. You have such a strong allegiance to your conscience. And you're so goddamned grandiose about it."

"I should stay humble?"

"Humble from insight, not fear. You give all your love to cockroaches and snakes, Alan, because they can't abandon you. You give it to dead geniuses, and historic events; you give it to hamburgers, even."

"How'd you know about that?"

"You told me once about McDonald's versus White Castle. I've never heard anyone talk that way about a hamburger."

"And you're a *psychiatrist!*"

"And I'm a psychiatrist! I know you can take that huge intelligence, and prodigious energy, and colossal libido . . . Alan, don't cry . . . I didn't mean . . ."

"Hey . . . psychiatrists . . . are supposed to . . . love crying. Don't you all . . . have stock in . . . Kleenex?"

"Here's some Kleenex. No, I don't have stock. It's OK. You can cry."

"You use . . . such big adjectives . . . for a furriner."

"What?"

"Huge. Prodigious. Colossal."

"That's why you're crying?"

"I don't know why I'm crying. I'm crying because you're gone."

"Are you serious?"

"Of course I'm serious. I just wrote a five-act epic drama about it. Want me to read it to you? Here, I have it in my back—"

"You feel this after everything we talked about?"

"You talked. I still want to get back together."

"Alan, I'm with Calvin. You and I were never together."

"Well then, I want to *get* together."

"No."

"Germans have to bond with Jews."

"Calvin is Jewish."

"I mean real Jews."

"Calvin is a real Jew."

"That's final?"

"That's final."

Though the only arms Alan wanted at that moment were hers, he had to content himself with the artist's classic three: silence, exile, and cunning. Without another word, he left the office, taking her box of Kleenex with him.

# 15. THE GOLEM OF PELHAM PARKWAY

*Das Ewig-Weibliche—zieht uns hinan!* Forty-eight, forty-nine . . . fifty, fifty-one, whew, I sound like a PSA for emphysema. *Hinan*. Hang on to that newel post, Alan, and gather your wind so Deb doesn't reconsider taking her clothes off for a fat old fart. N is for newel post. Who's Newel? Gotta look that up. OK, to the door, in my role as knocker-in-waiting on knockers-awaiting. That girl's bazoom keeps expanding. Is it courtesy yours truly or courtesy White Castle? Can knocker be singular, or do they have to actually knock together? *Siamo in due!* But then does that mean that Ursula, may her name be erased from the Book of Life, has no knockers since you couldn't get them to knock even if you pushed em medially with all your might? No-knock Ursula? Sounds like the early days of gasoline ads. *Oh, we're the men of Texaco, we work from Maine to Mexico*. . . . That's right, hide global hegemony behind a cheap rhyme!

All right: normal breathing pattern re-established. Next decision: a big bad knock, scare the shit out of her, or a teeny-tiny suckling-dove knock to arouse her curiosity? Arousal sounds good. Start soft and go to loud PRN. Standard procedure except for the FBI and the Exterminator. Knock, knock, knockey. No answer? Knock, knock, knock-o. Still no answer. She's gotta be home by now. KNOCK . . .

"Well, if it isn't the bad or stupid child."

"Isaac, what are you doing here? And lay off. Seder was five months ago. Enough already."

"What am I doing here? I live here."

"Occasionally."

"Jane's out of town."

"So you're forced to slum it back home."

"No, I'm taking care of my *tsatskeleh*."

"What's wrong with the *tsatskeleh*?"

"I don't know, Mr. Nursedoctor, you tell me. She's got the poops!"

"My Celia shits! That's Swift."

"I know. I'm the toast-and-tea brigade."

"Well, why don't we go in and see the patient?"

"After you, Doctor."

"Alan! I was hoping you'd come over."

"So why didn't you call?"

"Can I ever get you?"

"Well, here I am anyway. What's cooking?"

"My small *kishka*."

"Large *kishka,* if you've got the poops. How long? How many? How much?"

"Since eight last night, probably fifteen or twenty times, just water, less and less."

"Shame, shame, you're not drinking. Dehydration lurks: shrinking blood volume, thickening blood, eventually a little bolus of red glop limps around a huge circulatory system. Your brain won't like that. Isaac, the tea, please. Comfrey or peppermint. Dilute with cold water and bring the patient two large glasses. Like in the old country."

"At your service. Tea for you too?"

"Got any fizz?"

"Pepsi. Diet."

"That's my man."

"Alan, come sit down. You don't look so great yourself. You feel OK?"

"Just tired, Mère Ubu."

"No, really. You're actually looking haggard. Alan Krieger, haggard. Now there's a contradiction in terms. And you're all dressed in black. You never wear black. The sins of the world on your shoulders?"

"Who better? Also, I haven't slept for a couple of nights."

"Unemployment getting to you?"

"Yeah, I guess so. I can't stand looking for nursing jobs after getting so unceremoniously canned. No letters of recommendation. Can we call your former employer? What do I say?"

"It's getting to you."

"Yeah."

"But where have you been at night? I've tried to call."

"I know, my silly Charybdis. I got your messages."

"So why didn't you call back?"

"Here you are, children. Tea for two. Sleepytime. And for the caffeine addict among us, one Diet Pepsi on ice. Last two pieces of toast—for you, sweetie. And Alan, you'll have to make do with matzoh, your favorite."

"What is this? Honey-sugar matzoh? This is the bread of affliction? What's next, cherry matzoh? Root-beer matzoh? Say, there's an idea—cherry-strawberry matzoh. We could start the matzoh rumors again. Be great for AIPAC fundraising! You expect me to eat honey-sugar matzoh?"

"Take it or leave it. It's all we've got."

"Shame on you, Isaac. But maybe this is useful."

"What are you doing, Alan?"

"I'm just softening these horrendous slabs in Diet Pepsi. I happen to know the secret formula and can assure you that the interaction of the honey, sugar, and caramel coloring produces some mighty-healing antioxidants. Good for your poor little gutskins. Isaac, would you bring a medium-size mixing bowl, please?"

"Alan, what are you *doing?*"

"Patience, little pumpkin. *Pacience is an heigh vertu, certeyn*. Thank you. Now I'll just *potchky* the mess together with some of your warm tea, if I may, to make Dr. Krieger's Healing Slurry. OK, now pull up your jammy top there . . ."

"Alan!"

"Just expose the abdomen, please, what did you think I meant with your father standing here and all? And now let's just lower the bottoms over that sweet little mound of belly-blubber. Don't get upset—it's very lovable. There. An excellent less-than-sterile field, wouldn't you say, Dr. Goldenbaum? Not too embarrassed, even if it is your own daughter?"

"Every clinician needs a chaperon these days. Might as well be the father. You all right with this, sweetie?"

"So what else is craziness for? Would I go out with somebody normal?"

"You never have."

"Good, then we're all agreed and ready to proceed. Now I take this slurry, wait, let's crumble a litte more matzoh in to thicken it, there—that's the classical consistency, and ummm, nice and warm, let's make a little pile on your belly. . . ."

"Al-an . . ."

"Don't move, Miss Goldenbaum, or you'll muss the sheets. OK, a nice plop of warm Tao-flop, upper left quadrant, upper right quadrant, lower left quadrant, lower right quadrant . . ."

"That actually feels wonderful."

"Of course. You think I don't know what I'm doing? And last but not least, one final dollop on the omphalos, the naval that has never seen a ship. *Et voilà,* the slurrybelly, healing and being healed."

"You're going to clean this up?"

"Not just yet, Dr. Goldenbaum. First there is the heating, and then there is the shaping. The heat draws forth the *chi* or *prana,* energizing the third chakra, reshaping the etheric gut, and now we have to take that energy mass and shape it into a healing agent. Mind if I *potchky* it around on your belly?"

"If I minded, would you stop?"

"No."

"Then I don't mind. Saves energy."

"OK, now what symbolic figure do you want me to sculpt out of the presently amorphous masses on your belly? Here's the menu: a turtle. Supports the earth. Very stable. Better than Imodium. A snake. Yes, just like Shlong. The healing symbol of Aesculapius, shedding its skin, renewing youth and health, a transformed creature, as you will be."

"The caduceus has two snakes. What's the other one for?"

"Symbol of Mercury, messenger of the gods, and god himself of science and commerce. For some strange reason, it became the insignia of the U.S. Army Medical Corps, and thus mistakenly associated with the practice of medicine. Actually, it may not have been a careless error but the ingenious plot of some well-educated saboteur. After all, Mercury is also the patron of thieves, vagabonds, and rogues."

"How appropriate."

"Right-o. So a single snakey it is, if you want it."

"What's my other choice?"

"Oh. Almost forgot. Up, up, and away—out of the reptile kingdom to the top of the food chain—man. You'll forgive my sexism here in not proposing to shape a woman on your belly, but that might bring on double menstrual flow, or a preference for women over me. So how would you like a warm, gushy manikin embracing your midsection? A homunculus hug, arms and legs akimbo."

"Sounds nice and cuddly."

"OK by you, Doctor? Your daughter should have a man on her belly?"

"If it's OK by her. Sounds like very safe sex."

"Papa . . ."

"Well, fathers worry about these things."

"All right, here we go. Left upper quadrant becomes the left arm, with some left over for the head, right upper quadrant, the right arm, left lower quadrant . . ."

"Alan, now I'm cold where it's just wet."

"You'll warm it up, my little Nagasicki. Warm heart, cold left upper quadrant, as they say. Right lower quadrant, the right leg. Now a head and two little *feetselach* . . . you want hands? They're hard to do."

"No. Stumps are fine."

"Good. Now, Isaac, a towel, please, your daughter should be more comfortable. Deb, do you have a name for him? Thank you, Isaac."

"What was the golem's name, Yossel?"

"Isaac, you're brilliant! Who asked you, but you're brilliant! I was making a little golem and I didn't even know it. Well now, that changes things. Let's wipe really carefully, you shouldn't have wet skin, my dear, and then we'll just take the corner of the towel, and twist it around, and carve out a little tushie here, and some back-of-the-head curls, and just a suggestion of the scapular complex. . . . Would you like him to be wearing a bathing suit for propriety?"

"I would like it," Isaac said.

"Your father would like it."

"Go for it. A little one like in the Olympics. No boxer shorts."

"No boxer shorts, coming up. A little waistline, and left and right under-the-tush lines. Done. One Jantzen Supersport, $22.95, but for you, $8.95, you can pay me later. Very nice. Look at him."

"He's getting cool."

"So warm him up. You're the mammal. What's that belly for? Push. Push."

"Alan, I'm cold, take him off."

"Destroy the golem?"

"Yes."

"Just scrape him up before he does his thing?"

"He's doing his thing. He's making me cold."

"I'll go get a spatula."

"Always the gentleman, your father."

"Alan, you're an idiot."

"Now, now, my sweet. Who *knows* what good the treatment did?"

"Is this OK?" Isaac asked.

"Perfect. Would you like to perform the scrape-up?"

"No. Doctors are not supposed to treat their own children."

"All right. You can assist. Spatula."

"Spatula."

"Mixing bowl."

"Mixing bowl."

"Patient, are you still with us?"

"Just hurry up."

"Towel."

"Towel."

"OK, now you count the hemostats, and you snuggle in under the covers."

"No way. Now I have cramps again. I'm going to sit on the can."

"Don't fall in."

"Fuck off."

And off she waddled, contracting her bum against the dribble.

"She gets a little grumpy when she's sick," her father said.

"Not to mention vulgar. Isaac, I can't believe I forgot about golems. They're my totem animal. They haunted my adolescence. I tried to build one to murder my brother."

"It didn't work?"

"I was thinking of something with a bullet made out of frozen blood. You know—they'd inspect the wound—no bullet, mysterious. Got it out of a Charlie Chan movie. I even stuck my finger to see if I could make an experimental ice cube, but I only got a few drops."

"So the plan was called off."

"For want of a bullet," Alan nodded.

"And a good thing too."

Deb shuffled back into the room, her PJs askew.

"Hey there, bewitching, bothered, and bewildered, you're back. That was quick."

"It was mostly gas. I'm all pooped out."

"Cure courtesy of yours truly, poopet-master to the stars. This way to the gas, ladies and gentlemen. You're back just in time. Your father was about to give a lecture on the history and importance of the golem legend in postmedieval Jewish thought."

"Post-Renaissance."

"See, we're learning already. Everybody pile on the bed! SEM-INAR! Here, poopchen that poopeth not, I'll tuck you in. Dr. Goldenbaum?"

"What? What do you want from me?"

"Everything you know about the golem. Your daughter is an innocent, so start from scratch, and I'll kibitz with any additions from my gathering high school memories."

"You want to hear about the golem, Deb?"

"Why not? Live and learn."

"My motto exactly. How did Debbie, the busy and curious little bee, ever miss out on Father Isaac's golem lore?"

"Deb, I used to tell you bedtime stories about the golem. I remember we even had a picture book once. The golem looked like a cross between the Jolly Green Giant and the Pillsbury Doughboy."

"Hey, hey . . . what did the New Yorker say to the Pillsbury Doughboy?—What a great tan you have!" He waited for a rim shot. "Sorry."

"It's very vague." Isaac contemplating.

"The golem is in the Great Social Worker Hall of Fame." Alan being helpful.

"Wait—it's coming back."

"Ah, so. Proceed, Rabbi-san. The golem."

"I think we're back in Prague in the late sixteenth century."

"Fifteen eighty, I believe."

"You want to tell this?"

"No, no, go ahead. I'm sorry. The date just stuck in my head. Four hundred years to the minute before Reagan was elected."

"The Jews of Prague had suffered a series of pogroms . . ."

"So what else is new?"

". . . and there were rumors of another big one coming up. Christian child missing. Blood for matzohs . . ."

"And this is even *before* cherry-strawberry matzohs."

"So the great Rabbi Loew, blessed be his name, Rabbi Yehuda Loew of Prague, known as the Maharal . . ."

"You know what Maharal means?"

"No. There's no Hebrew word *maharal* . . ."

*"It's an acronym: Moreinu ha-Rav Rabbi Liva*—our teacher, the master Rabbi Loew."

"I see. Thank you. In any case, Rabbi Loew was one of the great . . ."

"Isaac. Excuse me for interrupting. And I don't want to get into another seder dispute. But for the sake of Enlightenment principles of truth-telling, I have to mention that all the stories about Rabbi L. were made up long after his death. There were no mentions of his feats—including the golem—in any contemporary writing, even in a family biography by his grandson. So it's kind of like the Jews in Egypt, isn't it? I'll shut up."

"Alan . . ."

"It was just a scholarly footnote. OK, Judah the Lion of Prague is about to . . . ?"

"Is about to make a golem."

"And why is Judah the Lion of Prague about to make a golem?"

"Interesting question, Alan. The easy answer is: to protect the Jewish community. But who knows what other motivations were lurking there? It's no accident that the golem reads as a very early version of the Frankenstein story. And what is that about? Faustian pride? The need to unlock the secrets of the universe, to put theory to test? Doubt? Did Rabbi Loew doubt God? Would God serve his purpose when the very same God was allowing the pogroms?"

"That wasn't in the book," the patient said.

Her father excused himself: "Not for a three-year-old, Debeleh, this level of speculation."

"Faustian pride. Excellent. More, Isaac, more."

"Yes. And then there are the questions about whether the golem was 'alive' in the sense that we are alive, whether he had a soul, or only a soul-like something."

"Three-fifths of a human. He couldn't talk."

"And that in itself, Alan, is significant. Speechless. For all his power, speechless. There was some disputation among later Talmudists about whether a golem could be a member of a Jewish congregation—would you have a *minyan* if the golem were the tenth man?"

"Goddamn, I love the Jews. Who else would worry about such things?"

"I remember now—the rabbi had to kill the golem," Deb put in.

"My girlfriend's earliest memory: rabbis killing golems."

"Right. But we're getting ahead of the story."

"So does killing a golem violate the prohibition against taking life?" she asked.

"Talmudic questioning in the DNA she has," her father boasted.

"It's a crucial question, Isaac."

"I know, I know. I wasn't kidding."

"Does taking the life of less-than-human-beings violate 'thou shalt not kill'? Buddha would say yes," Alan averred.

"And the Talmud would say no," Isaac returned.

"Bloodthirsty barbaric book, if you ask me. Joshua fit the battle of Jericho, Jericho . . . that's our song, baby. Up and atom."

"Exactly. Adam. The man made out of the dust of the earth. That's what the Maharal was up to. Scientific experiment. Can this be replicated? So he has his servant bring back barrel-loads of clay from the banks of the Moldau . . ."

"An incident not transcribed by Smetana. It's a good thing the Christians weren't into satellite surveillance yet."

"And they haul the clay up to the attic of the Old-New Synagogue."

"They?"

"Well, probably the servant."

"Wanna hear a joke?"

"I'm in the middle of the story." Isaac offended.

"Alan, quiet. This is getting interesting."

"No, no, it's relevant. A rabbi, to show his humility before God, cries out in the middle of a service, 'Oh, Lord, I am nobody!' The cantor, not to be left behind, also cries out, 'Oh, Lord, *I* am nobody!' The janitor, deeply moved, also raises his head and cries out, 'Oh, Lord, I am nobody!' The rabbi turns to the cantor and says, 'Look who thinks he's nobody.' "

"That's relevant?"

"Humble is relevant."

"No fighting, children. There's this huge pile of Vlatava clay in the attic."

"And Rabbi Loew shapes the clay into a man." Debbie remembering.

"The Jolly Gray Giant . . ."

"Yes. And then—there are various versions of the story here," Isaac continued. "One is that the Maharal wrote the Shem, the name of God, on a piece of parchment and put it in the golem's mouth."

"And the golem got up and did a little jig and said, 'Yes, Massa, what I can do for you?' "

"That's one version: Shem in mouth, active, Shem out of mouth, lifeless. On the Sabbath, the Rabbi would take the Shem out of the golem's mouth and it would sit quietly in the back of the shul all day, waiting . . ."

"Like my Uncle Stanley . . ."

"The more interesting version is that the rabbi carved the words YHWH ELOHIM EMET, 'God, the Lord, Is Truth,' into the golem's forehead."

"No, that story is about Jeremiah the Prophet and his son in their way-back attempt at a golem," corrected Alan.

"Yes, you're right, thank you. But still, the lesson is there. The first move the golem made was to—accidentally or not—rub his forehead and erase the E of EMET."

"A little psoriatic itch, perhaps?"

"So what was left would be God, the Lord, Is Dead. *Met* is 'dead,' right?"

"Right, Deb."

"Great story. I like it better. Don't you, Alan?"

" 'God is dead.' Scarier words were never spoken. I like scary. It was a warning about making a golem. Jeremiah killed it then and there. And advised any other serious chemistry majors to study all this just to know the power of the Old Man but never, never try to do this at home. What would John Dewey say?"

"But Rabbi Loew went ahead," continued Isaac. "And his Joseph was quite impressive—especially for the Christians. Saturday night, after sundown, in went the Shem, and Joseph patrolled the community for the rest of the week."

"Wasn't there some story about his doing the wash or something?" Deb asked.

"Return of the repressed!"

"Yes, daughter mine, but I think it wasn't laundry. Rabbi Loew gave explicit instructions that no one but he was to give the golem any orders."

Unable to contain himself, Alan barged into the story: "But one day the rabbi's wife thought, 'There's that big lug sitting around all day—just like all the other damn men—except he isn't even studying!—while I have to do all the shopping and cleaning.' "

"The more things change . . ." Deb said.

"So she told Joseph to fetch some water from the well while she went out shopping."

"Bet I know what happened."

"I'll bet you do. The sorcerer's apprentice had nothing on Yossel. It took two weeks to dry out."

"Hey! Seminar! Serious business!" Isaac chided.

"So?"

Isaac picked up the thread again."So the day came when Rabbi Loew forgot to take the Shem out of the golem's mouth on Shabbat . . ."

"That *was* serious business," interrupted Alan. "The goddamn thing went berserk. Take away my weekend, will you? No overtime even? We need a union! Don't cry, Yossel, organize! Oops, there aren't any other golems. OK, then, take it out on someone. Express your anger, primal scream and all that."

"He's making fun, but in the story it was serious business. For one thing, it proved the Jews *were* a threat to the larger community. Not good."

"Look," said Alan, "you throw boulders around, you tear up trees by the roots, it makes more goyish jobs. What were they complaining about? Any excuse, any excuse . . ."

"So Rabbi Loew ordered Joseph to come with him up to the attic of the Old-New Synagogue . . ."

"Did Joseph know what was going to happen?"

"That was much debated."

"Do not go gentle into that good night, Yossel."

"If he did, it must have been a deep understanding that kept him from killing the rabbi. In fact, there is a lot of later literature that develops themes similar to Frankenstein—the golem's loneliness, his need for love—even sex. It seems possible that he could have developed a full soul by grace, or experience. . . ."

"Four-fifths?"

"What's *golem?*" Deb asked the room. "I mean, what does the word mean?"

"Alan?"

"Isaac?"

"In Hebrew it means something like shapeless matter . . ."

"Something like primordial slime."

"Something that has potential but is not yet formed, not yet there."

"My mother, Krieger the Great, used to call me a golem when I was little."

"Right. In Yiddish it's a kind of affectionate insult."

"It wasn't so affectionate. Will you allow one more footnote? The last, I promise. There is, I believe, only one use of the word in the Bible. One of the psalms. Adam, in one of his more brown-nosey moments, praises God for having raised him from earth and made him into golem. Unperfected substance. Very humble."

"Unlike you, who is perfect."

"But very like you, Ms. Nulliparous. It can also refer to a woman who hasn't given birth to a child, my little *golemitchka*. How's your gut-skins doin?"

"Better, actually. I guess I got distracted."

"Unwilling, as usual, to give credit where credit is due."

"To you?"

"Not me. To the little hot mannykin . . ."

"Warm, then cold."

". . . on your little sweet bellykin."

"The real question," Isaac on track, "is not what the word means but what the story means."

"I would submit, Professor Goldenbaum, that what this story shows is the inevitable connection of power and destructiveness. *Nicht wahr?*"

"But isn't that what you're always bitching about," Deb observed, "about what Walter says?"

"What?"

"That military power has turned Israel into a destructive force that has to be stopped."

"Walter is an asshole. Excuse me, Isaac. To fill you in, my brother the associate professor of religion is a self-hating Jew with no comprehension of the fierce urgency of now, to quote a self-hating black."

"Alan . . ."

"Jews need power—to fulfill their mission in the world."

"And what might that be, Alan?"

"To stand in the way of any false messiah. To *protect* the world from idolatry!"

"What are you talking about?"

"What was the single greatest moment in Judaism?"

"Moses leading the people out of slavery."

"No! The greatest moment in Judaism was rejecting Jeshua, the carpenter from Nazareth, accusing him of megalomania, of leading the people astray, of being a threat to the state—all of which he was. Why the hell do you think we *needed* a golem? So we could keep hope alive. The moronic goys bowed down in salaam and danced around the golden crucifix. But we were steadfast. We learned our lesson. Never again!"

"But we're still waiting for the Messiah."

"Really? Who wants a messiah to come and stop history? Jews want motion, discovery, not boredom and closure of the unknown. That's our gift to the world: the genius of Jewish restlessness, the postponement of utopia. Without Jews, without the thirty-six hidden Lamed Vovniks, humanity would retire to the couch, the world would stop. But we say no to closing down history, and yes to hope, and the world finds that, finds us, intolerable. Well, I say tough shit. No fucking messiahs allowed. Ever!"

"What arc you talking about? Nobody's claiming to be the Messiah."

"Ah, but people are being *treated* like the Messiah."

"Who, what people?"

"Black people."

"Alan, you're crazy. People talk about blacks like the problem, not the solution."

"I'm telling you, if someone doesn't stop them, it's the end. Not the end days, the end."

"Stop who?"

"The blacks."

"You're going to stop the blacks?"

"You bet. *Someone* has to."

"Alan, please, I'm queasy enough."

"Stop them from doing what?"

"From taking over."

"What?"

"Their music. Their clothes. Their talk. Their drugs. Their values. Just listen to the kids."

"So you're the next false messiah?" asked Isaac.

"No way. I'm *fighting* the false messiah. I'm keeping the world open."

"You're the thirty-seventh Lamed Vovnik, then?"

"Maybe. I'm not supposed to know. Though I like that. Thirty-seven. A good prime number. The number of Shakespeare's plays. The number of Brecht's plays."

"So what are you going to do?"

"I don't know yet. But something."

"You and the golem, huh? Our protector."

"Look, Deb, did I cure your bellyache or not?"

"Not."

"Incorrigible. You get left behind when the ark leaves."

"So where does Noah get a Mrs. Noah to clean up the shit?"

"Alan," said Isaac, "I don't know what you've got in mind . . ."

"Neither do I."

". . . but violence only escalates."

"You can fight that with a fierce act of the imagination."

"And what would that be?" Deb asked him.

"Deb, out of bed. We're going to White Castle. I'm going to eat thirty-seven burgers without throwing up."

"I would throw up watching you."

"You don't have anything left to throw up. C'mon, up and Adam."

"Why do you want to eat thirty-seven White Castle hamburgers?"

"It's probably never been done," Alan proclaimed.

"Alan, I'm not going to watch you eat thirty-seven White Castle hamburgers. I'm not even going to watch you eat one White Castle hamburger. I'm sick, remember? And I'm staying in bed."

"You'll be sorry. Your father has no more toast, and though you may get better in your gutskins, your karma will suffer irredeemable damage for being present in a house with raspberry matzohs, and for *not* being present at the creation of Plan X. Personally, I'd rather have shitty cramps than shitty karma."

"Well, you're you, and I'm me. I'll call tomorrow to find out the late-breaking news."

"Sure you won't stay longer, Alan? I can find something else to cook up."

"Thanks, Isaac, but delirium calls. *Ciao, messieur,* chow, *mademoiselle*. I wish you the gentlest of farts."

## 16. THE JEWISH CHILD'S BOOK OF COGNITIVE DISSONANCE

People of the Book. People of the Film. They say the film is never as good—but it has its moments. At least that was what Alan thought when he stopped off at Blockbuster on White Plains Road, snuck back up to Alhambra apartment 4K, propped the little plastic container against the Deb door, rang the bell, then galloped around the corner and down the stairs like a herd of brontosauri.

Isaac opened the door, and the black box plopped back on the floor of the hallway, making a little *krechtz* as it slid back over the tiles.

The brontosauri were galumphing two flights down by now—still, Isaac had no problem identifying the source of the spoor. He turned back into the apartment and into Deb's sickroom.

"Your young man left you a present."

"What is it?"

He examined the box.

"*DER GOLEM Wie er in die Welt Kam.* Wegener, 1920. Two-day rental."

"He's so thoughtful," she said, "arranging a golem to nurse me along. Wanna watch it with me?"

"Not tonight, dear," her father said. "I have a headache. Want me to plug it in for you? Or have you had enough Jewish magic for one evening?"

"I'll take a look. 1920. Couldn't be too special-effecty."

"Except for the car chase at the end," her father warned.

He wheeled the TV to the foot of Debbie's bed, threw the switches, and popped the cassette into the VCR. The screen responded with dashed lines and loud static.

"Channel 4, Dad."

Channel 4 was better. The FBI made its usual appearance, giving Isaac confidence enough to shut out the light, leave the room, and close the door behind him. Deb was left alone with German Expressionism.

German Expressionism is nothing you'd like to meet alone in a dark alley. For it *is* a dark alley all by itself, a world of chiaroscuro images and distorted shadows where normal appearance seems abnormal—so abnormal is it. Abi-Normal, Deb thought, but not so funny. Here in front of her was a German view of the Jewish ghettoworld, frightened, but admiring. The sets made the buildings themselves speak in architectural paraphrase—as if with cabalistic power of flaming Hebrew letters—of twisted, tilted, cave-like homes and shops, breathing and breathed by unaccountable light, afflicted and blessed by menacing darkness.

And the Jewish people—despised inhabitants of that city—looked like nothing she had ever seen in the Bronx: sinister, rich concoctions of cultural stereotypes, their faces engraved with inwardness and anguish, strange beings of magic and mystery in wizard hats, wicked witches of the East. The unknown Jew.

Is that who I am? Deb wondered. Still? If I went there now? She watched the dancing goyishe children with flowers in their hair. Not one like me, she thought, dark and fat, fat little Jewish girl, stay in your place, Deborah, behind the curtain in the synagogue. Watch Jane light the candles and make gefilte fish, and help her set the table, learn to be a good *balaboosta* while the boys take on the spiritual tasks. Thank God Isaac said, no, no bat mitzvah. *Non serviam!* I will not be the next Jewish mother golemette.

Her cramps increased, and she lay back, eyes closed, while the film went on without her.

Title: *DECREED AGAINST THE JEWS:*

*We can no longer neglect the popular complaints against the Jews.*

*They despise the Holy Christian ceremonies:*

*They endanger the lives and property of their fellow men;*

*They practice black magic.*

*We decree that all Jews shall leave the city and all adjoining lands before the month is ended.*

*IMPERATOR.*

This plot device she did not see, nor did she need to. She had her own *tsouris*. As pain engulfed her being, she recalled another time upon her back, breathless upon her back, having been chased and tackled by three Italian boys on a raid into her neighborhood. Nine or ten years old they were, and she seven or eight—all without body hair, she with breathless, breastless chest exposed now to the summer sun. They had pinned her down. They had seized the star of David lightly chained around her neck. They had laughed and called her a Yid, a kike, then carved a cross onto her chest, just where a cross would lie, carved a cross with a point of her star and run away. Sharp scalpel, that.

She touched her breastbone, now defined by the mounds of her breasts. She fingered the *hay* that lay there now—softer, rounder, with no sharp points like Mogen David—*hay* for *hayim,* life. She pressed the life against her sternum and breathed until her colic passed.

When she opened her eyes, the great Rabbi Loew was shaping clay into a giant protector, a homunculus with an Asiatic face, tall, with a helmet of hair. The whole affair breathed *schwarze Kunst,* but zany, the rabbi a little *meshugge*. She remembered a joke Alan had told her: In a small Ukrainian village, it was rumored that a Christian girl had been found murdered and that a pogrom was in the offing. The community gathered in the synagogue to consider the dire consequences and plan a defense if they could. All of a sudden, the president of synagogue came rushing in, breathless. "Brothers," he said, "I have wonderful news! The murdered girl is Jewish!" Ha ha.

A community without women. Wonderful news in a synagogue without women—a murdered Jewish girl. Stop kvetching, Deb. It's a funny joke. Deep, sad, and funny.

She watched the rabbi-clown's alchemy, religion, science, magic all combined—the German fear of Jewish revolutionary power, she thought, their view of our demoniac forces. Awe-inspiring. They're in awe of us; they think we command supernatural powers.

She watched these medieval Jews create a shtick modernity: a robot, controllable, merging the fantasies of past centuries with the great appliances of everyday life. Golem Yossel, longing to be human—like Alan. But his superiority casts him out. My poor little golem. But also Alan the rabbi. *Everybody* in this film is Alan, she thought, maybe even those little girls. People are afraid of him—like of little girls. If they're not fat. Or if they're too smart. Of Alan and me. Everybody fears. God too? He makes Adam from dust, then he gets scared and runs away? But then, eventually, we're dust again. Servitude, rage, then back to dust.

The monster's jealous. Look, he's breaking out in pustules because he wants the girl. Big guy, there. I wonder if he has a penis. I wonder if the rabbi made him a penis. Did he make it circumcised? He's got to be circumcised or he wouldn't be a Jew, right?

I think he might like a fat girl. I like a fat guy. Boy, would Alan be jealous! He'd break out in pustules! But Alan's a pretty good deal, golem and rabbi rolled into one big, fat, persecuted reacher-outer. He even smells like a golem. The stench of his room. His room is like the belly of Jonah's whale, he said. What does *that* mean? His room spews him forth to preach? What does he preach? Zionism? Socialism? *Shtetl*ism? Mysticism? The *ganze geshichte?* No wonder he's so fat. No wonder he itches. Or is it fleas? That hovel room, his "road to excess," as he says, and "palace of wisdom."

When Deb came up for air, a little blond shiksa was offering an apple to the great big golem. Don't take it, don't take it. It's happened before. I wonder if Alan has a little blond shiksa with an apple. It's sweet, though, the way they cuddle.

Another cramp. Deb lay back. She missed the sweetie unscrewing the star, she missed the golem's death. Behind her eyes she saw a grotesque of her own: Alan the monster. What he did to that black man in the ER. How could he even make up such a story? What else could he do? What *wouldn't* he do? He thinks he's God, the *Übermensch,* some kind of Titan, puffed up and raving like a demon.

The TV screen, once black, shone blue. Blue like a sky exhausted by forms, images that might lead to freedom—or to Nazism, destruction of peoples, or mass barbarity. Deb rummaged in her own images: of "social work" in a failed system, of her client detritus, and herself, a gender pariah, unworthy of being counted in a *minyan*.

You make pariahs, you become one. The Germans. The Israelis, us Americans. Alan, with all his pariahs, he'll be pariah too. And after all those deaths—enter me, Debeleh—the Jewish mother to resupply the race! So I have to be fruitful and multiply? Why?

For every golem that falls, a hundred spring up. Seething with obscure emotions, Deborah Goldenbaum surrendered, and passed into chaos.

## 17. SHRINKING

Alan sat in his own waiting room, a small chamber bearing a striking resemblance to his kitchen. What was different now was the set dressing: a large potted *Dieffenbachia* (poisonous), the classic doctor's-office plant, brought in from the living room, and a stack of magazines, now several months old, borrowed permanently from St. Vincent's. All but one of the pile—*Sports Illustrated, Newsweek, People, U.S. News and World Report*, etc.—was, to quote Pooh-Bah, "merely corroborative detail, intended to give artistic verisimilitude to an otherwise bald and unconvincing narrative." The functional member, the active, enzymatic face, was an issue of *Muscle and Fitness* featuring on its cover the usual svelte yet bosomy woman clinging to the massive biceps of a smiling behemoth, any one of whose muscles, individually, might have serviced her as happily as a husband and a half.

The cover called out, "Twelve Steps to Bigger Arms" and "Lean and Hard Abs—a Ten Minute Routine"—the latter article especially annoying to Alan since he had actually tried the routine for two days running. Still, the magazine, its photos of cyborg-like humans, its ads for phytonutrients promising physiologic miracles, its articles addressed to the already-mutant, was essential preparation for the therapeutic moment about to begin.

A huge roach meandered over the kitchen table, surveying the Formica, antennae-wise, for smears, spills, or crumbs. So magnificent was he that he snagged his landlord's peripheral vision and interrupted his reading. Alan considered him, nodded his head, proud as a papa at the gleaming chitin coat, said, "*Ess, mein Kind, ess,*" and returned his attention to "Too Busy to Train? Workouts You Can Live With."

The timer had an attack of digital peeping, like the epileptic firings in Prince Myshkin's brain. Prep time over.

Alan walked into the doctor's office, which bore a striking resemblance to his bedroom. He closed the door, approached the black velvet slab with its half whole of Elvis (whose remaining eye was capable of following you around the room), and freed its two grommets from their hooks. There on the wall, glowing with sepulchral light, occupying the only non-booked slab of wall space in the room, was a long, narrow mirror, related to *Spiegel* on the medicine cabinet in the bathroom but only as a cousin once-removed. This power-object was named Zrcadlo, a fierce and mysterious evocation of Praguish alchemy and might. A good thing too. The patient needed all the help he could get.

Alan inspected himself closely. Tie, Windsor knot, one slight stain, belt invisible under overhang. Stately? No. But decidedly plump.

"Bishop of Hippo," he whispered at his image. "Not contrite enough. Let's try simply . . . Fat Pig. . . ."

An astute drama critic might have heard deep authenticity in the words. Or just good acting.

"Flabby, abdominous porker," he continued, andante. "Gorbellied, overstuffed, grungy and hideous swine. Nauseating, foul, endomorphically deformed porker." He began a slow crescendo. "Corrupt, steatopygous hog and bloatbelly." His eyes narrowed as his pupils adapted to the gloom. "Repugnant oinker, king of corpulence, distended Brobdingnagian poltroon." Mezzoforte now. "Quaking bog of oleaginous lard, lump of blubbery, monstrous, pachydermic, misshapen charlatan, waxing in all dimensions. Fake, fraud, overstuffed imposter." Forte now, accelerando. "Windbag know-it-all, cetacean blowhard, gross belugic phony! Threefold anathema and plague upon your grotesque, seam-splitting, foul mountain of flesh. I hate you, I hate you, I hate you, asshole prick! You deserve to die!"

Silence. The critic quite confused by now.

Alan watched the mirror and waited for his respiration to normalize.

"Thank you, Doctor. I'll consider what you say. See you next Monday."

The doctor nodded, as did Alan.

He hung Half Elvis up again, the other way round, and sat down in his reading chair.

"And now, part two, playback of last night's homily by Alan Krieger, RN, on 'The Heresy of Self-Regard,' with appended analysis of the myth of Narcissus as told by Ovid."

He reached for the Sony Walkperson on the floor next to the chair, took two deep breaths, closed his eyes, and pressed the play button.

Nothing. Dead as a doornail, though it had always been unclear to Alan why doornails were more deeply dead than other nail species.

"Shit!"

He banged the poor innocent on the arm of the chair. The cover to its battery case sprang loose and skittered over the floor. Pulling gently on the ribbon, he dislodged the Energizers and inspected them. He shook them next to his ear. He clacked them together and replaced them, urging them into spring-loaded cohabitation. Still, "play" played not.

"We'll give them a chance to rest, to sleep it off. Perhaps on the third day . . . though I really liked the line about my own riches making me poor."

He started for Ovid and then remembered: "No! No." He checked his watch, and then his Chevy calendar. "It's the last Monday of August, and therefore time for our bimonthly weigh-in. Does that mean every other month, or twice a month? In any case."

Down on hands and knees to extricate from beneath the skirts of the reading chair an ancient bathroom scale.

*"Oh, Detecto*
*How perfecto*
*Your effecto*
*Et expecto. . . .*
*Mmmm, mmmm, mmmm!"*

Kissing the rust-blushing machine, Alan sat down with scale in lap, and with moderate difficulty extracted his Swiss Army knife from his sandwiched right hip pocket. He looked the Detecto assuringly in the face.

"Be not afraid, my sweet child. I am not Father Abraham, you are not the laughing Isaac, and this is not mournful Moriah but only the Grand Concourse. Nevertheless . . ." He began undoing the four screws that held top to bottom . . ." Nevertheless, that does not prevent you . . ." He lifted the lid, exposing the mechanism and scale . . ." from giving our monthly gravitational research a local habitation and a name . . . which this month is . . . the planet Mars!"

He placed the gut-exposed machine carefully on the arm of the chair and made for the desk drawer, where he found a roll of economy cellophane tape and a paper disc cut from a three-by-five card, laboriously protractored, ruled, and labeled. He returned to the chair, and using the small blade of his knife, cut the "Venus" disc from the normal scale for earthlings. Proceeding delicately outward in the solar system, he taped "Mars" in its place, screwed the lid back on, and carefully zeroed the mechanism. Grabbing his one Gustav Holst out from between Hindemith and Honneger, he fired up cut one.

"And now, ladies and gentlemen, Mars—the Bringer of War."

Alan stepped on the Detecto to an ostinato of wood-struck strings and ominous brass.

"One hundred and eleven pounds, ladies and gentlemen, the opus number of the great last Beethoven sonata, down from 261 on Venus, and 290 on Earth. That's one hundred and seventy-nine pounds lost, ladies and gentlemen, one hundred and seventy-nine pounds in only four months. The Moon and Pluto coming up, in that order. By November, Alan, you will have achieved your final goal of nineteen pounds. Victory is at hand! Twiggy, eat your heart out, wherever you are!"

## 18. THE JEWISH QUESTION

"Got a cigarette, bud?"

Calvin eyeballed the panhandler.

"Sorry, I don't smoke."

It was a warm late-August evening, yet the man seated on his brownstone steps was dressed almost for winter it seemed, in heavy robe and wool-socked sandals. Calvin started past him up the stairs.

"OK, you got spare change? Spare bills?"

Calvin fished in his pocket.

"How's a subway token? That OK?"

"Sure. Thanks."

He began again up the stairs.

"To keep me from drinking?" said the voice from below. "You know what's good for me, right?"

"No, I . . . It's just what I had. I just bought a bunch of tokens on the . . ."

"Token gestures for the great unwashed?"

"Excuse me, I have to . . ."

The bum rose to his full short height, and faced his opponent, three steps above.

"Got any spare girlfriends?"

Calvin stopped his climb and turned to study his tormenter.

"Alan?"

"You caught me. But you'll never keep me."

"What are you doing here? And what is this getup?"

"What do you mean what am I doing here? This is a free country.

I'm a citizen. And this 'getup', as you call it, is my official hairshirt slash cassock, made for me by a certain Jewish *muchacha* with phenomenal seamstress skills."

"How long have you been sitting here? How'd you know where I live?"

"We have a certain girlfriend in common who lets me in on things—including, ahem, herself."

"What do you mean?"

"What do you think I mean? I, Calvin—like you—have known her in the biblical sense, and your address was part of our post-coital pillow talk."

"You made it with Urs?"

"Ahem. Well, yes. Or rather, she made it with me."

"She never told me that."

"Perfidy, thy name is woman."

"In fact, she said she never *had*."

"Liars have long legs, my friend. Tell you what. I'll take her off your hands, cheap. Damaged goods—you don't need em. Let's go for a walk. We can talk about it."

Calvin stepped uncertainly onto the sidewalk. Alan took his arm and directed him down the hill toward Riverside Drive and farther west into the park. They walked in silence north along the riverrun, the sleek black man in summer cords, the dumpy fat one in winter weeds, an odd couple.

"I was only joking, Calvin. We didn't fuck. Never."

"Really?"

"Really. But I still want her back."

An older woman, poodle on leash, picked up its turd most delicately in her plastic bag-gloved hand. She smiled at the two men and walked south with her treasure.

"Alan, you can't have her back. You never had her."

"Well then, it's my turn, don't you think? Now that you've had yours?"

A muggy dusk rose sluggish from the water, idly colonizing the sky. Alan hoped Calvin was seriously considering his request.

"Prague really brought us together," the black man said.

"What do you mean?"

Calvin sat down on a bench facing the Hudson, and Alan followed, suffused with a sense of loss.

"When we were visiting the Old Jewish Cemetery, we got caught in an astounding thunderstorm, and we ran for cover into the first place we could find—a grim burial society building that turned out to be an exhibition hall for kids' drawings and poems from Terezin—you know this?"

Alan nodded.

"Kids who would soon enough be sent off to Auschwitz. There was one drawing there of a family of mice, with a poem about a poor little mouse tortured by a flea. But Daddy Mouse came and caught the flea and popped it in a frying pan, and the little mouse called out, 'Brothers, sisters, come and see! For lunch we've got a nice, fat flea!'"

He paused. Streetlights danced in the darkened water.

"And we both started crying. We tried to hide it from one another—embarrassed, silly—but then we just couldn't hold it in, and we both broke out in tears and wept in each other's arms."

"What a spectacle, huh?" Alan almost whispered. "And I'll bet it was crowded with lots of other wet people, gawking."

"Maybe. Yes, it was crowded. But we weren't really aware of anyone else, just of ourselves and our connection to those Terezin kids."

"*Quel* triumphant father, ready to make a family meal out of his kid's blood! What do you think that nice, fat flea was nice and fat on? Typical Jewish rejoicing! I say get out the Xyklon B and kill em all—the fleas, I mean. I'm sick and tired of hearing about Jews as beautiful victims."

"But the mouse family wasn't just a victim. They caught the flea, and killed him and ate . . ."

"And then they got sent to Auschwitz. You think you'd be bawling over a family of German mice who'd finally caught the Jewish fleas gnawing at them and tossed them in ovens for dinner? It's the patheticness of the Jews you guys were crying over, and I'm sick and tired of Jewish patheticness. Exemplary victims, weak, passive, cowardly, timid and downtrodden, limp Jewish rags soaked in repulsive silent suffering . . ."

"Well, I'm not sick and tired of it," Calvin said quietly. "In fact, I know now I have to embrace that heritage. What you call pathetic is for me a unique gift and message to the world of violence out there. The whole *point* of Jews is in the tradition of scholars and loyal wives, gentle, mild, morally sensitive, embracing the high ground and the spirit in every aspect of life. . . ."

"Tell that to the IDF . . ."

"The IDF! That's Jewish? Jewish machine guns, Jewish tanks?" Calvin demanded.

"You bet!"

"You know what I love about Yiddish, Alan? Yiddish is a language that has never, never been spoken by people in power. There are no words for weapons or ammunition, no formulas for police tactics or expressions for military plans. . . ."

"And that's why they don't speak Yiddish in Israel. Yiddish is a language of exile, and we're not in exile anymore!"

"Yeah, well, I'm going into exile."

"What do you mean?"

"I've decided to quit my job. The BATF is feeling a little un-Jewish since Prague."

"And what does the Herr Doktor Fräulein think about this?"

"She understands completely."

"I suppose two can live on a hundred and fifty bucks an hour."

A seagull landed in front of them, hoping for something from Zabar's. Alan found a Tootsie Roll in his cassock pocket. The bird was happy enough, and carried it away, wrapped as if for takeout.

Alan was exasperated in four dimensions. He was frustrated knowing that he had now fully lost Ursula. He was disgusted too, kitsched-out, by the picture of the two of them blubbering over a mousie poem. He was affronted by the saintly, nasal-voiced *schlimiel* beside him, posing as the poster boy for Alan's team, the Servants of Yahweh! And finally, Alan was pedagogically exasperated. He needed to teach Calvin a lesson.

"Calvin? You think God is a sissy?"

"I think God has certain values."

"Bookish and gentle, meek and mild, ethically pure, hostile to violence, devoted to justice . . ."

"There's a Yiddish expression, Alan, 'One knows a Jew by his pity.'"

"I have a secret for you."

"Yeah?"

"Violence is as Jewish as potato latkes, Calvin. This world ain't *Fiddler on the Roof*. That was bad enough. But after the Shoah show, non-violence doesn't cut it anymore. For Never-Again-ists, we need force and power, and not just brain power. We need the fiber of Jewishness, that's our roots, don'tcha know, our Bible tales of conquest and organized killing, and vengeance."

"An eye for an eye and the whole world goes blind."

"Bullshit." Alan flared up. "You don't even *understand* 'an eye for an eye.' 'An eye for an eye' is about measure and moderation—you don't kill a man if he only took out your eye—you just take out his. But now we need to up the ante. I don't know about you, but I am directly descended from a great line of Old Testament kings, priests, and warriors. Krieger, y'know? But hell, why not a *new* testament—and I'm not talking about Paul's epileptic ravings and Jesus's *mishegas*—I'm talking the norm of a new kind of Jew, no more bent-over rabbis but patriotic, bronzed warriors, kicking ass and transvaluating values. It's time for the Viconian age of the post-*schlimiel*!"

Alan began walking, with Calvin close behind.

"Alan, you're so full of shit. You're the most bookish person I've ever met, a true Yid in your own personal *shtetl*."

"I'm not a *Yid,* Calvin! I'm a Hebrew! Alan the Lout, Rambowitz the Angel of Death, my son the Avenger. I am the ghost of Hanukkahs past, Judas Maccabeus, hero of battles. . . ."

"Sure it's not the other one?"

"Who?"

"Iscariot, the Betrayer."

"Who am I betraying?"

"Your people."

"The Yids? Are you kidding? This is the Bar Kochba guerrilla revolt, the kamakazi zealots at Masada, the cult of audacity. . . ."

A huge squawking in the sky as the gulls engaged in brutal birdly battle.

"Meyer Lansky, Dutch Schultz, Bugsy Siegel! C'mon, Calvin, let's dance, let's whore-a: *Hava nagila, hava nagila, hava nagila, mon-sterous Thou . . .*" Alan grabbed Calvin's hands and swung him around until he crashed into the railing, frightening the wits out of three joggers.

Calvin didn't know whether to laugh or be furious.

"Hey, man, I thought you guys had rhythm," Alan yelled. "I thought it was white guys who couldn't dance."

Calvin pushed him away, but Alan began again to assault the black man with words.

"You remember old Isaac Stern and his gang, toting around their Irguns, killing the Brits? The Torah and the sword, *mensch,* the Emet New Jersey Golems. 'There shall step forth a star out of Jacob, and a scepter shall rise out of Israel, and shall smite through the corners of Moab, and break down the sons of Seth.'"

Calvin stepped suddenly forward and caught one of Alan's waving arms and twisted it with ease into an immobilizing hammerlock.

"Hey, what are you doing?"

"Just calming you down, Alan, and maybe breaking your arm."

Alan considered his position. "Calvin?"

"What?"

"I'm going to have to kill you."

Calvin let go his wrist and set him free. The two men looked at one another as if for the first time.

"I'm going to have to kill you. You stole my girl. You spit on my religion."

Calvin pointed to the lump at his right upper pecs.

"What's that?" Alan asked.

".357 Magnum."

"Pretty un-Jewish to pack a concealed weapon."

"I haven't quit yet."

"OK, I'm not going to kill you."

"Sure?"

"But if I were, I'd have to use a silver bullet."

"You think I'm a werewolf—or a vampire?"

"I would never use anything but silver bullets to kill someone. You kill with lead, it's commonplace murder. But with silver . . ."

"You can't buy silver bullets."

"With silver, they die whispering Argggggg—for *argentum.* They die for redemption and righteousness, they die of goddess and magical purity, of the moon, the lovely, changing, cool and silver moon. They die for hope and unconditional love . . . serenity . . . nobility . . . they die of myth. 'The words of the Lord are pure words, as silver tried in a furnace of earth . . .'"

Calvin walked away but said over his shoulder, "May the world be protected from Alan Krieger."

"We'll see," Alan called out and followed Calvin upriver.

Another bench. Calvin wiped the evening dew off his side. Alan declined his offer to wipe the whole.

"You think you're some kind of free spirit, Alan. But I've never seen anyone as much a slave as you."

"Slave to what?"

"To your own rhetoric, to the flight of your ideas. Look where this stuff takes you. You're a nurse, not a cop or spy like me. You *pilpul* your way through the Talmud of life like the best of black-gabardined beards, a real smartass—but spiritual, and wise through disputation."

"So then can I have Ursula?"

"But what you are is some new kind of weird, self-hating Jew. Not a warrior. You can't live up to your own imaginative flights. Alan the Lout, Alan the Avenging Angel. That's not who you are. Now, I want you out of my life and out of Ursula's. Do you understand?"

"How do *you* know?"

"How do I know what?"

"Who I am. What I can do and not do."

"It's my job."

Two men, one black, one white, one in seersucker, one in burlap, two Jewish men parted ways under the New York sky.

New York, the Big Apple far, far east of Eden, a city whose first governor, Peter Stuyvesant, allowed small numbers of Jews to there reside, while denying them any "free and public exercise of their abominable religion."

Calvin looked up at the Milky Way.

While Alan studied the Gang of Stars.

Calvin hadn't dreamed this scene.

Perhaps Alan had.

# PAPER TRAIL 6

## ANSWER TO A PERSONAL AD IN THE NEW YORK REVIEW

(ad clipped to copy of response)

A VERY SPECIAL WOMAN, tall, enthusiastic, creative, warm, wise, lively and active, who is open and psychologically aware, is looking for a man who needs and appreciates the need for a close connection, who can laugh, enjoy himself and others, and who is warm, generous, thoughtful and wise, and is also psychologically aware. My interests are diverse, and include psychology, literature, music, nature, medicine, history and politics. My preference is for a non-smoker, age range from upper 30s to low 50s. NYR Box 7227.

840 Grand Concourse, Apt. 6F
Bronx, New York 10472

April 20, 1992

Dear Goddess,

What, my dear, are you hiding? (You asked for psychologically astute.) You didn't mention your age, but you want someone between 37 and 53, so you must be past forty, and that was hard for you, wasn't it? Turning forty without a man in your life? All those little wrinkles around the eyes? The flesh on the underside of your arms getting a little baggy?

And I don't notice anything about thin, or trim—the two most common words in opening statements of all female ads in the *NYR*. Isn't print wonderful? You can hide so much that isn't buoyant behind adjectives that are. But what happens when you entice a man to come have dinner? How embarrassing that moment when he knocks on the door, you open it, and you see the disappointment deep in his eyes! How many more times can you go through a dinner-that-has-to-happen-in-order-not-to-embarrass? Well, he'll probably pay the bill. At least you get a free meal out of it. Save enough to put that ad in for another week.

Do you think I'm being cruel? I'm not. I'm just trying to get our relationship off to an absolutely honest and realistic start. How we hide from one another in these *verdammte* ads! $3.95 a word! Only Satan could have set such a rate. Let's see. You're in for 85 words X $3.95/word. That's 335 dollars and 75 cents. That means you're either enormously wealthy or enormously desperate. Which, my dear, which? Perhaps both?

Well, you can breathe easy, tall, enthusiastic, creative, warm, wise, lively and active woman, open and psychologically aware. I can assure you that I am older, fatter, and uglier than you are. Wait. Stop. Not yet the circular file. Some open, psychologically aware thought will reveal the benefit of such a partner: You can be superior, the more attractive one. You can be sure I will not be tempted to graze on greener grass. You can count on the world's judgment: yourself as magnanimous, spiritual enough to ignore mere physical manifestation. You can copulate in the dark and imagine whomever you care to—in fact, I will help you fantasize partners you might never have imagined. You can assuage your barrenness (I see no mention of children) by mothering a social reject who will return your love without reserve, and with man-sized organs—every woman's fantasy for her male child.

In this, my offer, you may recognize someone "warm, generous, thoughtful and wise," ready to submerge himself, without being threatened, in the multi-leveled superiority of another, not needful of lording it over some fat, ugly, Jewish girl, grateful for any attention. I know my place, my dear, and that is more than can be said for our screen stars or religious and political leaders.

You may prefer a non-smoker, but the first lesson I bring you is that you can't have everything you want. I am a two-pack-a-day Marlboro man myself (sans firm jaw, leathery hands, and chaps, to be sure). Hard pack, if not hard abs. Think of Bogart, George Raft, all those cigarette-lipped '40s types that once made female hearts go pitty-pat under heaving bosoms. Little by little, *if* you are as open as you advertise, the secondhand smoke will perform its addictive wonders, and you will find yourself beneficiary to all the benevolence of *Nicotiana tobacum,* great gift of the much-vaunted native Americans, helping you deal with stress, calming down your tension, pepping up your lethargy, helping you to concentrate and overcome unpleasant feelings with a mild state of euphoria. Deep in our smoke-filled rooms, you and I will create a hazy world of seamless, creative harmony unknown to the abstemious. Let them divorce one another and abandon their children. Our union will be the stable oak in the great forest, faithful and content till premature death do us part.

I'm sure you are not afraid of a little death, my dear. Your interest in literature, medicine, nature, and history (not to mention politics!), if not superficial, should have taught this lesson: we must befriend our wily enemy, our redeemer, our relief. Such is the wisdom of the ages brought to you, free of charge, by your humble servant, Alan Krieger, who anxiously awaits your reply. I trust by now this letter has distinguished itself from the many others in your gloating, but anxious, pile. Do you have the courage to respond?

Sincerely,
Alan Krieger

P.S. Send photo, please. I need an image on which to fasten my affections.

*July 5, 1992 Not answered. Maybe write her again.*

*september*

## 19. SEPTEMBER 10: HAPPY BIRTHDAY TO WHO

*Knock, knock, knock.*

KNOCK, KNOCK, KNOCK.

"Who the fuck is it?"

*Knock, knock, knock, knock, knock.*

"Whad'ya want? I'm on the can."

"Western Union."

"Just a minute. I don't know any Western Union. We don't want any."

"Telegram."

*KNOCK, KNOCK, KNOCK.*

"I'm coming, I'm coming. Don't have a cow. Jesus H. Christ, a man can't take a shit in peace these days. Lock number one. Lock number two. Police bar. Chain . . . Deb!"

She stood there, looking lovely, holding three cardboard boxes, arranged vertically in size place.

*"Happy birthday to you,*
*You were born in a zoo,*
*You look like Oswald Spengler . . .*
*And you smell like him too."*

"What's with this birthday crap? You know I don't celebrate my birthday. What are these, presents? I don't *do* presents for me."

"But I do. Besides, you'll like them. More besides, I won 25 bucks in the lottery."

"You buy lottery tickets? That's for po' folks to support the rich."

"My nephews give me lottery tickets every birthday."

"But your birthday's in April. This is September"

"I just found them at the bottom of my bag. Scraped them off, and voilà, free lunch."

"Besides, I can't stand the 'Happy Birthday' song, though I have to admit that Oswald Spengler made it more palatable. Hey, wait a minute, he's the world's ugliest man."

"I swear to God I never saw his picture."

"No, really, here, wait, look. These two books were the only things my father left me. Think Pop was up to his old symbolic tricks? Look at this picture."

There he was, chief don of the *Untergang,* Mr. Decline of the West himself, looking fierce and bald, and you wouldn't want to marry him.

"Yikes," opined Deb.

"You betcha. I actually did write another birthday song. I sent it in to *Reader's Digest* hoping it would be adopted by the whole country, beginning with the semi-literate lower classes."

"What happened?"

"I've got the rejection slip in a cheap frame in the bedroom."

"Oh, *that's* what that is."

"Wanna hear it?"

"Sure. Do you think I should sit down first?"

"Yeah. Pull up a couch. You can put those ridiculous boxes down. Ready?

*A semi-happy birthday*
*to you, ma'am* (it could be "sir"), *while you can,*
*for happiness is fleeting*
*and death does have his plan.*
*Though now you're able-bodied*
*and full of life and vim*

*your body will be sullied*
*and taken o'er by him—*
*Deb-bie.* (You put the person's name in there.)"

"They didn't accept that? I'm shocked."

"Yeah. And the tune is even from the 'St. Matthew Passion.' It's the chorale when Christ is up on the cross."

"More the pity."

"*O Haupt voll Blut und Wunden.*"

"Sounds messy."

"I'm nailed right in."

"What's that?"

"Over the cross. INRI. I'm nailed right in."

"Never knew what that meant."

"Stick with mc, babc."

"It doesn't mean that. You think I'm dumb? Where's your mother on your birthday?"

"Whoops. Didn't I tell you?"

"What?"

"Alice doesn't live here anymore."

"Who's Alice?"

"Sorry. Florence doesn't live here anymore."

"What do you mean?"

"She moved out."

"When? Why?"

"I don't know. A while ago. She decided to move in with Walter and Anne. I'll kill them if they hurt her."

"Why didn't you tell me?"

"I forgot."

"You forgot?? How long did you know this was happening?"

"Right after my Mother's Day sermon."

"What was that?"

"I told her the story of Oedipus."

"That was in May. May, June, July, August, September. That was six months ago. And you haven't told me?"

"I didn't want to worry you."

"What am I, your mother? I'm your girlfriend, your helpmeet, your soulmate! You're supposed to talk to me about these things!"

"So hit me. I was just trying to minimize your contact with Krieger *mishegas*."

"Listen, it can't get any more *meshuga* than just being with *you*."

"Wanna bet? You're not going to believe this. When I was teasing her about my having an Oedipus complex, you know what she said?"

"What?"

"'Oedipus, shmedipus . . . as long as you love your mother . . .'"

"You're making that up."

"Swear to YHWH."

"I don't believe it. Anyway, that's no reason to kick her out of her own house."

"I didn't kick her out. She left voluntarily. She's always wanted to be a country girl."

"Are you kidding? She'll trip on rocks and break a hip."

"I got her a snakey cane."

"What do you mean?"

"A cane carved like a snake, complete with red, forked tongue. Like hers. She loved it. Said it would help her remember Shlong. Look, what are you, my mother? Don't bug me about it. What's in the boxes, even though I don't want any presents? Nicely stacked. Like you."

"Open them."

"Let's see if I can guess. Three boxes, arranged in a ziggurat, such as was built at Ur during the neo-Sumerian age in the third millennium B.C.E. and dedicated to the moon god. At the top was the temple. So I suspect this little package on top is something holy. A new set of phylacteries for me? Wrong, Alan! It's . . . a bottle of sake."

"For your Buddhist studies. For your Kurosawa studies. So you can get drunk like Toshiro Mifune."

"But you know I don't drink. Except Manischewitz, and that as little as possible."

"It's time, Alan, it's time. *In vino veritas*."

"I went to CCNY, not Harvard. We didn't believe in *veritas* there. Couldn't afford to."

"Try it, you'll like it. It's like Manischewitz."

"But I don't *like* Manischewitz."

"All right, I'll drink it. I don't suppose you have any sake cups."

"No, but we have an old eye-washing cup in the medicine cabinet. Wait, I'll get it. It's slightly filthy, but I'll wash it out and it'll be good as new."

Deb steeled herself for what might be coming.

"Here. Classy glassy!"

"Yuck!"

"It's clean."

"It's had roaches peeing all over it."

"How do you know?"

"Your bathroom is Roach Central."

"So? I washed it. Here, I'll pour you some, and I'll even take a sip first like they do in Renaissance dramas about the Borgias."

"Stop. *I'll* wash it. Then I'll feel comfortable."

"Suit yourself. Can I proceed to the mid-floors of the ziggurat?"

"Guess first."

"Can I feel? Hmmm. Feels like a moderately heavy rectangular solid. Bends like a paperback book. I like your wrapping. The *New York Times* financial section."

"It's the part we throw out first."

"So, let's see. Midsection of the ziggurat was dedicated to routine maintenance and administration. I would therefore guess this to be a new paperback edition of Irma Rombauer's *The Joy of Cooking*. And . . .

wrong again, Alan. It's . . . Aaaargh! *War and Peace*. Touch it with only the tips of thumb and forefinger, Alan, and quickly deposit it in the trash!"

"What do you mean, the trash? It's one of the great works. You *like* great works. You don't have it."

"Do you suppose, my sweet, that it is an accident that I do not pollute my shelves with this overrated piece of Slavic shit?"

"But it's Tolstoy's birthday today. Your birthday is Tolstoy's birthday. I looked it up in the Book of Days."

"Do you also think I am unaware that the Imps of Perversity have eternally linked Alan Krieger with that abominable imposter and cosmic fraud? Alan Krieger, faithful disciple of his antithetical archrival Fyodor Mikhailovich Dostoevsky? I've carried this cruel fate around with me for . . . how many years?"

"Thirty-six."

"Thirty-six years. And now you have to remind me of it on this of all days, my birthday?"

"But it's *his* birthday."

"Sha! Ptui! Don't mention that pronoun in my house again."

"What have you got against Tol—"

"Stop!"

"You've read it?"

"You think I would criticize something I didn't know anything about? You think I am my brother or his keeper?"

"But what do you have against you know who? My father loves him."

"Your father is an Enlightenment dupe. How can anyone prefer his lawful, rational universe to Dostoevsky's anarchic, mystical, hallucinatory one? We're ruled by Zohar, not Talmud! Your father thinks the peasants are noble? No, the peasants are sick, violent, and corrupt to the soul. Tolstoy—ptui!—is like Walter living up in the beautiful countryside with his beyuuu-tiful wife and his beyuuu-tiful children."

"There you go with Walter again."

"Hey, I'm for stark realism—like the sewers of Leningrad, or the

IRT at rush hour. Tolstoy never rode the IRT in his life. He was sipping chai from a silver samovar when Fyodor Mikhailovich was facing a firing squad! You think we need more smiley faces in this world? And the fucking irony is that Tolstoy, may his name be erased from the Book of Life, set himself up as a god. He challenged God—while Dostoevsky groveled in front of Him. God, that is. Makes me want to puke."

"I loved *Anna Karenina*."

"Of course. It's a girl's book, a book for sissies. A heroine named Kitty. Might as well be Barbie! Give me a man's book anytime. *Moby Dick* . . ."

"Dostoevsky didn't write *Moby Dick*."

"But he could have. He just didn't know from whales. Ahab is as mad as Dimitri."

"Well, maybe *I'll* read it, then," she said, turning the book over and over again. "I never have."

"Neither has anyone else. They just say they have. Who could get through it?"

"You did."

"Just to nourish my hatred."

"You better get to your last present before it gets really cold."

"You know what he did to his wife?"

"Who?"

"Count Tracula."

"No."

"Made her copy that damn thing over, first word to last, six times. No xeroxing allowed. Then he wanted to give all their money away to the poor."

"OK. Shut up and open the big box."

"He wants to sacrifice himself, so he arranges to starve her? Nice. Finally, he runs away from home. She's up all night worrying. And you know what he takes with him? A copy of *The Brothers Karamazov!* On his deathbed, there he is, reading Dostoevsky! QED! Question Enswered Definitively."

Alan picked up the third and final box and eyed it at arm's length.

"So, pizza! It's warm. It says PIZZA on the box, that's a pretty broad hint. Look at that guy. No chef would eat his own pizza. Whoa! It's not pizza."

"Tricked you."

"Six times six—thirty-six—White Castle hamburgers—they are White Castle, aren't they? Nothing else is so small and cute—individually wrapped . . ."

"By yours truly."

". . . in aluminum foil. And still warm. And all that for my aluminum-foil ball, too. Now there's a present I can get my teeth into!"

"I thought so. But then again, I thought you'd like the sake and the Tol—the book."

"May I serve you?"

"I just had dinner. They're all for you."

"You won't even have one?"

"Half. I'll just have a half. A symbolic gesture of sharing."

"Half a White Castle hamburger? They're quantized. There's no such thing as half."

"You need to eat thirty-six."

"Why? Lurianic kabbalah?"

"No, because nobody ever has."

"But I'm only going to eat thirty-five and a half."

"At least you'll be up there."

"Thirty-five and a half it is. Cleverest of girls. I'll get a knife. Or you want to rip one in half with your Amazon teeth?"

"A knife will be fine."

"Yeow!"

"What's the matter?"

"Nothing. I cut myself."

"My little klutz! Let's see your hand, bubbie. Oooh, nasty."

"I'll stop the bleeding; you cut up a Band-Aid and make a butterfly."

"Where are the Band-Aids?"

"In the medicine cabinet."

"I'm not going in that bathroom."

"Why not? You've already slurped the worst of it."

"I washed that glass thoroughly. Eye-cup."

"Go get me a Band-Aid before I bleed to death. There are scissors in the medicine cabinet. Just cut four strips out of the two ends. And bring one more Band-Aid to cover the whole thing. I'll press on it with paper towels."

"What kind of blood do you have?"

"Blue. Red. I don't know. Regular blood. All-American."

"I mean what type. What blood type?"

"O-negative. Universal donor. I'm so sweet and kind."

"What a waste."

"Why's that?"

"Who would you give your blood to?"

"I wouldn't give it to. But I'd give it for."

"For what?"

"Can you pull the ends of the wound together? Good. Now add the other butterfly. Excellent. Now the other Band-Aid. Debbie Goldenbaum, Jewish EMT. Now we can grapple without fear of staining the upholstery. This reminds me of when I cut my hand when I went to visit Walter. I was peeling a hiking stick with my hunting knife so I could be a real *Wandervogel,* and I almost sliced my thumb off."

"You have a way with hunting knives."

"You are referring to my slicing up my bedroom walls and Walter's bed—and my left shin—when I was an overexuberant youth?"

"What would you give your blood for?"

"I knew you would ask that! Let's see. To carry out the mission of the Jews."

"And what may that be?"

"To stop the children of darkness. 'The horse and the rider hath he drownéd in the sea.'"

"That's God, not you."

"Me too. God and me."

"Alan Krieger . . ."

"Krieger means warrior."

". . . golem of the Grand Concourse, savior of the Jews."

"A little grandiose, but it'll do."

"Alan, you're nuts. What are you thinking of?"

"I'm thinking of this old guy I saw last week at his mom-and-pop store in Canarsie, where he used to serve the Jewish community, joke with people, commiserate with people. I walked in there last Thursday, and there he was shaking helplessly in front of two black teenagers who wanted some of those little Mrs. Smith's apple pies, you know them?"

"Sure."

"He was out of them."

"So?"

"So what would you say if someone was out of apple pies? 'Thanks,' maybe, 'I'll take a blueberry,' right? You know what they said? 'You got no apple pie for us? You in deep trouble, Jew man.' Storekeepers have been shot to death for less. They split when I came in, and I hate to think what would have happened if I hadn't."

"What did he say to you?"

"He spilled out his heart and his guts. He cried in front of me, a stranger come into the store. It's happening all over, all these little old Jews, fearing for their lives, losing their businesses, their pitiful life savings. Do the country-club Jews understand this? They haven't been anywhere but Nordstrom's and Starbucks for twenty years. They can afford to be liberal. 'Oh, yes, we understand the reason for your kicking us in the teeth.' Lenny Bernstein raising money for the Panthers, the prick. Couldn't conduct either."

"So what do you have in mind?"

"I have in mind the call we got from a single mom—black—my last day at the ER: 'Uh, how much bourbon is too much for a two-year-old?'

You think things will be better the next generation? I have in mind blacks chanting, 'More lampshades!' at a cannibal demo in Crown Heights. I have in mind my little Jewish nephew singing gangsta rap. Makes marrying a non-Jew look like yeshiva. I have in mind this poem I've been carrying around in my wallet. Julius Lester had a kid read it on BAI during the Ocean Hill-Brownsville strike my father was killed in. Damn, I've got a lot of shit in this wallet. Here, it's a little smushed. Wanna read it?"

"Another gem from the Krieger Hate Archives?"

*"Hey, Jew-boy, with that yarmulke on your head*
*you pale-faced Jew-boy*
*I wish you were dead.*
*I see you, Jew-boy*
*now you can't hide*
*I got a scope on you*
*yeah, Jew-boy, you gonna die."*

"Scary."

"Know what Lester's comment was afterward? 'Beautiful.'"

"Lester's Jewish, isn't he?"

"All the worse. Black Jews think they're superior even to Jews. But when the shit hit Lester's fan, which won out, you tell me, black or Jew? Here, gimme, I'll put it back."

"That's lunatic-fringe stuff, Alan."

"Oh yeah? When was the last time you interviewed the good people of 125th Street?"

"When was the last time *you* did?"

"What do you think I do with my newly-free days?"

"I haven't the slightest idea. You're a bit secretive, you know."

"Research, my dear, investigative research."

"You keep it all in your wallet?"

"Only the gems. I've got enough derriere problems already."

"This is all hateful, Alan. You're turning hateful."

"*I'm* turning hateful? What about *them?* They have to be stopped. And we are going to stop them."

"There's no *we* in this, Alan."

"Man and wife are one."

"I'm not your wife."

"Man and soulmate are one."

"Not with a racist . . ."

"Debbie the bee, you have to learn to sting."

"I don't *do* violence. Jews don't do violence."

"Listen to you. Tell it to the Palestinians."

"You sound like Walter."

"Ooof! Anything but that. OK, *don't* tell it to the Palestinians. You ever hear of Sid Luckman? Years ago, there was this football player by the name of Sid Luckman, I think on the Chicago Bears. He was the first professional Jewish quarterback. Imagine. The first. With all our brains. So one time, when his team came to the Polo Grounds to play the Giants, he invited his immigrant Jew father to watch him play. The old man didn't know from football, and he watches—completely confused—he watches from the stands while Sid drops back to pass and every once in a while Sid gets totally creamed. Every time his son goes down under two tons of goys the poor old man *oi-oi-oi-oi-ois,* and when halftime comes, he runs to the dressing room, and there is Sid, sitting on the bench, bruised and exhausted. His father rushes over to him and says, 'Sidney, Sidney, you big *schmegeggie,* just give them the ball.'"

"That's a funny story. So?"

"Debbie, this I will not be. I will not just give them the ball."

"Who's *them?* Who's *them?* We're not talking football. We're talking potentially serious racial violence."

"You bet your sweet ass we are. And it isn't coming from us. 'I got a scope on you, Jew-boy, you gonna die.' Never again, say I. We don't hand over the ball."

"Alan, blacks and Jews are in it together—the same boat. And you'll never get Jews to solve the differences with violence. It's not the way we . . ."

"Are you kidding? Violence is as Jewish as apple *charoset*. In fact, violence was the cement that held us together, memories of our victories. Victimization, you couldn't live on. 'Let the high praises of God be in their mouth and a two-edged sword in their hand to execute vengeance upon the heathen, and punishments upon the people.' Psalm 149—check it out, check it out. And our hero Joshua, the mass murderer, for whom so many of our sweet little Jewish boys are named."

"But Alan, you . . . you're totally nuts—besides being a Buddhist. You don't even kill cockroaches. You've never spilled a drop of blood except your own."

"You don't think I can transform into the Lion of Judah?"

"Maybe the Cowardly Lion. 'Put em up, put em up!' "

"Wizardry will fix everything, my Debeleh."

"Meaning?"

"Meaning that's what we have to do. The Cowardly Lion of Judah and his Girlfriend with Sensible Shoes. We have to scare the shit out of enough of those flying monkeys that they'll pull back, and we as a people will take heart and come to our senses."

"The Wizard is a phony, Alan."

"So? So is everyone. It's the way the world works. Some would call it Art. And you wanna know what else? You have to become Deborah."

"I *am* Deborah. Pass the sake."

"On your birth certificate. But who calls you Deborah? No one."

"Mr. Finkelstein in the sixth grade used to call me Deborah."

"Perhaps he knew something."

"Why Deborah?"

"Ruth they know, Rachel they know, Sarah they know, Irma Rombauer they know, but Deborah they don't know."

"All right, Alan. So who was Deborah?"

"Deborah was the only female judge in Judges. She was also a prophetess. Early twelfth century B.C.E. Long enough ago for a revival, don't you think?"

"What did she prophesy?"

"What did she prophesy? When Israel was oppressed by the Canaanites, she prophesied victory in a war. She ordered General Barak to assemble ten thousand men and destroy the army of Sisera, the Canaanites' main man. She even gave the attack order: '*Chaaaaarge!*'" Alan screamed it out and whooped around like a banshee. "And General Sisra, all tuckered out, wound up in the kitchen of a little sweetie named Ya'el, buddy of Deborah. This verse, the oldest poem of Israel, is so good I committed it to memory:

*when he asked her for water*
*she gave him milk*
*her hand was on the spike*
*her right hand on the heavy hammer*
*she brought it down on Sisra*
*she smashed his head*
*she crushed it*
*struck the spike into his neck*
*he bent down at her feet he fell*
*he fell he lay down at her feet*
*he bent down at her feet he fell*
*fell where he bent*
*he bent down at her feet he fell*
*he lay there ruined.*"

Alan got up from the floor.

"It's all there in Judges 5, one of the great slow-motion scenes in paleocinema. Thus was Israel delivered from the oppressor. And that, my dear, is who Deborah is, *no* extra charge for Ya'el, and that singing, stinging bee is the bee you must become. So be it."

"This is wonderful sake. You should try it."

"So just help the Cowardly Lion of Judah, the golem of the Grand Concourse. We can be the salvation of the Jewish race."

"*You* the salvation of the Jewish race?"

"You'd rather have Henry Kissinger?"

"Alan, listen to me. Can you just settle down enough to listen to me? You're so excited, you haven't even eaten any of your hamburgers. Are they even still warm?"

"Uh-huh. The wonders of space-age radiation reflectors."

"OK. Unwrap one. Good. Sit down. Good. Eat, eat. Chew your food. Fifty times a bite. Well, twenty-five."

"Three?"

"Five. Don't just gulp it down. You want something to drink?"

"Whattaya got?"

"What do you mean what have I got? It's your house."

"Oh. What have I got? I'll have a Diet Pepsi. In the fridge."

"What am I, your slave?"

"Hey, it's my birthday, remember? I'm eating your somewhat weird version of a birthday cake. You won't bring me something to wash it down?"

"All right, all right."

"Thank you, Ya'el."

"Deborah. Here's your drink. Care to sniff the tab?"

"Oh . . . yes. Um, very nice. Very nice."

"Thank you. Now . . . are you listening?"

"Ummmm."

"Is your mouth full so you can't talk back?"

"Mmmmm. Ummmhummm."

"Alan, you are fishing in dangerous waters. I'm not kidding. This is false-messiah stuff big time."

"*They* are the false messiah, not me."

"Have another burger. They're just thrashing around being resentful."

"Wook, Miz Oldenbaum . . ."

"Don't speak with your mouth full."

"How am I not upposed to eak with my mouf full when you are making me eat thirty-iks White Cawoo hamburger before they get cold?"

He washed the remains of burger 13 down with Pepsi.

"OK. My mouth is not full. Can I speak?"

"*May* I speak. Go ahead. You have one minute."

"I've never said anything in one minute."

"Time to try. Topic sentence?"

"Topic? Great false messiahs of history. Can I have just one more bite? It's my birthday."

"I'll wait."

"I will skip over the obvious and odious Shabbatai Z'vi . . ."

"Whom even I have heard of. Joined the Nation of Islam, didn't he?"

"Way to go for false messiahs. I want to get right to Jakob Frank, about a hundred years later, who, with all his disciples, converted to Catholicism."

"Is that better or worse than converting to Islam?"

"Who cares where false messiahs go? They're false. They go to False Land. The question is where they've been before they get there, and Frank was at a pretty interesting place."

"Your minute's up."

"Let me finish. You may like it. Have some more sake. Relax."

"More sake sounds good. Sure you don't want some?"

"I'm naturally high. Besides, I want to be able to take advantage of you later, after you get trashed."

"Maybe I *will* have a burger."

"Have two. They're getting cold. So anyway, Jakob Frank."

"What about him?"

"I'll tell you in a minute. But first . . . 'The Shards of God.'"

"Another Krieger soap opera?"

"No. Kabbalah. Kabbaaaaaaaaaalah. Woo wooo woooooo. Mysticism! Stop yawning."

"I'm sleepy. It's all this alcohol."

"You've had two eyecups full of sake."

"Three. And I'm small and delicate."

"No. Wake up, *wake up,* this is important for our future."

"Mysticism is important for our future?"

"Hey, you think this world is real? This is it? The all-shopping channel?"

"I'm awake."

"'The Shards of God,' Version 1. By Anonymous. Once upon a time, when God was finishing up the universe, He hired . . ."

"She."

". . . She hired an angel to distribute the divine effulgence out into the world and gave this angel a great big crock from Her Grandmother's kitchen, and the angel was supposed to sprinkle divinity out of the crock, a little here, a little there. . . ."

"What was Her Grandmother's name?"

"We'll file that under koan. Keep quiet and listen. So the angel flies down out of the hangar with the crock, and it hits about 13,000 feet above sea level when all of a sudden there is this huge bang."

"Satanic terrorists?"

"Close, but no cigar. No, the power of the contents was too great for the crock. Even covered with Saran Wrap."

"Bad, bad . . . You're not supposed to use Saran Wrap. Dow Chemical. Napalm."

"That was thirty years ago. How long do you want to punish an innocent international corporation? Competitiveness. America. Anyway, I'm not the one who packed it in Saran Wrap. God did."

"I thought you were God."

"You must be drunker than I thought. Have another eye-cup."

"Don't mind if I do."

"So the crock shatters into numberless pieces, like a fragmentation bomb, speaking of terrorists, and these pieces fly out into creation, and anywhere you look you might find, sometimes hidden, sometimes not, a Shard of God."

"Even in the cat's doody-box?"

"Even in the cat's doody-box. A Shard of God."

"Maybe we shouldn't empty the cat box, then."

"Maybe not. End of story number one."

"That was nice. Tell me another one."

Deb tottered into the living room and flopped down on the couch.

"You get another one if you eat another burger. Need to dilute that blood alcohol with fat globules for better comprehension. This is a deep one."

"Just one hamburger?"

"Yes. I don't want any divine vomit fragments on my divine couch. I'll stick the rest in the oven."

"This is good. I *like* White Castle hamburgers."

"I know, dear, I know. Ready for the second story?"

"The Shards of God."

"No. We just had that. This one is called 'The *Sparks* of God.' It's the original of 'The Shards.' Deeper."

"Why didn't you tell me that one first if it was the original?"

"We proceed from the surface to the core. This is original Isaac Luria, echt kabbalah. According to Isaac . . ."

"My father?"

"No, my pixillated poppet, Isaac Luria, most brilliant student of the Zohar. According to Luria, the reason God wanted to spread the divine effulgence throughout creation was because He wanted His light to illuminate creation."

"In the doody-box."

"The doody-box of existence. Yes. Now. Here comes the hard part. You still there?"

"Debbie Goldenbaum reporting for duty."

"That's not the snappiest salute I've seen. Better. What are the consequences of the scattering of the divine light?"

"I dunno. Sparks in the doody-box? Hard to clean? Can't flush em down the toilet?"

"Even at your worst, you're right on. Consequence number one: in this world, God's light is broken, nothing is perfect, everything is awry."

"Sliced, without seeds."

"Very funny. No, sliced *with* seeds, the sparky seeds scattered at random in the created world. Not in their places. Just scattered any old where."

"An unruly mess."

"Yes, an unruly mess."

"Like your room."

"And that's why. Things aren't where they should be. Above, below, to the side, but never right on. Listen, now. Are you listening? As a result of the shattering, all being is in exile—just like the Jews—disjointed, displaced from the homeland. Do you get that? All being is in exile."

"ET, phone home!"

"And what's more, since the divine sparks even fell into the forces of darkness and evil, there they are—feeding and supporting them, the forces of evil. Are you starting to get my drift, or are you too far gone?"

"No, I get it, I get it. The whole world, not just us, the whole world is in exile. . . . From the very beginning."

"Right. McDonald's wins out over White Castle . . ."

"Oreo over Hydrox. Windows over Mac."

"It's a mess."

"Goldtooth over you. My $90 shoes give me blisters. And all this crappiness in the world is because—everything is in exile!"

"You are one smart little chicken. And now the plot thickens. We need to heal the flaw, repair the universe. *Tikkun*. Luria says that God needs human partners for this job, and that *that* is the meaning of history. Pretty interesting."

"Helping God gather up the sparks."

"Exactly. And *that* will be redemption."

"Not five cents a bottle."

"Not *ten* cents a bottle. And where do we have to go to gather up the sparks, to pry them from their shells and put them in their places?"

"Into the doody-box."

"You're so good. Into the doody-box exactly. And where is the doody-box?"

"In the bathroom."

"In the bathroom and the bedroom, and even in the pants of all those shvartzas out there."

"Right in their pants."

"God is there."

"But She needs to have her booboo fixed."

"And her nose wiped. We need to take on evil where it lives, some bigtime fall cleaning, straighten up the house, even if it means getting messy."

"Change the doody-box."

"And when we do—*that* will be the messianic age! When all things will be in their place, that's the Messiah! Who needs Christ?"

"Christmas. Keep Christ in Christmas."

"But we can't be afraid of getting dirty, really dirty—and that is where Jakob Frank comes in. Remember?"

"Jakob Frank is dirty, really dirty."

"*Oi,* so dirty you wouldn't believe it. He taught that in order to gather the sparks, Jews, good little Jewish boys and girls, had to descend into the abyss of sin and pass through the 49 gates of abomination. Here, let me take off your blouse."

"Why do you want to do that?"

"And your bra. Oh, my goodness, the holiness of sin, my big-boobed beauty. Sin as service to God. You know what Jakob Frank said?"

"Here, let me take off my pants," Deb mumbled.

"He didn't wear pants. He wore a gown."

"Was he gay? I mean transvestright?"

"He said we have to hurl ourselves into sin in order to get at the holy sparks down there. He wanted to break through the rules of Torah into the superconducting, frictionless world of Zohar. In the new world, the old rules don't apply: all is allowed, and all is holy. Even killing."

"Thou shalt not kill, thou shalt not kill."

"Old baggage. The warrior messiah needs to kill. 'Without ye die, ye shall not be born again.' Sex and murder and salvation. Praise the Lord who permits the forbidden."

"Is it forbidden for you to come inside me?"

"No."

"Alan, wanna come inside me?"

"As soon as I get your signature on the dotted line."

"What dotted line? I don't see a dotted line."

"And you don't even have a pen. It was a metaphor. I want you to agree to help me."

"I'll help you. I'm your helpmeet. Helpmeets help. Help you what?"

"Help me gather the sparks of God from the doody-box."

"Come inside me, big fella."

"Promise you'll help me."

"Take off your pants."

"If I do, will you help me?"

"Look how little you are. C'mere. Get that little weenie over here. I'm gonna do Debbie magic on it."

"Promise."

"I promise."

"What do you promise?"

"I promise to help you."

"Help me do what?"

"I don't know."

"Promise to be a little golem."

"I promise to be a little golem."

"To save the Jews."

"To save the Juice."

"To gather the sparks."

"To gather the sparks."

"And clean the doody-box."

"And clean the doody-box."

There was silence as the seals came undone.

"Is that it?" she asked.

"Yes."

"Then get over here."

## 20. ALAN AWAKE

Heart beats *andante* into right ear on meaty right shoulder, arm extending up . . .

Lub-DUP, lub-DUP, lub-DUP, lub-DUP, lub-DUP, lub-DUP . . .

*When you're LYing awake with a DISmal headache, and rePOSE is tabooed by anXIety . . .*

But I'm not anxious. And I have no headache.

*Um, da da da daaaaaaa* lub-DUP, lub-DUP, off. Lub-DUP, lub-DUP. *Um da da da daaaaaaaaaaaaaaaaaaaaaaaaaaaaaaaaaaaaaaa-aaaaaaaaaaaaaaaaaaaaaaaaa* how many, my heart? It could last forever, out of time, out of space, God's eyebrow raised in infinite fermata. Wilder than the fifth of Johnny Walker. Fate knocks at the door, then discovers the doorbell. . . . No thank you, I gave at work. . . . lub-DUP, lub-DUP.

Left knee slightly bent, limp cantilever off right leg, extended underneath.

Left arm limp along left side, left hand scratching left buttock in an absent Parkinsonian way. Yet not so insentient as to miss the micro-pleasures of bumps excoriated, follicles picked, and scales upturned and flicked in epidermic exploration.

*Thuuuurrrrrupp.*

Good one, Alan. I'll roar you as gently as a sucking dove. Not sucking. The opposite. Fair fecality and tuning of the tail.

Fucking Walter, always exposing my clandestine farts. "Does someone in this car need to go to the bathroom? Mo-om, Da-ad!" Three is not only the number of the Trinity but also the minimum number of people among whom a fart is not definitively ascribable. The miracle of three . . . the stable stool.

*Um da da da ddaaaaaaaaaaaaaaaaaaaaaaaaaaaaaaaaaaaaa-aaaaaaaaaaaaa*

Cooommming! But what if I can't move? What if I can't move my leg? I can't move my leg, I can't move my leg. Hey, I can't move my leg! I really can't. It's disconnected. It's just lying there like a long slab of meat. With the bone in. C'mon, Alan, move it. You can move your leg.

Whew. I thought I couldn't move it. I thought I was turning into . . .

I can't believe that letter. Walter makes her a birthday video of all the old home movies for which there are no longer any working projectors except if you pay a zillion bucks to have them put on cassette? It was wonderful? Baby me is crying and crying and Walter is no doubt looking at me with a smirk on his innocent face and she thinks it's wonderful? I'm crying for an hour, two hours, and my fucking father is filming the whole thing like Ingmar Bergman?

I remember when Walter blew pepper in my eyes when he was "taking care of me." As in the Mafia. "Mom, I just wanted to see if it would make him sneeze like in *Alice in Wonderland*." Why didn't he just bring me in as a science-fair project? Set me up manacled at a table and let parents blow pepper in my face, and keep track of the results? A typical straight-A Walter move.

My nose is stuffed. I can't breathe. Nosers. Nosers. What if I couldn't breathe?

He turned on the light on the floor next to the bed, and, white-blinded, groped around among the bottles for the plastic one with the nipple top. Snort. Snort. Twist cap back on. Twist switch back off. Wait.

My nose is clearing, but my *head* is stuffed. My skull is stuffed—with brains! I need more nosers.

Twist, twist, snort, snort, twist, twist.

There it goes. *Laudate,* Merck Sharp and Dome for the sharpness of your shrinkers. Oxymetazoline hydrochloride, when I am sent to the gas chamber, let it be you that takes me down, shrinking my brain to the size of one of Walter's official American League baseballs signed by the warden, the executioner, and Mickey Mantle. O it's so nice to breathe again, to feel the cerebrospinal fluid wafting across my sulci.

I never *could* play baseball, much to Walter's delight, as I would have beaten the shit out of him if I could have. One more notch in his superiority belt—he and Pop out there in the park, fungo-ing to each other, while I invented Weight Watchers and sulked.

Fungo. What the hell kinda word is that? Have to look it up.

Paw around for pad and pencil, write, "Look up fungo" illegibly in the dark.

Always on my case. Filling our room with his mirrors, just the thing for the overweight child, and I kept warning him about vampires. Goddamn sadist. Telling me about sex, which I didn't believe, but ruining my faith in grownups anyway. *Soooo verfluch ich die Liebe.*

Good man, that Alberich. Probably plump—but stately in a dwarfish kind of way.

As his eyelids grew heavy and his breath slowed, Alan drifted down into the greeny depths of the Rhein. But there, in a great slimy clearing, surrounded by eels and bones was—Mrs. Melnick, the underworldly miasma only Walter could shield him from should the elevator ever stop at five on their way down. The ominous thumping, banging, knocking in the floor of their apartment, a threatening, fierce rebuke from Mrs. Melnick, the "old witch" in the apartment below as she—what?—beat the ceiling with her broomstick, as they imagined? Protesting the peregrinations of normal, active, good little Jewish boys, circumscribing their play, a menacing presence, intimately lurking.

"If you don't do what I say, I'm going to call Mrs. Melnick!" Ma would threaten. That brought us into line—fast—though not quite as quickly as her "I'm going to call the Institution" routine, which usually involved picking up the phone. Presumably, the Institution had to be reached telephonically, while Mrs. Melnick could be called on in a chummier fashion. Mrs. Melnick, secret ally of my mother, contactable at any time . . .

*You're a regular wreck with a crick in your neck,*
*And no wonder you snore, for your head's on the floor.*

We usually went up and down the stairs for fear that the elevator would stop at—five! *Da da da daaaaaaaaaaaaaaaa!*

*You've got needles and pins from your soles to your shins*
*And your skin is acreep, for your left leg's asleep.*

Say, it *is* asleep! My leg is asleep.

*You've a cramp in your toes*

I do! I have a fuckin cramp. Yeooooowch. Retroextend. Ah. Better.

*And a fly on your nose.*

No flies. Yet.

*And some fluff on your lung and a feverish tongue*
*And a thirst that's intense . . .*

Reach. Drink. Glug, glug. Push button down so when you knock it over in the middle of the night, it doesn't soak old Bigger Thomas there.

*And a general sense that*

There were three other tenants on five who might need the elevator. But what if it were—Mrs. Melnick? What if *she* got into the elevator with us—just the three of us, me and Walter and her—locked into that tiny space together.

*And a general sense that you haven't . . .*

Once the elevator did stop at five, and—it was Mrs. Melnick! It was the only time we ever saw her. I thought she might have three heads and the legs of a chicken. But there she was, Mrs. Melnick, the duchess, getting into the elevator—with us. How did we know it was her? We just knew. A fat fifty-year-old in a grubby pink bathrobe, wearing bedroom slippers, with curlers in her hair. She got in without acknowledging us: perhaps she didn't even see us shrinking into the elevator walls, and when the car stopped at G we oozed around her, opened the gate, pushed the door, and made a break for freedom. And she continued silently down to B, the dark, labyrinthine basement, her natural abode.

Alan shut his eyes and pushed them, Oedipus-wise, deep into their sockets.

*. . . general sense that you haven't been sleeping in clover.*

Who *was* Mrs. Melnick? *What* was she? Did she have a family? What did she do for work? Why did she go out so seldom that we only met her once? One might ask the same about God.

The old testacle God, not the new testacle God, she was just as mysterious.

A dark, amoeboid dollop of transcendence—right on the Grand Concourse.

Alan turned on his back and stared through the ghast-lit ceiling, out into the celestial dome of the west Bronx.

*For now we see through a glass, darkly; but then face to face.* The old days, way back, when gods walked the earth, bodhisattvas pushrolling up and down the Concourse, ringing prayer bells, and delivering the body and blood of the Eternal—in little cups. God! The Good Humor men, like a secret society of *tsaddikim,* holy teachers silently teaching, the white-garbed last of the Just. Their "Dixie cups," ostensibly from the South but almost certainly deriving from *dixit*: "it is spoken."

You hold the cup in sinister hand, feeling its coolness in your summer palm, and with dexterous fingers, you pry loose the tab that lifts the cover.

Open sesame, and behold! Underside the cover, the imprint of the universal mystery—the Tai Chi, the great Manichaean yin/yang of complementary opposites—chocolate and vanilla. But wait! Under the brown and white—lick them off, *te absolvo*—yet another manifestation. A layer of waxed paper—not the ordinary waxed paper Ma wrapped soggy cream-cheese-and-tomato sandwiches in—but a special waxed paper, thicker, nonwrinkly, found nowhere else in secular experience—under this layer, semiopaque eyelid of the Frog of God—an image, barely discernible. Blue of the beyond, the mountain's foggy mists—someone, something, was under there.

Now the moment of joy, ecstasy, known only to me and Saint Teresa: Using the waxed-paper tab, I s-l-o-w-l-y peeeeel away the barrier. Not too fast, keep it coming, now. And lo and behold, there is a face. A blue face, blue as Krishna's. Where have I ever seen blue faces since? Clark Gable, Lana Turner, Alan Ladd, Dorothy Lamour—*l'amour!*—clear and luminous stand-ins for gods and goddesses.

But it wasn't the *existence* of the face that was so impressive. It was the *revealing* of the face, the implicit lesson: behind the manifested world, beneath and beyond even its most pregnant brown-and-white sweetnesses with their abrupt and arbitrary color line, lay still another domain—the god domain—which I could glimpse by peeling away, peeling away. . . .

The rest? Anticlimactic by comparison. I spoon my way down the border, awash in the contrast of sweet white and bittersweet brown. Bliss—yet anticlimactic. Once the border was consumed, I could push the two remaining hemicircles together for a repeat at smaller radius, fat boy Alan thus intuiting, without Klaus Fuchs even, the mechanism of Fat Boy, the plutonium bomb. Thus, smaller and smaller, too soon disproving Zeno's paradox.

Good Humor man, where are you now? Has the Grand Concourse become too petite? Are you afraid of getting rolled, mugged, kicked in the fudgsicles?

He reached again for the water bottle and nearly lost a canine trying to pull the nipple into drinking position.

Fuckin dentists' lobby.

Suck glug suck glug . . .

"*Oi,* vas I toisty!"

Was that her a couple of years ago in the supermarket? That old woman in slippers and babushka? She shuffled the same way—mirthless and mean. I should have asked her. But I was still afraid, Lordy, Lordy. Maybe it wasn't Mrs. Melnick—but maybe it was. And no Walter to protect me. And was that Stephanie London turned middle-aged hag on the subway today along with her daughter, the spitting image of Stephanie London the unattainable so beautiful I could never look at her so how do I know what she looks like, or even looked like? Was she a goy? What was she doing in our neighborhood?

Alan's nose turned into a snorting proboscis. A Jewish tapir. He swung over and buried it in the well-bemucused pillow. His canines ached. He felt fullness draining from his superior face to his inferior one, in this case, right to left. What was draining? Fluid? What kind of fluid? And how did it get across the inside of his face? Maybe it was the blood-dimmed tide, drowning the ceremony of innocence temporarily at home in his left maxillary sinus.

Walter had sat him down on a bench in the park across the street, maybe even the same bench on which he oozed toward Calypso. It started as a typical Walter put-down: "You mean you don't know where babies come from?"

"I know, I know."

"Where, how?"

"I know."

"You don't know."

When he told me, I didn't believe him. "Grownups would never be that dirty." But they are, they are. They're dirty. Why would I have shit stains on my underpants if I wasn't dirty? I'll bet Walter has them too, though with that blond shiksa wife, who can say?

He wasn't always so bad, my big brother. Protected me from Ronnie Mergler anyway, that fat-prick bully, stepper-on-er of all anthills, killer of kittens and puppies. . . .

Alan's mind pullulated in his head, a bag of worms and slithering brainial nerves. But slower and slower . . . *Langsam, Wozzeck, langsam. . . .*

Your eyelids are getting heavy, Alan, heavy, becoming meat, slabs, help, my soul is drowning in . . . polypep . . .

Deb rolled over. Her knees engaged his gut.

Oooof.

Shift southward. Knee to knee.

Anisotropic human molecules. Levo. Sinister and gauche. Better than dextro, though. Rotate to the left, *mon fils.*

He shifted concave to her convex. She snaked her arm up over his girth and spread her drowsy fingers north of naval.

Trapped. Ooooooo. Do no arm. Weighing me down. Too hot. Sweet arm. But too hot.

He pushed it back along his flank . . .

Whew, better.

. . . and laid his arm along it, flank, arm, arm, like the Federal Aeronautics Administration.

I miss my Myshkin, lying there, along me, kneading. Little Myshkin of the too-sharp claw. Great massage when it wasn't an acupuncture session. His was a noble fall, however.

*Thwaap.*

Oooooo, Mère Ubu . . . a stinker. One for the books. *Repeating in her amorous fits, Oh! Celia, Celia, Celia shits.*

Arm. Nice arm. Soft arm. Snoring arm along my side. O arm that ever is when leg is not. I have to pee.

Easy does it. Do not wake the sleeping beast.

To his hands and knees. Rising backward, creeping hands up his own thighs toward verticality.

Look at her. Isn't she cute, my own little Mrs. Melnick? How would I know? It's too dark, and I don't have my glasses. Up, up, and ooof-away. My, Alan, but your head is high off the bed. Practically an out-of-body experience. Now a few steps backward. Beep, beep, beep, beep. Turn right, don't fall. Now shuffle-o, shuffle-o, shuffle off to Buffalo.

He ricocheted off the doorjamb into the bathroom.

Oh, ghostly receptacle, white in the night. Position via shins. Icy porcelain kiss, and kiss. Ahh, the little death. Lean forward against wall to create verticality of flow. Close eyes. Ahhhhhhhh. And then ah . . . ah . . . ah, let go, little prostate, let em through, let em through. Now flick the old putz. Flick, flick. No matter how you jig and dance, the last drop's always on your pants. Or in this case, on your leg. Now back to my sweet patootie. Lower yourself slowly, o weighty object. Cuddle her up a little. Scratch of scalp and squeeze of tit. Mmmm, she likes that. I wonder if she thinks it's old Falstaff here squeezing or if it's Brad Pitt. Brad Pitt? The treacherous slut!

Alan rolled over. Twist, *the light gleams an instant,* burrow around in books and papers, pack, Zeppo, flick, suck, *then it's night again.* Ahhh. 3:40. Twist. *No lack of void.*

Inhale deeeeeeply. Hold. Aaaauuummmmmm.

Nothing like a drag after copulating with Brad Pitt.

Alan lay on his back, his Deb snoring gently on his left, his right arm extended comfortably in half-crucifixion position, coffin nail emitting its darkling trail along the y-axis.

You blockheads and dung-chewing varlets . . . you liars less studied in philosophy than baboons . . . the pugnative choler of St. Fatgulch here (for from the paunch comes the dance) will inflict such punishments upon you as will cause you to beshit your britches. . . .

Sound bethwacking . . . unjointing of the spondyles . . . impaling at the fundament for your pernicious lies! May St. Anthony's . . . fire roast you. May Mahoom's . . . disease . . . spin you. And may you fall, bewildered . . . into bottomless . . . mayhem!"

*Da da da daaaaaaaaaaaaaaa*

They fall . . .

*Da da da . . .*

The earworm of the Fifth metamorphosed into a butterfly of old Beatles song. It crawled along his flattening convolutions, fanning them to sleep with Peter Max wings.

*You're a real Marlb'ro Man,*
*Short and fat like Ca-sals, an . . .*

The tempo changed, *allargando*. . . .

*Blind as bat like Serkin an*
*diminuendo sempre*
Serkin an . . .
*morendo*
for nobody
*lunga pausa*. . . .

Off, he was, to the land of downy sleep, death's counterfeit, chief nourisher in life's great feast. The *New York Review* birthed a cigarette hole but didn't catch fire, thank God.

*october*

# 21. A WALK ON THE WILD SIDE: CELEBRATING ZELENKA'S 317$^{TH}$ BIRTHDAY

Well, Lenox and 125th. Still Indian summer. Still sunny. You'd think Shvartzaville would have its own weather. "In Darkness let me dwell. The ground, the ground, shall sorrow, sorrow be." Indian summer—is that still politically correct? Look at this place! Good thing all those vendors got kicked off the street; it'd be a thousand times worse.

Well, here we go. This is it.

"God? God, are You listening? This is Your chance to show Your stuff. Here's the mission plan. I'm gonna walk west on 125th from here over to the Eighth Avenue subway, and I'm gonna cross the street back and forth a couple of times and get into whatever crowds are the biggest and maybe do some window-shopping. Now—here's where You come in. Pay attention: if You don't like my plan for *Kristallnacht*—You know, salvation through abomination, teleological suspension of the ethical, and all that—then I want You to *strike me down*. I'm serious. Dead. I mean, You don't have to do it Yourself. I'm sure there are many Freakin Merkins in the next two blocks who would be willing to do it for You, free of charge even. You get what I'm talking about? I'm either going to get from here to Eigh8th and down into the subway safely en route to Fordham Road, or I'm not. If I make it, I'll figure that's a blessing, that You want me to go ahead with Plan X. Clear? And although those *occhi chorni* are already staring at me, probably because of the color of my skin, or my Popeye forearms bulging out below my rolled-up shirtsleeves, or maybe it's just my propeller yarmulkea, I will help clarify the issue for You and for posterity by acting somewhat outrageous so as not to disappear into the crowd.

"Did You know that October 19th is Jan Dismus Zelenka's 317 birthday? Of course You knew that, You know everything, but maybe You weren't keeping track. But now that I mention it, I'm sure You're as happy as I am. It's the little things in life that keep you going, don't You think? So, because it's Zelenka's birthday, and because it's thematically appropriate, and because when in Rome . . . , I've got my big CD boom-box here that my brother Walter sent me out of pity and terror of my being any less than up-to-date—and thereby evading comparison with his material acquisitions—I've got my big black box with its sub-woofing attack dogs to boom out Zelenka's 'Lamentations of Jeremiah' to the locals of color who of course don't know jack shit about classical music, well, not exactly classical, since Jan Dismas ain't exactly classic, more's the pity, but You know what I mean. They probably also don't know jackshit about Jeremiah, so I'm trying to kill three birds with one stone here—a music appreciation session, a Bible lesson, and of course seeing if You need me to get myself killed.

"Now, was Jeremiah stoned to death, or what happened to him? So I'm going to stand in for the old boy here in this miserable resemblance to Jerusalem—similar only to the extent that it has mosques, and damn well better convert to God—or Sodom and Gomorrah, here we come. Alan the Prophet doesn't sound as good as Jeremiah or Eziekiel, but it's better than Bruce the Prophet, wouldn't You say? Or Chip? Chip the Prophet. Anyway, You only have to put up with it for two blocks, OK? Gimme the benefit of the doubt; I don't have much practice. I'll talk loud. So, You ready? Does this interest You? Lemme just get this fuckin machine on to the right mode, let's see, CD, up the volume, up the bass equalization, whatever the hell that is . . . and push play! Mm, mm, mmm, that man sure knew how to scratch them viols.

*Incipit lamentatio Jeremiae Prophetae.*

"*Incipit* is right. It's only the beginning, my melaninic friends, only the beginning. *Bereshyt*. Stuff up your ears with earwax if you care not to hear, or tie yourselves to your own mast cells—because if you don't, it's—

*ALEPH.*

"And standing in today for Jeremiah the Prophet, who was unavoidably detained on the way to the theater, is none other than Alan Krieger, Boy Wonder and Sometime Healer, for your edification and his own.

*ALEPH.*

"*Aleph*. The first letter of the Hebrew alphabet, my friends. And where are all the Hebrew children? Must be out there weeping by the waters of Babylon and 125th Street.

*ALEPH.*

"Now, ladies and gentlemen, such as you are, surely you know that the Hebrew letters, unlike your own paltry ABCs, such as they are, are not just transliterations of vocal sounds, but symbolic projections of energies in different stages of organization. What? You didn't know that? What *do* they teach you in your crumbling schools?

*ALEPH.*

"*Aleph*. Number one. The sound before all sounds. The archetype of the unthinkable, unrepresentable life-death. The abstract principle of all that *is* and all that *is not*.

*Quomodo*
*sedet sola*
*civitas*
*plena populo: facta est*
*quasi vidua*
*domina gentium:*
*princeps provinciarum facta est*
*subtributo.*

"Whoops, I stepped on a crack there. Break your mother's back. My mother, not your mother. Hope she blames Walter, not me. Walter's my shit-ass brother, my mother's current keeper. But that's not your problem. *You* all are *not* my mother's keeper. Or my brother's. Step on a crack, you will find a black (selling crack, of course).

"Step on a black, you will get the sack. Not you. You don't work. I suppose I don't work anymore either—but we digress.

"The city is lonely that was once full of people. The Harlem Renaissance down the tubes. Cain't get whitey up here any more without gentrification. He don't believe in spooks; he don't believe in spooks.

"*Facta est subtributo.* Oh, my goodness, you have become vassals, servants, slaves. Sound familiar, my friends? Why is that? Why have you always been, why will you always be, the underclass, you people? Think there's any reason?

"Or is thinking too hard?

"Oop—here comes *Beth*. No, not that Beth, not the twenty-year-old hot stuff with the six kids. Beth the second letter, the archetype of all dwellings, though you folks don't seem to care much about dwellings. But consider, too, the archetype of all containers, nickel bags, hair-pomade cans, prison cells. The physical support without which nothing is, without which Aleph life-death can't manifest. That's m-a-n-i-f-e-s-t to you literacy-impaired-niks. It means to show or display itself. Even as you do, half a million show-offs displaying yourselves in three square miles. Intense, intense. Like overcrowded rats.

"Do you like this music?

"Hey, ma'am, you like this music? You do? Well, praise the Lord!"

"Praise the Lord, too, bro."

"I'm not your bro. I'm Walter's bro. And won't he be sorry? Sorrow and pity and terror. And here we are crying in the night. You, not me. I cry in the day only. You cry in the night because your deadbeat lovers have all split sans child support and there is none to comfort you, ceptin maybe the next lover.

"Oops, step on a crack, they'll call you a quack, though you, not I, are the ones into voodoo. Quack, quack, quack—you've said the magic word, Alan. Voodoo. Voodoo? We do. We charge you yield, in Queen Victoria's name. Sylvia's Restaurant is around here somewhere. And if you listen very carefully, you can hear the duck quacking inside the wolf's stomach, because in his hurry, he

*BETH.*

*BETH.*

*BETH.*
*BETH.*
*Plorans*
*ploravit*
*in nocte,*
*et lacrimae ejus*
*in maxillis ejus:*
*nos est qui*
*consoletur*
*eam*
*ex omnibus*
*caris ejus:*
*omnes amici*
*ejus*
*spreverunt eam,*
*et facti sunt*
*ei inimici.*

mistook her for a plate of CHITLINS. Hey, even my mother's food tastes better than soul food, and she doesn't even *have* a soul."

*GHIMEL.*

Better cross the street. People seem to be avoiding me on this side. Besides, those kids have to hear

*GHIMEL.*

about how everybody has become their *inimic*eys

"WATCH OUT, YOU FUCKIN IDIOT! Humans before vehicles! Top of the food chain! Give these apes a '62 Chevy, and they think they're Mario Andretti.

"*Ghimel,* you on the south side of the street.

*GHIMEL.*

Ghimel, the organic movement of every Beth goosed by Aleph. You ought to understand that, you jiggling jelly-rolls. If you get them big, black aleph-ends inside you, you squirm around like Ghimel. Ghimel that old, soft, shoe. A one, a two,

*GHIMEL.*

a doodly-doodly-doo—like that.

*Migravit Judas propter afflictionem, et multitudinem servitutis: habitavit inter gentes, nec invenit requiem:*

"I say there, sir, do you speak Latin?"

"Watch out, muthfucka, you gonna get fucked over."

"Are you threatening me, sir?"

"No, man, you too big an asshole to take my time."

"And a pleasant day to you, too, sir. In exile, that is. Among the nations but *sans requiem*. Damn! Step on another crack, you'll become a hack. Me? Never! You'll turn into a macaque, and get AIDS. Only if I have sex with the locals. Step on a crack's an aphrodisiac. Maybe that explains this semiotic semierection. Hey! *Omnes persecutores ejus apprehenderunt eam inter augustisa.* Blame it on the Jewish landlords!"

*omnes persecutores ejus apprehenderunt*

OK, made it to Seventh Ave. Adam Clayton Powell Boulevard. I can't believe they'd name anything after that crook, the prince of dubious practices. Keep the faith, baby.

"Hey, you. Big black guy! Keep the faith!"

"You too, brother."

"I do, I do. You should only know. Look at that fucking state office building. Mario Cuomo shows his good faith to his loyal blacks. HEY MAN, you like this architecture?"

Well, that was a withering sneer! Hates it so much he won't even answer me. With architects like that, who needs Albert Speer? And ah, the Teresa Towers, a.k.a. the Teresa Hotel, once the largest hotel in the world open to blacks.

"Hey, old mama, remember when Commandante Castro stayed here?"

"Sho do. He come dance at the block party."

"How come he stayed here?"

"Didn't want to stay with the rich people."

"You like that?"

"Don't you?"

"The gates are destroyed, Grandma, the virgins are dragged away."

"What you talkin?"

"Seventh Avenue ain't what it used to be."

"Well, ain't that the truth."

"Nice talkin to you."

"Peace, brother."

Cross on the green, Alan. *Fart shittr,* by my green candle, this is too easy. What do I have to do to get struck down? I'll yell louder.

"*OPPRESSA EST. OP-PRESSA EST!*"

Old Z knows whereof he speaks. I skipped *Daleth,* no problem, only the symbol of all physical

*eam*
*inter augustias.*

*DALETH.*

*DALETH.*

*DALETH.*

*DALETH.*

*Viae Sion lugent,*
*eo quod non sint*
*qui veniant*
*ad solemnitatem:*
*omnes portae ejus*
*destructae:*
*sacerdotes*
*ejus*
*gementes: virgines*
*ejus squalidae,*
*et ipsa*
*oppressa*
*est amaritudine.*

*HAY.*

*HAY.*

*HAY.*
*HAY.*
*Facti sunt*
*in capitae,*
*inimici ejus*
*locupletati*
*sunt: quia*
*Dominus locutus*
*est super eam*
*in multitudinem*
*iniquitatum ejus:*
*parvuli ejus*
*ducti sunt in*
*captivitatem,*
*ante faciem*
*tribulantis.*
*Jerusalem,*
*convertere ad*
*Dominum*
*Deum*
*tuum.*

existence. Pop dismissed it all. But *Hay,* here, Hay, number five, the archetype of universal life. Make Hay when the sun shineth. Where would the Universal Life Church be without Hay? And all those guys that manufacture Hay pendants? Hay mucking around with Daleth can play the game of existence, together with Aleph, the intermittent life-death.

"What do you think of that, sir? Do you believe in intermittent life-death? I'm interviewing for the *New York Times*. Damn."

"What's the matter?"

"Stepped on another crack. Break your mother's back."

"What you talkin bout my mutha?"

"I was just saying the poem: Step on a crack, break your mother's back. You say that poem too? Not just melanin-deprived sons of Jewish mothers?"

"Man, it don't mean nothin. It's just a poem."

"Ah, I see. Poetry don't mean nothin. Something inherent in poetry, no doubt."

"No, man, it's just a kid poem, not a poem poem. Don't you know nothin about poetry?"

"I'll go home and study, my friend. Thanks for reminding me."

"What's that? It's a fuckin rat! It's four feet long! I thought it was a giant dachshund, but it's a fuckin rat. HEY KIDS, look at that rat, just strolling along Martin Luther King Jr. Boulevard. *Iniquitatem ejus.* Hey, man, look, there's a rat there. Aren't you going to do anything about it? You see that rat? Oops. Into the alley Did you see him?"

"How you know it was a him?"

"There aren't any girl rats. Rats are hims, and mice are hers. What do they teach you in biology? It was a big, sharp-toothed, guy rat."

*VAV.*

"Well, shit, man, go call the CDC. Here's a dime."

"CDC? CDC? Whatta you know about the CDC? I'll take the dime, thanks."

*VAV.*

"My mom lives in Atlanta. Don't spend it all in one place."

What is this? I come down here with my boom box to preach to the heathens, I expect to be killed, and I wind up getting spare change. Without asking. And I missed the end of the first Lamentation. *They* missed the end of the first Lamentation. Should I rewind? *Fart shittr,* I never get the right button, and I always just go back to the beginning of the cut. Onward. Anyway, there'll be more bawling about conversion to the Lord later. CDC. Do Re Do. Now there's a sequence Zelenka would never use.

*VAV.*

*VAV.*

*VAV.*

"Hey, my little chickadee, am I in the vicinity of the famous Apollo ballroom?"

"Up a ways, right across the street."

"Thank you. As you can see, I'm from out of town. Did you know that *Vav* expresses the fertilizing agent, that which impregnates? I wouldn't get too close to this boom box if I were you."

"What's vav?"

"Oh, Doctor, I have no idea how I could possibly have gotten pregnant."

"I'm not pregnant."

*Et egressus*
*est*
*a filia Sion*
*omnis*
*decor ejus:*
*facti sunt principes*
*ejus*
*velut arietes*
*non invenientes*
*pascua:*

"You will be, you will be. With bazoomers like yours, before the year is out.

*et abierunt absque*
*foritudine*
*ante*
*faciem*
*subsequentis.*

*ZAIN.*

*ZAIN.*

*ZAIN.*

*ZAIN.*
*Recordata est*
*Jerusalem*
*dierum afflictionis*
*suae,*
*et omnium*
*desiderabilium*
*antiquis,*
*cum caderet*
*populus ejus*
*in mani hostili,*
*et non esset*
*auxiliator:*
*viderunt eam*

"Oh, Alan, any kiddie in school can love like a fool, but hating, my boy, is an art. Step on a crack, get ready to attack. Avoid the cul-de-sac. Don't go slack. If needed, sit on a tack. And he thought I didn't understand poetry!"

"Hey, man, I like your beanie. How much you want for it?"

"My dear dark sir, this here is no beanie. This is a propellered yarmulke. Interstellar propeller, I believe. It represents the foreskin detached from the eight-day-old, the covenant in the flesh. The propeller represents *Ruah,* the breath of the Lord hovering over His people. The elephant represents the Republican Party."

"So how much?"

"Not for sale to the uncircumcised, my friend. I have not been mentally stripping you, but fifteen cents to your dime your shlong is *ganz geputzed.* And you're missing *Zain,* the seventh letter, the achievement of every vital impregnation, the opener of the field of every possibility, including the Seven Deadly Sins and their secular variant, the Seven Deadly Enemies of Man. Remember Billy Batson walking down that long hallway to meet Shazam? Those statues: Pride, Envy, Greed, Hatred, Selfishness, Laziness, Injustice? (You'll note the remarkable absence of Lust.) Don't look stupid at me. Captain Marvel. Why do you think Billy Batson the crippled newsboy was turned into Captain Marvel, the big red cheese? To combat the Seven Deadly Enemies of Man. And Woman. Look around you, sir. You see any problem? Nuff said?

And no, you can't buy the beanie. Go kill some kid for his sneakers.

"Gotta cross the street. See what's playing at the Apollo. Round many western islands have I been, which bards in fealty to Apollo hold. Oh, Billy, Ella, Duke, Count, Aretha, where are you now?

"What the . . . yikes . . . Yeeeeeowwieeeeeee!

"*Oi.* Shit!

"Thus far in his great mercy has God led me. Look at my goddamn arm. It's bleeding. It's scraped. I can't believe this."

"You OK, sweetie?"

"I don't know."

"You look disheveled."

"Sorry. This is a new experience for me. Don't they put guards around open manholes? I'm gonna sue the shit out of the city."

"There was a guard, sweetie. You bumped it aside. You OK? None of your parts damaged?"

"Scraped off a piece of my psoriasis. Where are we? Whoops, Jerusalem sinned grievously and therefore she became filthy. Well, that couldn't be me, I'm serving the Lord."

"Not filthy. Ignominious."

"A Latin speaker!"

"Well, the cognates anyway."

"OK. You're right, then—merely ignominious.

"But the beginning of *Teth* is coming up. The archetype of primeval female energy. Makes things clearer. *'Sorde.'*"

"Like sordid."

"*Sordes,* thou good Samaritaness: dirt, filth,

*hostes ejus*
*et desiderunt*
*sabbata ejus.*

*HETH.*

*Peccatum peccavit*
*Jerusalem,*
*propterea*
*instabilis*
*facta est:*
*omnes, qui*
*glorificabant,*
*spreverunt*
*illam, quia*
*viderunt*
*ignominiam ejus:*
*ipsa autem gemens*
*conversa est*
*retrorsum.*

*TETH.*
*Sordes ejus*
*in pedibus ejus, nec*
*recordata*

*est finis sui:*
*deposita est*
*vehementer,*
*non habens*
*consolatorem: vide*
*Domine, afflic-*
*tionem meum*
*quoniam*
*erectus est*
*inimicus.*
*Jerusalem,*
*convertere ad*
*Dominum*
*Deum*
*tuum.*
*HETH.*

*HETH.*

*Cogitavit Dominus*
*dissipare*
*murum filiae Sion:*
*tetendit funiculum*
*suum,*
*et non avertit*

squalor. It *would* take primeval female energy to notice that."

"Well, you *are* filthy, sweetheart. Don't take a woman to see that. Filthy clothes, filthy mind. Can I pull you out, and we can be filthy together?"

"I weigh a lot."

"I weigh 220, darling."

"Women don't weigh 220. You're not even fat."

"I'm not even a woman."

"Whoa . . . what's going on here?"

"Grab on to my boa. I'll haul you up."

"Thanks but no thanks. I'll climb out myself."

"Now, don't be silly and prejudiced, a smart Jewish man like you."

"How'd you know I'm Jewish?"

"Who else knows kabbalistic meanings of the Hebrew alphabet? Besides, you look Jewish."

"Well, you don't. Actually, you do dress a little like Miami Beach. And that patch, *echt* Hathaway cyclops."

"Ah, *c'est moi, chérie.* And on the first guess, you smart cookie, let me eat you up! And Miami! The most exquisitely beautiful people in the world! Here, grab hold."

"That thing will never support my weight."

"Specially reinforced with steel chain for self-defense. One can never be too careful with these violent, transvestophobic masses. I've killed three people with it. Up you go."

"Wait. Three people? Ooof."

"*Into the wild blue yonder . . . Flying high, into the sky.*"

"*Oi.* Thanks. You sing beautifully—for the Air Corps."

"My name is Jack. You can call me Doreen. Jack—black, Doreen—queen. And shut that damn thing off, darling. I can barely hear myself think."

"Now? Just when we're starting the 'Lamentations for Good Friday'?"

"It's October, silly."

"Of course it's October. October 19th. Zelenka's birthday."

"Who's Zelenka? Shut it off."

"No. Zelenka's the greatest composer in the history of the world, as you could *tell* if you weren't so ego-involved."

"*Nobody* can tell. There's too much distortion. It sounds like the underground works at Mount Pinotubo."

"I have to crank it up so they can hear. HE THAT HATH AN EAR, LET HIM HEAR. ARE YOU LISTENING OUT THERE?"

"What do *you* think?"

"No."

"Correct. So what are you doing?"

"I'm making a test."

"What are you testing?"

"None of your business."

"You're cute."

"You're repulsive."

"No, *you're* repulsive."

"How can I be cute and repulsive at the same time?"

"Cabbage-Patch Dolls are cute and repulsive at the same time."

*manum suam*
*a perditione:*
*luxitque*
*antemurale,*
*et murus*
*pariter dissipatus*
*est.*
*TETH.*

*TETH.*

*Defixae sunt*
*in terra protae ejus:*
*perdidit,*
*et contrivit*
*vectes ejus: regem*
*ejus*
*et principes ejus in*
*Gentibus:*
*non est lex,*
*et prophaetae*
*ejus non*
*invenerunt*
*visionem a*
*Domino.*

"Well, you're just repulsive."

"Why?"

*JOD.*

"Cause one-eyed men shouldn't dress like women."

"Why, darling? You think Socrates wore a three-

*JOD.*

piece suit? Or a black leather jacket?"

"But you also act like a woman."

"Hauling 200-plus pound putzes out of the sewer?"

"I don't want to have sex with you. I'm normal."

*Sederunt in terra,*
*conticuerunt senes*
*filiae Sion:*
*consperserunt*
*cinere capita sua,*
*accincti*
*sunt ciliciis,*
*abjecerunt*
*in terram*
*capita*
*sua virgines*
*Jerusalem.*

"You're normal? On what planet?"

"Look, Jack . . ."

"Doreen."

"Look, Doreen. I've gotta finish my plan here. I've got a lot hanging on it."

"I've got a lot hanging on me."

"There are more important things in this world."

"Like what?"

"Like trying to influence the struggle between good and evil."

"Which side are you on?"

"What do you think?"

"It's a *little* hard to tell."

"*Chacun a son gout, mon ami,*" Alan muttered.

"Chacun a son goo, too."

"Look, I can't tell you what this is all about, Doreen. I just have to see if I can get over to Eighth, get onto the A train, and get to Fordham Road in

*CAPH.*

one piece. A third of a block to go."

"That's the test?"

" Well. Yes."

"OK. That's fine. You give me a call when the grade's posted. Here's my card."

"IBM?"

"Why not? Big building. Plenty of closets."

"I'm not into sex with men."

"You said that. But I'd love to know more about your experiment. I'm a good listener. I ask good questions. Personnel consultant— it's right there on the card."

Tap tap.

"Well, maybe I will. I have to see."

"Oh, and if you decide to sue the city, leave me out. I'm just a Good Samaritaness. Despised and rejected by all, but worthy nonetheless."

"Gotcha. You'd only testify against me anyway."

"There *was* a guard rail, hon. You were just too whacked out to see it."

"Thanks. Maybe I'll catch you later. Doreen."

"Bye, whatever your name is."

"Alan. Krieger."

"The warrior. A dangerous profession. You can get killed being a warrior. Take it from an F-16 pilot. See you later."

"*Jerusalem, convertere ad Dominum Deum tuum. Jerusalem, convertere ad Dominum Deum tuum.* HEY, YOU KIDS, *CONVERTERE AD DOMINUM TUUM,* and I don't mean crack."

He walked down the rancid subway stairs, still alive, if slightly bruised. Take the A train, man, Take the A train. God and Billy Strayhorn must believe in you.

*CAPH.*

*Defecerunt prae lacrimis oculi mei, conturbata sunt viscera mea: effusum est in terra jecur meum super contritione filiae populi mei, cum deficeret parvelus et lactens in plateis oppidi. Jerusalem, convertere ad Dominum Deum tuum.*

# *november*

## 22. RITUAL BATH

He checked his Casio.

"OK. Four of the clock P.M., November 9th, 1999. Sixty-one years to the minute from *Kristallnacht*—given six time zones—and thus the hour for cleansing."

Alan put down his Fanon, got up from the reading chair, and walked down the book-lined hall into the bathroom. He closed his eyes, inhaled slowly through snottish nostrils, exhaled meditatively, and turned to his image in the mirror.

"Boo!"

The image jumped.

"Scared you, didn't I? Pretty terrifying man-mountain, don't you think? Grrrrr."

The mirror didn't seem convinced.

"Man-hillock? Mound?"

Alan stopped, as he was no longer ahead. He reached down and pulled his inside-out sweatshirt laboriously over his ponderous paunch (right-side-out was already used), peeling it up over his head and arms, revealing to the mirror the silk-screened portrait of Jan Dismus Zelenka—which then went crumpling to the floor. It was a custom-made present Walter had given him in days preceding the struggle over Zion. DISMUS BE DE BAADEST, it read. And on the back, CZECH IT OUT. He wore it nearly every day. His "warm."

Next came his t-shirt (GOD CAN SHAVE WITHOUT SOAP), more pliable, and then his pants and socks, both removed by stepping on cuff and toe and pulling out. It was easier than bending over. He stood in his underpants and turned again to the mirror.

Gruffly:

*"Spiegel, Spiegel an der Wand,*
*Wer ist die schönste im ganzen Land?"*

Then in a high mirror voice:

"Oh, Queen, you are, you are!"

The tub was unspeakably filthy, though Alan didn't think so. Just soap scum, he reasoned—"The Filth of God," he called it. Filthiness is next to godliness. Filthiness is a sign of health and wholeness, or holness, as the alternative-health community spells it. Filthiness makes for a strong immune system, oh so important these days.

"*O Filth of God most hoooooh-ly,*" he sang and turned on Tigris, the left faucet. The water gushed from the Spout Called Sargon the Great, and Alan tested it with the back of his hand as though it were milk from baby Gargantua's bottle.

"Yeowch!" he screamed as Tigris switched quickly from cold to scald. He opened Euphrates on the right, and adjusted for optimal temp. One thing about old New York apartments—they don't stint on water. Or heat. And this was ooold water, living water, *mayim hayyim,* running full-hearted, like the original HOH from the primal sea, the womb of the world, the amniotic tide—perfect for a ritual bath. Why do you think so many Jews live in New York?

Alan watched the tub fill, level by level. At bathtub ring four, halfway up the side, he shut down the stream. This was the height he could submerge in—almost—without overflowing the tub. Alan pulled down his underpants, kicked them off into a corner, placed one foot into the liquid heat, next the other, and then, grasping the soap dish on the left and the rim of the tub on the right, he lowered himself like a cadmium sphere, into the molecular flux.

"Waaaaaaaahhhh." His tush touched bottom. And,

"Aaaieeeeeee." His back touched the cold porcelain. And then,

"Wuuuuuaaaaahhhhhh!" His body slid down the frictioning tub, knees up, chest covered, belly an omphalic island, neck bent acutely at C7. It was his incarnate approximation of a sine wave. In half a minute his forehead broke out in sweat, and he knew he had arrived.

"*O lacryma Christi,* I humect!"

Reaching out with his right hand, he grabbed his red rubber duck, which had been perched on the bathtub rim, watching.

"Devvvvvil Duckie! My own! Come swim with me."

And he set the bird afloat. He grabbed the psoriasis soap from the dish, black and smelling of tar.

"Come, Deathbuoy Soap. Come scrape my integument, that I may be worthy of a great deed. But first, a moment of prayer."

He closed his eyes, and wallowed in the heat now comfortably caressing his body.

"O, water which dissolves all things, and breaks all forms," he muttered, "submerge my past as in the Flood, And purify me, regenerate me, restore me as at the dawn of my existence. Yowsah!"

His opening eyes took in the abdominal mound ahead. A gay, martial tune filled his memory.

*My* belly, he thought with love, and began to sing:

*"Laudate belli principem,*
*Qui nobis dedit gloriam . . ."*

Wait a minute, that's the wrong kind of belly. But then again, maybe it's not. What *is* that tune? Soprano singing—*Jephthe!* Jephthe's daughter—singing about Israel's victory.

*Qui nobis dedit gloriam*
*Et Israel victoriam . . .*

High voice: "What's up, Dad?"

Low voice: "Um . . . unfortunately you have been selected to be sacrificed so that Israel might conquer the Ammonites."

High voice: "Whad'ya mean sacrificed? Who selected me?"

Low voice: "Weeeelll . . . I did. No, I take that back. I mean *you* did. I mean it wasn't my fault. All I did was promise to sacrifice the first whatever that would come forth from my house to meet me if I won. A burnt offering—you know. If we could cream the Ammonites."

High voice: "So who did you think would come to greet you, Dad, Gruff the goat?"

Low voice: "Dear, you *have* to make offerings to the Lord if you want to . . ."

High voice: "Daa-ad! I'm your only daughter. A virgin, yet."

Low voice: "Look. You can't make an omelet without breaking eggs. . . ."

Omelet—that sounds yummy. But not till the unemployment check comes. Christ, only a month or so left, then what am I gonna do? I've used up all the ERs and ambulances in town on three fraudulent job queries a week. Good thing I don't have a daughter. Forget the omelet, Alan. Tighten the belt. I do have Shlong, though. But how can I tighten my belt if my belly's getting bigger from starvation and kwashiorkor?

"Huh, Devil Duckie, huh, what am I to do?"

Duck voice: "Take the soap . . ."

"The soap . . ."

Duck voice: "The Deathbuoy . . ."

"Ah, the Deathbuoy . . . and wash myself, right?"

He gave Devil Ducky a squeeze. It squeaked.

"Yes, the mitzvah, the ritual. That's why we're here in the bathtub. All right, ladies and gentlemen, it's time for the actual cleaning in preparation for the cleansing. Or is it the other way round? In any case."

He rose up slowly, *de profundis,* and lathered the soap upon his hairy body.

*"Puß on rye, da* DA *da, oomp, da* DA *da*
*Puß on rye, da* DA *da, oomp, da* DA *da a*
*Puß on rye don't make you spry,*
*Puß on rye, right in the eye,*
*Pu* . . . what's this?"

Alan stared at a brown spot on the back of his right hand, the hand holding the Deathbuoy. "Out, out, *verdammte* spot. Lessee . . . round, smooth borders, less than six millimeters, monochromatic, so probably not melanoma—wouldn't Eddie like *that*? But what if it's . . . the beginning of stigmata . . ."

He checked the back of his other hand.

"There! There! There's another little spot. And another one! Stigmata, I told you. They won't even need nails. They can just push the pegs right through the holes. But maybe I'm just getting old, getting liver spots. On the other hand, they could be the tiny surfaces of *tsimtsumed* Gods. Let's hope so."

*Gir-irth and width, da* DA *da, oomp, da* DA *da*
*Gir-irth and width, da* DA *da, oomp, da* DA *da*
*Makes it a gift to take a pith . . .*

He examined his circumcised penis and decided not to comment, though he had strong opinions about how the constant friction on the exposed glans desensitizes the old shlong so that, unlike a shvartza for example, the Jewish boy is not so violent in puberty.

*Departed hence, my innocence*
*Oi, Gott,* from whence experi-ience?
*Oi, Gott,* from . . .

He put the soap back in the dish, both drooling.

"And now for the grand rinse. Total immersion, with holding of the nose."

Down into the water he collapsed and crashed, creating a tsunami that flooded the floor and soaked Jan Dismus Zelenka. Head under, he rolled onto his side like a great amniotic whale, shook his head and blew bubbles to aerate the waters. He thrashed in restricted space with the kinetic intensity of Mr. Brownian Motion himself. Then, with the momentum of a breaching leviathan, he sprang once again to standing position and looked around him. The mirror was too steamed to comment. So Alan did.

"Blessed art thou, o Lord our God, King of the Universe, who has made us holy with Thy commandments and commanded us concerning immersion. And now sweatless in Gaza. Also oilless, tearless, pissless, semenless, mucusless, salivaless, vomitless, milkless, pusless, and without dingleberries. Cleaned in arse-pipes and conduits. Squeaky clean. Right, Devil Ducky?"

"Squeak, squeak."

"And thus we issue a call, like Marat in his bath, a call not to the People but to the Almighty, Who has already approved our project by not destroying us on 125th Street though He had plenty of chances to do so. And now, a small specimen of the petomanic art to push things along."

Poot.

"Joseph Pujol, are you listening?"

"Squeak."

"Ducky, did you ever consider that yours is the color of blood, symbolizing at once life and death?"

"Squeak."

"Oh, Devil Ducky . . ."

He broke into adoring song:

*"Devil Ducky, you're so swell,*
*You guide me on my path to hell . . .*

"Ducky, did you know that in 1259, in Gloucester, England, a Jew fell into a cesspool on a Saturday and asked—in observance of the Sabbath—not to be helped out until the next day? The Earl of Gloucester heard this and commanded he not be fished out on Sunday either, so that he would observe the Christian Sabbath with similar reverence. On Monday, Ducky, alas, they discovered him dead. This is not Alan's problem, for he knows how to transform cess into bless and mess into yes. Right, Ducky?"

"Squeak."

*"Devil Ducky, yes, you're a friend of mine . . .*
*De doo, de doo, de doody doody do . . ."*

Alan took three fingers of holy water and let it drip upon his crown.

"*Baptisio me in nomini Yahwehi.*"

Then he took a deep breath and sang,

*"O welche Lust! in freier Luft*
*den Atem leicht zu heben!"*

and reached down to pull the stopper from its bunghole. The water went from calf to ankle to instep, gurgled its last, and disappeared.

"Impurification. I am ready. I will dress and await my little Debeleh so that we may celebrate the season at the supermarkets of our choice."

## PAPER TRAIL 7
## HIS SUICIDE NOTE—JUST IN CASE:

*To Those Who May Come After*

Genocide is no fun—on either end.
Otherness is the primary challenge to Being. At least to my Being.
Damn all those too cowardly to act.

First, it was necessary to identify the problem and the enemy.
Otherwise, I might not have conceived so clearly what to do.
Rage is past. I act out of coolness and clarity.
Give me the benefit of the doubt.
I act to try to make things better—for all of us.
Virtues lie in the interpretation of the time.
Evil unheard, unseen, unspoken will triumph.

May you all help finish the work I have begun—
Even our black brothers, for no one is beyond redemption.

> Beings are numberless, I vow to save them.
> Delusions are limitless, I vow to cut them off.
> Dharma gates are boundless, I vow to enter them.
> Buddha's Way is unsurpassable, I vow to become it.

Alan Krieger, Kristallnacht, 1999

# 23. *KRISTALLNACHT* ON THE GOLEM HEIGHTS: A NIGHT OF FAITH AND INFINITE RESIGNATION

Alan and Deb arrived at his house with bags bulging.

"Oof. Good thing we don't have a siege every month."

"You're expecting a siege?"

"Goes with the territory. I'm all out of breath. Close the door, will you? Wah! And Wah! Should have had these delivered. But then they'd know where I was. Put yours down here. It'll be like a three-bag Christmas—a month and a half early."

"Hanukkah."

"Christmas. I don't do new-fangled wannabe holidays. Though it *is* a war celebration. None of this Prince of Peace stuff, Ms. Goldenbaum. Beat your plowshares into swords, lest ye be fucked by agribusiness."

"You bought twice as much as I did."

"I eat twice as much as you do."

"But mine is twice as inspired."

"*Oi.* Just what we need. Staples, we need staples! Whad'ya got?"

"You first. You have more."

"OK. Four large Diet Pepsis."

"No wonder your bags were so heavy."

"You can go for months without food, but you can't go for a day without Diet Pepsi. Dehydration. Lowered blood volume. Anoxia of the brain and testicles. Not to mention I need the caffeine. Three boxes of Pop-Tarts, assorted flavors."

"What if they shut off the electricity?"

"So?"

"So no toaster."

"So who toasts? Mothers of nine-year-olds. I eat em straight. OK. Whad'a *you* got?"

"Wise Potato Chips. You like wisdom. The Owl of Minerva and all that. There he is, right on the package."

"But better than Wise is Lay's. They made me think of you, little scootchem. And?"

"A bottle of Manischewitz Matzoh Ball Soup."

"Excellent. In case I catch a cold. But it reminds me of my mother, who made me feel like a matzoh ball."

"Give her a break. You kicked her out of her own house. . . ."

"I did not. She left voluntarily."

"Right. 'A Jew's joy is not without fright.'"

"What fright? She wanted to live in the country, see her grandchildren . . ."

"Uh-huh."

"Entemann's Reduced Fat Chocolate Donuts."

"Going on a diet?" Deb inquired.

"No, they're to make up for these Yodels and Little Debbie Devil Creams. I just love biting into Little Debbies. Aaarrg!"

"Hey, cut it out. Human bites are dangerous."

"The Augmentin samples are in the bathroom. Your turn."

"Let's see. Here are some snake treats."

"What do you mean, snake treats?"

"I got them in the gourmet pet food section. Little balls of I don't know what, ground mice and chemicals and flavoring. I thought Shlong might like them."

"He's still fasting from Yom Kippur. *We* need the food."

"Then maybe *you'll* like them. Here, I'll cook them up in that canned gravy you've had in the cupboard since three Dostoevsky's birthdays ago."

"Deb, cut it out. This is serious."

"What is serious?"

"What are we doing tonight?"

"Some kind of *Kristallnacht* ritual. I don't know. You're in charge. As usual."

"And is *Kristallnacht* serious?"

"Yeah, but that was sixty years ago."

"It's gotten less serious?"

"OK, OK, no more joking around."

"Spaghetti-Os. Six cans."

"That's serious?"

"Complex carbohydrates are damn serious. You can't run a revolution on Little Debbies. Besides these have a free hologram under the label. I'm going to collect all six. And look here—protein! Prince Edward sardines, for the icthyophageous. Baloney, thick sliced, lower sodium."

"Gotta watch your blood pressure."

"Damn straight. Hypertense decisions are flakey decisions. And, continuing the protein theme, a comparison shop of Oscar Mayer versus Kahn's All-Beef Franks versus the gold standard, Hebrew National Zion."

"Always the scientist. But great minds do think alike. I got you a looooong Polski kielbasa."

"In honor of the six million."

"In honor of the six million."

"A beautiful object! The tight boomerang shape says, 'Up Yours!' to that fucking antisemite Eliot: 'Up yours, T. S.; we thought of it first!'"

"Thought of what?"

"'The end of all our exploring . . . To arrive at where we started.' A Jewish idea, don't you think? Especially in its kielbasa manifestation. Heinz Tomato Ketchup in a new easy-squeeze bottle."

"Alan Krieger! How unclassical! What's become of your standards?"

"They were out of glass, narrow-mouthed."

"You won't be able to take out your aggressions."

"Oh, yeah? Just wait and see."

"Oh, I bought you some vitamin C."

"I don't take vitamins. No American needs to take vitamins."

"Some oranges, a cantaloupe—*au naturel*."

"You know I don't eat fruit."

"And a large frozen OJ."

"No more OJ! I've had enough with OJ. Haven't touched it since the trials."

"What if you get scurvy during the siege?"

"The better to bite me with, my dear."

"The less better to bite you with. Your teeth fall out."

"Yes, but it's colorful and dramatic. Ah, Chef Boyardee! Chef Boyardee, *mon semblable, mon frere!* Chef Boyardee Beef-a-Roni."

*"Beef-a-roni's full of meat.*
*Beef-a-roni's fun to eat.*
*Beef-a-roni, what a treat.*
*"Hoo-RAY for Beef-a-roni!*

"Isn't music wonderful? Also I got some Barnum Animal Crackers so I can eat my totem bear before I go to war."

"Why didn't you go to Zabar's and get some real bear?"

"Are you kidding? It's forty bucks a pound!"

"So how often do you eat bear?"

"I'm fucking unemployed!"

"I'll stand you to some bear."

"It's too late. It's already *Kristallnacht*nacht. By the time we get down to Zabar's and back, it'll be tomorrow."

"So? You got to be at work early in the morning?"

"Deborah Goldenbaum, what did I ever see in you? Don't you understand the meaning of applied symbolism? Tomorrow is no longer Turgenev's birthday."

"I thought you said this was a *Kristallnacht* ritual."

"Yes, but it's both. We have to celebrate Turgenev's birthday. Even though he's a second-rate writer, he's still better than you know who—the T word—my birthday cohort."

"Why Turgenev's birthday? Isn't celebrating *Kristallnacht* enough?"

"Here, look. Rudin. Last page. 'On the broken body of an overturned bus there appeared a tall man in an old frock-coat with a broad red scarf tied round his waist and a straw hat on his grey dishevelled hair. In one hand he held a red flag, in the other a blunt, curved sword, and he was shouting something in a strained, high-pitched voice, scrambling up the barricade and waving both the flag and the sword. A Vincennes sharpshooter took aim and fired. . . . The tall man dropped the flag and fell face forwards like a sack, just as if he was falling at someone's feet. . . . The bullet had passed through his heart.'"

"Aren't you lucky to have the complete works of all Russian novelists . . ."

"Except onc."

". . . at hand. What's so special about this old man?"

"It's me. Rudin. He's me. On the barricades."

"What barricades?"

"That's next. Let's finish unpacking. Aunt Jemima Pancake Mix."

"But you don't cook."

"I bought it for the picture. Hey, my bags are almost empty, and yours is still looking robust."

"Got some staples here. Cereals, Alan. The staff of life."

"Let's see. Oh, yum, Count Chocula! And Lucky Charms, just what I need. And what's this? Kaboom. Toasted oats with marshmallow. Sounds good enough to eat. And Life! You bought me Life. To life, to life, *l'chaim! L'chaim, l'chaim,* to life. I can eat it with my Cool Whip."

"Then I have a little stash from the dented-can store. Malta Goya."

"Malta Goya? What's that? Must be for goys. This bottle looks like it's right from the Spanish Civil War. It's still got 1930s dirt on it."

"Goya. I thought you'd like the name."

"Antiwar creep."

"All right, it was only fifty cents."

"And it's alcoholic. You know I don't drink."

"Zero point five percent. You couldn't get a canary drunk on this."

"I have to stay pure. Keep my immune system strong. And my mind clear. Like here, with this, my last purchase: Breyer's Take Two, chocolate and vanilla brick. Now almost melted for maximum bouquet. It reminds me of the black-white divide. Keeps me on message. Besides, I like the little black specks in the vanilla. My father told me it was ground-up cockroaches, and I've felt tender about them ever since. An entomological Babi Yar."

"OK, then. I win the prize for most egregious entry."

"What do you mean? What's in that bag?"

"A package of Dye Hard Lollipops."

"What's that? Lemme see. Lewd Lime. Radical! Lewd is for me."

"Read the color alert."

"'Color Alert: Your entire mouth will turn bright green and shock everybody.' I can't believe they actually make this stuff. I always wanted a green mouth!"

"Oh, and a little checkout-counter book."

"*Really Silly Pet Jokes*. $1.09. That's a really silly price."

"I thought they might have some snake jokes."

"'Why are dogs such bad dancers?' Huh? Huh? 'Because they have two left feet.'"

"Maybe it gets better."

"Unlikely. But I love the lollipops."

"Good. Why don't you take off your coat and make yourself at home?"

"Coat. Yes. Empty Schaunard's pockets of some nonfood items here. No-Doz. Playtex Living Yellow Gloves."

"What are they for?"

"Fingerprints, my dear. Absence of."

"Alan, what kind of craziness are you plotting? What are you up to?"

"All in good time, my little chickadee. Let's get all this stuff into cabinets."

"Ice cream in the freezer," Deb advised.

"Oh, yuck, it's leaking on the clean tablecloth."

"Filthy tablecloth."

"Clean. And while we are getting our aerobic exercise, squatting and standing and reaching, I will introduce you to the next event in the evening's entertainment, Kostuming for *Kristallnacht*."

"Oh, hey, there's one more thing in my bag. Stick out your hand."

"Are you kidding? You think I trust you?"

"Just do it."

Deb placed her offering daintily on his outstretched palm.

"What is this? It's a can."

"Open your eyes."

"It's a can without a label."

"What's in it?"

"How the hell do I know? It doesn't have a label."

"I thought if you closed your eyes, you could intuit what's in there."

"Like the blind Tiresias."

"Yeah."

"Well, I can't. Tiresias didn't *do* cans."

"OK, so we'll eat it whatever it is."

"You want me to eat something I don't know what it is?"

"Sure. Why not?"

"What if I don't like it?"

"Then don't eat it."

"But then I'll have to throw it out. If I open the can, I'll have to throw it out."

"If you don't like it. But if you do like it, you can eat it."

"I don't throw out food. I'm a member of the clean-plate club. What about the starving children in, where are they now, in the former Yugoslavia?"

"Alan, it's only a ten-cent mystery can. It's no big deal."

"It *is* a big deal! You *don't throw out food*. And you know I don't like many foods. Why do you make me go through this?"

"Alan, Alan, I'm sorry. I'll take it home. I'll eat it—whatever it is—I promise."

"You'll tell me what it was."

"I'll tell you."

"OK, then. Now it's time for costuming."

"Clothes make the man."

"And superclothes make the Superman. You know who said that?"

"Superclothes make the Superman? Nietzsche's mother?"

"No. Clothes make the man."

"Uh-uh."

"Mark Twain. 'Clothes make the man. Naked people have little or no influence in society.'"

"Do you think that's true?"

"You're supposed to laugh."

"I think naked people have a great deal of influence on society. They *make* society."

"Are you propositioning me with your lewd remarks? We have other ways tonight. We are going to remake society."

"How is that?"

"Dressed in the *Übermensch* costume you and I are about to create. You brought the felt?"

"I brought the felt."

"You brought the needle and thread?"

"My little handy-dandy travel kit with six colors of thread, courtesy the Statler-Hilton, Washington, D.C."

"What the hell were you doing in that den of corruption?"

"AASW meeting."

"American Association of Sexy Women?"

"Nah. Social Workers, what else? Completely unsexy."

"Don't give me that crap. I know what goes on in those hotels at night."

"What?"

"Hanky-pank, that's what."

"You don't trust me?"

"I trust you. I trust you. Why else would I choose you as a partner in crime?"

"What's our crime for the evening?"

"Wait. First costumes. You strip from the waist up."

"We won't get very far after that. Maybe we should save that for later."

"What do you think I am? Some sort of sexual pervert? You think just because I have your 38D bazoom pendulating around in front of me, I will be distracted from the greater work? I don't fuck with Earth Mothers."

"That's me? The Earth Mother?"

"Not *the* Earth Mother. *An* Earth Mother."

"There are others?"

"Thirty-five more."

"Why thirty-five more?"

"For the thirty-six Just Men. So no one gets left out. Justice on Earth. That's the gift of the end times."

"Do I get to dance with you?"

"Who else? Some fancy male social worker from New Brunswick, New Jersey? C'mon, blouse off. Bra too."

"No."

"C'mon, I brought you these little screw-on dangling earth-earrings."

"Oh, they're beautiful."

"But they're not for your ears. They're for your titties. You screw the little screws onto your titties, and voilà—earth mother."

"Not on your life. It'd hurt."

"You don't screw them hard. Just enough to hold under conditions of moderate swaying, bumping, and grinding."

"Alan. Forget it. Couldn't I just put mascara on my cheeks?"

"You don't like my earrings? I paid 21 bucks for them. Plus tax and shipping."

"I have some green mascara."

"Also from your Slut Wenches conference?"

"I wear it when I'm not around you. It's part of power dressing."

"You need power to visit the down and out?"

"I'm expected to dress professionally."

"OK, so put two green circles on your cheeks, like Clarabelle the morning after. Here . . . I'll paint them on."

"I can do it. Will there be roaches if I use the bathroom mirror?"

"Naw. They're out at a PTA meeting and won't be home till ten."

"I'm always afraid to go into your bathroom."

"Not afraid, my sweet. Merely disgusted. Do it here, then. Nice shade of green. A little bigger. Left side a little bigger."

"They're both the same size."

"I know. But we want to bring out your right brain."

"How's that?"

"God has given you one face, and you make yourself another. You jig. Do a jig. Good. You amble. Amble."

"I don't know how."

"Just amble back out into the bedroom. No, no, don't be frightened. I have no designs on your body."

"So what's *your* costume, madman?" Deb asked as they ambled themselves to Alan's *chambre à coucher.*

"Well, we just so happen to be standing in front of my chest of drawers. I've given some thought to this. I've rummaged down through the strata of old underwear and have found, buried in the 1970s—this!"

"An old 'I love Ludwig' t-shirt."

"When was the last time you saw one of these?"

"When people still loved Ludwig."

"That's true. Very astute. They *have* stopped loving him."

"He's been replaced by Mozart."

"And Tupac Shakur."

"Why do you suppose that is?"

"No more room for noble heroes in late-capitalist postmodernism?" Alan suggested.

"Could be."

"But tonight is the night of the rebirth of the noble hero."

"You?"

"Who else?"

"You gonna do something heroic, or just wear your 'I love Ludwig' shirt?"

"Patience, patience. I am not the man to squander such an opportunity."

"Your doctrine of the extreme and fanatic?"

"Doctrine of the extreme and fanatic, you bet. Now, out into the living room, picking up, on the way, my cape."

"That's a towel."

"The classic design."

"Used by four-year-olds. You're gonna have a cape?"

"Did you ever see an *Übermensch* without a cape?"

"Do they all say St. Vincent's Hospital Emergency Department on them?"

"Enough of your fashion fascist commentary. It's time for praxis. You got the felt?"

"I already told you I do."

"OK. Let's lay out the towel . . ."

"Cape," she corrected.

"Cape . . . on the floor. Now cut out two triangles about this big."

"I need a scissors."

"Here."

"That's not a scissors. That's a kid's scissors."

"You shouldn't poke yourself in the eye. Very good. What are you kvetching about?" he asked.

"I like to have good tools."

"OK. Now lay them like this."

"A yellow star of David."

"Looks good, huh? So sew them on the towel."

"Cape."

"Cape."

"Here. Try the cape on so I can see where to sew the star."

"How will we fasten it?"

"How did you fasten it when you were four?"

"I don't remember."

"Safety pin, probably. Statler-Hilton to the rescue again. This pin is a little small. Did your mother do this for you?"

"I don't remember."

"Now turn around. Let's make a little mark right here. Got a marker?"

"On the table. Don't mess up the towel. It's not mine."

"Just a little dot. OK, you can take it off. Give it here."

"*Der gelber Stern.* Twinkle, twinkle little star, on a Jew's heart in a jar. . . ."

"Black thread all right?"

"Excellent. Symbolic. Did you know that Jews had to wear yellow stars in the early thirteenth century?"

"No. I thought it was Nazi stuff."

"1215. Fourth Lateran Council. Pope Not-So-Innocent the Third."

Alan watched the iconic star take shape on St. Vincent's towel. The oxymoronic juxtaposition took the wind out of his levity. His gaze darkened as he was drawn back through the painful centuries. After manic comes depressive. He would fight it.

"This can be rough, right?" Deb asked. "We're not going for any quilting contests."

"Listen, if you don't want to do it, I'll glue it on."

"No. We need at least a little craft here. Or why did I learn to sew at Jewish camp?"

"After craft comes art," he returned.

"What's the art?"

"I am going to draw a U with an umlaut in the center of the star."

"How about an S for more comprehensibility?"

"We don't lower our standards to appease the masses. That's what this is all about."

"Whad'ya mean?" She sensed his change of tone. "Are you OK?"

"I mean Western civ is going to the dogs. To black ones. With the gold chains."

He went to the window and cranked it open.

"Alan." She held him by his thick shoulders. "What is this all about? You're not going to jump out the window in your *Übermensch* cape, are you?"

He looked outside to the park—six floors and a long hypotenuse below—and recalled Myshkin's leap into the netherworld.

"You think I'm whacked? Just getting some air. We've got work to do. I am appareled merely for protection . . ." He made a Cyrano bow and doffed his hat to his troubled queen. ". . . as is demonstrated by my Interstellar propeller yarmulke of many colors, which, by the way, has been market-tested on 125th Street. Guy wanted to buy it off me. Got a bobby pin? No. Wait. I saved the one you gave me on Passover as a souvenir of how hard it is to pin Jews down on their scriptural interpretations. I got it in this little box over here.

"There! Yarmulke as securely situated as those earrings would have been if you'd put them in their proper places. Which is to say, not very. It's why I could never be a good Jew. I could never get the damn yarmulkes to stay on."

"Well, you look very nice in your Ludwig shirt and *Übermensch* cape and rainbow beanie."

"Lunatic?"

"Maybe. But cute."

She was trying hard to feel relieved.

"OK. So. Get me that box over there. The blue one."

"What next?"

"It's my priceless collection of Captain Marvel comics. From volume 1, number 1, 1941, til Superman sued the red tights off him in '53 for plagiarism. This one comic is worth $350. Swear to God. I saw it posted in a comic-book book."

"Is this normal for a 36-year-old man? What are you going to do with Captain Marvel?"

"Do you remember SHAZAM?"

"I was into Little Lulu."

"SHAZAM—the magic word that turned the crippled newsboy Billy Batson into the almost invincible Captain Marvel, the big red cheese. SHAZAM. The wisdom of Solomon, the strength of Hercules, the stamina of Atlas, the power of Zeus, the courage of Achilles, the speed of Mercury—" And then Alan did something strange even for Alan. He took off his shoes, stepped out of his pants, and began stuffing the comics into his Ludwig shirt and down his long johns.

"Alan? What are you doing?"

"Help me stuff this stuff in. Don't crease them. They're your dowry. I mean my dowry."

"Alan . . ."

He kept to his work.

"Men don't do dowries," was all she could come up with.

"They certainly do, my lovely ignoramus. Check it out in *Webster's*. It's just that in this sexist, patriarchal society . . ."

"I never thought I'd hear you utter those words."

"You never thought a lot of things about your local *Übermensch*. OK, now right over my heart, left side, let's have a third layer. Here, maybe this one. Good. How about a fourth? This one."

"What are you *doing*, Alan??"

"The famous story of the shirt-pocket Bible stopping the bullet? I want to be shielded by the archetypal struggle between Captain Marvel and the evil scientist Sivana."

"You look like the Elephant Man."

"As opposed to the Elephant's Child? Good. But it's hard to move.

If I could flex my biceps . . . that's better. Now for the makeup. While I'm putting this on, I want you to stand outside the bathroom and tell me everything you know about *Kristallnacht*."

"You have makeup?"

"Tell me about *Kristallnacht,* Ms. Goldenbaum."

Pop quizzes had always made her nervous.

"Well, *Kristallnacht.* Let's see—1938."

"Good."

"Today, November 9th."

"Lasting into the 10th. Good."

"Some Jewish guy killed some Nazi . . ."

"Seventeen-year-old Herschel Grynszspan blew the brains out of Ernst vom Rath, third secretary of the German embassy in Paris, albeit by mistake, since he was actually looking to kill the ambassador, Count Johannes von Welczeck. Revenge for his father's deportation to Poland."

"And the Nazis used that killing as an excuse to organize a huge nationwide pogrom against Jewish shopkeepers."

"Not just shopkeepers, my sweet child. 'A spontaneous uprising of the German people to the news from Paris.'"

"Goebbels," she conjectured.

"You know what was the funniest part?"

"I didn't think there were any funny parts."

"There are always funny parts—to anything. Guess who was pissed off? The German insurance companies who had to pay for the broken glass and burned-down buildings. Those Jewish shops were rented in German buildings, and the owners filed insurance claims. 25 million marks' worth of damage instigated and organized by the government. The companies claimed they couldn't pay. It would break them and bring down the recovering economy."

"So what happened?"

"Bail out, bail out! Goering and the insurance guys decided they could blame the Jews for the violence—which they did—and demand a cleanup contribution of a billion marks. Which they did. And then they used the Jewish money to pay back the insurance companies."

"Why did the companies pay at all? Why didn't they just use the Jewish money?"

"The companies had to pay to maintain their credibility. Sound familiar?"

"That's funny? It's disgusting."

"*De gustibus non est disputandem. I* think it's funny."

"Alan, I'm scared. You look like a ghoul with that green mouth."

"This is just the color base. To make a golem, you have to mix the four elements. So hand me that little bag over there."

"What do you mean make a golem?"

"I'm gonna be a golem. Protect the Jewish community."

"What kind of *mishegas* is this?"

"This clay represents earth. And the water I'm smooshing it with represents water. Now for my forehead: gray slurry of clay."

"Alan. Golems are dangerous. Rabbi Loew said you shouldn't muck with golems."

"True enough, my sweet, as far as it goes. Now here is the Krieger advance on all of this. Why did the golem get out of Rabbi Loew's control?"

"Because the rabbi forgot to take the shem out of his mouth on the Sabbath."

"Correct. You get busy with rabbi stuff, and you can forget little things like that. But what if the rabbi *was* the golem? What if there were no separation between the two? He wouldn't have forgotten the golem, because he would *be* the golem. He'd feel everything the golem would feel. And the golem wouldn't fly off the handle, because he'd *be* the rabbi, and rabbis don't fly off the handle. They don't have handles. Get it?"

"So you want to be the golem and the rabbi combined."

"Precisely. Don't you think it's a breakthrough?"

"And you want to protect the Jewish community in a wise and controlled manner."

"Wise and controlled and effective. Can you light up this sage for me? The matches are in the bag."

"Fire and air."

"You got it."

"You can't be wise and controlled and powerful in an 'I love Ludwig shirt and a propeller beanie . . ."

"Yarmulke."

". . . and a stolen towel for a cape . . ."

"An *Übermensch* cape."

". . . and Halloween makeup . . ."

"Earthly clay."

"Alan. . . ."

"You have to consider my personal power . . ."

"Ha!"

". . . and add to it the power of the moment, the power of the media, the power of the deed, the power of onrushing justice, the power of almighty God . . . not to mention the power of Shlong."

"Shlong has power? He just lies there."

"He's been preparing for his moment."

"What moment?"

"But before we bring in Shlong, we have to build the fortress. *Ein Festeburg ist unser Gott.* The Walhall Arms. The Castle of Perseverence. *Das Schloß Kafkas.* The well-walled homes of Bluebeard and Donald Trump."

"Alan, time out. Let's slow down. I'll fix us three varieties of franks, and you can tell me what all is going on."

"We are about to construct the New Great Wall—made of the Great Books of the Western World, and maybe a couple from the Eastern. We have to seal this window with books and leave just a little peek-hole, a little poop-hole."

"Alan, this is starting to make me uncomfortable. You're really starting to act crazy. Crazier than usual. There's a crazy tone in your voice."

"Let me tell you a story. This is true. Hand me some of those Will Durant volumes over there. They take up a lot of space."

"No," she said. "Come here and sit down."

But Alan began to move books from the shelves to the windowsill.

"*The Story of Civilization.* That's what we need to protect us. Volume I: *Our Oriental Heritage.* Only three million left in the Book of the Month Club warehouse. So I have this friend, Becky Nichols, who teaches piano at the North Carolina School of the Arts, and she told me this story, swears it's true. *The Life of Greece.* Ah, yes, the polis of well-educated mutually responsible citizens . . ." He placed it in the stack. "Not counting the slaves they held . . . Wait, wait, music, I forgot music! We need background music for this event. Let's see, what do we have? Not Zelenka—he should never be background—something nasty and fierce, though, in a melancholy way. The early Gould Goldberg? Too optimistic. 'Bluebeard's Castle'? Too slow. Besides, those idiots don't speak Hungarian."

"Alan. Stop."

"No. But if it's choral it'd better be in English. At a certain point, I'll turn it up. Ah, perfect! Perfect! 'Israel in Egypt'! The Ten Plagues! Gift of Jaweh to the People of Thoth. Can you rattle them off?"

"I don't specialize in plagues."

"I do. Blood. Frogs. Lice. Flies. Murrain. Know what murrain is?"

"No."

"It's bad. Boils. Hail. Locusts. Darkness. And last, but definitely not least?"

"The killing of the firstborn."

"Good for you. You know, you can remember them easily if you use a mnemonic. Bflfmbhldfb."

"That's a mnemonic?"

"Yeah. Bflfmbhldfb. I've used all my life. It works. Didn't I get em right just now?"

"You need to eat something."

"If that's too hard, you can always use 'Before flushing, let fully matured bowels hang loosely during football break.' It could be easier to remember. For you. Though it's more information bits."

"This music doesn't sound fierce."

"Wait. It's just the overture. A little organ concerto. I need another book. *Caesar and Christ.* Good one. Remind me to tell you some good Nero stories. And Caligula."

"Finish the story you already started."

"Oh, yeah. Becky Nichols. So anyway, she's on the admissions committee, and entering piano students have to audition. And they're usually asked to bring one piece of Bach, one piece of Beethoven . . . *The Age of Faith.* That's a good one. This requires faith. Faith and infinite resignation."

"What?"

"One piece of Beethoven and one contemporary piece. So this guy comes in, blond kid, nice-looking young man, well dressed, and he says . . . *The Renaissance.* Ah, yes. Renaissance popes. They understood the theater of cruelty. He says, 'I don't have any Bach or any contemporary piece, but I'll play you any Beethoven sonata you name.' . . . *The Reformation.* These fit very well on the windowsill, wouldn't you say? So Becky, being a reasonable type, thinks this is pretty impressive for a seventeen-year-old, and she waives the requirements and says OK."

"Why are you telling me this?"

"Someone crazier than me."

"Oh, yes."

"So he asks which sonata do you want to hear, and Becky tells him to play any one he wants. . . . *The Age of Reason Begins.* Uh-oh, there goes the neighborhood! . . . So he sits down and starts to play Opus 10, number 3, and after about fifteen seconds, Becky asks him to stop and start again. . . . *The Age of Louis X-I-V.*"

"That's *quatorze.*"

"I know, sweetheart. I've seen his furniture at Bloomingdale's. So he starts playing again, and again Becky stops him."

"Why?"

"Very cautiously, she asks, 'Do you know you're only playing on the white keys?' . . . *The Age of Voltaire.*"

"Alan. What did he say?"

"Well, he said, 'Sure, I know. I never touch those black mothers.'"

"I don't believe it."

"Hard to believe, I admit."

"So what did Becky do?"

"Well, Becky is never one to take the superficial approach. . . . *Rousseau and Revolution.* . . . She sat down next to him and asked, 'What if we painted the black keys over—white?' 'Ohhhh no!' he warns. 'I'd know they was there!' . . . OK, here we go."

*Now there arose a new king over Egypt which knew not Joseph.*
*And he set over Israel taskmasters to afflict them with burthens, and made them serve with rigor.*

"Am I a burthen to you?"

"Yes, Alan. You are."

"*The Age of Napoleon.*"

"It's like having him as a boyfriend."

"Who?"

"Napoleon."

"What do you mean? Have you been going out with Napoleon behind my back?"

The judge could not judge, and the prophet could not predict where this was going.

*And the Children of Israel sighed, sighed, by reason of the bondage.*

"Well, that's a good pile," Alan declared. "Two-thirds of the way up the left side. Let's do the right with the *Britannica* up to the same height, and then between the sides up to that little whatever-they-call-it opening, and then we'll fill in the top with smaller books, but philosophically dense. *The World as Will and Idea* could stop a .44 magnum at ten feet, wouldn't you think?"

"Are you expecting bullets?"

"You can never tell who's coming for dinner."

"Alan, *you have to tell me what you're doing!*"

"Come on, now, let's start with *A to Antarah* and work our way to *Vase to Zygote,* hopefully not getting pregnant, and ending with *Atlas* for strength and *Index* for all the shitty books that should be banned. You'll forgive a 1963 edition since it's been downhill from there, and I never could afford one of those big new jobbies."

*He turned their waters into blood.*

"Mmmm. Ve vill see you at dinner, Mr. Harker."

*They loathed to drink of the river. He turned their waters into blood.*

"I wouldn't drink out of the Harlem River even if it was water. Would you? Or the East River. *Antarctica to Balfe*. What's Balfe? No time to look it up now. I'll do it tomorrow—if there is a tomorrow."

"You going to stop the sun in the sky?"

"No. There'll be a tomorrow for you. *Balfour to Both*. Just maybe not for me."

"Alan, what do you mean?"

"Oh this is my favorite."

*Their land brought forth frogs, frogs, frogs, their land brought forth frogs. Yea, even in the king's chambers.*

"And that was the origin of my spiritual father, the frog prince. C'mere, Creeping Beauty, lemme give you a little kiss."

"Frogs don't have lips."

"No, it's chickens who don't have lips. Frogs do have lips. See? And tongues. *Botha to Carthage,* two interesting subjects to think about, and where are they now?"

*He gave their cattle over to the pestilence.*

"That's the murrain. Told you it wasn't good."

*Blotches and blains broke forth on man and beast.*

"The dermatologists wracked up, let me tell you. *Carthuscans to Cockcroft*. Can you handle two at a time? You know who Cockcroft was? First guy to transmute elements. Unless you count the alchemists. 1932. Made helium out of lithium in a particle accelerator and opened a lucrative psychiatric practice changing manic-depressives into airheads. *Cocker to Dais, Daisy to Educational*. I used to have a Daisy air rifle when I was a kid. Walter gave me his old one when he started using Occam's razor. It was my first gun."

"I didn't know you did guns."

"I haven't for a while. But I've been rescherching my temps perdoos. Check out what's in that package in the corner."

*He spake the word, and there came all manner of flies and lice in all their quarters.*

Alan in his best *Bahnhof* loudspeaker voice: "Calling the Exterminator, calling the Exterminator . . ."

"Alan! What *is* that?"

"It's not a Daisy air rifle, that's for sure. It's a Galil ARM .308 semiautomatic."

"Ugh. Ug-ly."

"What do you mean ugly? It's top-of-the-line Israel Military Industries special. Tritium night sight. 6X40 Nimrod scope. How can Jewish be ugly? It cost me my last five years of savings."

"What are you going to use it for?"

"I'm going hunting."

"You'll shoot yourself in the foot before you're five minutes out. In the foot if you're lucky."

"I'm not going out."

*. . . and the locusts came without number, and devoured the fruits of the ground.*

"Are you going to hand me *Britannicas*?" he demanded.

"I want to know what you are planning to do with this gun."

"If there's a gun in the first act, it better go off by the third. I'll do it myself. *Edward to Extract, Extradition to Gambrinus, Gamebirds to Guittone . . .*"

"You're building a fort."

"With a peephole."

"You've got a rifle . . ."

"With a telescopic sight . . ."

*He gave them hailstones for rain; fire mingled with the hail, ran along upon the ground.*

"Are you planning to kill someone?"

"Listen, listen, this is my favorite . . ."

*He sent a thick darkness over the land . . .*

"Are you planning . . ."

"Shhhhh! Listen to that. C to A-flat to D-flat! Is that dark or what?

*. . . even darkness which might be felt.*

"It's like people whispering to one another across black, huge, scary rooms."

*Rrrrrring. Rrrrrring.*

"Damn, the phone."

*Rrrrrring.*

"You stop. I'll get it," Deb said.

*Rrrrrring.*

"No!"

She got it anyway.

"Mrs. Krieger, it's Debbie."

"I don't fucking believe it!"

"I'm good. Yes. They're good too. Busy. Yes, he's right here."

"I'm not home."

"You are. She knows it. You can't get out of it."

"Hello, Ma. I'm fine. How are you? Good, good. Nothing much. Just listening to some music. No, I don't particularly want to talk to Walter."

*He smote all the first-born of Egypt . . .*

"I don't have a lot to say to him at the moment. Maaaa. I said . . . Hi, Walter. Yeah, fine, and you? Hey, Walt, listen to what's on the radio here, I'll hold the phone up to the speaker."

*He smote all the firstborn of Egypt, the chief of all their strength, the chief of all their strength . . .*

"Is that a reference to you? I don't know. If the shoe fits . . . *Gamebirds to Guittone, Guizot to Hydrox* . . . I said, '*Gamebirds to Guittone, Guizot to Hydrox.*' They're volumes 10 and 11 of my *Britannica*. I know you have the new one, but I don't have a full professor's salary. Well, actually, I was thinking of going hunting, but not gamebirds. Actually, it was the Hydrox I was interested in. I want to see if the *Britannica* takes a position with respect to Hydrox versus Oreos. I do too. It's one of the few things we agree on. Well, let's just see."

Alan turned his back on the rising rampart and switched into emergency research mode.

"Goddamn. My older brother, straight from Central Casting, is right again! In fact, they don't even fucking *list* Hydrox. The last entry is Hydroxylamine, $NH_2OH$. 'Used in the manufacture of dyes, plastics, synthetic fibers and medicinals.' You think it's symbolic? Of what? Oh, Walter, get your head out of your asshole and lemme know when you hit land. Gimme back to Ma. Nice talking to you."

He rolled his eyes at Deb and, with a screwed-up mouth, flipped a *digitus impudicus* Vermontward.

"Ma, don't do that to me!! If I want to talk to Walter, I'll call him up. . . . I know you want us to be friends, but you don't get everything you want in life. . . . What? Debbie, turn that thing off, I can't hear a thing. What did you say? . . . I miss you too. Do you want to move back here? . . . Good, cause I wouldn't let you. . . . No, no, it's just that you wouldn't like it any more, dirty air, dirty people, I'm sure you'll think it's horrible. . . . I know, I know. You can take the girl out of the Bronx, but you can't take the Bronx out of the girl. I believe Kierkegaard said that. . . . Who's *Kierkegaard?* I'll tell you next time I see you. A melancholy Dane . . . No, Dane, not dame—Dane as in Danish . . . Yeah, like a Danish . . . Ma, I gotta go. I'm in the middle of something. Maybe you'll read about it in the papers. . . . Now, now, curiosity killed the gnat. I'll send you a clipping. . . . Soon, soon . . . OK, Ma, see ya. . . . I love you too."

He gave Deb the phone to hang back up.

"You're pretty mean to Walter," she said.

"His immortal soul to infinite wrath and despair for all he's done to me."

"Like?"

"Like I don't want to go into it. We've got other things to do."

"Count me out. I ain't on this team, Alan. Not without knowing exactly what you've got in mind."

"*Do not forsake me, oh, my darlin . . .*"

"It's not our wedding day. And I'm not marrying you."

"I need you, is all."

"For what?"

"We have to dress up Snakey-wakey. Lemme just finish quickly piling the *Britannica,* and then we get to the Great Shlong Event."

"And what is that?"

"It's jointly sponsored by the International Ouroboros Society and the American Salami Association. In the end is the beginning, you know."

Deb regarded him suspiciously.

"But first, there are some really difficult theoretical problems that have to be solved, and I'm sure only a woman can solve them."

"Like what?"

"Like how do you keep a yarmulke on a snake's head? Bobby pins won't hack it."

"You make a tie under his chin."

"But then the yarmulke will, you know, pop up in peaks or something."

"So?"

"But then he'll look like a bishop."

"So?"

"A Jewish bishop?"

"He's a Jewish snake?"

"When you get right down to it, I don't even know if he's a he. His name is Shlong because he's longer than he is wide."

"I'm not helping you with this anymore, Alan."

"You won't even help me with his makeup?"

"No, Alan. He already has beautiful markings. Stop all of this."

"You have to paint sacrificial beasts. It's done all the time. Little Shlongyskull, filled with dew, with skin of air and open eye, and nostrils breathing life . . ."

"Why is he a sacrificial beast? I mean, why would you sacrifice him?"

"He's been chosen."

"For what?"

"Sacrifice."

"Alan! What do you mean?"

"I'm going to kill him."

"What?"

"I'm going to kill Shlong."

"Oh, Alan, why?"

"Because it will be a test of faith. If God wants Shlong to live, he'll send a ram or something else."

"Just how is this ram supposed to get in here?"

"He'll knock on the door. Or bleat outside or ring the bell or something."

"And God told you to do this . . . whatever you're doing?"

"Not exactly. It's an extrapolation back from deed to preparation."

"But it's a horrible thing to do."

"Teleological suspension of the ethical."

"Alan. Shhh. Listen. Shlong is your pet."

"Isaac was Abraham's *son*."

"Abraham didn't kill Isaac."

"But he would have."

"So what faith are you testing?"

"That Jews are the Chosen People."

"So you have to kill Shlong?"

"It's important to fight back—for the good of the Jews and for the good of the world. Someone has to do something to start the rollback."

"What has this got to do with Shlong?"

"By killing him, I demonstrate my faith, I become a real-world warrior, not just a theoretical Krieger, I do something Walter would never do, and I prepare myself for the main event."

"Which is?"

"Hand me my hunting knife. It's over on the table."

"I certainly will not."

"Wait, Shlong, I'll be right back."

"Alan, put that down."

"Do this with me, Debeleh. Have some faith."

"Give me that knife."

"Deb, stay out of my way. Hey, let go. Ouch! Damn it, wench, you made me cut myself! I'm fucking bleeding to death!"

"You have a little cut."

"It's right in the tendonis thumbus opposingus, or whatever they call it. I'll never play piano again."

"You don't play now."

"Gimme that knife! No, go get me a Band-Aid first."

"Quit ordering me around, Alan. You've become someone else."

"I can't put a Band-Aid on my own hand."

"I'll bandage you if you'll stop all of this."

"I'll stop."

"OK. Wait. Let me wipe it off first. And I have some first-aid cream in my purse. There."

"Thanks. And now for Shlong."

"Alan, you promised!"

"No. I didn't. Deb, don't unman me. It took me months to work up to this. *Baruch atoh adonoi elohaynu melech ha'olum,* Blessed art thou, O Lord our God, King of the Universe, who has given us snakes and commandment to sacrifice them, spilling their blood in atonement for sin, and in hope of redemption."

"Alan! Stop!"

"Bye, Shlong. Thank you for agreeing to do this. Eh-la!"

He passed the blade across his trusting pet's throat.

"Alan!"

"Don't Alan me! You think Moses' girlfriends gave him grief when he went off to do sacrifices in the desert? Just hold up his tail while I hold his head over the sink."

"I'm out of here."

"Deb! Deb, don't go. It'll be OK. You'll see. Deb! Come back! Take the note. Deb, on the table, you have to take the note! Deb!"

Never had Alan felt so alone, his soul seething wildly in the void. He had come to the mountain, and the mountain was Moriah. Nothing in his life had ever seemed more important, yet there was a strange, hollow resonance to the room, an emptiness that threatened to engulf him. The snake began to twitch as the great terror dawned upon him.

"Shlong. Shlongy, it's all right. Don't thrash like that. Just relax, let it fade away. Easy, boy. Nice Shlongy. Good Shlongy. That's a good boy. Easy does it. Good boy. Here, let me wipe you off. Now just lie down here on the rug where it's soft. Good boy. Gentle into the night. Gentle. Gentle."

Alan stroked his head and back as Shlong began to go slack.

"I'll just turn out this light so it doesn't shine in your eyes."

He did so and then he waited.

"Didn't think I could do it, Calvin, did you?"

And Alan Krieger began to cry.

"Stop it, Alan! *Ridi, Pagliaccio!* Where's my snot rag when I need it? Ah! So . . . now I'll finish our fortress, and no one will be able to get us, Shlong. *Hydrozoa to Jeremy* . . . Stop crying, goddamn it!"

*Jerez to Liberty*, to Liberty! . . . Blowing of the nose encore.

"*Ridi, ridi.*"

*Libid to Mary*, et Spiritu Sanctu, and that will do if for the right side.

"*Ridi del duol che t'avvelena il cor.*"

Shut up, Alan. Stop slacking off! Now the bottom. God! Just fits! Four across exactly. Yet another sign! What a bitch to walk out on me! *Maryborough to Mushet* and *Mushroom to Ozonolysis*, *P to Plant* and *Plants to Raymund*. What am I gonna do without Deb AND Urs AND Shlong—not to mention the accursed Mom? *Raynal to Sarraut* and *Sasparilla to Sorcery*, God knows it's not far, *Sordillo to Textbook* and *Textile to Vascular*. Shlongy, don't worry about vascular, it's OK. And last but not least, *Vase to Zygote* and *Atlas* . . . and *Index!* Perfect, just perfect. Right up to the bottom of the pop-out whatchamacallit. Now all I have to do is build a little bridge across from *The Age of Napoleon* to *Libid to Mary,* then I can fill in the top with other power books. This better be worth it.

Let's see, this *Britannica* bookshelf doesn't come apart, and there are other things on the Will Durant shelf. I know! The kitchen table, it's got those screw-on legs. Two or three of those guys should fit right across the space. Eat your heart out, Joseph Strauss. Let's see if I can get these wingnuts off without any tools since God knows where the tools are. Could my mother have taken them with her? That's ridiculous. Yes! The mighty hands of Alan Krieger succeed in loosening wing nut number one. And number two. And . . . let me bang it with my knife handle . . . there goes number three. Four will be too wide. Let's get these things off. What to do with a table with one leg? I suppose I could use it as an easel, if I were Toulouse-Lautrec. OK, three legs across Dr. Durant and Dr. Britannica, and voilà—you could jump on that baby. Shlongy, you would have appreciated this—the supreme value of that which is longer than it is wide.

Now, on this firm foundation, we cut to the quick: Proceeding alphabetically through the library, we find, yes! Harold Bloom and his *Western Canon*. And good old Martin Buber for the solidity of the I-Thou bond. Shlongy, Shlongy, look at you! *Heart of Darkness,* why not, though in this case the jungle has come to Mohammed, *Crime and Punishment, The Brothers, The Idiot,* let's just cram the old boy in, *Short Stories, The Possessed, Notes from the Underground, Poor People,* oh Fyodor, your destiny is achieved! And of course my stolen copy of Andreyev, what's he doing out of order? Of course he didn't experience order—ever, Father Vassily, you poor *zhlub,* Oblomov, good, Rudin, Gogol, *Dead Souls, Stories,* what a maniac! Add him to the short list of people crazier than I, but I'm humbler. Humble, humble, where is that? Ah, Peretz. 'Bontshe Shvayg.' My favorite. Humbler than Alyosha. Euripides, two volumes, for *The Bacchae* if nothing else, Sophocles, for *Antigone,* Shakespeare for everything. And from the foreign-lit section—though why don't I think of Dostoevsky as foreign?—we have the great *Don*

*Quixote,* which someday, but not today, I'm going to read in Spanish, and we're running out of room, Yukio Mishima, hara-kiri, kitchy-koo, we'll stick these little guys in there, and there's just enough space to jam in René Daumal, *A Night of Serious Drinking,* though I don't drink.

Perfect. Unlike the world at large. Solid. A little working peephole just at shoulder height. And beautiful too, don't you think, Shlong? All those multicolored spines? Mr. Spine, I know you're probably dead, but give a last look if you can. Here, I'll hold you up. Good boy. Back to sleep.

And now let's have a little break for refreshments, even though we may throw up our food. In honor of you, Shlong, I'll cook up a plate of kielbasa, for extension and reflexiveness, and wash it down with Diet Pepsi for clarity and sweetness. Shlongy-shlong. And while this is cooking, would you like a little Bach to console the heart, inspire the mind, and enthuse the soul? 'He hath put down the mighty from their seat, and hath exalted the humble and meek'? That's me. Not the humble and meek, Shlongy, the one who hath exalted them, the putter-down of the mighty.

*Deposuit potentes de sede*
*Et exultavit humilies.*

Yowsah! Yowsah! And a little sip of soda . . . umm, those cold, fierce bubbles. O, celestial libation—I adore you! But you make me pee. Thirty seconds after, I need to pee. Whoops, I need to pee. But I'll hold it. Retain precious bodily fluids and stay fierce. Better get this music off before *Esurientes* fills me with good things and satiation.

OK. Now let's peep out the peephole, and what do we make of the great Grand Concourse? The Loewes Palace that has been forsaken, a temple that has been demolished, fences that have been breached, sanctuaries that have been burned, roads that have been uprooted, bolts that have been snapped, killers who have conquered, shame that has grown great, stones that have been scorched, friends who have been scattered, and here we sit alone and weep. By the waters of Babylon. Alan Krieger, pour out thy wrath upon the nations that know not the Lord and upon the kingdoms that call not upon His name, for they have eaten Jacob and laid waste his dwellings: pour out thy wrath upon them: and may the kindling of thine anger overtake them: pursue them with anger and destroy them from under God's skies.

Sounds pretty good. I can get into it. Just do it. Into biblical head. And now David takes his trusty sling, which, this being the very late twentieth century, is, in this case, a Hebrew .308 semi. And he is ready to go up against Goliath, ladies and gentlemen, or at least the colony of Goliathoids swarming below.

Shlong, look how beautiful this machine is. Look. Shiny. And if I just crank open the window behind it, the barrel fits right through this hole, with enough room for the sight. . . . Oh, I forgot the music. Let's face the speakers this way. . . . Damn, I could have used them for the bottom pillars. No, not as much protection as from *The Story of Civilization* and the *Britannica*. But let me turn up the volume way loud, and now, let's see, Handel this time. Handel turns out to be the composer of choice here. And for the true Messiah, disc two, number 17, and play! Yes! Where's my lollipop?

*Thou shalt break them with a rod of iron.*

I'll just do some practice aiming here to get my bearings. . . . Hmm. Hermes and Calypso out for a stroll. Is that a good-looking little family or what? Even through the scope . . .

*Thou shalt smash them in pieces, like a potter's vessel.*

And . . .

*Hallelujah, Hallelujah . . .*

"OK. Stand up everybody. You on the benches out there . . . hold the breath. Still. And then squeeze. Don't pull. Squeeze."

*KNOCK, KNOCK, KNOCK*

What the fuck! The nether regions speak?

*KNOCK, KNOCK, KNOCK*

The Commendatoress below? I'll pretend I'm not home. No, the fucking "Hallelujah Chorus" is blasting away. She knows I'm home.

"SHUDDUP, DOWN THERE!" What if she can't hear me yelling, the music's so loud? Better turn it down.

*For the Lord God omnipotent reigneth*

"I SAID, SHUDDUP, YOU'RE INTERRUPING 'THE MESSIAH'!"

*KNOCK, KNOCK, KNOCK, KNOCK, KNOCK*

"WHAT ARE YOU DEAF? I turned it down." Goddamn Philistine! I suppose she'd prefer Barry Manilow or something. Henry Kissinger singing "*Ach Du Lieber.*" "PERRY COMO'S DEAD! DEAD AS A DOORNAIL!" But *is* Perry Como dead? He seems dead. Have to look that up tomorrow.

*KNOCK KNOCK KNOCK KNOCK KNOCK*

"Whence is that knocking? How is't with me when every noise appals me?"

*The Kingdom of this world . . . is become . . .*

Jack up the volume, then.

*THE KINGDOM OF OUR LORD*

*AND OF HIS CHRIST, AND OF HIS CHRIST*

"Take that, you gibbering Melnicky ghost, with your broomstick on the ceiling!"

Enough.

He turned the volume down to normal.

She stopped knocking. Jeez, it's effective. Take that, VAMPIRE!

*KNOCK KNOCK KNOCK*

"Mother of God, preserve us! It's like having Ahab for a downstairs neighbor—walking around on his ceiling. Of course that makes me—"

*KNOCK KNOCK KNOCK KNOCK*

"—one great white Jewish WHALE AND I'M OUTA WATER, YOU HEAR? BEACHED! LIKE BABY JESSICA. I need a drink."

Alan hit the Pepsi bottle.

Ahh—it's the real thing. Or is that Coke? At least I'm not the coke generation. Crack, that is.

*KNOCK KNOCK KNOCK KNOCK KNOCK*

"Here's a knocking indeed! Knock, knock, knock! Who's there, i' the name of Beelzebub?" Oh God, maybe the Exterminator! Alan, don't answer—no Exterminators, please! But I should maybe turn the volume down just a bit, just in case. Pascal, et cetera. But not too much.

*And He shall reign for ever and ever*

For ever, and ever, hallelujah, hallelujah. But what if Mrs. Melnick comes upstairs *with* the Exterminator? She never has, but she might. Gotta hide this gun. How will I explain my green mouth? Debbie did it. Halitosis. Her chlorophyll gum. She left. To get more. But Shlong. Too big to hide. I can say I had to kill him. He was going to strangle me. In his coils.

*I know that my Redeemer liveth*

She does seem to have stopped knocking. But what if she's calling the cops? They'll find the gun. But it's legal to have a gun. I was just cleaning my rifle, Officer Friendly. No, I never shoot it, I just like it.

I'm a good Jewish boy. Good Jewish boys don't shoot guns. We believe in the sanctity of all living beings. And silver bullets are hard to get, and . . .

*And though worms destroy this body, yet in my flesh shall I see God.*

Worms? What worms? Oooooh, Shlong. Shlongy, the *Wurm*. See, I have to loosen the knots of the demonic powers, and I have to make war against them. So I took the strength out of the piercing serpent. See this cape? And this propeller hat? And this is clay for earth and water, and can you smell the fire and air. It's sage. For wisdom. Have a nice day, Officer Friendly. A nice night, I mean. *Kristallnacht.* Clear as crystal.

*. . . that he shall stand at the latter day upon the earth.*

Alan plunked his Galil .308 down on the kitchen table, poured himself a Diet Pepsi, and lit up a Marlboro.

*Since by Man came death . . .*

I had Officer Friendly pretty confused there, I'd say.

*. . . by Man came also the resurrection of the dead.*

Alan walked over to the window.

But what if she does send the cops? Noise complaint. Hear that, George Frideric? Maybe I'd better cool it till tomorrow. Ninth, tenth . . . the fires were still burning on the tenth. Getting too dark out there anyway . . .

*For as in Adam all die . . .*

TB continued on *Kristallnachtmorgen*. All the time in the world, Herr Krieger, all the time in the world. I'll clean up tomorrow. They'll never know.

*Even so in Christ shall all remain alive.*

He plopped down in his reading chair, suddenly spent.

"Debbie, Debbie, *lama sabachthani?*"

There was no answer.

Rifle across his knees, cigarette dangling from his lips, Diet Pepsi in hand, eyes closing as upon some oddly failed chapter, he drifted into the arms of Morpheus, the god of dreams, the giver of form to airy nothings.

*Behold, I tell you a mystery,* sang the bass.

*We shall not all sleep, but we shall all be changed. . . .*

He wet his pants. He slept.

*Amen.*

Over and over, *Amen,* until the grand pause, the most pregnant silence in the history of music, a womb swarming with all possible worlds.

And then—*Amen . . . Amen.*

## 24. HIP HOP

"OK, kiddo, into your jammies. It's past your bedtime."

Hermes pulled on his pj pants and top.

"Come here. Your hair is still wet."

Calypso picked up the towel he had left next to her on the bed. Hermes plopped down, kneeling, and suffered the final rub. When it was over: "Story?"

"No, Mom. Song."

"You sing with me?"

"Maybe."

Hermes climbed up on the bed beside his mother.

"This has got to be a bedtime song, now . . ."

"OK."

She sang in a low, velvet voice.

*"Duerme, duerme, negrito,*
*que tu mamá está en el campo, negrito."*

He joined her, his voice an octave above.

*"Duerme, duerme, negrito,*
*que tu mamá está en el campo, negrito."*

Then he listened again, closing his eyes.

*"Y si el negro no se duerme*

*Viene el diablo blanco y ¡zas! . . .*
*Le come la patita checapumba."*

He joined in

*"Checapumba, checapumba, checapum.*
*And if the negro doesn't go to sleep,*
*the white devil will come and zap!*
*he'll eat your little foot,*
*checapumba, checapumba, checapum."*

*Checapumba, checapumba* . . . The rhythm was so persuasive, he wiggled up off his mother's lap to dance. Calypso sang to his dancing form:

*"Duerme, duerme, negrito*
*Que tu mama está en el campo, negrito.*
*Trabajando sí, duramente*
*Trabajando sí*
*Pal negrito chiquitito*
*Pal negrito sí*
*Trabajando sí*
*Trabajando sí.*
*Sleep, sleep little black one,*
*your mama's in the fields, little one.*
*She's working hard, working, yes,*
*for her sweet little black one,*
*for her little one, yes."*

"Mom?"

He stopped dancing and kneeled back down in front of her.

"What is it, *p'tit garçon*?"

"Can I have a snake?"

"What kind of a snake?"

"Like that fat man with the whipped cream in the park."

Her mind went back to Alan. Pathetic, she thought. Bankrupt. Like unto death. But she too had seen the boa in the pet-store window.

"Why do you want a snake, *mon fis*?"

"To dance with. Watch. *Siveye* . . ."

He rolled the pink-and-green bath towel up into a flamingoed tube and began a Salome dance to *Checapumba, checapumba, checapumba, checapumba.*

"What will you call it if we get it?"

"I'll call it Shlong, Mama. That's a great snake name, don't you think?"

"Perhaps. Perhaps it's a very good snake name."

"Hip hop, Shlong, hip hop," he said to the towel as he bounced its tail along the floor. "Hip hop, hip hop, hip hop, hip hop."

Had Alan been there, he would have thought *Wozzeck*:

*Du! Dein' Mutter ist tot.*

But he wasn't there.

# PAPER TRAIL 8
# A POEM DATED 11/99 FOUND IN A DESK DRAWER

SHARDS OF GLASS AT *KRISTALNACHTMORGEN*
(after Whitman)

for Calypso

*A child said,* What is the glass? *fetching it to me with*
*chary hands,*
*How could I answer the child? I do not know what it is*
*any more than he.*

*Perhaps it is the flag of the inquisition, from*
*telling mirrors cloven.*

*Or perhaps it is the aping of a word*
*A poisonous gift and warning deftly dropt,*
*Bearing the Hashem someway in the corners, that we may*
*see and remark, and say,* When?

*Perhaps the glass is itself a child, multiplexed babe*
*of an alien nation.*
*Or perhaps it is a uniform hieroglyph;*
*And it means, sprouting alike in broad and narrow*
*fronts,*
*Growing among blond heads as among brown*
*Goldman, Glimmerstein, Himmelmann, Klein, I give them*
*the same, they all break the same.*

And now it seems to me the stubbly, five-o'clock
  shadow of graves.

Tenderly will I use you, shattered glass,
It may be you seek out the breasts of young men,
It may be that if I had known them I would have loved
  them,
It may be that you are for old people, or the offspring
  taken soon out of their mother's laps.
And here you scar the mother's laps.

This glass is very sharp to be from the white heads of
  old mothers,
Sharper than the wiry beards of old men,
Sharp to come from under the faint red roofs of mouths.

## THANKS . . .

First of all, to my tireless and doughty editor, Fred ("Momma Bear") Ramey, who licked this distasteful cub into shape from its golemesque beginnings.

Then to the nonfictional folks who have kindly allowed their faces, facts, and creations to be here appropriated:

- Martha Nussbaum, for her openness to and good humor about being attacked by my would-be hero;
- Arthur Naiman, who continues the mischievous good humor of his *Every Goy's Guide* with his kind permission to quote therefrom;
- Tom Robbins, whose Sissy Hankshaw makes an unscheduled appearance on the Grand Concourse;
- My daughter, Mario Trabulsy, MD, whose ER skills are matched only by her unfailing good humor in the face of it all;
- Roger Gillim, violist extraordinaire, for his endless jokes and ribald stories on carpools to rehearsals;
- Joel Meltz and Dennis Jakob, for their articulating and modeling of the doctrine of excess;
- and last, but also first, the gentleman unnamed who started me writing, and writing this book in particular.

Finally, thanks to my faithful wife and partner in crime, Donna Bister, first reader, gentle critic, and walking dictionary.